Kingdom of Denall: The Troven

By

Eric Buffington

Kingdom of Denall: The Troven

Published by Dragon Scale Publishing

ISBN:1943183309

ISBN-13: 978-1-943183-30-2

Other Books by Dragon Scale Publishing

Jonathan Haymaker

The Sorceress of Aspenwood Series:
Dimwater's Dragon
Dimwater's Demons

Tales from Terramyr (Short story anthology)

The Annals of Esparia Series:
The Protector of Esparia

The Dragon's Champion Series
The Dragon's Champion
The Warlock Senator
The Dragon's Test
Erik and the Dragon
The Immortal Mystic
Return of the Dragon

The Netherworld Gate Series
The Tomni'Tai Scroll
The King's Ring
Son of the Dragon

The Dragons of Kendualdern
Ascension

Acknowledgments

From the initial idea to publishing this book has been an adventure! An adventure I could not have done on my own.

A special thanks to a small group of people who read through early drafts of the story and gave feedback: Dave Chudleigh, C.M. Mullane, George Macialek, EmmaLeigh Buffington, Laura Sushoreba, Shawn Buffington, Jill Petty, Julia Chudleigh and Marial Lewis. The advice, edits, and excitement that you shared when reading the book inspired me to keep going especially when the end seemed a distant, unreachable dream.

Sam, Rachel, and the team at Dragon Scale Publishing have been amazing. When we started, the story had a good direction and some fun characters but when we finished it was a full well-rounded book series. It really is amazing how a couple sets of talented eyes can see greatness and help it to come out. Thank you for bringing out the best in the Kingdom of Denall. I look forward to working with you for many more great books.

Saying, or writing, thanks will never be enough to properly recognize my wife for all that she has done to help make this possible. MaryBeth has read and reread every phase of this book. In addition to hundreds of edits she gave me advice and perspective that changed the entire course of the Kingdom of Denall. From her honesty, patience, and support, this has become a reality.

Thank you to everyone who helped on this adventure!

To MaryBeth, my perfect match in every possible way.

CONTENTS

In the third era a leader shall arise, to save he must destroy.
The one without a mark, without a gift, without strength,
he shall become the one with all marks save one, all gifts save
one, all strengths save one.
The marks shall be gained at a great cost, forged in the fire
of the mountain, when he overcomes death.
He shall rise or fall, when the Stones of Power are united
again, he shall be the force of Change.

PROLOGUE

Water echoed off the walls of the long, dark corridor. The abandoned mine deep in the Egtharnton Plains had long been the meeting place for Mordyar's stone seekers, and tonight they were gathered together in a large, underground room for an oath ceremony. The light from the lanterns was absorbed into the roughhewn rock walls, leaving the room dim.

Twenty-seven seekers stood in a large circle all dressed identically. They had long, white, nondescript robes, and bottles of liquid hanging around their waists on white sashes. They circled left two steps, then back to the right three steps. This motion continued as the large circle shifted until they made a full rotation. It was dizzying for the young man standing in the center as he watched and waited.

Young Franklin had been raised by two stone seekers, and now that he was of age, they wanted him to take the oaths and become a seeker like them. He had learned all his life about the great power of Mordyar. He knew that Mordyar would one day come to Denall, and when he arrived, he would appoint rulers from those who faithfully served; those who sought the Stones of Power throughout their lives, and especially any who found the stones. But despite being taught the truth about Mordyar daily at home, he still did not know if he was ready to become a seeker at such a young age.

The circle came to a stop and five seekers were chosen to ask Franklin some questions. He knew that he could ask anything he wanted for clarification, but now that he was in the center of the circle, failure to correctly answer any question would mean death for him.

The head seeker, Melna, began, "Who is the rightful ruler of Denall?"

"The Great Sorcerer Mordyar," Franklin answered automatically.

Melna nodded in satisfaction. "Well done, Franklin."

Although it was an easy question, Franklin beamed at the compliment. He had heard of Melna, but he had only met the head seeker two times, and he was pleased to be in her good graces.

The next assigned seeker stepped forward. "What is the sworn duty of a stone seeker?"

"A stone seeker will scour the world in search of the Stones of Power," Franklin replied. His parents had been through this ritual, but they were forbidden to share any details with Franklin. Although they had not shared the specifics, they had prepared him as best as they could without neglecting their sworn duty. This answer came almost as quickly as the first as it was taught in his home from the time he could walk.

The seeker did not nod or acknowledge whether he was correct, but merely stepped back into place in the circle.

A third seeker took a pace forward. Franklin recognized this seeker. He called her Aunt Kham although she was not his aunt. She was a wandering seeker. She went from village to village looking for anyone who had an exceptional gift, or anyone who stood out, and she made a note of it and looked for opportunities to search that person or his belongings. Though each person in Denall was born with at least one of the six gifts bestowed by the ancient sorcerers, some were endowed with more advanced gifts, and it could be difficult at times to distinguish whether a display of great strength, or perhaps of outstanding listening ability, or even the appearance of a particularly skilled magician was due to a level four or five gift, or to the enhancement the seekers knew could come through the use of a Stone of Power.

Sometimes, following one of Aunt Kham's 'investigations', a body would be found, and other times there would be complaint of a house or cottage having been mysteriously ransacked, but she was never caught. When she was close to Franklin's village, she always came in and spent a day or two resting at his home. It was tiring work being a wandering seeker, and she was one of the best.

"What are you willing to do for the Master?"

Franklin was not sure how to answer this question. "I do not understand," he said cautiously.

"To what lengths are you willing to go?" Kham added as clarification. She tried to keep her head steady, but could not stop herself from giving an encouraging nod.

"I would do anything the Master required of me. I would give up my own life, or take the life of another," Franklin answered. He had heard his mother and father talk of the dedication required, and they often told him this exact phrase. He had said the words, but until recently, didn't know if in his heart he truly believed he would be willing to give his life for a cause.

Aunt Kham nodded and smiled in satisfaction as she took a step backwards into the circle of seekers.

The next person to step up to him was his father. "Are you willing to give your sight for Master Mordyar?"

"Give up my sight?" Franklin repeated. "What do you mean?"

"Your vision, are you willing to give up your vision?" his father reworded the question.

"Do you mean I will never be able to see again?" Franklin asked. His father did not answer, but stood still with his hands behind his back. The way he stood, Franklin knew he was holding something concealed in his hands, but he could not see what it was. Trusting his father, Franklin nodded. "Yes."

The four seekers who had asked him the questions lunged forward and held him down as his father kneeled over him.

"This ceremony is not only to test if you will say the words, but if you are willing to support your words with actions." His father said. Then he revealed the knife that was concealed behind his back. "I will now take your eyes for the Master's cause."

Franklin looked around him at the seekers who held him down. He knew resisting them would be futile as they held him fast. He also knew that every seeker he had ever seen had both eyes. Franklin couldn't believe that his father would actually cut out his eyes, but looking up at his dad he wondered if he might be wrong. At that moment he made a decision. He decided that despite his youth, he was completely dedicated to Mordyar. If it would help the Sorcerer's work, then he was willing to give his eyes. If he said the words, he needed to demonstrate his resolve with his actions. Franklin did not struggle; he laid back and took a calming breath.

Aunt Kham released his arms and the other seekers followed her example. Franklin was left lying on the ground as his father held the knife high above his head.

His father kneeled down next to him and slammed the knife into the ground next to his son. Franklin jumped slightly at the sudden movement, but did not try to get away. "You will need to give up your sight, my son, but not like this." He lifted his son from the ground and returned to the circle. Franklin stood up, waiting for the final question.

Franklin's mother stepped forward. He could see the look of pride in her eyes as she reached out with a small bottle.

"Franklin, when you first drink this you are making an oath. You are dedicating your life, and your sight to Mordyar. When he returns he will give you wealth and lands, and restore to you your natural sight. This is the promise he gives for your loyalty. Drink and join the seekers."

Franklin took the flask from his mother. He had been taught all about the promises that Mordyar made to his faithful seekers. He smiled at his mother, and then tilted his head back to take a long drink. The liquid burned as it went down his throat, but he continued to drink until every drop was gone. As it entered his body, he could feel heat pulsing through him, intensifying, until he felt like he would be burned from the inside. He began scratching at his arms and legs, trying to fight the terrible fire that was burning within him, but it only intensified.

The boy screamed out in agony and thrashed on the ground, sweat pouring from him, soaking his clothing. Slowly the pain began to subside; it became an uncomfortable itch, then warmth, and finally it was gone. He breathed out in gasps and stayed lying on the floor for a long time trying to recover enough strength to stand.

When he opened his eyes the world had changed. He could still see the natural surroundings of the underground room, and the people standing in a circle, but now he could also see on each seeker glowing balls of light everywhere they had magically enchanted items. Inside his body he could feel only one desire; a power pulling at him, the desire to please his master and find the Stones of Power.

From the time he took the oath, Franklin searched diligently for the Stones of Power. He started out working in his parents' fletcher shop, but then moved north to Hillside to set up his own business. As he grew, he traded with local merchants and often spent his nights in the tavern listening to tales from those who arrived from distant parts of the country.

One evening, as he walked down the main street of Hillside, he was greeted by the innkeeper. He was a kind man, always willing to talk, and often a good source of information.

"Hello Frankie," the innkeeper greeted him in a friendly tone.

"Hello, my friend," Franklin replied, grasping his hand and giving it a firm squeeze.

"I thought of you the other day," the innkeeper said, resting his hands on his large belly. "I heard the story of an exceptional archer. He doesn't even have fuzz on his face and he shot an eagle out of the sky."

"You don't say?" Franklin said with sincere interest.

"I swear on the life of the king," he replied, while holding his open left hand out in a sign of honesty. "He's in the next village over. They say he saved a small child as an eagle dove down to scoop it up." Much to Franklin's amusement, he moved his hands in a downward motion acting out the scene as best he could.

"Well that is a rare talent!" Franklin replied. "I'll have to make some special arrows to match his skill, and deliver them as a gift for being such a young hero. Where did you say he lived again?" Franklin looked eagerly at the innkeeper.

"He's over in Dungan; the village just down the hill."

It frustrated Franklin that people in Hillside described

everything not in Hillside as 'just down the hill,' but he simply nodded and took a mental note.

"Do you happen to know his name?" he asked, trying to keep the conversation as casual as possible.

"No, didn't catch his name, everyone's just taken to calling him Eagle Eye. Quite the name, isn't it?" Franklin smiled, but it didn't reach his eyes. He was thinking that a boy so young would need some help to make that kind of shot. Even if he didn't have one of the Stones of Power, Franklin determined that at his first opportunity, he would make a trip to Dungan.

The sun had barely risen the next morning, when he was on the road to Dungan riding his sturdy horse. He had packed a small bundle of arrows as a gift for Eagle Eye, a gift he intended to use as an excuse to get some time alone speaking with the boy. Before nightfall, he entered the village and went straight to the largest building he could see, hoping to find a place to rest and perhaps, if he was lucky, learn about the boy. As he approached the building, he saw a young boy sitting on the roof holding a bow.

"Hello, up there," he called out in a friendly tone. "Do you happen to know where I can find a place to stay for the night?"

"Sure do," he replied with a large grin. "But it'll cost you."

"Really? How much?" Franklin asked, somewhat amused by the boy's behavior.

The boy sat bolt upright, clearly not having expected an encouraging response. "A copper." His words were more of a question than a statement or a demand and Franklin chuckled.

"What's your name, boy?"

"It's Bendar," he answered too quickly, and Franklin knew he was lying, but decided to play along.

"Bendar, that's a really nice bow you have there. I am a fletcher from Hillside. I actually have an entire bundle of arrows here that I specially made." The boy almost fell off the roof, leaning forward to get a look at the arrows. "I will give you one of these arrows, Bendar, if you will tell me where I can find a place to sleep tonight, and if you will tell me where to find Eagle Eye."

The boy raised his hand excitedly. "I'm Eagle Eye," he declared. "I was just kidding about the whole Bendar thing, my real name is Kaz, and you can stay in the inn right here." He pointed down at the entrance of the building he was watching over.

Franklin pulled a single arrow from his bundle. "Come on down and get your reward."

The boy disappeared off the roof, then popped out beside the inn with an expectant look on his face and his hands outstretched.

Franklin looked the boy over, but there were no signs of any magical items on him. He sighed dejectedly before handing over the arrow.

"How about you show me what you can do with that bow of yours," Franklin said.

"Pick a target," Kaz replied confidently, looking out across the village green.

"How about that fence post over there?" Franklin raised his hand to point, but before he had stretched out his finger, an arrow stuck in the post with the back vibrating from the impact. "That was very good," he said, sincerely impressed. "You have a great gift." Franklin then turned his horse around and trotted back out of the village.

"Wait a minute," Kaz called after him. "Aren't you going to stay in the inn?" There was no response. "Who were the other arrows made for?"

Franklin heard the cries from the young boy but didn't turn around to answer.

It was difficult every time he had his hopes up, just for them to lead to another dead end. *Maybe one day I'll find something worthy of sending a message to Mordyar, then he'll know all the work I have been doing, and I'll be rewarded when he comes.*

On his ride home in the dark, Franklin made a decision. He was finished with this part of Denall. Perhaps there was a Stone of Power closer to Pike Point.

CHAPTER 1

Dune focused on keeping his breathing quiet and steady. Any sudden movements, or even a change in the rate of his heart beat, could set off a magical trap and alert the stone seekers of his location. The robe that hung from his shoulders to the ground blended into the surrounding night forest, keeping him hidden from even the keenest of eyes. But that was not enough to get past magical traps. He inched his body into a crouching position, picked up an acorn, and brought it up to his mouth. He quietly whispered an enchantment into his hand as if telling the small nut a secret. When he performed the magic, the five red marks on his left wrist flared into a deep maroon color.

The acorn shell silently cracked as a green root began pressing its way out, searching for some fertile soil. Dune opened his hand into a cup and watched the root grow until it was an inch long. The live root was what he needed. He opened his hand, fully spreading his fingers apart, and with hardened air, magically threw the acorn up and away to land in the clearing that separated him from the seekers' campsite.

When the acorn hit the ground, a ball of fire engulfed it. The acorn was burned to ash instantly. The stone seekers jumped into action, grabbing their weapons and rushing into the opening. Dune watched as they cautiously examined the open space, and found only ash. "What was it?" Edgar asked. This particularly vile stone seeker led the small group, and he had a special liking for magical items and traps.

"There's not much left," answered a younger man. He was new to their crew, but seemed to be the most intelligent. "It had to be alive, or it wouldn't have set off all the traps."

Edgar kicked the ground, and grunted in disapproval. "Those traps were expensive! You're telling me it was just some squirrel that set them off?"

"Probably more like a mouse, or a small bird" the young man corrected. "There's literally nothing left, so it couldn't have been very big."

"Ahhh!" Edgar screamed as he turned around and punched

a tree. Dune was pleased at how frustrated Edgar was getting at the loss of some of his traps, but he was also delighted at the prospect that perhaps they wouldn't use so many next time they made camp. Getting established as a hunter in the small southern village of Eaton had taken several months, and still he had failed to get very close to this group of stone seekers. They were polite with other villagers, but seemed wary of Dune as a newcomer. The only time he was able to get information from them was when he tracked them like this while they were camping out, doing some hunting, or visiting nearby hamlets. Dune was beginning to think that there wasn't much he could learn from this group, and he would soon set his own traps to capture them and turn them in.

The stone seekers moved back to their campfire, with Edgar still grumbling about the loss of his magical traps. Dune circled around the edge of the clearing, ducking in and out of the darkest shadows. He cast a small spell of sound dampening on his feet before he got within earshot of their campfire.

"We can't be sure," came the voice of a woman in her forties, not much older than Dune. "What if she comes back here? Many years ago she did live here."

"That's just rumor. Nobody actually knows where she is," Edgar responded. Not sure who they were talking about, Dune continued to listen from his secluded hiding place in the trees, careful not to touch any branches or make any noise. "Besides, it doesn't matter," he added. "We'll be seeing all of them soon enough."

"What about the man from Norwell?" the young man asked. "We have to look into the blacksmith, and besides, it's on the way."

Edgar audibly scoffed. "It's just another dead end, like the cooper from Pike Point, or the carpenter from Gulpond. There's nothing unique about a blacksmith staying up all night to work the forge, especially this close to the tournaments."

"What if it's not just the tournament?" he protested.

"It was your lead, you go look into it. I'm heading north." Everyone around the fire remained silent for several minutes.

Dune could hear Edgar's loud, smacking lips as he chomped on his evening meal. He didn't like how they were talking about a blacksmith in the capitol city of Norwell, but at least they seemed to have decided they would leave him alone.

There was a shuffling of people as they pulled blankets over themselves and settled in for the night. Dune was about to leave when he heard the woman speak again. "You know what I wish?" she mused. "I wish I could see the look on that magician's face when he goes back home."

Edgar laughed out loud, "That would be a sight, wouldn't it, to watch that fool when he realizes he's not as clever as he thinks?"

Dune stood frozen in place. *How did they find me? What did they do to my house?*

"Speaking of traps," the young man added, "do we have anything else to keep us safe tonight?"

"I've got something," Edgar answered. "Everyone come here." Dune watched as they all gathered around their leader. "It will trap anything that breathes in our camp, anything that's not touching it when we activate it." The three seekers touched the small artifact, and Dune quickly sucked in a deep breath.

"There," Edgar said. "Now go to sleep. Maybe we'll have a few squirrels caught by morning."

Still holding his breath, Dune began walking away from the camp as quickly as he could. He didn't know the radius of the trap, or how it would react to magic, so he kept walking in the dark shadows of the trees. After walking almost half-way around the clearing, his lungs were burning.

"What was that?" the woman asked. Dune stopped moving, forcing his lips to remain closed, his lungs begging for air. "I thought I heard something in the woods."

"It's probably one of Jeff's mice," Edgar responded in a tone that was beyond indifferent.

Not knowing how much longer he could wait, Dune began moving again, hoping they thought he was a mouse.

"There it is again," she said. Firelight danced around as she pulled a burning log from the fire and began moving in Dune's direction. He took longer strides, trying to quickly get away, but he knew she would reach the clearing before he could escape it. Not knowing if he was outside the magically defended area, and with his head throbbing from the lack of oxygen, he dropped to his knees, silently released his breath, then began gasping for air, as quietly as he could manage.

As he knelt low to the ground, the female seeker came into the clearing with a piece of wood in her hand. It had a small flame on the end, but it cast very little light, and went out when she waved it around searching for Dune. Dune remained completely still. Not only was it the best way for him to remain hidden, but his breath had sprung the magical trap and now it held him in place. He watched the seeker as she stalked around the clearing. She was not looking into the trees, but pausing every few yards to listen. Dune calmed his breathing until it was completely inaudible.

With his robe covering him, and his inability to move, he was quickly overlooked as the seeker checked the clearing. While she was searching, he reached out with magic and touched the trap that held him. Although it was serving a purpose for him at the moment, he knew he would need to escape as soon as the woman was gone.

The magic that held him was not overly complicated. It was air that had been hardened into an invisible barrier around his body. What was interesting about this trap was that it was still connected to the object Edgar held. By connecting his magic to the hardened air around him, Dune could manipulate the object and it's magic. For a brief moment he considered reversing the magic so it would capture only the people who were touching the object when it was activated, but that would ruin all he had worked for. Instead, he patiently waited until the female seeker was done looking through the clearing, took a deep breath, and then he touched the hardened air with a weave of magic that unraveled the spell.

He quietly stood up, looked out into the night, and teleported away as far as he could see into the woods, landing a safe distance from the clearing and the camp. When he was sure he was safely out of the range of the trap, he began breathing like normal. He looked out to the north, the direction the seekers were heading. He didn't know why they were going, or how long they would be gone, but after several months of waiting, he felt like this trip might bring him to their leader.

But first he needed to get one thing from his booby-trapped house, the one thing that he couldn't have while standing next to a group of seekers. The Magic Stone

CHAPTER 2

From his vantage on the roof of the Dungan Inn, not much escaped Kaz's keen eyes. From the moment he climbed up onto the roof in the early hours of the morning, he watched the sun come up, spreading shades of reds and oranges across the clouds. With his enhanced vision he scanned the distant forest line and watched squirrels dodging about on trees as if they were excited to see the morning. He looked up into the sky, watching as swallows flew in erratic patterns, catching insects as they made nearly impossible turns in the sky.

Now with the sun rising into the sky, the villagers began to appear on the packed dirt streets. The tall young man shifted slightly to ease a cramp in his leg, then rubbed his hands quickly through his short, light brown hair, and over his face to keep from falling asleep during watch duty. Like most people he observed walking through the small village, Kaz wore sturdy, undyed wool clothing that was a mix of natural colors.

A movement near the tree line outside the village caught Kaz's attention, and he focused his sight, the four maroon dots near his left eye standing out as he did so. The leaves of an oak sapling shimmered in the breeze, and the shadows along the edge of the woods danced in the morning sun, but he kept a close watch on the spot where he had seen an unnatural movement. Something was there, just outside of his view, and when it moved again he would be ready. He shrugged his bow off his shoulder and eased an arrow to the tight string. Another scamper of movement to the left, then to the right, made him dart his gaze back and forth. *What are you?*

Without warning, a bundle of hay flew out of the woods over a thick wall of thorns. Kaz drew his bow and released an arrow. His broad head arrow pierced the hay just as it hit the ground. "Nice try!" Kaz called out through cupped hands, though he wondered if the men in the woods could hear him.

From the woods emerged two members of the town council, the inn keeper, Barrels, and the owner of the general store, William. Barrels carefully pulled Kaz's arrow from the hay and nodded in approval as William took dutiful notes. *Always keeping the watchman on high alert, even though there hasn't been the slightest bit of excitement in years.* He understood the need to keep the men sharp, but sometimes the town council's tests seemed absurd.

Kaz climbed down the ladder from the roof far enough to take his arrow from Barrels' outstretched hand.

"It's a beautiful morning for a walk in the woods," Kaz said, knowing that their test of his skills had probably taken them on a mile long hike through the dense forest to ensure they stayed out of his enhanced sight.

"It is a nice sunny day, and the woods were pleasant," William replied in a monotone voice that sounded like he was bartering a deal in the general store. *Sarcasm is lost on that one.*

"You do understand why we're out here, don't you?" Barrels asked.

"To keep the village safe from bears and drams and…"

"Partly," he interrupted. "However, it's also to keep *you* safe. In just a few days you'll be out there," the large inn keeper pointed out of town to the east. "Your eighteenth summer is upon you, and your Troven will begin soon. You'll need your sharp eyes, your fast hands, and your keen wits." Kaz looked down at the ground, scrunching his eyebrows in concentration. It had never occurred to him that all the tests over the past several months were all to help him. The inn keeper tucked his hand under Kaz's chin, lifting his gaze until they met. The older man smiled broadly and nodded at Kaz in a fatherly way. "You'll do just fine. You're a good lad."

Barrels and William continued on their survey of the village, Barrels greeted people fondly while William paid more attention to his book of notes than the people he passed. When they were out of sight, Kaz climbed back up and sat down on the roof, taking a drink from his water skin as he watched the villagers go about their business. He wondered how many of them had played a part in his 'training?'

The cooper took some cured wood from the lumber mill and the baker's son pushed a small cart filled with clay pots down the main street. He kept looking back and forth between the packed dirt streets of Dungan and the distant forest until Herleva came into view. *The most beautiful woman in the village! It's just too bad she got hitched before I could finish my Troven!*

Kaz kept his eyes locked on her until she passed by the inn and disappeared behind the blacksmith's shop. Seeing her pass by was the highlight of the morning. With the streets now empty, Kaz looked out past the village limits to Tunkin Lake. He knew there was a fish or two waiting for him there as soon as his shift on the roof was done.

After several more hours of observing familiar people pass through the streets of the quiet village, Kaz saw something that caught his attention and promised to provide some entertainment.

While the village council met, Fenn, the daughter of the village council president, sneaked behind the inn, probably on her way out of town to the Sigris farm again. Kaz snickered at her as she lifted her green dress just above her ankles so she could walk through some sawdust without getting any on her. He almost laughed out loud when she paused to check her reflection in a puddle of water. Although he and Fenn were casual friends, she was far too uptight and proper for his liking.

Kaz moved quietly to the edge of the roof and picked up a large pebble. He looked down at Fenn who was smoothing a loose piece of hair and trying to incorporate it into her long dark braid. While she focused on her reflection, Kaz tossed the small stone in her direction and ducked out of sight.

Kaz listened carefully to hear the stone splash, followed by Fenn's fearful squeak. Although he couldn't see her face, Kaz grinned from ear to ear thinking of the glare that was certainly directed at him.

"Where are you Kaz?" After a minute she continued, "Kaz Kinsley, I know it's you up there!"

Kaz popped his head into view and casually dangled his legs over the edge of the roof. "Hi, Fenn."

"Kaz, what are you doing?" she demanded in a hushed, yet angry tone. "My heart is about to pound out of my chest!"

With a smirk he responded, "That's what all the girls in the village say about me."

"You wish!" she retorted, wiping her hands down her dress to brush away any droplets of water that were still there. "The only time you make hearts beat is when we're rushing to get away from you."

"Now, Fenn, be nice. I didn't notice you there," Kaz lied.

Fenn narrowed her eyes and folded her arms across her chest. "I'm sure Gran will be thrilled to hear about your morning activities," she threatened.

"You're probably right," he said sarcastically as he began to stand up. "In fact I'd better go right now to the village council meeting and report all the *interesting* things I've seen this morning." He gestured toward Fenn. "I'd hate to get in trouble for missing anything."

"No, Kaz. Don't!" she said, obviously not wanting her trip to the farm to be reported. "It's probably best if we just go our separate ways and forget this whole thing happened."

Kaz smiled down at her. "Sounds like a good plan." He reached down into his tackle box and pulled out a special surprise. As Fenn turned to continue her secret trip he called out to her, "Hey, Fenn, can you make sure this gets delivered to your boyfriend?" Kaz tossed a small handful of worms at her.

The frightened girl shrieked and ran out from behind the inn, no longer concerned whether she was noticed. Kaz couldn't help but laugh as he watched her make her way down the road. Every few steps her body shook like she was having a spasm and she rubbed her hands through her hair as if checking to see if one of the worms was somehow lodged in her perfect braid. Before she was out of his sight, her hair was teased into a complete mess.

* * * * *

The smell of fresh hay was one of Garin's favorite things in the world. He inhaled deeply before tearing the bale apart, throwing some food into the stall for the lamb. While cleaning the stalls was not the most glamorous job around the farm, he tried to enjoy every minute he spent here before he had to go.

He moved one lamb into the clean stall, then turned and looked at another animal. "No complaining, little girl. You're moving next once we get a clean place for you."

"Baaaa," it responded.

Garin patted the lamb tenderly, then paused before he made his way to the final stall. Through the thin wooden walls of the barn he heard some unusual sounds. The farm workers out far in the field were greeting someone who approached. While he couldn't make out the specifics of what they were saying, he knew it was probably Fenn coming to visit, and they would send her in his direction.

He quickly began cleaning out the final stall so he would be done before she came in. As he heard her footsteps approaching he called out, "Just wait out there for another minute, maybe two. I'm almost done. "

The door swung open and Fenn stepped through it just as he tossed a pile of woodchips down for bedding. The wind from outside caught the small chunks of wood and sawdust, and threw them up into Garin's face, past him, and all over Fenn's dress on their way out the door.

"Oh no!" Garin said, raising his hand to cover his mouth. "I told you to stay outside; now you're a complete mess."

"It's all right," Fenn said between coughs.

Garin rushed over to her and started pulling loose pieces of woodchips from her hair. "Wow, that wind sure blew your hair all around too, didn't it?" he observed as he worked to clean it out.

"No, the wind had nothing to do with my hair," she countered. Her tone was very stern and she scowled as she looked over her shoulder in the direction of the town.

"Well I like it this way," Garin said, trying to smooth over anything wrong he might have said. "I just have to move the last lamb over to this stall, clean out that one, and put the tools away. Then we can go for a walk down by the creek, or go check on the calves," he offered as he reached down and moved the last animal into the clean stall.

To Garin's surprise, Fenn walked into the small, dusty barn and grabbed a second pitchfork. "Wait a minute," Garin protested. He reached out and tried to take the tool from her.

"It'll go faster if I help," she insisted. Despite the dirty work and her inappropriate attire, she walked into the dirty stall, dug the pitchfork in and began throwing out the old hay.

Garin smiled as he grabbed the other pitchfork and worked next to Fenn. *This girl is amazing!*

Together they cleaned the stall and filled it with fresh bedding. Garin loved working with Fenn, and imagined how things might be after he finished his Troven. He hoped that they would spend every day working side by side. When the work was done, he looked at her in complete dismay. Her dress had some dark brown smears, a layer of dust covered her entire body, and her hair was a disaster. "I think we need to get you cleaned up," Garin said as he reached up and pulled a piece of hay from Fenn's hair.

They stood face-to-face and she looked right into his eyes. "It's okay, Garin," Fenn began, "I don't mind farm work. Besides, I came here to spend time with you, and if that means I'm mucking out stalls all day, then that's where I want to be."

Despite his feelings for Fenn, Garin stood awkwardly for several seconds, not knowing how to respond. He reached out to take the pitchfork and Fenn playfully moved the tool behind her back. As Garin reached around her and grabbed for the pitchfork he unintentionally placed his hand over hers.

With the tool in his hand he looked up and noticed he had closed the distance between them. He stood within inches of her, looking into her bright green eyes. She stood still, no longer playfully moving the pitchfork away, and slowly closed her eyes, tilting her head to the right. Garin closed his eyes and leaned in closer. He could feel his heart pounding and he instantly forgot about everything else but Fenn.

He soaked in everything about her; the way her hand felt beneath his, the intense beating of her heart, the rhythm of her breathing, and how her body felt against his. Then he felt her nose bump into his.

"Oh, sorry," he said bashfully. "I guess one of us should keep our eyes open."

Without saying a word, Fenn reached up and placed her hands on either side of his face and pulled him toward her. This was the moment Garin had been anticipating for years.

The door of the small building swung open abruptly.

"Hey Garin, we need to-" the intruder stopped talking and just stared at Fenn's arms around his twin. "Hi Fenn," he said, looking somewhat embarrassed.

"Hello, Farin," Fenn replied as she quickly put her hands down by her side and took a step away from Garin.

"I'll just be leaving." Farin said, as he backed up slowly out of the building.

Just then Garin heard their father calling, "Is he in there?"

"Just lambs in there," Farin shouted in return. "I'm sure he's out by the old well. Don't worry Dad, we'll find that obnoxious beast before it gets too far." Then he added in a whisper. "You owe me big time for this one." Farin turned around and let the door slam closed behind him as he left.

"Well, I guess you have to get going," Fenn said with disappointment clearly written on her features.

Garin felt like there was more he needed to say and do, but he couldn't think of anything that would make the situation better. Leaning in to continue their kiss seemed completely out of the question after the interruption.

"Yeah, I'd better go."

"Fine," Fenn said abruptly, then turned and quickly left the barn. Garin stood still, holding a pitchfork, dumbfounded at how agreeing with her had made her so upset. He returned the pitchfork and left to find his brother.

*****

The sun stood high in the sky as Farin and Garin silently searched in the underbrush for the runaway lamb. On their father's farm they were always the ones sent to find the missing livestock because they were the best listeners. They squinted to see as far as they could for the stray animal, but to better play to their strength they would, from time to time, stop and listen. Having enhanced hearing was often considered the most versatile ability because it was always active. Listeners could, with sharp concentration, hear almost twice as far as they could see, however, this made their hearing so narrow that, much like a tunnel, they lost the sense of their surroundings. To maintain an awareness of their immediate area while straining to hear farther distances, the twins took turns focusing their hearing. They had searched for stray livestock, or played in the dark so often, they alternated seamlessly without needing to speak a word.

After putting some distance between themselves and the farmyard, Farin twisted his walking stick in his hand and held it out like a sword. He swung the stick in a few practice strokes, then turned to face Garin.

"So, what was that I walked in on?" he asked with an expectant look. Catching his brother in an embarrassing situation was something he couldn't let go.

"I'm sure you can figure it out," Garin replied curtly and continued to walk past his brother.

Farin swung the stick around and stopped it in front of his brother. "I covered for you; I think I deserve more of an explanation than that," he responded.

Garin rolled his eyes and pushed the stick away. "Covering for me once doesn't even come close to how many times I've had your back," he replied, holding his index finger in the air for emphasis.

Farin's face split into a smile. "Well I guess you do have a point," he regretfully conceded. "But I'd still like to know the details."

Looking deflated, Garin stopped and concentrated on the ground. "What you saw was all that happened."

"What?" Farin asked in complete shock, "You're leaving tomorrow and you didn't even give her a kiss goodbye?"

Garin threw his arms up in frustration. "Well if you'd given me another minute or two," he countered. Garin began walking again, searching through the woods for the stray.

Shaking his head, Farin responded, "You waited until the last possible minute on the last possible day to do something you've wanted to do for years. I can't believe you!"

"Thanks for rubbing it in." Releasing a breath, Garin continued, "At least we'll be back in a year."

"Back in a year? I can't believe what you're saying. It's just a good thing you have me as an older and wiser brother, or else I don't know what you would do," Farin said with a grin. He started formulating a plan to get them together for a secret rendezvous.

Garin rolled his eyes at his brother, who constantly rubbed in the two minutes that made him Garin's senior. "What are you talking about?" he asked, looking back out into the woods.

"We'll find a way for you to get to your dearest love."

Clearly tempted by the prospect, Garin paused for a moment to consider, then shook his head. "You know we can't sneak out tonight. It's the night before the Summer Festival; we're the guests of honor, and Mom would never forgive us. Besides, we'll need all our energy for tomorrow. We can't be out all night."

Farin held his hands up in a sign of surrender. "Fine, Garin. If that's what you want." Although he acted disappointed, Garin was probably right. Getting out that night would be nearly impossible.

"I'm not saying it's what I want," he replied angrily. "I'm saying it is the right thing to do."

"You really do have a talent for ruining all my fun," Farin replied.

They continued to search for the lost animal in silence. From time to time, Farin glanced over mischievously at Garin who consistently looked back with a stern, serious face. These exchanges spoke louder than words between the twins who had a strong bond, and often carried on entire conversations without needing to speak at all.

While searching for the lost lamp, Farin snagged his hand

on a briar and immediately placed his fresh wound in his mouth. "If I don't find that four-legged-good-for-nothing beast soon, I'll break its neck."

"Probably wouldn't help much," Garin countered. "A dead lamb can't grow into a full-sized meal."

"Well, at least I wouldn't have to search for it again and again. Besides, I'm not going to be here to enjoy it when it is full-grown." He pulled his finger out of his mouth and looked to see if it was bleeding.

"Shhh! Do you hear that?"

As Farin strained his heightened sense of hearing, the two marks on his ear lobe deepened to a maroon red. It was faint, but he could hear the sound of bleating in the distance. "Over there." He pointed to their right.

Farin led the way down the hill, but stopped short when he saw his friend coming with the runaway in his arms. Even at this distance he knew it was Kaz. Kaz was one of the few people in town who always had a longbow strung and slung over his shoulder, and he was taller than most men.

Kaz's kind face brightened into a boyish grin as he saw his friends. "I saw her coming over from your farm and I thought I'd save you some time."

"Thanks, Eagle Eye," Garin said as he took the lamb from Kaz. "With you on guard we'll always be safe from bandits, forest fires, or wandering sheep. But your keen eyes missed that it's a male."

"Guess I didn't concentrate on looking between its hind legs. I'll leave that to you," Kaz said jokingly. "Farin, what about you? No thanks? I just saved you wandering all the way to the village."

"Thanks a lot! Now we'll be back to work in the fields with those brainless, walking muscles Dad hired from out east." Kaz and Garin exchanged a confused look, but Kaz just shrugged and let Farin continue his rant. "Did you see that strongarm Dad hired? He's a level four. What a monster."

"I'm a level four," Kaz interrupted.

"It's not his level, it's his… I don't even know." Farin started walking briskly through the small stand of trees back to the farm, not sure how to explain his frustration, not even sure if he fully understood it. "Well, for one thing, none of his shirts have sleeves and he's always flexing when anyone walks past. Just to show off, he pulled a full grown tree right out of the ground without needing a horse team, and yesterday he pulled out that rock in the south field we've been trying to remove for years. It's not that he is a level four, it's that he wants us to always remember the strength of his gift." Farin's friends jogged to keep up with his determined gait as he continued to moan about his father's hired laborers.

Finally Garin interrupted. "Far, can you stop complaining? I don't think I've had a moment of silence since the day we were born. You complain about farming, you complain about sheep herding, then you complain that Dad hired people to do the farming, next you'll complain if he gets someone to gather the sheep."

Farin stopped walking and turned to look at his brother. He knew farm life was important to Garin, and hadn't meant to offend him, but now that it was time to leave, the things that had once seemed annoying were unbearable. Before he could apologize, Kaz interrupted with a mischievous smile.

"He was quiet once. You remember don't you, Garin? He concentrated so hard to hear if the girls in the…"

"Seriously, do you have to bring this up?" Farin responded as he playfully punched Kaz in the gut a little harder than he needed to. "Every time we talk you have to remind me."

Half coughing, half laughing Kaz continued. "You were concentrating so hard on those girls three hundred paces away that you didn't notice the stinger land on your lip. You looked so funny; your mouth swelled up so big you couldn't talk for a week!" Kaz puffed his lips out trying to imitate what Farin had looked like, but stopped when Garin did not join with him in the joke.

Farin did not feel like joking around, and he appreciated that Garin sensed his mood and had not encouraged Kaz. Farin glanced at Garin and gave a slight nod of his head. Garin returned the gesture.

"I'm just messing around," Kaz began, oblivious of their unspoken communication. "Come on Farin, you've never let me live down the fir tree incident." Now Farin did crack a smile, even if it was somewhat forced.

"It's not the girls, or the stinger, or even the muscle heads Dad hired, and it's certainly not your inability to climb trees in your birthday suit. I'm just ready to be out of here. The only thing I'm going to miss about this place is you two." He continued in a lighter tone, "And you'll have plenty of silence when I set my back to this village, because I'm never coming back."

"I think you're forgetting we're going with you," Garin responded.

"Do you know what's funny?" Kaz asked. Not waiting for a response, he answered his own question, "How different two people can be who look exactly alike." Kaz paused a moment as the twins turned to glare at him. "You see? Even your attempt at making nasty faces at me is identical." He reached up and playfully rubbed Farin's sandy brown hair into a mess. "There, now I can tell you apart."

Farin swatted his hand away and grabbed Kaz in a headlock. He knuckled Kaz's head until he was able to wriggle free. Kaz scowled at Farin while he tenderly touched the top of his head. "I like this one better than you," Kaz said, pointing at Garin.

"Too bad he's not terribly fond of you," Farin countered. "Especially after what you…"

Garin shushed them with a wave of his hand. "There's something moving." Everyone paused as the two dots on Garin's ears darkened. "That way," he said pointing over a small ridge.

The twins ducked behind a tree and Kaz leapt to the top of a nearby boulder to scan the woods. From behind the tree Farin couldn't see anything, so he focused his hearing and watched as Kaz widened his stance and silently drew a long, wooden arrow from his quiver.

Kaz smoothly nocked his arrow and drew his bow. The dots

on his left temple darkened as he strained his sight to focus on what he saw.

As the feather from the arrow brushed his cheek he released the bowstring. The arrow soared through the woods, and there was a high pitched, frightened scream. Farin laughed out loud as he realized Kaz had found Bendar.

Garin, who was the least fond of Bendar, wondered aloud "Should we go get him or let him figure it out on his own? I know you like him, Kaz, but seriously, do we have to take him with us?"

Kaz shook his head as he called and waved to Bendar, answering Garin over his shoulder. "You know we need him. If he's not with us, Farin and I would only have you to pick on the whole way to Norwell. Besides, he has the route all planned out and all the rations calculated. We need his brains as much as any of our gifts if we're going to succeed."

"I just don't get why you seem to like him so much. He talks like everyone around him is an idiot."

"He is a level three intellect," Kaz responded as if that was explanation enough.

"Yeah, and I'm a level two listener. That doesn't mean I act like everyone else is deaf." Garin put one finger to his mouth when Bendar came within ear shot.

The three bright red dots on Bendar's forehead were the first things that came into view as he stepped up over the ledge. He was, as usual, wearing brightly colored clothing, the way the professors did at the capitol city of Norwell and in the universities. Farin didn't remember Bendar ever wearing anything different, or trying at all to fit in with the other boys in the village.

His round face wore a stern frown when he closed the distance to the three boys.

"Have a good laugh, pea-brains?" he asked as he held up the arrow. He reached out as if to hand it back to Kaz, but when Kaz moved to take it Bendar snapped it in half and tossed the shaft into a small briar with a satisfied smile.

"Sometimes I wonder why I even agreed to help you all

survive on your Trovens. I presume you at least gathered the supplies on the list?" Bendar asked in a condescending tone.

"We got everything," Kaz called from behind the thorn bush. He carefully moved his hand farther into the briar, trying to retrieve the arrowhead.

"We have everything you've asked for and we even decided to pack our own underpants," Garin replied with a sarcastic, you're-not-my-mother tone as he turned and left with the lamb.

"Don't listen to him. He's just mad he didn't see Kaz's arrow hit your pants," Farin said. With a quick focus to see if Garin was out of earshot he added. "You could help things by not being so condescending all the time."

"It would be a lot easier to be friendly if I was not always the butt of your jokes." The words were emphasized by reaching down and poking his finger through the hole in his trousers. "Despite the unnecessary nature of this venture, I am looking forward to testing the words of Emer, the head scholar from Norwell University. He wrote, 'Traveling can separate the strongest of friends and unify the worst of enemies. Through miles together, true character is forged, formed, and brought to light.' I wish I had space in my belongings for even a portion of his writings."

Farin had no interest in writings from scholars, and even less interest in hearing about them from Bendar for the next year.

"I have one question, Bendar. Who is this Emry guy and has he ever left the walls of the university? I've heard you talk about all these wise guys, but I've never heard of them leaving their cozy apartments in the capitol. I'll tell you one thing: I'm not wasting my strength carrying scrolls, books or anything I don't need."

With this final insult Bendar shook his head and paused. "First off, you asked two questions. Secondly, it is *Emer*. I am sure with some concerted cognitive effort you will be able to pronounce it correctly. And thirdly, I do not think it necessary for you to carry a single transcript, text, manuscript or writing of any kind unless it has bright picture drawings." Bendar smiled wide with satisfaction at having outwitted Farin. He looked to Kaz and back to Farin for some kind of reaction, but all he received was a dismissive head shake.

Returning from the thorn bush, Kaz broke the silence, "Bendar, was that a joke? We really need to work on timing and delivery, but other than that, you nailed him." Kaz clapped Bendar on the back and brought him over to a nearby rock where they sat down to make their final preparations for their departure.

*****

Bendar began his return trip to the village with many thoughts on his mind. The walk would only take him a short time, and with the rate the sun was setting, he calculated he would have just enough time to go to his father's store, gather the perishable items he had left until the last, and hide them outside the village where he would collect them after the Troven ceremony.

While he walked he continued to think over his entire plan. Bendar had everything figured out; the rations each person would collect, minus the amount eaten each day by the average person, times the number of people and number of days. He also took into consideration the approximate amount of meat, fruit, berries and roots they could gather while traveling, the travel time for the average person, and the distance they needed to travel each day to reach Norwell by the end of summer. He knew the best route to avoid unnecessary dangers while making good time.

In his mind there was always a calculation of some kind being made, and in most cases the solutions came very quickly, leaving him satisfied. Bendar felt exactly how he liked to feel: in control.

As he passed down the main street of Dungan, his thoughts were unexpectedly interrupted.

"Hi Bendar, are you okay? You're talking to yourself."

Although surprised by this intrusion, Bendar answered as

politely as he felt protocol demanded. "I did not realize I spoke aloud. Sorry if I bothered you."

"Not at all, Bendar. I was just worried you might be nervous about tomorrow," Bendar looked up and saw it was Fenn who addressed him. Unlike most of the youth in Dungan, Fenn was always kind to Bendar, and the tone of her voice was sincere.

"I am not nervous," he clarified, "I just have a lot that needs to be done. Thank you for your concern." Thinking the conversation was at a logical conclusion, Bendar continued walking down the street.

Before he could walk far, Fenn called out after him. "Bendar, take care of yourself out there." Bendar nodded and continued to walk away.

Although this was a nice gesture, he knew she didn't care one way or another about whether he did 'take care of himself.' Nobody in this town truly did. Nobody in the town really knew him at all.

He spent the warm seasons with his father's family in the harbor city of Pike Point where his parents had met. His mother had been born and raised in Dungan and insisted they all live there during the colder months.

Because of his time spent away from the village, his heritage coming from the sea dwellers, and his gift of intellect, he was different than most of the villagers. As such, he questioned many of the traditions of the small village, including the rite of passage into manhood that would send the boys off on their own at the Summer Festival to "find themselves."

Bendar's father who, like Bendar, was gifted with intellect, found this tradition both antiquated and illogical but also saw the merit in keeping his wife happy, so he consented to the tradition.

When that decision had been made years ago, Bendar had had a realization of his own. He needed to look out for himself. When he had met a professor during his summer holiday in Pike Point a few years ago, he knew a great opportunity had come his way. The young professor had been travelling to take up his new position at Hanger University, far away in the south. During the three days the man had been staying at the inn belonging to Bendar's uncle, Bendar had taken every opportunity to speak with him, and had eventually gotten the young professor to agree to take him on as a sort of project pen pal. What had begun as an opportunity to have his questions answered and reading material referred to him had turned into a serious offer to come to the university. Although he never said it out loud, as Farin did, Bendar had his own agenda. After the Troven, he would never see this quaint place again.

CHAPTER 3

"Wow! This bread is wonderful!" Garin announced as he grabbed another slice and dipped it into the runny yolk on his plate. The warm bread let him know that his mother had been up before the sun, stoking the brick oven and baking. She had also collected fresh eggs, and cut thick slices of ham from the storage in the smoke house. On the table there was also a small bowl of fresh strawberries she insisted were only for the twins. She had probably searched for half an hour just to find those few ripe strawberries this early in the season.

"Yeah, thanks Mom," Farin cut in, unceremoniously spitting out a piece of half chewed ham on the table.

Swatting Farin's hand, his mother scolded, "Don't talk with your mouth full." She looked down at her hand then, and with a pained look in her eyes, she unexpectedly stood up from the table and walked into their living room where she sat on the sofa, buried her face in her hands, and began to quietly cry.

"What's wrong?" the boys asked in unison. She tried to wave them away, but they dropped what they were eating and rushed to her side.

Their father lovingly joined them in a huddle around their mother and put his hand on her shoulders.

"She's just going to miss you both very much." He sat down next to his wife and placed his arm around her. He soothingly whispered into her ear. "It's going to be okay. They understand how important it is to find themselves through this tradition. They know how to hunt, fish, plant and harvest." Then with a slightly raised voice, obviously more for the boys than for his wife, he continued. "They also know the best idea for survival is to either go up into the Northern Forest, build a small log cabin and live off the land, or go to Hillside and work with Baron Omer for the year."

Looking somewhat surprised, their mother turned on him. "You can't tell them what to do for their Troven! You know that." She emphasized her words by slapping his arm and pushing it off her shoulder.

Somewhat sheepishly he continued, “I wasn't telling them to do anything, I was just speculating and making some general statements.”

Farin moved around the sofa so he was facing his parents and cut in before their disagreement escalated.

“It's okay Dad, we have a plan. We'll be all right. But, thanks for the advice.”

Garin took his mother’s hand and held it tightly, “We love you, Mom. Thank you for everything. We're going to be fine.”

With this declaration of love from her teenage boy she couldn't keep the tears from flowing. She pulled Garin in for a tight hug with one arm while she motioned with the other for Farin to join with them. For several moments she squeezed them tightly to herself, refusing to let go. As she held them close, she spoke through her sobs, “Just be safe out there. Don't travel at night. Always have your bows ready. Keep to the main roads and…”

At this point her husband cut her off, “Now who's telling them what to do?” He quickly held up his hands in surrender against a deadly glare.

* * * * *

Bendar’s feet hitting the wooden floor was the only sound in the house as he walked down the hall to the dining area at exactly seven thirty, just as he did every morning. His father sat at the table, and his mother stood by the fire preparing the morning meal.

“Good morning,” his mother said with a smile.

“Hello Mother, Father,” he said while he retrieved three wooden bowls and spoons from the cupboard and set them around the table. As he set the table he wondered whether any of the other boys leaving on their Troven today were still doing their daily chores like it was a normal day.

His father had his spectacles on and was reading through a supply list for restocking the general store. He only put his glasses down when his mother began filling the bowls with porridge.

"Any news from the west?" Bendar asked, nodding his head at the paper his father placed on the table. Bendar's uncle in Pike Point often included some updates with the supply lists he sent, and Bendar was always interested in foreign relations, especially since there was some tension growing between the islands in the Hogden Ocean to the west.

"No new political developments," his father replied in his usual, level tone. "However, my brother tells me that the sea level this year is a handspan lower than last year. While this is not a major concern in itself, when combined with reports he sent of storms in the desert and the unnaturally long winter in the eastern mountains, I am starting to see some very strange weather patterns."

Bendar leaned forward on his chair. "Do you think The Changing is happening?" Bendar had an interest in almost all academic pursuits, but he had been especially fond of reading prophesies about the end of the world. As a child, it was the only thing he could read that felt like fiction, and over the years it grew into a mystery that he felt compelled to solve. *How would all the prophecies be fulfilled? Was it through natural causes, or man's own choices? Where did the ancient prophecies come from? Could they be substantiated?*

His father shook his head. "Bendar, you will not need to worry about that coming any time soon. According to those scrolls you have read there are so many things that need to happen before The Changing, they could not possibly happen in your lifetime."

"I know," Bendar said, somewhat deflated. "I just find it fascinating that so many things from the Hanger University scrolls I've been reading are happening. The rising tension in the western islands, Mordyar invading and conquering in the far southern seas, the strange weather patterns I just find it interesting. That is all."

From across the table, Bendar's mother looked up from her bowl at Bendar, then to her husband.

"Bendar," she began, "You are right. Some unusual things

are happening, and you are also right to be cautious when you leave the safety of Dungan. In the village council meeting, William brought up the exact things you are talking about."

"That is enough, Ellen," Bendar's father said in a matter-of-fact tone.

"No, it's not enough." She said with a hint of agitation reaching her voice. "We need to make him aware. There are dangers out there that are hard to predict. With knowledge, he will be better able to grow from his Troven experience." She paused a moment, and when her husband did not object she continued. "The bandits are more aggressive than ever. Wild animals have been spotted where they usually don't roam. It is more dangerous than ever for us to send out our children." Then she looked right at Bendar and in a rare moment of emotion she spoke tenderly. "Please take extra care of yourself and those other boys."

Nodding his head he promised, "I will."

Then Bendar's father said, "You do need to exercise caution, but there is no cause for alarm, or worry about the world ending. Before The Changing there must be wars and invasions in every land. Denall is a peaceful country with no enemies. Our king is currently working to negotiate peace among the Hogden Islands, and many wars are coming to an end as we speak. Mordyar hasn't been heard of in several years, and he is very far away. We are safe for quite some time from having any enemies or anyone wanting to invade Denall. And of course there is the part in all ancient writings about the magical stones gathering."

Bendar interrupted his father, excited that he was speaking so openly about a topic he usually avoided. "I have always wondered about that part. Do you know what it means?"

"Nobody knows for certain, it says the stones will gather, and that the gathering will shake the earth. Some scholars speculate that it is continents coming together, while others have compiled some legends about magical stones. But there is so little written about it that any emphatic statements can be dismissed as speculation. The important part is that you have nothing to worry about for many generations to come. Right now you need to focus on being safe and finishing your Troven. You may learn something from this experience that will shape the rest of your life, and that is much more important than studying the end of the world."

* * * * *

"Kaz! Get up out of that bed and come in here!" Gran called from the lower level of the home they shared. Kaz heard the older woman shuffle to the dining room to wait for him. It was the last breakfast he would have with Gran before his Troven, and it was shaping up to be a memorable meal. He slowly climbed down the stairs, gripping tightly to the hand rail. Every few steps he moaned audibly.

"What's wrong with you?" Gran called up to him.

She was still at the table, until Kaz got to the ground level and turned around to face her. The older woman's eyes looked like they were going to bulge out of her head when she saw Kaz. His hair was disheveled and he had dark red spots all over his pale face.

"Are you okay? What happened to you?" she asked as she hurried toward him.

Kaz spoke in a croaky voice in response. "I don't know Gran, I just don't feel well."

She tenderly helped him to a seat. "Is it your stomach? Your head?" she asked reaching up to touch his forehead.

"I think it must have been those vegetables you forced me to eat last night." Kaz couldn't keep a straight face any longer and he cracked a wide smile.

"You really are such a pain, you know that?" Gran said as she reached up and gave Kaz a playful twist of his ear. "You get to the table or you'll start your Troven with an empty stomach."

Kaz wiped his face clean as he joined Gran at the table for breakfast. "Do you think when I come back, I can, you know, stay here again?" Kaz asked between bites.

After his parents' death, Kaz had moved from house to

house in town. He had spent the last year living with Gay, who most people in town fondly called Gran. Because she lived on the far outskirts of town and her husband had passed away, the villagers agreed Kaz should live with her to help keep up the home and watch out for her. It was a modest home with a small garden in the back, but because of her age, Gran tried to remain on one level of the house as much as possible. Kaz had helped her to convert part of the first floor into a bedroom, and feeling uncomfortable using her old room, he had made a bedroom for himself in the loft upstairs.

During his time with her, Gran had taught Kaz to sew and knit and promised to not tell the other boys how skilled he was. She said he'd thank her one day when he had warm socks on cold winter nights. Although he did not like feeling as though he was the property of the village to be passed around where there was a need, he did like Gran, and the feeling of being needed and useful and genuinely loved. He really did want to come back to live with her when he finished his time away.

Gran looked to Kaz with a wide grin on her face. "As long as I don't have to put up with more of your silly pranks," she replied as she took her napkin and wiped off a smudge of red that remained on his face. "I was actually thinking when you return you would be looking to get married, set up your own homestead, and raise children. I thought you could take over this place as long as you took care of me until I go."

"Come on Gran, don't talk like that," Kaz replied.

"I'm serious. When you come back, the place is yours and you'll be taking care of me for a change." She gave Kaz an affectionate wink and looked at him across the top of the teacup she had just raised to her lips. She waited for a moment as he processed that thought, and then briskly began piling his plate with food. "Now let's get eating or we'll be late for your own ceremony."

Kaz began eating his breakfast quietly as he thought about Gran's offer. He did want to return here when he was done, but he didn't know how he felt about settling down in Dungan forever. This was the place where he had grown up after his parents had been killed, but before that, he remembered how his father had always told him to 'search for his place.' He had wondered from time to time what that could mean, especially being moved from family to family as he had grown up. Villagers who had known his father told him that it meant for him to find his place in their community – to be useful. Though he knew their words made sense, aside from helping Gran, he didn't really feel like he actually had a place here in Dungan.

✢ ✢ ✢ ✢ ✢

Village Council President Gib stood center stage, with the town council in perfect symmetry on either side of her overlooking the town square. She was dressed in a bright red, full traditional formal gown which stood out in contrast to the yellows and oranges worn by the other council members. Gib looked much like an older, but still strikingly beautiful version of her daughter Fenn. Tall and slim, with dark hair and green eyes, she was much slimmer than the previous council president and had not been in office long enough to have the ceremonial robes tailored. Her ear marks darkened as she made regular audio scans to check that all was in order before she began. In her oversized gown she began the Troven Ceremony.

"Welcome one and all to this momentous occasion." With that brief introduction she opened the scroll and began to follow the script:

"Two hundred-forty three years ago, a young man named Dungan was eighteen. While young and not yet considered a man he left Kinstock with his new bride to seek their fortunes in the world. Exactly eleven months and three days from the time they left Kinstock, they arrived at this very spot and determined they would make it their new home. While time has erased their original homestead it has not erased their memory. From his humble beginnings he built a homestead, planted fields of vegetables, fruit trees and grapes. With the pelts he trapped he purchased and raised sheep, cows and horses. In time others joined him to settle this land and it has grown into a populous town that is proud to have taken his name." Farin let out an audible sigh and Kaz almost burst out laughing when he saw the death stare Farin's mother shot at him.

The village council president continued. "In memory of his journey into adulthood, each boy in the summer of his eighteenth year *must leave Dungan*, for four seasons, with the intent of discovering his own place in the world, proving he can survive on his own. When he returns he is accepted into the village to take up his place as a man. The Troven is a tradition of our ancestors that has served each generation well in teaching our young men to find themselves, and to find a purpose in this world."

The way she emphasized the words 'must leave Dungan' made Kaz think back to the time when he was very young, when Tomas had tried to outsmart the tradition by living just outside the village and snuck into his parents' home from time to time for warmth and some food. When his parents found him shivering and thin from lack of food, they took him in. As soon as the snow melted they left the village in shame with their son -- who would never be considered a man in Dungan.

In preparing for his Troven, Kaz had talked with some villagers who had built temporary cabins and lived off the land, and others who had joined the King's army. It seemed that every young man had his own idea of the best Troven experience, but what each had in common was that after a full year away from their families most boys returned, never to be called boys again, but men. Others found new lives in distant places and returned briefly from time to time, having earned their place as equally honorable men who were simply better suited for other places. There were also a few who never returned. When one year passed with no return, the sons were tactfully declared men who had gone to other realms.

When Gib had finished her part of the ceremony, Kaz released a moan as Check Mizar stepped forward to give his words of advice.

"Boys, every year the seasons change. The summer becomes fall and then the fall becomes winter. Winter gives way to spring which then changes into summer…" If previous years speeches were any indication, Kaz knew Check would go on for far too long. Kaz's part in this ceremony would not come for quite some time. One great advantage of not being a listener was that Kaz could tune out the boring monotone speech given by the graying member of the village council while he surveyed the audience.

He saw Garin and Farin's mother fighting back tears -- trying to put on a strong face for her boys. Their father stood taller than normal, filled with pride as his boys made the final step into manhood. They both made eye contact with Kaz and nodded in approval. After his parents died four years ago, Kaz had lived with Garin and Farin for a time. Scanning the crowd, he saw many families who had taken him in. He saw Ion and Sacks -- the town blacksmith and son. While he lived there for six months, they had taught him some of their trade, but he did not have the disposition for blacksmith labor, so they passed him to another family. He had tried livestock, farming, cleaning the inn floors, and even clerking at the general store with Bendar, but he never found his place in this town until Gran took him in.

As Kaz continued to look into the audience, he saw so many of the families who had been kind to him or helped him get through the difficult time after losing his parents. He also began to notice more and more eyes were looking back at him. When he saw Gran in the audience, she urgently pointed for Kaz to look to the center of the stage. He turned his head and realized they were all waiting for him. In a moment of panic Kaz's mind went blank. *What's my line?* With a priceless grin for the crowd, Kaz sought through his mind for anything he may have remembered Gib or Check saying. He was at a loss, so he did the only thing he could think of.

"I'm sorry, did you say I could go yet?"

Kaz began to walk off the stage, which made the adults in the audience shake their heads or silently laugh while they restrained their children from open laughter. At the bottom of the stairs Gran met him with a stern look and turned him around.

"Go back and tell them your oath."

With that reminder, he walked to the center of the stage. There he raised his left hand and opened it for all to see his empty palm. This universal sign of honesty was made before making an oath, as a symbol that he was not hiding anything. With his hand outstretched he loudly began his oath.

"I swear in my travels to always do that which will bring honor to the places from whence I hail: the kingdom of Denall, the Western Realm, the village of Dungan." Then with a pause uncharacteristic of Kaz, who was always a show off for a crowd, he emotionally added, "and most of all, the family name of Kinsley." Kaz stopped speaking, and took a step back as Garin, Farin and Bendar repeated the oath. They stood silently on the stage as the villagers took one final look at the boys who would, in one year, return as men.

After a moment of silence, the audience clapped and cheered, shouting words of encouragement.

Kaz raised one hand and waved to the onlookers, then turned left and walked to the edge of the stage. He slowly stepped to the side, allowing the others to leave first. Kaz watched as the other boys met with their parents. Garin and Farin were met with solid hugs from their father and a fit of uncontrollable weeping from their mother. Bendar's father gave his son a sturdy handshake and his mother gave him a strong hug while she dried a stray tear that escaped her control. Kaz was happy for the support his friends had, but felt a sharp loss at not having parents to bid him farewell. He also wondered what it would be like to get a parting gift. Garin, Farin and Bendar's parents handed their sons each a small bag of items to help with their journey to manhood.

Kaz took a step forward when he saw an unexpected movement from the corner of his eye. Fenn was weaving her way through the crowd. Kaz stopped moving, knowing something fun was about to happen. *What is she thinking?*

He looked back over his shoulder at Gib. Her dark gaze was a clear indication that she had also noticed her daughter's trajectory, but in her position on the stage all she could do was watch as things unfolded.

Kaz took a slow step into the middle of the narrow stairs, making sure nobody from the town council could stop what was about to happen. Fenn was no longer slowly making her way forward, she had broken into a very unlady-like trot. She burst through the crowd of onlookers and threw her arms around Garin's neck. Kaz covered his mouth to stifle a laugh that threatened to burst from him.

"What are you doing?" Garin asked, looking around awkwardly, knowing the eyes of the entire village were on him.

Without giving an answer Fenn pulled him close and their lips met. Kaz knew that this was the moment Garin had been anticipating for years, and he seemed to drink in every second. When she pulled away he gulped in a calming breath, and for a brief moment seemed to forget that he had an audience.

"Wow," was all he could force out of his mouth.

She subtly slid her hand down Garin's arm and placed something into his hand before she turned and darted off back into the crowd.

Kaz finished descending the stairs and patted Garin on the back playfully, his momentary grief replaced by amusement. His friend was now red-faced and facing the stern scowls of his parents.

Kaz made his way past his friends and began down the path when he heard his name being called. At first he thought he was hearing things, but after his name was repeated more urgently, he turned around. Gran called for him and slowly pushed through the crowd. When she caught him she reached up and gave him a tight embrace around the neck and placed in his hands a hand-knit sock that served as an unorthodox 'bag' of gifts.

"Kaz, care for this gift and it will care for you."

Kaz looked up to the village council. "Gran I thought only parents could meet us before our Troven."

Gran made a determined face and replied. "I don't care what they say. You are my boy and I'm seeing you off. Besides, if they let that girl give him a kiss, they'll indulge an old lady." She then kissed him on the cheek.

"Thank you, Gran," he said, his voice choked with emotion. He thought that he was prepared to walk off the stage alone, but as he held the small woman tightly in his arms, he realized how wrong he was. He didn't want to let go.

When Kaz opened his eyes he realized, for the first time, he was being left behind by the other three boys who were making their way out of the village green. He whispered in her ear as he released her embrace.

"Goodbye. I will see you in four seasons." Then he turned, and over his shoulder in a much more characteristic manner he added, "And don't forget to feed my pet mice, I've been raising them on your finest cheese."

"You'd better get going now or you'll not only find yourself on this trip, you'll find my wooden spoon across your hind quarters!" She scolded with a playful slap on his rump. Seeing her playful scowl was exactly what he needed as a final farewell. Kaz turned and jogged to catch up to his friends as they turned their backs to the village.

CHAPTER 4

As they left the village, Kaz heard the band begin to play. The post-Troven-ceremony party had officially begun. He grabbed his stomach and tried to suppress a loud growl.

"Barely out of the village and you're already starving," Farin commented with a smirk.

"Give me a break!" Kaz demanded, then he sighed and continued. "I was just thinking of Mrs. Henchin's strawberry pies, and fresh-baked sticky buns, and..."

Farin grabbed his own stomach, "Stop it!"

Kaz only smiled and playfully shoved his friend. "Speaking of things that are sweet to the lips," Kaz said with an exaggerated pucker, "that was quite a memorable ceremony for *you,* wasn't it, Garin?"

Garin's cheeks burned red, but he quickly recovered. "Make fun while you can. You'll probably forget about it soon, just like your lines while on stage." Kaz noticed Garin rub his hand over his front pocket and smile like a love-sick fool. *What did she give him?*

"That *was* pretty sad, Kaz," Farin added, "It was actually good that Fenn showed up so people won't just call it the year that Kaz stood looking around like he didn't know where he was."

"Very funny," he replied. He knew when the twins started ganging up on him it was time to change the subject. "So Bendar, what's the plan?"

Bendar looked back at Kaz. "I thought it was *your* village's tradition for those being sent on Troven to be *silent* as they exit the village."

Garin rolled his eyes and shook his head, and Farin just stayed quiet. "I think we're safely out of the village, unless that was just a clever way of telling me you don't feel like talking." Kaz replied, looking expectantly at Bendar for a response.

When Bendar didn't answer he looked around at the Segris twins, who seemed content to walk in silence. Kaz continued to hike for several minutes before he couldn't stand it anymore.

"Come on guys, we can't just wander along like this for the next year! This is supposed to be our time. We're out on our own. Every year we've watched people leave the village, but we've never known what they do when they get out of sight. This is our journey into manhood, our chance to have some fun. What do you want to do?"

"Anything," Farin responded, as he broke off a small branch of a tree and began swinging it around. "Whatever we do out here is better than being back there." He pointed back at the village that was disappearing in the distance. "I just wish I had left sooner."

"Me too," Garin agreed.

All three boys turned to look at Garin, but it was Farin who spoke. "I thought you hated the idea of leaving."

"I do. I wish I had done this last year because then I'd be back by now," he replied.

"Come on, like she'd have waited for you if you had left then!" Farin laughingly taunted as he jumped around Kaz and Bendar to get further away from Garin.

Shaking his head at the petty exchange, Kaz interjected, "You two are really amazing, you know that?"

"Thanks Kaz, I think you're pretty great too," Farin said with a smile.

"That's not what I meant. I meant you're just so different." Then, seeing that Garin was still walking with his head down, Kaz added, "And sulky." Garin looked up with a glare and swung a wide, playful punch at Kaz who easily evaded it and then grabbed Garin in a headlock. "Besides," Kaz added when Garin was able to struggle free of the hold, "doesn't Fenn have a younger sister?"

With a look of mock sincerity Farin nodded. "That's right, Garin, and by the time you come back as a man, she'll be out of diapers."

"Seriously guys, do you really not ever think of what it will be like when we come back? The village will welcome us, we'll be able to build our own homes, grow our own crops, and start raising families. I can't wait to be done with this and moving on with life. Don't you ever think about what you want in the future?" Although Kaz would never admit it out loud, in many ways he looked up to, and envied the fact that Garin seemed to be so grounded and have everything figured out.

"I think about the future all the time," Kaz interjected. "Like when will we get to the first food stash?"

"We have only been walking for twenty-three minutes," Bendar said in a monotone voice. "Perhaps I should reconsider some of my calculations about your food consumption."

"You've calculated my food consumption?" Kaz asked in disbelief.

"Eating is an important part of survival," Bendar replied.

"What else have you calculated?" Farin asked.

"Hopefully everything." Bendar stepped off the path and pointed to a hollow under a large cherry tree. "Just up ahead on the left is the first stash. That one should have been pretty easy to discover." The first stash of supplies was covered with dried leaves, carefully camouflaged to blend in naturally.

The boys threw the leaves to the side and uncovered the large, wooden box. Kaz reached under the box to lift it up, but nothing happened.

"Are you going to pick it up?" Garin asked.

Kaz turned on him with a sour look, "Why don't you try helping? This thing weighs a ton!"

The larger farm boys hefted the crate out of the ground easily and then pried off the lid, excitedly sifting through the supplies.

"Something must be wrong." Bendar cut in, pushing his way to the crate. "Perhaps I have misunderstood this part of your tradition. If adults in the village find the food stash, do they not take some of the supplies, to help promote self-reliance among those who are sent on Troven?"

"That's only *if* they find the stash." Garin responded. "You must be better at stashing than you thought." Although it seemed to irk Garin to admit Bendar was good at something, he also looked very satisfied to point out that Bendar was wrong.

"No I am not. This was found." Bendar knelt down at the

base of the tree and searched for tracks. Looking up at the others he continued. "I know it was found."

"What are you talking about? Here are all the apples that I collected and all the salted dry pork Farin borrowed from Dad's smoke house. Two bow strings and a hunting knife. This is great!"

"Something about this is just not right." Bendar looked concerned. "My parents knew about this stash. They should have taken at least half of the materials." Kaz could see the worry creasing Bendar's face, and it clearly bothered Bendar that the stash was intact, but the other boys just kept pulling out supplies.

"I'm telling you they didn't find it," Garin insisted, gesturing to the undisturbed surroundings. "Can't we just be happy for what we have? Your calculations were wrong, but your stashing was perfect."

"Let us gather what we can fit into our travel bags," Bendar said, handing out the small burlap sacks from the supply crate, "We can reach the second stash by nightfall and that will be our campsite." They filled the bags with the food and supplies, hefted them up, and continued down the dirt road.

At about noon Kaz was exhausted by the hours of walking down the dirt road carrying the heavy pack.

"I need to get this bag off my shoulders for a bit. Can we stop for lunch?" Kaz looked at the other boys pleadingly. He knew Garin and Farin worked on the farm and expected them to be in good shape. Trying to appeal to Bendar, Kaz added, "It's logical to stop now, so our bags will be lighter after we eat."

Bendar shook his head at Kaz's remark, but seemed to be happy to shrug his bag off his shoulder and set it on the ground.

"We can stop for a little rest, but not too long. It is still a half day's trip to the second storage crate."

"Is there any way we can rest somewhere else today?" Kaz asked, wanting to have some fun on the first day of his Troven. "Perhaps right here. There is a stream we can collect water from, and we can sleep in that small stand of trees over there."

Bendar looked unsympathetic. "That would be fine if you

want to sleep without any shelter. Those supplies are in the second crate."

"Why did you put them so far away from the village?" Garin asked. Kaz was happy that he wasn't the only one not wanting to walk all day long.

"When we discussed it, everyone agreed that we wanted to get moving away from the village quickly."

"I guess that was before we realized how boring it is to walk all day long," Farin interjected.

Bendar exhaled loudly. "Next time, decide to make the camp closer, before I haul all the supplies so far away from the village."

The boys were silent. Kaz looked apologetically at Bendar. He hadn't thought too much about all the work Bendar had done over the past few weeks to get the supplies in place, and the more he thought about it, the more petty it seemed to be upset that he had to walk the distance one time.

"Thanks for getting the supplies in place," he said.

Bendar nodded, "Let us eat so we can be on our way."

While he chewed on a piece of dried meat, Kaz silently fingered the 'bag' Gran had given him. Although the tradition was for the boys to not open the gifts until they stopped for their first night, nobody said anything about feeling through the bags. The knitted sock contained some items that he could identify through the dense wool. First off, there was the second sock, and a small rectangular box. Knowing Gran it was probably a sewing kit. If the other boys asked about it, he could tell them it was to stitch up any deep cuts so he didn't come home looking like the latticed top of an apple pie. There was no way he was telling them that Gran had taught him to sew and insisted he mend all his own clothing. No matter how much time he spent fiddling with the gift sock, he couldn't figure out the last two items. One felt like a long, thick string or chain. It could be a snare or sling, but he couldn't be sure. The last item felt like a small, smooth stone. *What could she have meant by her farewell statement? One thing is for certain, I am not going to take up precious space in my travel bag to carry a 'lucky' rock for the next year.*

The rest of the day was spent walking nearly due east on the main road from Dungan to the nearby town of Hillside. The journey was monotonous as they walked through the Woller Plains. Although they did pass some small stands of trees that provided shelter from the sun, most of their day was spent exposed to the direct sunlight while open fields spread out in every direction as far as they could see. Kaz tried to initiate some conversation, but it always fizzled, and they returned to walking in silence. The only real excitement was when Farin stumbled over a tree root and twisted his ankle. They needed to stop walking for exactly eleven minutes, as Bendar insisted on pointing out.

As the day came to a close, Bendar, without giving any notice to his companions, headed left off the road, awkwardly climbed over a short stone wall, and continued into an open field. In the field he counted eight paces west from a large stone and began to dig with his hands to unearth a wooden crate. All four boys hauled the crate up.

"This is even heavier than the last one," Farin said through gritted teeth. "What's in here?"

Offhandedly Bendar listed the supplies. "Food, a flint, three more hunting knives, four longbows, arrows, quivers, travel bags, wood for one night of fire, spare clothing, a sheet of canvas for a shelter, a sword, and some other supplies that I thought would be discovered and taken away. We cannot take all of this." Bendar anxiously rubbed his forehead, as if he was more deeply worried than before. "If the second supply stash is undisturbed, then the third was, in all probability, discovered," he said to the group.

"Either that or nobody knows about any of the stashes," Kaz countered. "That was an amazing hiding spot. Nobody could have found that."

Ignoring Kaz's comment, Bendar addressed the group, "I have selected a campsite in that stand of trees on the far side of this field." He began to explain the reasoning for this location, but the exhausted group hefted the crate and walked the remaining distance without waiting for a full explanation. When they reached a small, flat spot, Bendar indicated they would stop. The boys dropped their heavy bags and the large crate. Farin and Garin massaged aching limbs, and Kaz simply collapsed onto his back looking up into the canopy of trees. He heard Bendar shuffling around getting the campsite set up, but couldn't bring himself to move another inch.

"What are you looking for?" Kaz asked when he saw Farin haphazardly rummaging through the crate.

"This," Farin responded, pulling out the sword.

Garin shook his head and threw his hands up in the air, "Are you kidding? Why did you have Bendar pack that?"

"It's for protection," Farin said as he drew it from the sheath and swung it around.

"What are you going to protect us from, mice? You've had like four lessons when you were a kid."

"And I've practiced every day since, and worked with some of Dad's hired help," Farin countered. He thrust his sword forward to punctuate his words.

Kaz looked up from the ground, and from his vantage Farin didn't look half bad. "I can't believe you have the energy for that," Kaz moaned. "Bendar, I'm not sure anyone has ever made this much distance on their first day of Troven."

"Actually, I have read of some who claimed to travel through the entire night to arrive at Hillside and enjoy a restful night in the comfort of an inn. Three returned men wrote of Trovens that never involved sleeping a single night under the stars."

"They're liars!" Farin chimed in. "Bendar, although you are the reason that we walked halfway to Norwell in a single day carrying a mountain of supplies," he exaggerated, "I'll give you this much: now that we're stopped, I'm glad your stashes have everything." He sheathed his sword and placed it next to the spot he had picked out to sleep.

"I actually wanted to talk to you all about that," Bendar began. "I had a special surprise at the third stash, and I fear it will not be there when we arrive. I think I have been outsmarted."

"Impossible. You're the highest level intellect in the entire village," Kaz reassured.

"That does not mean I am the smartest person in the village."

"What are you talking about?" Garin asked.

"The development of a gift is just as important, if not more important, than the strength of that gift." Bendar said with a satisfied nod of his head. Kaz looked around the campfire and was happy to see that he wasn't the only person with a confused look on his face. Bendar stopped opening his gift sack and continued. "My father is a level two intellect, and he has had forty years of life experience," he explained.

Kaz leaned forward, anticipating Bendar actually making any sense, but after a long pause Kaz waved his hand for Bendar to finish his point.

Bendar put his hand on his head as if puzzling out how to explain a simple concept to three dense students.

"Is a level four strongarm child stronger than his level three father?"

"No," they all answered almost in unison.

"Exactly my point. If one uses his gift daily and develops it faithfully, one could become more powerful than a person with a higher level who is slothful. Does that make sense to you?"

"Yes, school mistress," Garin answered sarcastically.

Kaz wished Bendar's question didn't sound so condescending, but fortunately Bendar ignored the comment and continued. "Do you remember your father's level four strongarm from the Eastern Mountains?"

"So I see you noticed him too," Farin said with an I-told-you-so look to Kaz and Garin.

"He is constantly working on his strength. This could be because he lost an arm wrestle to a level three, or he was raised with a level five in his village or family and always wanted to keep up. Either way, he is much stronger than any strongarm I have ever seen, and he is probably as strong as the average level five."

His logic was beginning to sink in with Kaz and he saw Farin nodding.

"That makes sense," Farin said. "Our dad always sent us to find the stray animals, and we've become the best listeners on the farm, maybe in the entire village." Kaz remembered his conversation with Barrels, and wondered if Garin and Farin's father sent them out to help prepare them for the Troven.

"How long have you known about this?" Garin asked.

"I do not know for sure. It just seems logical. This is one of many hypotheses I have constructed and intend to research further."

"One of many?" Kaz said. "What other ideas do you have?"

Bendar stood up and took his place standing in front of the group like a scholar addressing his pupils. "All of you turn around for a moment." Kaz, Garin and Farin turned around and looked out into the field. After a few minutes of sitting, Bendar instructed them to turn back around. "Now tell me what you noticed out there."

Kaz was the first to speak. "I saw some trees, and then an open field with freshly planted crops. What's your point?"

"Tell me what you noticed," Bendar said turning to Garin.

"I noticed that I was sitting on a log with my back to the fire," Garin replied curtly.

Farin cut in, "I noticed that the trees are creaking as they sway back and forth. An owl hooted as it flew over the field just outside of the trees."

Bendar smiled from ear to ear. "Do you see?"

"See what?" Garin asked.

"They both experienced the same thing, but Kaz told me what he saw, and Farin told me what he heard," Bendar nearly danced with joy. "I think that there is so much more to our gifts than just enhancing a single characteristic. I think it determines so much more about who we are," Bendar spoke quickly, and waved his arms around like an excited child who had just received a long awaited gift. Kaz didn't ever remember seeing Bendar so happy.

"That's nice," Garin said, clearly uninterested.

"Even the way you are acting proves my point. I am so

excited about this and you do not seem to care at all. I have always had a natural love for learning. I see the world through academics, and logic. Each gift seems to be connected to how we experience the world around us."

"What about magicians?" Garin asked.

Shaking his head Bendar answered, "Admittedly, at present my hypothesis is inconclusive. I have never seen a hound and I have only once met a magician. There are also so many other unanswered questions: Why are some gifts more common in certain regions? What determines the strength of a gift? Why are so many more people born with the gift of hearing and sight than anything else? Why are some people born with two weak gifts instead of one strong one? If the gifts originally came from powerful sorcerers, can a powerful enough magician give someone a gift now? There are too many questions without answers, but that will all change when I get to Hanger University," Bendar clamped his mouth shut, then looked around the group guiltily.

"Where did you say?" Kaz asked. "I thought the plan was for us to go together to Norwell, then Farin would join with the King's army, and the three of us would return together, not head off to the Southern Desert."

"It is the best university for studying marks and gifts," Bendar began to explain.

"Wait a minute!" Garin cut in. "What about working together? You plan the route, we do the heavy lifting. I guess your plan is to just use us to get what you need, then leave us in Norwell as you go south," Garin's voice rose as he spoke.

"I will not abandon you," Bendar started sounding sincere, but Kaz knew there was nothing he could say that would change Garin's low opinion of him.

Kaz put up his hands to stop the argument before it escalated. "Let's just open our gifts and call it a night."

Grumbling, the others agreed and silently sat around the fire opening their gift bags.

* * * * *

Bendar moved to sit on a log alone, frustrated that in his enthusiasm he had let it slip that he planned to go to Hanger. Although Hanger University did have scrolls and scholars who could help him study various gifts, he also knew they had the most comprehensive library about The Changing. Of all his academic pursuits, he felt most drawn to this topic of study, and for a reason that logic could not justify, he felt that The Changing would happen sooner than anyone thought, maybe even in his lifetime.

Despite all his reasons for choosing Hanger University, Bendar knew his companions on this Troven would never understand him. Nobody truly understood him. Accepting that his current situation as a social outcast was out of his control, he opened the bag he had received from his parents.

In his small bag was a travel sized book, and a note from his parents:

Bendar,

We are very proud of the boy that you have become. As you lead your friends, please be kind and understanding. Always remember that wisdom can only come when knowledge is applied in the real world. Sometimes you will need to make decisions that do not make sense, but feel right. These choices will help you in becoming a man. Follow your head, follow your heart, and live by the values you have been taught.

Mom and Dad

P.S. We hope that you are not too disappointed that the two stashes are left as they were. We thought it would be a better challenge for your group to choose which items you would take and what you would leave behind.

Bendar read over the note again, searching the words for any hint that they had found the third stash. Did the mention of two stashes mean that is all they think I have? How would they know it was more upsetting for the stashes to be left alone? And perhaps the most confusing part of the note was that in his father's handwriting the message told him to follow his heart.

After examining the note until he had it memorized, and was certain he couldn't learn anything useful from it, he opened the small book. The Changing. Bendar opened the book and began reading. He smiled as he thought of his conversation with his father earlier that day.

*****

Garin sat close to the fire using the light to closely examine the contents of his bag. It contained three items: a knife, a gold coin, and a note:

Garin,

We know that you are coming home to us and we will probably not see Farin again. Please watch out for him. He needs your stability and you need his passion for life if you are to grow into the men you need to be. Dad included the knife he has told you about, but you have never seen. It was given to him by his father when he started on his Troven. He used it every day he was away, and hopes it will play a role in you becoming a man. Stick to the main roads and travel by day if at all possible. Remember to keep your ears sharp; they will protect you from danger. This coin will help you get started on your journey. Dad says to not spend it all in one place, and I say not to waste it. Now put this note away and get some rest.

We love you very much,
Mom and Dad

After he read the letter, he reached into his pocket and pulled out the gift from Fenn, the greatest treasure he had received at the ceremony. Garin looked at the drawing. It was a perfect resemblance. He wondered who had drawn this picture, as he knew Fenn was not much of an artist. He turned the drawing over to see on the back a few words in Fenn's graceful handwriting.

"I will wait for you," was all that was written.

"So what did Mom say to you?" Farin asked him. "Probably the same stuff Dad was writing to me. I bet they were writing two letters at the same time. Listen to this part: 'Be strong, Son.

Mom says she loves you, remember your oath. Also, Mom says be careful, and take care of your brother.'"

"Yeah mine is basically the same; 'Take care of your brainless brother so he doesn't get himself killed.'" With a smile, Garin showed Farin the knife. "What did they give to you?"

"Oh you know -- the usual -- a note, a gold coin, Dad's scarf from his Troven, and a love letter from Fenn."

"I can't believe you were looking over my shoulder!" Garin yelled as he turned to grab Farin's bag and have a look for himself. Although he knew Farin didn't have a picture of Fenn, he couldn't help but take a look just to be sure. The twins wrestled on the ground and only stopped when Kaz stood up and made an unexpected announcement.

"I want to tell all of you that I am very good at knitting."

This surprise outburst from Kaz silenced everyone. Kaz lay down as though nothing had happened and closed his eyes as if he hoped to avoid the razzing that was sure to follow.

"I'm so glad that you are opening up to us after all these years, Kaz," Farin began in a sarcastic tone.

Garin picked up right where his brother left off. "Is there anything else you'd like to tell us? Do you want me to tuck you in?"

"Did you knit those socks?" Bendar asked. Although his tone was serious, and Kaz raised his head up off the ground and looked like he was about to answer, the twins laughed even harder.

"Remind me to thank Gran when we get back," Garin began.

"I always knew I liked that lady," Farin said, then he turned and saw Kaz throw something into the supply crate. The object caught the firelight as it flew and Garin saw that it had a metallic, reflective surface.

"What is that, Kaz?"

"It's nothing, goodnight."

"Seriously, it looks-" Garin began

"Expensive," Farin finished. "What is that?"

By trying to avoid the topic, Kaz had drawn all attention to the small gift Gran had given him. In answer to their question, Kaz pulled out the note from Gran.

"Dear Kaz, I hope these socks keep your feet warm. In this note I am to give you counsel, at least one piece of advice that you should follow and one piece that you must follow. You should dry your socks every night by the fire. One of the most important things on your Troven is to have dry feet." Kaz paused and smiled at the other boys, then he held the socks up near the fire before he continued reading. "The piece of advice that you must follow is that you will, as soon as you are done reading, announce to your friends that you are talented at knitting. You may think that there is some hidden reason for this request, but there is not. I'm just getting you back for all the tricks you played on me when you lived here. They always kept me smiling and this is to remind you that I'll always get the last laugh. I hope this trick will help you remember all the fun we had. Love, Gran."

"It didn't say anything about that thing you threw away." Garin remarked.

Kaz turned the note around and Garin could see a short scribble at the bottom, as though it was not going to be on the letter. Kaz turned it back around and continued, "When my husband passed away he gave me this necklace with instructions to pass it on to the owner it chose. I have worn it every day since he passed. I didn't understand how a necklace could choose an owner until today. I felt the necklace pull toward you as you stood on the stage. Wear it well."

Bendar had sat up and joined the conversation. "Can I take a look at the necklace?"

"It's over there in the crate. You can do whatever you like with it," Kaz answered.

Bendar and Garin both looked through the supplies for the necklace. Bendar found it first and began examining it by the firelight. Garin sat close and looked down at the piece of jewelry. The necklace was clearly made for a woman. It had a beautifully hand crafted silver chain with a small, polished stone. The chain looked well-worn as though it had been passed down for many generations, but the stone was what caught Garin's attention. It was completely free of any scratches. It was perfectly smooth, and reflective as a still pond.

Turning it over in his hands Bendar commented. "Are you going to keep it?"

"I don't mind telling you guys that I was great at something, but I'm not wearing women's jewelry," Kaz replied.

"You can't just leave it here," Garin said in a serious tone. "It belonged to her husband, it's really important to her."

"I'll pick it up on my way back home," Kaz answered. "Gran will never know the difference." He squirmed on the ground trying to find a spot where the ground didn't dig into him.

"What if something happens to it? You can't just leave it," Garin protested.

"If you like it, why don't you wear it?" Kaz rolled over, grabbed the necklace from Bendar and tossed it to Garin who put it around his neck, but made sure it was hidden by his shirt. Garin didn't want Kaz to throw it away, but he also was not comfortable wearing jewelry so everyone could see.

"I'll keep it for you for now, but when we get back to the village, you're going to be wearing it."

"Deal, you wear it in public, and I'll wear it for Gran," Kaz said as he rolled over to get some sleep.

Farin surveyed the campsite, "Just so I'm clear," Farin said looking deliberately at each boy around the fire. When all the boys were looking at him, he made a confused face as though considering something very important. "Bendar has been quietly moping all day because his stashes were not disturbed and he got exactly what he wanted, Garin is wearing women's jewelry, and Kaz revealed that he likes to knit. I wonder if all journeys to becoming men start with three guys pretending to be ladies." Before he could even finish his thought several small tufts of sod were thrown at him.

CHAPTER 5

Dune walked into the tavern of the small hamlet in southern Denall and gave a friendly wave to the owner, a tall man in a white apron.

"Hello, my friend," the man replied, reaching out a hand in a friendly gesture. "How did your hunting expedition go?"

"It was unfortunately not as successful as I would have liked," Dune replied as he removed his leather hunting coat and placed it on a wooden peg on the wall, leaned his longbow up next to it, and looked at himself in a reflective shield that hung on the wall. Although the disguise made him look like a local hunter, his dark, almond-shaped eyes and thick, black hair were a giveaway that he was from even farther south.

"What are you serving tonight?" he asked. He needed a quiet place to sit and think before he proceeded. When he had arrived in Eaton he had set up two cabins. One was close to town, known among the locals, the other was more of a single room hideaway—a safe house for when things went wrong. He needed to figure out which one was surrounded by traps.

"Roast mutton stew," the tavern owner gestured to a simmering pot over the fire in answer to Dune's question, then began to wipe down a nearby table. "A friend of yours arrived today and said it was your favorite, and that you'd be returning tonight."

Dune searched the room for any familiar people.

"Where is he?" Dune replied after surveying the tavern for his mentor. Kire was the only man who would claim Dune enjoyed mutton stew, but he lived in northern Denall, a distance that would take several months to travel. *What is he doing here and how did he find me?*

"He said he'd meet you at your cabin later today." He smiled wide as he added, "I hope I didn't ruin any surprises."

Dune tried to act casual, while his mind was racing. "How long ago did he leave?"

"Not long at all," he responded.

Dune nodded, and tossed a coin to the man. "Thank you.

I've got to go."

The man nodded as he placed a large bowl on the cleaned table in front of Dune. "What about your stew?"

"Save some for me, I'll have some later." Dune grabbed his bow and coat, and headed to the door.

"There's one more thing," the inn keeper said, but Dune did not wait to hear his message. He needed to find Kire before he inadvertently set off any magical traps. Knowing Kire was in the area made him very uneasy, and he needed to make sure he was safe, then find out the reason for the visit right away. There was no time to think this one through. He needed to move. Dune darted around behind the tavern and looked out in the direction of his cabin in the village. He teleported out into the night. He landed next to his cabin near the village. It seemed quiet and undisturbed, but he cautiously approached.

"Kire," he called out in a hushed voice. He kept a safe distance from the building, but reached out with a hair-thin strand of magic. "Kire, are you there?"

While he circled around the entire cabin he continued to reach out with magic and call for his friend. When his magic touched the outside of the building, he could feel several spells, but didn't have time to check what each of them would do.

Dune released a relieved breath. Kire was okay. Then he scrunched his eyes in confusion. *If Kire is not here, he must know about the other house, but how?*

He waved his hand and vanished. Teleporting in three jumps he brought himself up next to the small, rough-sawn log building. Crouching under the open window, his back against the wall, Dune tried to listen for any movement inside. When he didn't hear anything, he began inching up so that he could peek in through the opening, and was unexpectedly rapped on the top of his head.

"Ouch!" he protested, dropping back to the ground and twisting quickly to peer up at the old man who was now leaning on the window frame, looking down at him with a wide smile. "What was that for?" Dune asked, rubbing his head and standing up.

"For old time's sake," replied Kire. "You really need to be more cautious."

Dune vanished from outside the house, and appeared inside, standing in front of his old mentor. Though his head still smarted, and his pride more so at having been so completely unable to sneak up on Kire, even after all these years, he was happy to see the old fellow.

Dune embraced Kire and motioned for him to sit down. The older man had not changed much since they last saw each other. He still had salt and pepper hair, and he wore a large blanket with a hole cut in the center as a poncho.

"I think you are overly cautious," Dune replied, pointing at a red dot on Kire's nose. "Do you honestly think it is safer to travel as a person with the rare gift of enhanced scent?"

Kire shrugged his shoulders, "It makes people feel more at ease than thinking I might be reading their thoughts," he said with a significant nod of his head toward Dune. "Besides I think the nose mark goes very well with my outfit, don't you?"

"What are you doing here?"

Kire took a seat at the small table in the cramped space. "I was travelling south on my way to the desert. I heard that there are some lost records hidden in the desert dunes," Kire answered, then he spoke in a hushed tone, "Is it safe to talk here?"

"I thought it was safe, until you came here. How did you find me? How did you find *this* place?"

Kire waved him off, "That's not important now. What is important is that you are in danger. We all are."

"We?" Dune asked lifting his eyebrow quizzically.

"The stone holders," Kire clarified. "Anyone holding a Stone of Power needs to be extra cautious. Mordyar's stone seekers are getting more bold. I've seen four while travelling here to meet with you, all of them wearing their special elixir bottles on their belts." Kire held his hand out for emphasis, "Ten years ago, I could go almost anywhere in Denall and I was safe. Now they are popping up all over the place."

Dune rubbed his chin thoughtfully, trying to put together

the pieces. "I've been keeping watch on a group of stone seekers here in Eaton for almost six months trying to gather information about their leaders. Then about two days ago, for no reason, they packed up their things and left town."

Kire leaned forward in his chair. "Where did they go?"

"They are heading north, but that's not helpful, everything is north from here."

"Hmmm," Kire said as he raised his hand to his chin.

"What are you thinking?" Dune asked.

"It's possible there are more to be seen because they are all abandoning their marks, traveling somewhere. That could explain why so many are on the roads. If you're looking for their leadership you might find it, but if I were you, I'd stay as far away from their gathering as possible. I wonder what would cause the stone seekers to swarm together."

Dune thought back to the conversation he had overheard about a blacksmith in Norwell, "Perhaps they've found one."

Kire nodded thoughtfully "It is possible they think they know where they will find one, but it seems that there must be something even more compelling to bring them all scurrying out of hiding en masse. The whole clan of seekers could hardly expect to be rewarded for delivering a single stone. At any rate, I'm going back home, and I suggest you do the same."

Dune stood up from his chair and walked slowly around the small room, trying to piece together what he could do. So much had changed for him in the last day that he was still trying to figure it all out. For years he had been trying to stop the stone seekers, and now they seemed to be on the move. If he followed them he might learn what he needed to stop them, but he also risked being in the middle of a crowd of stone seekers while in possession of the Magic Stone. Kire was obviously scared by the seekers, and he was going into hiding, but that wasn't an option for him. He wasn't ready to go home yet.

While pacing the small room, Dune kicked a floorboard near the corner, and popped up one end. He waved his hand, deactivating the magical trap, and reached into the opening to retrieve the Magic Stone. The small black stone was glossy and polished with an almost metallic sheen. He placed it in an internal pocket in his robe. He stopped pacing and sat back down across from Kire.

"You think you are invincible," Kire said, pointing his finger at Dune. "You need to be more careful." His tone was reminiscent of the days when Dune had been under his tutelage. "If I can find you this easily, others can too." Kire stood up and walked to the small, window-like opening in the wall.

"They did," Dune admitted. "I was following them and overheard them saying that they set up something around my cabin."

Kire stood up, "That's not good."

"What?" Dune asked, joining him at the window.

"The inn keeper agreed to deliver a message to your house for me," Kire answered solemnly.

Dune waved him off, "Don't worry. I saw him at the tavern, he's…" An explosion erupted, blasting high into the sky so that even at their distance from the village they could easily see it. Dune shuddered and turned to Kire. "He's dead."

The older man nodded his head, "Ironic," he muttered under his breath. Dune looked quizzically at his mentor who then squinted thoughtfully and grunted, "Fitting might have been a better word."

"Fitting? What are you talking about?" Dune asked, not liking either of the words Kire used to describe a tragic loss of life.

"He's their informant," Kire explained. "He told them about you. They set a trap, and it sprung and caught him." As he spoke he spun his hand in an arch coming full circle at the end.

Dune let the truth of what had happened sink in. The inn keeper had always been kind. Hearing it from Kire made perfect sense, but he felt foolish for not realizing it earlier. He looked at Kire and placed a hand on his shoulder.

"You have the greatest mind I've ever seen. You can unravel any mystery. Come with me. Help me stop the seekers." Kire was shaking his head before Dune's words were out, but he pushed on, "You are always trying to find answers. This could be the chance to really solve an important puzzle."

"It could also be a chance to get myself captured and killed." Kire responded decidedly. "I can't solve any puzzles if I'm dead."

Dune turned from the window and grabbed his bow, "Well, I'm going after them. I'm going to find out what the seekers are doing, and if possible, I'm going to stop them."

Despite Dune ignoring his recommendation and caution, the older man smiled. "Can I make a suggestion or two before you begin?"

"Absolutely," he responded, happy for any help he could get.

Kire took a seat at the table. "For starters, don't trust inn keepers, and use better disguises." He smirked before he continued. "But you might want to try to recruit someone you do trust to help you."

Dune looked down at his mentor and exhaled in frustration. "I just tried to."

Kire laughed lightly. "You need someone who is younger, adventuresome, and can help you in a fight. I'm not the best option for that kind of thing. Besides, if you are going to survive a gang of stone seekers, you'll probably need to do some reckless and foolish things, which you might not try if I'm around."

"I think I know just the person." Dune said.

CHAPTER 6

Garin opened his eyes the moment the sun began to rise. It was difficult to find a comfortable place to sleep, but now that he was lying on the ground, he didn't feel any desire to get up. He gingerly pulled the small picture of Fenn from his pocket and straightened it against his leg. When he looked at her, all his aches, pains and discomfort seemed to evaporate. He looked over his shoulder to make sure nobody else was stirring, then leaned close and whispered to the picture.

"I love you."

Shortly after his moment of silence, Bendar got up off the ground, dusted the dirt off his pants, and looked around the camp. When he made eye contact with Garin, the other boy pointed out into the trees and whispered,

"Scouting ahead. I will be back soon."

Garin nodded slightly, then put his head back on the ground. He listened as Bendar clumsily made his way through the woods. *Good thing he's not trying to sneak up on any unsuspecting animals.* Knowing that Bendar's blundering in the woods would rouse the others, Garin put the picture of Fenn away.

From next to him on the ground, Farin moaned as he rolled over to greet the new day.

"I think I slept on every root and rock in all of Denall," he said loudly, destroying what peaceful calm was left of the morning.

"Nope, you must have missed one," Kaz said as he tossed a small stone at his friend.

"How 'bout you brother?" Farin said, turning toward Garin. "Are you alive?"

Garin rolled over and glared at his brother. "Yeah, I'm awake. Just trying to enjoy the silence of the morning. Then you two woke up."

"So you've been up for a while?" Kaz asked, while rubbing his eyes and stretching out his long arms. "Where's Bendar?"

"Said he's going to scout ahead. You might have mistaken him for a stampede of cattle," Garin responded. "Do you think he'll actually come back?" Garin asked sarcastically, exchanging glances with the others.

Kaz was the first to reply. "He is just out scouting like he said. You really need to give him a break. He has plans just like the rest of us, and his plans are bigger than Dungan."

"Fine, I'll give him a break if he comes back." Garin responded.

"Well, if he is planning to leave us, at least we have all the supplies," Farin said, gesturing toward the crate. "Let's get some food and we can decide what to do with Bendar later."

While Garin built up the fire and started boiling some water, Kaz and Farin looked through their supplies for breakfast. The boys came to the fire with a small wooden bowl filled with dried fruit, nuts, grain for porridge, honey, and some jerky. The jerky was put aside for lunch and they continued rummaging through the supplies. While they were searching, they heard a rustling from behind a small bush. Kaz took three steps to grab his nearby bow and had an arrow nocked and drawn before he saw Bendar emerge from behind the bush.

"Put that away," he began, "I only have one spare pair of pants." Despite his dislike for Bendar, Garin found himself smiling, and the other two boys laughed out loud. "Look what I found," Bendar began, as he lifted a medium sized bowl to show the group. The bowl was filled with wild raspberries. "I thought they would be nice with the porridge."

"That's great!" Kaz answered enthusiastically as he pulled out the oats and made his way over to the fire.

Bendar followed Kaz and looked at the pot of water that was just beginning to boil. "With that much water we'll need about…"

Grabbing the oats from Kaz, Garin interrupted. "I know how to make it." Garin dumped the oats into the pot and began stirring.

Bendar backed away from the pot and looked at the other boys, seeming to sense some tension, especially from Garin, he addressed the group.

"Can we talk about last night?" When no one responded, he

continued. “I was always planning to tell you about Hanger, I just needed to wait until we left Dungan.”

“Why does it matter that we’re outside of Dungan?” Kaz asked.

“I do not think my parents would have let me leave if they knew my plans,” Bendar answered. “My father wants me to settle down in Dungan and take over his general store. He feels it is the most logical thing for me to do.”

“Let me get this straight,” Kaz interjected, “your parents don't know?”

“No, I have only told you,” Bendar said, gesturing to them. He rummaged through the supply crate and pulled out a small piece of paper that was neatly folded and had a dried wax seal on it. He held out the note to Kaz, “It has been difficult not sharing this with anyone.”

“What is it?” Kaz asked.

“Just read it,” Bendar responded, as he sat down, using the corner of the crate as a seat.

Kaz took the paper and carefully unfolded it.

“Bendar, my friend,” Kaz began. “The information you have collected from Pike Point, the observations you made in Dungan, and the conclusions you have come to, show your potential. Let this note act as an official acceptance into Hanger University as my research assistant. On your journey to Hanger, keep your eyes open for any data to substantiate your hypothesis in regards to the sixth gift. We will discuss more when you arrive.” Kaz turned the note over and looked at Bendar. “Who is it from?”

Bendar reached out and took the note back. “It is from Professor Exovia. He has spent his life studying the enhanced gifts we have and their corresponding marks. It is fascinating how the region you are born in and your parentage do not always determine the gift you will have. From some of my research and observations, I have begun to question the existence of the gift of scent. Have you ever seen anyone with a mark on his nose?” The boys shook their heads. “Exactly. What if that gift is not real, or maybe it has gone extinct…”

As Bendar droned on about some professors he had been in correspondence with, and about theories he had, Garin began to be filled with some remorse for how he treated the other boy. He turned back to stirring the thin but lumpy porridge, and the others sat down around the fire. After he finished talking about his studies, Bendar moved next to him.

"Garin, can I help with that?" he asked, indicating the mush.

"I don't need help with the food," Garin responded, then he looked up to see Kaz and Farin. The two boys looked down at the pot of food, then back up to Garin pleadingly. "Fine, maybe I do need some help with the food," Garin admitted, cracking a halfhearted smile. He turned to Bendar and continued in a lower, somewhat embarrassed tone. "Let's just forget about last night. I just don't like being here. I'm tired and sore."

"I understand," Bendar said, then he moved to the pot over the fire and began crushing the small lumps to make a smooth porridge.

"Besides," Garin said as he stood up, "the thought of coming all the way back here with just Kaz for company turns my stomach." He made a gagging gesture.

"The thought of you cooking all the way back turns mine," Kaz responded.

"So what are we taking with us?" Farin asked as he rummaged through the crate.

"We need the weapons, tools and food," Bendar began, "we won't get far without that.

Kaz pulled a small knife from the crate and strapped it into his boot.

"I also think we can leave the canvas shelter behind. It is very heavy, and we can sleep in the open, or make a lean-to when it rains," Bendar observed as the other boys shifted the shelter to remove their supplies.

Farin nodded, and Garin was also happy when they placed the bulky fabric into the crate.

"Your book," Garin said, pointing down at the gift from Bendar's parents. "I guess it wouldn't be too bad for you to take one book from Emer."

Bendar smiled kindly. "I thank you for your consideration, Garin. However this is not Emer, it contains prophecies about The Changing." Noticing that the topic piqued their interest, he opened the book, "The section I am reading now has some old legends and myths about magical stones. Perhaps I can share them with you while we travel."

"Fine by me. It'll break up the monotony of the walk. Speaking of stones," Garin interjected as he made sure he had Kaz's attention. "I've changed my mind about your gran's necklace. I think I rolled over it about a hundred times last night. I'll keep it during the day, you keep it at night."

"It'd be easier to just throw it away," Kaz argued, but Garin glared at him until he conceded, "Fine. I'll take it at night. By the way, I think it looks very good on you," he teased, and Garin shoved it under his shirt.

As they discussed the necessities of their journey, the boys filled up their backpacks, strapped knives to their belts, filled their quivers, and each took a bow for hunting. With their packs ready, they buried the rest of the supplies and hid the signs of the fire, then set out on the second day of their trek.

The second day of trekking was much different than the first. There was no initial excitement of heading out, and no farewell ceremony; only walking. After walking for almost an hour, the pack straps were digging into Garin's shoulders, and he was starting to get bored, "Hey Bendar, got any good stories from that book of yours?"

Bendar looked over his shoulder, "Yes, actually there was one I think you all might find interesting. Although the origins are unknown and the authenticity cannot be verified, it is rather entertaining."

Kaz tapped Bendar on the shoulder and shook his head sadly at his friend. "You can't start a story like that."

"I was just giving some background so you could…"

"We don't need background," Kaz interrupted. He stepped up on a rock and held his hands out dramatically. "Unless it's 'On a dark and stormy night deep in the northern maple forest' or something like that." He dropped back to the hard packed road.

Bendar stopped walking for a moment and looked at Kaz in complete confusion. "This is why oral history is so inaccurate."

The twins burst out in laughter. "While that is true," Kaz admitted, "It's still a lot more fun that way."

Bendar began walking again, and the others gathered around expectantly. "While I have not yet committed the tale to memory, I will relate it as accurately as I can from what I read. More than two hundred years ago, six magicians were charged with delivering six magical stones. Each stone was connected with one of the special abilities granted to mortals by the ancient sorcerers. The magicians traveled to all parts of the known world delivering the stones to each owner the stone seemed to choose. When the stones were delivered, the magicians were done with their tasks and were never heard from again." Bendar looked to the other boys. They waited in silence for a moment as they continued to walk.

"So what happened?" Garin finally asked when it seemed Bendar was not going to add anything else to the story.

"I just told you," Bendar replied. "The stones were delivered, the magicians were never heard of again."

Farin shook his head, "I can't believe I'm saying this, but I liked Kaz's version better."

Not waiting for approval from Bendar, Kaz stepped up onto a stone wall that lined the road and dramatically began making up his own version of Bendar's more factual tale.

"In Gulpond village just north of the Coffall Desert, the hot sun rose early as the mysterious rider dismounted and walked through town toward the inn. His purposeful walk drew every eye that his peculiar tan robes and snow-white desert stallion had not already gained…"

Throughout the trip, Kaz continued to entertain the boys with made up stories about the magical Stones of Power. After the first tale, Bendar stopped protesting the historical inaccuracies and quietly kept pace with the others. They continued until late afternoon when Bendar announced that they would be stopping for the night in a stand of trees just off the main road. They dropped their packs and sat for a time on the ground before moving to the tasks that needed to be done.

"Which do you want more -- food or sleep?" Farin asked to nobody in particular.

Kaz was the first to respond. "I don't think I care about food at this point. I could just lie down and sleep for three days."

"I know what you mean," Garin added. "I don't care if Mordyar himself came into this camp, I'm not getting up."

Bendar turned toward the idle conversation and sternly silenced them. "SHHH! Do not talk like that!"

"Calm down Bendar, it's not like he can hear me," Garin said with a smirk.

"You have no idea what he is capable of, Garin Sigris, nobody does. Mordyar is the most powerful sorcerer who has ever lived, and we are lucky his attention is not drawn to our island." Garin looked quizzically at Bendar, waiting for him to crack a smile or give some kind of sign that he was joking, but it never came.

"Are you serious?" Farin asked. "You really think Mordyar is coming here?"

"I did not say he is coming here, I said we should not do anything to draw his attention." Bendar answered in a hushed tone.

Farin covered his mouth trying not to laugh out loud. "I don't think he knows every time someone says his name. Besides, I'm pretty sure the king and his army could stop anyone or anything that steps foot on Denall."

"I wouldn't be so confident. Unlike any of you, I have traveled beyond the Northern Plains. Many merchants who trade at Pike Point tell of the destruction that Mordyar leaves in his wake when he sets his mind on conquering."

The twins burst into laughter at Bendar's pronouncement. They were rolling on the ground uncontrollably. "Now he starts--" Farin began.

"--telling good stories."Garin finished.

"Fine, do not believe me! But do not curse our entire trip by mentioning his name repeatedly," Bendar yelled. The volume increased with each word he spoke.

Kaz interrupted. "Quit it! All of you! I think we can safely say this is a topic that we don't agree on. Let's just agree to not bring it up again. Can we at least do that?" The twins stopped laughing and Bendar took a deep breath. "Good, I'll take that as agreement."

Despite everyone's desire for sleep, they slowly moved around collecting fire wood, setting snares, and unpacking the food and sleeping supplies. After a short meal of some nuts, dried fruit and some jerky, Garin laid down on the ground on his back, squirming to find a comfortable position when Kaz's necklace dug unto his shoulder.

"I almost forgot," he began as he removed it and threw it over to Kaz. "Have a nice sleep with that thing on your neck." He rolled over and fell happily into a deep sleep.

CHAPTER 7

The fire was dying down and the four boys slept soundly, recovering from two days of unusual physical exertion. Having two strong listeners in their group, they all rested, relying on Garin and Farin's enhanced hearing for protection. Although Kaz could see farther than either boy could hear, it did no good during a night like this when the moon's light was hidden by thickening clouds.

Kaz rubbed his eyes when he heard one of the boys roll over on the ground. Farin threw some small sticks on the fire, and a slightly larger log.

"Is something wrong?" Bendar asked sleepily.

"I thought I heard some dry grass crunching. Maybe a deer walking in the woods. It's probably nothing," Farin responded. "Hey seamstress, do you see anything out there?"

"What?" Kaz groaned from his sprawled position on the other side of the fire.

Garin sat up and rolled his head, stretching out his neck. Kaz saw the marks on his ears darken as he made an audio sweep of the surrounding area.

"Get up now!" Garin reached for the long bow and nocked an arrow.

"What is it?" Bendar asked as he scrambled to his feet and joined the other boys standing in a small circle with their backs to the fire. Each had a longbow in hand, and Farin had his sword strapped to his waist.

"What's out there?" Kaz asked as he searched the darkness for any sign of movement.

"Drams," Garin and Farin announced in unison.

"They must be very hungry to attack so close to the road." Bendar observed. "When they get that hungry, they usually don't stop their attack until they get some meat."

"That's not helpful," Kaz said as he anxiously pulled on the bowstring. "I can only see to the first row of trees."

"The rest of us can't see anything at all. It's so dark, we can't see beyond the firelight. We need to seek shelter." Bendar said, moving to the edge of the clearing. "Get up into the trees." He began running for the closest tree.

"There," Farin said, pointing out into the night. Kaz shot an arrow in the direction Farin pointed, but he heard it thud harmlessly into a tree. He nocked another arrow and waited while the other boys began scampering up some nearby trees. When the dram came into sight he drew his bow, and in a fluid motion released the arrow. The shaft protruded out of the animals head, a perfect kill shot.

"Get over here!" Farin beckoned. "Two more drams are coming." Kaz turned and ran toward a tree where Farin was hiding. As he came close to the tree he could hear the deep, gruff pants of the large animals that were now in their camp. He pumped his arms for more speed, and at the last minute he threw his bow to the ground and jumped up, grabbing on the highest branch of the tree he could reach.

He wrapped his arms and legs around the branch, frantically trying to stay out of reach of the dram that was now underneath him. From a nearby tree an arrow flew and found its mark in the dram's body. The creature howled out in pain, but continued to claw at the tree. With a massive lunge, the dram's front paws reached Kaz and ripped open his left leg, throwing him down from the tree onto the ground. When he hit the ground, Kaz turned over, and covered his arms over his face as the dram approached. Trying to ignore the pain, he kicked out, hitting the dram in the snout. The creature howled out, then arched its back as it cautiously advanced. Kaz pushed against the ground until he backed into a tree.

"Take him down!" Garin yelled from up in the tree, and Kaz saw an arrow strike the dram. The powerful dram lunged forward but was stopped as Farin dropped down from the tree with his sword blade driving down into the creature's torso.

Kaz looked out over the campfire and saw another dram charging into the camp. Bendar and Garin took it down with arrows before it was able to cross over to Kaz.

"Can you climb?" Farin asked as he grabbed Kaz under the shoulder and pushed him to standing.

Kaz nodded, and reached up to grab the branch of a tree. The pain from his legs throbbed as he pulled himself up, but he quickly fell back down again. He shook his head. "I can't do it."

Garin jumped down from a nearby tree, and ran to his side.

"Lift!" Kaz pulled up while Garin and Farin pushed him from underneath. His leg sent shooting pain all over his body as Farin threw his legs up over the first branch and then continued to push even harder, forcing him up higher into the branches.

"I'm up!" Kaz shouted down to the twins and they began climbing up to join him.

Bendar shot an arrow at another dram that was running through the camp toward Garin, giving him time to get up out of range.

With the arrow still lodged in its side, the dram scratched at the tree, and jumped up in the air, snapping its jaws at the boys who were just out of its range. Farin grabbed his bow and shot an arrow into the dram's open mouth, sending it falling backward onto the ground.

Garin tore the sleeve off his shirt and wrapped it around Kaz's leg. The material quickly soaked dark red.

"We need to get down to our supplies," Garin called out to Bendar.

"We can't do that with them down there," Farin said pointing at the dram. "How many arrows do you have left?"

Bendar looked in his quiver quickly before calling back. "I have eight. How many do you have?"

"Three," Farin called back, his voice filled with frustration. "I dropped the rest when I went down for Kaz. There are at least fifteen more drams in the pack. Even if we took one out with every arrow, we can't kill them all."

"And we can't wait up in the trees all night. Kaz is losing too much blood," Garin added.

"What if we kill this one, and make a run for more…" Kaz stopped talking as he saw some glowing eyes approaching the camp. More drams were congregating in the campsite, smelling blood and waiting for some meat. "Never mind." Kaz dropped his head to the side and fell limp on the branch he was sitting on. Farin and Garin reached out and stabilized him.

"Wake up!" Garin encouraged. He pushed Kaz up to a sitting position. "You don't want to lose this," Garin joked as he shoved Gran's necklace into Kaz's shirt.

Kaz smiled weakly and forced himself up against the tree. He blinked several times, and tried to focus on his breathing.

"I think I'm okay," he said. "What are we going to do?"

"We need to kill the alpha," Bendar called out.

"What are you talking about?" Farin asked.

"The pack always follows their leader. We need to kill the leader first, then when we begin attacking the remaining drams they might disperse."

"They might disperse?" Farin asked, "What if they don't? Couldn't we just kill all we can, and let them eat each other?"

"Until their leader is dead, they will not retreat. It's our only hope," Bendar replied.

"They're all circling around randomly, which one is the leader?" Garin shouted.

Kaz watched the drams in the camp. Some were digging through their supplies, others were circling the base of the trees they were hiding in, and some were beginning to eat the dead drams, snapping at any other dram that tried to share in the feast.

"I don't think the leader is here yet," Bendar answered "Can either of you hear the sounds of one dram that is larger than the others?"

Garin and Farin looked at each other, then back at Bendar, tilting their heads in confusion.

"What do you think a larger dram sounds like?"

Kaz looked out into the night, and although his mind was foggy, he thought the moon was coming out, because he could see clearly out past the trees.

"I think I can see him," Kaz said in a voice filled with pain. He pointed out into the darkness. "He's right there; he's circling around the others. Can you hit him from here?" Kaz asked Garin.

"I can't even see him," he answered.

"Are you serious?" Kaz asked, shaking his head to clear the

fogginess. "Okay, give me the bow." Kaz grunted as he twisted his body on the large tree limb. Kaz clenched his jaw and drew his bow, aiming out into the darkness. With a final grunt, Kaz released the bowstring and the arrow flew through the trees and found its target. Kaz slumped down and would have fallen out of the tree if Garin hadn't caught him.

"I got him," Kaz whispered to his friend.

Hearing Kaz's announcement, Farin called out to Bendar. "The alpha is dead!"

"Take out as many as you can," Bendar called back. He fired an arrow down at a dram that was rummaging through their packs, then aimed at another that was pawing at his tree. The injured drams winced, then ran away.

"They're retreating," Bendar shouted, "The leader must be dead." Bendar kept loosing arrows at any dram that remained in their camping area until his quiver was empty and the site was relatively quiet.

"I'll be right back," Farin said to his brother. Without waiting for a reply, Farin climbed down the tree, retrieved his sword from the fallen dram, grabbed a handful of arrows, then put on Kaz's travel pack. He quickly returned to the tree and handed up the arrows, then climbed up to sit next to Garin and Kaz.

Garin began rummaging through Kaz's pack and pulled out Gran's sewing kit.

"I'm glad someone thought to include a suture kit," he commented as he pulled out Kaz's water skin and began to clean the cuts on Kaz's leg.

Kaz cringed, "Yeah, good thing."

"Get some rope," Garin said to his brother.

"To tie on the bandages?"

"No to tie us up in this tree, I don't feel safe on the ground, not with those drams roaming around."

Without argument, Farin climbed down again and quickly gathered some supplies. He also retrieved some food and water. Bendar joined him in the campsite, and filled up his quiver and supply sack. He threw some more wood on the fire for light before they both climbed back up into the tree for the night.

CHAPTER 8

On the cobblestone streets of Kinstock horse hooves clopped and boots fell as people went about their business. Through the wall, P could hear each person as they approached the inn, and could distinguish the softer footfalls as they passed into the distance. Some people slowed down as they passed the rented out room in the inn, but most kept walking at a consistent pace. As she listened to the people in the streets of Kinstock she kept her eyes on the people in the room with her, not sure who she could trust.

She was the first to arrive, and from her seat in the far back corner she watched each man as he entered. The loudest of the men were eight strongarms, mostly large men who moved slowly, and many of whom opened their mouths enough to show that they were not overly bright.

When a heavy set of footsteps approached their room, she raised her hand up and nodded to the level two intellect sitting at the front of the room.

"Looks like our tardy friend has arrived," Dunkan said as he stood up at the front of the room ready for their meeting to start.

As he spoke, a tall, broad strongarm named Scar pushed open the door and entered.

"Sorry I'm late," he said slowly, his thick accent a sure mark that he had been born outside of Denall. "When Flick told me where we were meeting I forgot how to spell 'inn', so I was lost outside for a while." He grabbed a drink from the small serving table at the side of the room, and stood, slowly drinking it as if he didn't notice that everyone was waiting for him.

Waving for Scar to sit down, and giving him a slight scowl, Dunkan began their meeting.

"Let's get started, men," Dunkan began.

Derft, a large, level two strongarm sitting on the front row interrupted, "Men? What about the skirt in the back?" he asked in a low voice, then turned around to look at her with an arrogant grin.

P hated men like him. The kind who ogled at her, then

dismissed her usefulness at every opportunity. She considered walking to the front of the room and clobbering him right there, but decided to forgo his humiliation for now.

"First off, I never wear a skirt. Second, I'm a listener, so sitting up at the front and whispering isn't going to make a bit of difference."

Derft continued to address Dunkan. "I don't like it. We need to know we can trust her, and I've never heard of her before." Some others nodded in agreement.

Dunkan silenced the murmurs with a wave of his hand.

"She is a level four listener, she's the highest level in this room, and she will not let us down. The fact that we haven't heard of her is a credit to her work. She's been working Kinstock for several years. Any other objections?" With that said he looked over the group. Nobody voiced their concern, but P could see Derft shaking his head and tapping the man seated next to him. "For those of you who haven't met the 'skirt' in the back of the room, that's P. She's our listener."

"P?" Derft asked from the front of the room. "Did they give you any other letters to go with that?"

"I find that one letter gives me more flexibility and anonymity…" She paused and raised her hands apologetically, "sorry Derft, those are some really big words. Let me speak in your language. If you don't like my name, you can come back here and we'll have a talk about it." She not only wanted to keep her real name a secret, but she wished she could forget it herself. She wished she could forget a lot about her past.

Derft leaned forward, beginning to stand. "Now settle down," Dunkan interjected, placing a hand on Derft's shoulder and pushing him back down into his seat. "We're on the same team here. Let's all try to get along." He made eye contact with P, then shook his head subtly. "The past few months we have stationed Ortis and Derft at the mine," he pointed to the two men, the largest in the room, who nodded their heads. "Flick, Scar and Rod were working in transportation, but a recent accident has left us without Rod. Ashley and Stash have been working with the smelters. This is the process we have learned:

The mines are a day's travel northeast of Kinstock with a reliable mount. It can be done as quickly as…" He searched his papers.

"Six hours, the fastest I've been able to do it is six hours," Horse announced. "That was alternating between two horses in good weather."

"Thank you, Horse," Dunkan continued. "To eliminate that daily trek the miners have their own community near the mines. Many of the miners felt more comfortable in their little hamlet as they were mostly strongarms hired from the east who had settled with their families in the area. These people are all powerfully strong. Some are significantly larger than Ortis and extremely handy with picks and blunt instruments." Dunkan paused and looked at the large men in the room with him. "If we tried to take the gold from them, they'd tear us apart. Flick and Scar have been working transportation of ore for three months. Tell us what you have found."

Flick was a tall, thin man, uncommon for a strongarm, but despite his slender build he was known for having strength comparable to men twice his size."To prevent anyone from trying to steal the gold bars, the exact location of the refinery is kept secret from everyone except the local soldiers and guards." Flick smiled at the crew as they all grunted in response.

Scar, a tall, well-built man wearing a bandana, continued in a slow drawl. "The place is secret 'cause there is two delivery routes. The first delivers half way and the second delivers the second half way." Scar scratched his head and counted on his fingers, perhaps wondering if his math was accurate. After a moment of serious thought he looked up to Flick.

"Scar and I have been working on section one for three months, and in a strange turn of events, a man who was working in section two has gone missing, and they needed a replacement." Flick smiled and raised his glass as the men returned the motion.

"I think he means to say we killed the guy," Scar put in. Several men with their glasses raised shook their heads at Scar's stupidity.

Saving his friend from any further embarrassment, Flick

took over once again.

"Scar was placed on the second rotation, and we have mapped out the entire route to the refinery."

Before any questions could be raised, Dunkan stood up.

"Thank you, Flick and Scar. While on a hiking trip in the forest, Com got lost and 'accidentally' passed by the refinery. Before the soldiers escorted him blindfolded back to the main road he was able to make some observations."

Com, the slim visor in the group, stood up and walked to the front of the room. He quickly scanned the room and pointed to Ortis.

"I thought we were supposed to check our weapons at the door?"

"What you saying, little man?" Ortis shouted in a guttural voice.

"I'm saying that I can see the small blade that you have concealed under the armguard on your left arm." Com stood calmly in front of the crowd. "There are also two others who slipped weapons in. Would you like me to point them out, or will you give them up willingly?"

Dunkan stood and looked over everyone. "If you want to be in this crew, we need to count on each other. Put your weapons at the door or you're out."

Ortis and Derft stood and dropped their blades at the door. Everyone in the room looked around expectantly for the third person. No other person rose, but everyone turned to the door at the sound of metal on metal as a third blade, this one much smaller than the first two, landed on the pile. Com met eyes with P, then continued.

"There are fifteen guards outside the refinery." This news made the entire crowd gasp, but Com continued. "Inside I counted five, but there are more. My best guess is at least double that." Dunkan stood, nodding to Com, but Com continued standing and spoke. "By the foot marks and treads that were on the trails to the refinery I can also tell you that an armed guard of fifty men accompanies each full shipment of gold from the refinery to the keep in Kinstock." Com returned to his seat.

This last piece of news began an outburst of objections, questions and dissentions.

"How are we going to pull this off?"

"Fifty, are you sure?" Horse asked.

Ortis shook his head. "This will never work."

"That's a lot; it's even more than we have here," Scar added after counting on his fingers.

Dunkan resumed his place at the head of the room and waved everyone to silence.

"This is also what Ashley and Stash reported. The shipment is guarded heavily from the refinery to the keep, because that is where they pay their taxes. After they collect the taxes, they seem a lot less worried about protecting the gold." Dunkan smiled, then continued. "After the gold is counted and the taxes are collected, the gold bars are delivered to the merchants almost completely unprotected and that, my friends, is when we'll take it."

On the street just outside the building P heard many footfalls as people passed the shop, but one attracted her attention. The person stopped outside the inn and then began walking again in an irregular manner. In response to this person, P raised her hand cautiously with two fingers extended. Dunkan, seeing the sign, copied it and seamlessly began a monotone lecture on the history of Kinstock for the benefit of the eavesdropper.

"Kinstock is a large town in northern Denall. It is large enough that it could rightly be called a small city, but most people still think of it as a town, as it has only been in the last generation that a nobleman of any significant rank has controlled the barony to which Kinstock owes fealty. The current Baron Tran was awarded the barony following an illustrious career in the king's guard, and, it is rumored, as a way to ensure that the king's sister, the late Baroness Tran, would be cared for in the manner to which she had grown accustomed while growing up in the castle at Norwell. Kinstock is located ten days north of Lexingar, the great city." Scar raised his hand and looked like he was going to ask a questions, but was promptly silenced by an elbow from Flick and a second showing of the sign.

Flick, playing the part of an interested student, asked, "Why would the region of Kinstock be so much more a desirable place for the sister of the king?"

"Wonderful question," Dunkan said in his best scholarly voice as he shook his head toward Flick. "There are two commodities that are easier to find in Kinstock than anywhere else in Denall; Maplewood lumber, and Kinstock gold. Baron Tran has a right to take a percentage of the taxes due to the realm on that gold, and those taxes add up quickly." P put her hand down when the coast was clear. and Dunkan continued. "The Kinstock goldmines are the richest in Denall, and that's why we're going to rob them," he concluded with a smile.

While Dunkan laid out the plan, all present made careful mental notes so they knew their parts exactly. They all left the meeting speaking of the wonderful history of Kinstock, never to see each other again until the appointed time. P made her way back toward a small apartment under a jewelry shop. The rain started to fall, turning the streets into a slippery layer of thin mud over stones. The falling rain was an advantage to a well-trained thief as it obscured most of the regular sounds of the city. In the rain people were also more careless, concentrating on staying dry more than on the weight of their purses. Despite people pulling their coats up to their necks and shrugging their shoulders up to keep away the cold, P was quickly able to pick out one target to help fill her pockets.

Strongarms were the easiest prey. They often relied on their brute strength to solve problems and trusted that nobody would dare steal from them. P stepped up next to a large man under an awning. While he was looking out into the rain she slipped her hand into his satchel and relieved him of two coppers and a silver coin, exactly half of what he had.

As she dropped the coins into her purse, he looked down at her and tipped his hat before he ran out into the rain. She quickly looked around. There were no other obvious strongarms in the vicinity. As with most areas of Denall, the majority of people were level one or two listeners or visors, with an occasional intellect. Although there were other opportunities for her to snag a coin or two, she didn't want to risk getting caught taking a penny when she was on the verge of a huge heist, so she left them alone.

P turned down the street toward her room and instantly ducked back behind the cover of the jewelry shop. Engaging her enhanced hearing, she could make out a conversation between two familiar voices that was happening in front of her door.

"I thought I just saw something at the end of the building there," came Ashley's voice.

"She shouldn't be back for another half hour, it can't be her," came the reply from Ortis. If she had been anyone else, that exchange would have put her mind at ease, but she had learned not to trust the words people said. She focused her hearing even further. In the alley, there was a distinct sound of fabric brushing against fabric at a quick rate, as if he was waving his arms around or pointing while he spoke. Next she heard the pounding of feet. They were coming after her.

P walked back past the front of the jewelry store, trying to look casual until she passed the edge of the building. She ducked down the alleyway between the shop and a bakery. Knowing she could be outmatched in a face-to-face confrontation, she decided to remain completely still and silent, allowing herself time to approach from a more advantageous position. She crouched for several minutes while monitoring all she could see, and doing regular sound scans of her surroundings. The two men walked together past the opening of the alleyway. In a short time they passed again going back toward her apartment.

When she felt sure that nobody had discovered her hiding place, she made her way quickly to the back of the shops and silently climbed up over the fence at the back of the alley. She moved two blocks down so that she could scale the apartment building across from the jewelry shop. Without making any noise, she climbed up a tree that would allow her to step directly onto the apartment roof. When her eyes reached the level of the roof she saw two men standing guard on the roof, watching over the entrance to her quarters. Their backs were turned toward her as they looked intently down onto the streets below. P climbed a few more branches up until she was able to step directly onto the flat roof. She focused her hearing to learn what she could of their plans.

"I just don't trust her." It was Derft's voice she first heard. "I think she brought the third knife."

"That is a stupid argument," Horse answered. "You brought a knife in with you."

"That's different, I have worked in this crew for three jobs. Everyone knows where my loyalties lie. Besides, without me, they can't move the gold," he added flexing his muscles for emphasis.

P began silently walking toward the two men. She cringed at the slight scraping sound of her boots on the tiles, but Horse and Derft didn't seem to notice as their conversation continued. "I'll tell you one thing, my loyalty lies with gold. I'm sticking around until I get paid, then I'm leaving."

Derft turned from the street and looked at Horse, P froze, not daring to move and draw any attention. "Horse, you can do what you like, but I'm telling you, working for Dunkan is about the best chance you'll have to make a go of it in this area. He'll take an extra cut for himself as the brains of the operation, but you can bet he's thought it all through."

Horse shook his head and they both looked back down at the street. P inched forward until she was standing within striking range of the men. "I'll stick around until I can afford to leave, and as for the girl, well, once the job is done, I think I may find a way to inherit a double portion of the spoils."

"Really?" P asked. Both men turned suddenly to find P standing practically on top of them with a curved short sword drawn in one hand and a throwing knife in the other.

Before they could sound an alarm, she threw the knife at Derft, hitting him with the blunt handle so that he fell unconscious, then she stabbed Horse through the heart, placing her hand over his mouth to stifle any sound he made.

Hefting Horse's limp body up to the edge of the roof, P

spied over his shoulder, looking down at the two men who were standing by the door of her apartment. She raised his lifeless arm in the air, and they waved back. After making a scan of the adjacent rooftops and feeling confident that they were clear, P dropped back to the street level and casually walked down the street to her apartment.

Closer to her home she greeted Ashley and Ortis. "Hello gentlemen," she said, while giving them a winning smile. "What brings you out tonight?"

"We're here to deliver a message," Ashley said as he brought a small club up from the ground. His large arms bulged as he flexed his grip on the club.

"What message could that be?" she asked, giving an innocent, bewildered look that had worked to her advantage many times over the years.

"We only work with the best, and if you couldn't figure out that something was wrong tonight on your way home, you are not fit for our crew." Ashley stepped closer to P.

"Ashley, wait. What are you going to do to me?" she asked, looking vulnerable and scared. If he had known anything about P, he would have known that vulnerability and fear were two emotions that she rarely felt and never showed. He would have also realized that his answer might be the last words he spoke.

"Let's just put it this way," he said, with a wave of his hand toward the rooftop. "I don't think we need a listener to finish this job."

"You can't make that decision. That is up to Dunkan," she said, taking a step back to stabilize herself for the forward attack while looking like she was retreating.

"Who do you think sent us?" Those were Ashley's final words in mortality. Before he could even register what was happening, he went from being the bully in charge to the dying man grasping wordlessly at his throat where a throwing knife protruded.

Ortis looked desperately at the roof, then back at P. In a panic he stammered, "What are you going to do with me?"

"Well I want to let you know something before you die."

She slowly drew a second throwing knife. "This little stunt of yours has become *your* test, and you are no longer needed for my crew."

When P entered her room she saw Dunkan waiting for her, two cups of tea laid out on the table in front of him. He glanced over her blood spattered clothes and unsheathed weapons.

"So, how did it go? I take it you ran into some trouble on the way home?" he asked while sipping some tea.

"Our shares in the operation will be slightly higher," she replied with a flat look. "The men you selected seem to have unusually strong objections to having a 'skirt' on the crew. I kept Derft alive; we'll need his strength to move the gold, but the others will need to be disposed of. Horse had exceeded his usefulness, Ortis had no courage, and Ashley, well, Ashley had a girl's name."

"The bodies will be taken care of," Dunkan said as he took another sip of tea. "It's so hard to find good help these days."

"I was rather impressed with Com today," P noted as she crossed the room and pushed Dunkan's feet down from resting on her end table. "We now have our visor, four strongarms, one listener, and our brain." With this last note she gestured toward Dunkan.

"What do you think about Scar?" she asked, not wanting an incompetent fool on their team any longer than necessary.

Dunkan scratched his head for a moment and took a deep breath before responding. "He's strong as an ox, and easy to fool. He'll help load the gold, then we'll dump him off a cliff."

"If he can remember where he's supposed to be," P corrected.

"Just let Flick keep him in line. Imbeciles are the easiest to keep under control."

P wasn't sure if she agreed, but there wasn't time to look for another strongarm for this mission, and she knew he was strong enough to help with loading the gold. "So when are we making our move?"

"We'll see how Derft is feeling in the morning."

With a final smile Dunkan placed his empty cup on the

table, stood up, and left the apartment. P followed him to the door and bolted it shut to ensure there would be no more intrusions, then sat on a chair absentmindedly cleaning and sharpening her knives while she thought through every detail of her plan, and what the acquisition of this gold shipment would mean for the families of Hess.

CHAPTER 9

Despite the sun rising, Farin remained in the tree, looking nervously into the woods. Through the night he had jumped at every sound, and during his watch, had constantly been looking over his shoulder for drams. A movement on the tree limb made him jerk his head over to look at Kaz, who was pale from loss of blood, but thanks to Garin's stitches, Bendar's supplies, and a night of rest, was half lucid. "I think I can walk on it," Kaz said as he slowly moved to the edge of the branch, and untied the support strap that had held him in place through the night.

"I highly doubt that," Farin argued.

Despite the protests of his companions, Kaz gently moved his foot to a lower branch and shifted some pressure onto his right leg and winced in pain. "Yeah, I'm going to need some help getting down from here," he said, pain clear in his voice. "Maybe I'll be good to walk with you after lunch."

Bendar was the first to speak. "We are not convinced."

"We'll help you down," Garin said to Kaz in a no-nonsense voice. He climbed behind Kaz, and with Farin and Bendar holding his legs, the three boys were able to awkwardly lower Kaz down to the ground. "We need to boil some water and check for infection," Garin said when he was able to look at Kaz' leg. "The wounds are not too deep, but they need to be kept clean, or he could lose his leg."

"Lose my leg?" Kaz said in a panic. He struggled to move and bumped his leg on the tree and screamed out in pain.

"Hold still!" Garin said sternly. "You have nothing to worry about if you hold still and let me take a look at you." He opened the dressing on Kaz's leg and shook his head when he looked up at his brother.

Farin, knowing what his brother was thinking, looked up at the sun, then east toward Hillside. "It'll be at least a couple of hours before we can get moving today, and we'll be moving very slowly."

"What else can we do?" Garin asked, looking at Bendar.

"We have to get to the third stash in Hillside. I have

arranged for us to have a pack horse that can help with our journey."

"A Horse! Are you serious?" Kaz was ecstatic. "How did you manage that?"

"That is what I have been working on for the past six months. Now do you understand why I'm so concerned about the third stash not being disturbed?"

With a renewed determination Kaz clenched his teeth and tried to stand. Garin pushed him back down.

"Don't try it!"

"If I can't walk," Kaz protested, "It will take a week to get to Hillside with you dragging or carrying me."

Farin shook his head. "I'm not lugging you around on my back. We'll just have to give it some time to heal."

"How long do you think this will take to heal?" Kaz asked as he patted his leg. His eyes watered and he winced slightly.

"I have no idea, I've only ever stitched up animals, and they walk away from it the same day. With a baby like you, it could take months," Garin replied with a smile. "We also have to think about our supplies. With your leg injured we'll need to double up our packs," Garin added.

Farin held his head between his hands in concentration, then he looked up as an idea came. "Once we have a horse we could pack it down with these supplies, and go back for our buried supplies."

"What if you leave me here with the supplies and you go get it and then come back?" Kaz suggested.

"I can stay with you," Garin offered. "I know how to change your dressings, and together we can defend all of the supplies so you both can travel faster," he looked to Farin and Bendar as he finished.

Farin chimed in. "We need two people to get Kaz back up in the tree if the drams come back. Why don't we all stay here a couple of days until Kaz is up to traveling? We can slice some of the meat up and dry it out for jerky, and roast some of it over the fire.

Bendar's forehead crinkled as his dots darkened. "We can't

stay here while Kaz heals," Bendar argued, "The dram meat will go bad and attract scavengers, some that can climb trees. It might not even be safe here for one night. We need a clean bed for Kaz to heal properly, not the ground, or tied up in a tree. I can make the trip to Hillside by mid-afternoon. I will collect the horse and come back for all of you. We can spend one final night here together, then move on tomorrow morning to Hillside. I'm sure the animal can carry Kaz as well as some supplies."

"Bendar's plan makes sense to me," Farin agreed, looking around at the others. "I think you should go."

Kaz nodded without any protest, and then all the boys turned to look at Garin. "It seems like the only way," he admitted. "You'd better get going."

Bendar nodded to his companions, and grabbed a walking stick and a light pack with supplies that would get him to Hillside. "I will come back for you soon."

With Bendar out of sight down the road, Garin looked down at his friends. "We need to take care of that meat. I'll slice it up, and Kaz, you can dry it by the fire."

Without saying a word, Farin began walking into the woods. "Where's he going?" Kaz asked, before he was out of earshot.

"To get more firewood, of course," Garin answered as if it should have been obvious to anyone. Farin smiled as he passed out of sight. His connection to his brother was so natural that sometimes he felt like Garin could read his mind. He knew Garin wasn't completely trusting of Bendar, but after the past few days, it seemed like things were improving. He hoped they would all be able to get along long enough for him to get to the capitol.

Farin returned to the campsite a short while later with his arms full of wood for the fire. "You know guys," Kaz started as he sat turning the dram meat over the coals. "Getting attacked by a dram really makes you think a little, doesn't it?"

"Sure," Garin answered. "I thought about home, and my parents, and…"

"Fenn," Kaz cut in, "We know you were mainly thinking about her." Garin blushed slightly, but didn't deny it.

"I was actually a little excited," Farin said, putting the wood down by the fire. "In all the time we've lived on the farm, I've never really been in that kind of danger. I've thought about life in the King's army, and now I'm more certain than ever that that is where I belong." He drew his sword and sliced it through the air.

"So what did it make you think of?" Garin asked as he sat down next to Kaz.

Kaz shrugged his shoulders, then took a deep breath before responding. "I don't really have any idea what I want in life." The twins sat silently, not sure how to respond. "I mean, look at you two. Garin is practically married, you know what you want, and Bendar has his own plans, but what about me? I don't know where I'm going to go, what I'm going to do, or who I'm going to become. It's all blank."

Farin finished stacking the fire wood he had brought in to camp, and sat down by the fire. "That sounds like a great adventure to me," he remarked. "Just going forward, not really knowing what's in store."

Kaz nodded and added under his breath more to himself than anyone else, "It's also kind of empty." Then he perked his head up and added with a smile, "Well, wherever I end up, I don't envy the other guys there."

"Garin, is he delirious again?" Farin asked, as he reached for the medical supplies. "I'll check for infection on his leg."

"I'm fine," Kaz said, swatting Farin from touching his leg. "I'm just saying that when I get to wherever it is I'm going, I'll have the normal things I've always had – good looks, charm, and a sharp wit—but I'll also have the greatest battle scar ever."

With a roll of his eyes Garin commented. "Too bad it's so far up your leg that if anyone were to see it you'd be stripped down to your birthday suit. "

"Which strengthens my point," Kaz said without missing a beat. "I feel sorry for all the other guys in all of Denall."

"Now you're sounding a lot more like yourself," Farin said with a smile.

When Garin finished butchering the first dram, the brothers

dragged the carcass out across the field to a larger group of trees a safe distance away. "We'll need to start a second fire to dry out all that meat," Farin observed when they were on their way back. "And it'll take all day to drag the others over here."

Garin didn't respond, but just nodded as they walked. Before he took the next dram carcass he used his knife to wedge out a large tooth. The off-white tooth was long and slender, coming to a point at one end. "Want one?" he asked, gesturing to Kaz and Farin.

"Why would we want one?" Farin asked, confused by his brother's odd interest in a dram tooth.

"It's just a little keepsake from my Troven. Something I can show my kids." Garin placed it in his pocket.

"Nope," Farin said with a disgusted look on his face. "But thanks for thinking of me." Kaz just shook his head.

"Suit yourself," Garin said, grabbing one leg of the dram to drag it away.

"Besides," Kaz added, looking up from the drying meat. "First he'd need to convince a girl to settle down with him."

"Now be kind," Garin said, holding up a hand in protest. "It's not nice to say things like that. His kids will already be at a disadvantage."

Sensing an insult coming, Farin cut in, "He's right. There is at least one thing his kids will have that mine won't."

"What's that?" Kaz asked.

"A good looking uncle." Farin laughed as he grabbed the dram's leg and began to pull it out into the field.

With the dead animals far away, the boys organized camp, feasted on dram meat, and waited for Bendar's return. As the afternoon turned to evening and the last rays of sunlight slipped below the horizon, Farin could tell Garin's initial annoyance had turned to frustration as there was no signs of Bendar.

"Where is your friend now?" Garin demanded of Kaz.

"Garin, with all he's done for us, can't you at least give him some benefit of the doubt?" Farin asked, trying to calm his brother down.

"Seriously, Garin." Kaz added, "We should be worried for

his safety, not…"

Garin cut him off, "If you were in his shoes, would you come back for us?" He looked around at the other boys expectantly, but Kaz and Farin remained silent. "He wants to get far away from here, and we're slowing him down. He thinks of everything in logical terms. He needed us for protection, but now we're a liability. Maybe it's time we made up our own plans."

"Let's just get the supplies tied up in the trees, and ready to go in the morning. There is still time for him to get back," Farin countered, but as the moon rose in the sky, Garin's words began to sow seeds of doubt in Farin. One wounded companion would slow down Bendar's travel to Norwell, and he had stayed up in the tree during the dram attack rather than getting down to help the others. While doubts grew in his mind, darkness fell and they all tried to get some sleep in the relative safety of the trees.

"Your shift!" Garin called out to Kaz as he tossed Gran's necklace at his wounded friend. "I'll take it back in the morning."

Kaz grinned and hung the necklace over the end of a tree branch. "I think I'll let Twiggy here take a shift," he said patting the branch. "Just don't forget it in the morning," he added with a grin.

Garin rolled his eyes, "Now even the branch is doing your work for you," he joked.

"Be nice," Kaz insisted while making a pathetic face, "remember, I'm injured, practically on the brink of death."

"You'd better watch it," Garin warned, "if you keep making that face, I'll leave you behind tomorrow and take Twiggy with me." He jumped down from the tree and made sure their camp was prepared for the night. During the dark hours of the night, Garin and Farin took shifts climbing down to keep the fire stoked and make periodic scans of distant sounds. The restless night was passed with only one alarm, but it turned out to be just a curious squirrel checking out the campsite.

The darkness began to fade away as the growing light gave evidence of the coming day. Farin couldn't remember a time when he felt more sore, tired or miserable, and in his mind he had already spent his gold coin for a night or two at an inn with a bed. Despite the discomfort of the tree digging into his legs and back, he resisted getting up until the sun was fully up in the sky. "Time to get going," Farin finally said when he couldn't stand sitting in the tree any longer.

When on the ground, Kaz tried to walk, but it looked more like a pained hobble. Farin climbed back up the tree to where they had slept. "Since you've become such great friends," he said, as he grabbed the branch next to where Kaz had slept, "I think we'll take Twiggy along with us." He grabbed Gran's necklace and tossed it down to Garin, then snapped the branch off for Kaz to use as a crutch. While it helped Kaz take the weight off his leg, he was still only able to move along at a painfully slow pace. After deciding what supplies they could manage to carry, they tied the remaining supplies in their tree and headed toward Hillside.

Through the morning they made their way down the road. It was painfully slow with Kaz grunting in pain every few steps. Farin dropped some supplies from his backpack and walked next to Kaz, allowing his injured friend to lean on him, but the extra weight of his friend pressing down on his shoulder only emphasized the weight of the pack on his back. Farin clamped his jaw tight and kept walking, hoping that around each bend or over each small hill he would see the village they were trying to reach.

At mid-day they stopped at the side of the road for a break. Their lunch consisted of dried meat, water, and some fresh fruit they picked off the trees and bushes near the road. Eating gave them the encouragement and energy to get up and move forward. Just as they did, Garin perked up his head. Farin focused his hearing down the road and caught the sound of wagon wheels. Over a distant hill Farin saw a cloud of dust and he pointed. "A wagon's coming. Can you see anything?"

The red dots next to his eyes flared to life as Kaz zoomed in on the coach. "It's a stage coach; it has some baggage on the top, but it looks like it's not filled to capacity. The driver is speaking to the people in the coach. They seemed to be in a hurry about something, but I'm not sure what it is. I've never seen people ride a coach with their heads out the openings to talk with the driver before." Kaz shrugged his shoulders. "Honestly, I don't care what they are excited about, I'm just glad to finally see someone."

As the coach neared, the boys waved their arms, and it slowed down. From under the brim of his sweat-stained brown hat the driver looked down on them. The man had a beard that was well overdue for a trim, and the boys could see that he was missing several teeth as he gave them a reassuring smile. "We're heading to Dungan. Want a lift?"

Farin's heart sank, and he felt Kaz slump more heavily on his shoulder. The one place they could get the care they needed, the one place to which they had a ride, the one place they could not go. "How far are we from Hillside?" Garin asked hopefully.

"We left about an hour ago," the stage driver answered. "It's about twelve miles down that road. Walking at a good pace I guess you'll get there before nightfall." With his answer their hopes crashed.

"Please, sir. We need to get to Hillside as soon as possible. Drams attacked us on the road, my friend is injured. We can pay you for transportation to Hillside," Garin offered hopefully, holding out a coin in his hand.

Perhaps the mention of earning some money perked his interest because the coach driver turned to his patrons. "Is there anyone who can't spare some time to take these boys closer to Hillside?" Some heads appeared in the window of the coach and Farin saw men who looked like they were workers. Perhaps one of these men would work on his father's farm. Some of them expressed words of sympathy, while others looked completely uninterested in the turn of events. "Well I guess that settles it, we'll make a detour through Hillside, again, on our way to Dungan," the driver announced.

The coach driver pulled the break and jumped down to help the boys load into the coach. He held out a hand for support and helped Kaz into the coach. "Thank you, sir." Kaz said while giving him a winning smile. "I don't know what we would have done if you hadn't come."

"Up we go!" he said as he helped Farin into the coach. Then to Kaz, "No need to go on about it. We'll have you taken care of in short order."

As Garin stepped up into the now crowded coach, the driver started to close the door. "Watch your fingers, son. Last thing we need is another injury." He smiled and closed the door as the passengers found room for everyone.

The driver nimbly got back up onto the coach and grabbed the reins. The wagon began moving down the road, bobbing back and forth as they headed toward Dungan. Farin leaned out the window and craned his neck to look down the road. He sat back down and looked at the other men in the carriage. "So, what are you doing when you get to Dungan?" he asked, wondering if any of them had been hired by his father.

"You know," one of the large men said with a gruff voice. "Working in the fields and farms, maybe at the lumber yard."

Farin shook his head, "There's no lumber yard in Dungan. There's not much of anything there if you ask me."

The man looked to his companions questioningly, then shrugged his shoulders. "I guess we'll just look for work in the fields."

"Well, if you tell Mr. Segris that you met his sons on the road, he'll probably find something for you to do," Kaz added.

"Mr. Who?" one of the men asked.

"That's odd," Garin chimed in. "There isn't a lot of freelance work available in Dungan. I'm sure you would have heard of the Segris farm if you are heading to Dungan for work."

Farin looked at his brother and saw an almost imperceptible shake of his head. Garin thought something was amiss. Farin began really observing the men in the carriage with him.

They were all well-built and could work on a farm, but now that he thought about it, they were not dressed like farm workers; they looked more like ragged wanderers. He also noticed that they each carried long hunting knives, and most of them had a hand resting on the hilt. "So, when are we turning this wagon around?" Farin asked as they continued down the road west.

Instead of an answer, the man who sat next to Farin began pulling out his knife.

Kaz was the first to react. He lashed out at the nearest passenger in the coach. He struck the man on his right so hard, he heard a cracking sound. The man was clearly stunned.

Farin cocked his arm back, ready to punch the passenger next to him, but Garin held his arm from moving. Farin looked around the coach and saw that the other 'passengers' were all holding their weapons up, ready to attack. The man next to Kaz had recovered enough now to look Kaz right in the eye. He pressed down hard on Kaz's thigh. A deep red blotch appeared on Kaz's pants where the man was pressing.

"Is there more fight in you?" the criminal asked as he eased the pressure on Kaz's leg. Kaz winced in pain. "Didn't think so." His wicked smile widened as he saw the pain he had caused.

"Stop it!" Garin shouted at the bandit, but the man just reached out and cuffed Garin across the head.

The bandit beside Farin pressed the point of his knife into Farin's side. "Don't even think about moving." His soft, evil voice made Farin want to throw up, but all he could do was sit silently.

"Nobody speaks a word, or I'll finish the job on your friend's leg." The man who was speaking wrapped a leather band around Kaz's eyes and the other passengers produced their own bands for Garin and Farin. They covered the boys' eyes and ears as best they could. The carriage turned to the left off the road, and they bounced in the rough field for several silent minutes that seemed like hours. Kaz, from time to time, would moan as they hit an unusually rough patch. This continued until the coach came to a sudden halt.

The bandits removed the blindfolds and shoved Garin and Farin out of the coach onto the hard earth. Kaz was thrown roughly from the coach and fell into unconsciousness when he landed squarely on his injured side.

"I don't know who you think you are," Farin started. He

stopped when the coach driver drew a bow from the packs he had taken from the boys to store at the top of the coach, and pointed it right at his chest.

Frozen with fear, Farin stared wide-eyed at the arrowhead he felt sure would be the last thing he saw in life, then Garin stepped in front of him. "What do you want from us?" he asked.

"This is a nice bow," the man began. "We'll take it. Let's see what else they have for us." The thieves took the boys' weapons and backpacks, and then they began searching the boys while the marks on the driver's ears flared red as he kept a look out.

One man searched Kaz while the other two grabbed Farin. "I don't have anything," he insisted, but they turned his pockets inside out, then moved on to Garin.

As one of the large men reached for Garin's pocket, he slashed with his father's knife. The knife left a long cut on the robber's forearm. The bandit retaliated with a solid punch that knocked Garin to the ground and made blood run down his nose. The man grabbed Garin's knife and quickly patted him down for anything else of value. When his eye fell upon Gran's necklace hanging around Garin's neck, his eyes widened for just a moment, and he took a quick look around. Seeing that the other bandits were busy harassing the other boys or getting the horses turned around, he ripped the necklace off Garin's neck and quickly bent down to slip it into a pocket hidden in the inside seam of his pant leg. Then he dropped the boy to the ground, kicking him in the stomach.

Unexpectedly, the coach driver's head snapped up and he looked out into the distance.

"Let's get out of here!" he shouted as he pointed out into the distance. Farin watched as the men loaded back up into the wagon, which was now pointing toward a small path that would carry them deeper into the woods. He focused his hearing in the direction the driver had been looking. Suddenly he knew why they had broken off their activities so abruptly. He heard horses, and they were coming fast.

The man who had taken Gran's necklace threw Garin a wink, and with a triumphant look, climbed into the coach, which took off as quickly as it could go.

Knowing that they could not move Kaz out of the horses' path, and with Garin still nursing his bloody nose, Farin stood up so he could clearly be seen and braced himself for whatever these horsemen would do. The fact that whoever was coming was intimidating enough to send a small band of thieves running in the opposite direction without putting up any fight made him nervous. Garin slowly stood up next to Farin, and the two looked toward the approaching horses.

"How's the nose?" Farin asked as he put his arm around his brother for support.

Garin looked over at Farin and smiled. "It was worth it." He then held out the picture of Fenn. "They didn't get everything."

Farin shook his head.

"Well, you'd better put that somewhere safe. These ones might not be as generous."

When the horses came into view, Farin felt some relief. The patrol of a half dozen soldiers were riding in rigid formation, and they were all dressed alike. The lead horseman wore a solid breastplate that reflected the sunlight.

"They look like soldiers," Farin remarked.

Garin squinted and shaded his eyes with his hand. "I think they have a blue bear crest. Farin, am I seeing things?"

"Or is that the crest of Omer?" Farin finished Garin's thought.

They recognized the crest from the few times they had gone with their father to trade crops for Omer's wine. Baron Omer controlled Hillside's surrounding area, and most of the Woller Plains, extending many miles in every direction away from his massive castle complex which, even after generations of expansions and additions, was still referred to simply as "the keep" in this region of Denall.

Omer had the best vineyards in all of Denall, not to mention the best of everything that was to be had through his extensive trade agreements. Although it cost him dearly, their father had willingly made the trip and paid the price for that wine that would only be opened on special occasions, though on the last trip he had groused all the way home about having to wait with twenty other similar farmers and merchants for a hearing with the steward. The regular schedule of trade interviews had been put on hold when a representative from the king's guard had been ushered in to demand a tour of the barony to "establish the continued security contribution the barony was making to the realm."

Now experiencing firsthand the efficacy of Baron Omer's "contribution to the security of the realm," Farin didn't mind at all that they had been kept that entire day standing in the courtyard of Omer's Keep. As the soldiers drew up in front of them, Garin fell to his knees, and in complete relief whispered under his breath, "We're saved. We're saved."

As they drew near, the patrol leader held his arm up and brought it into a tight fist. In perfect unison, Omer's men came to an abrupt halt.

"What are your names and what is your business?" the hazel-eyed patrol leader asked them.

"I'm Farin, this is Garin and Kaz," Farin answered, as he gestured to Kaz who was now awake, wincing as he held his leg. "We're from Dungan and headed to Hillside."

"You're quite a bit out of your way," he responded with a grin. "Hillside is that way, you know," he pointed into the distance. "What are you doing out here?"

Garin explained about the coach ride while the man thoughtfully nodded and listened.

The man replied, "You're lucky we passed this way. There isn't a lot of traffic around here, so the bandits always prey on single travelers or small groups. We'll get you safely to Hillside. Stay there until you are healed up and then go home." He motioned for three of his men to carry the travelers.

"Thank you, sir," Farin replied.

"You can call me Commander Aldis," the man responded with a tilt of his head. The three riders carefully lifted the injured boys while Commander Aldis urged his horse forward and rode next to the man who looked like the second in command. He leaned in close to his companion, but Farin's heightened hearing picked up what he said.

"Don't know why all these kids are out on their way to Hillside."

"What did you say?" Farin asked from behind his rider. "Excuse me, Commander Aldis, are there others going to Hillside? Did you find Bendar?"

"We picked him up yesterday. He was beat up pretty good. We dropped him off late last night at the Hillside Inn. I told him to stay there for at least a day or two 'till he was fit for traveling. We've been tracking the bandits since that time, and that's when we found you."

"Can you take us to the inn?" Garin and Farin asked in unison.

Commander Aldis nodded his head and kicked the horse into a trot. "Let's get you boys to Hillside."

After bouncing along on the back of the horses for some time, the party reached the road and turned right toward Hillside.

"How far are we from Hillside?" Garin asked his rider.

"It's just up over that hill, maybe a mile. Why do you ask?"

"This is where we met the coach. They told us we were hours from Hillside."

"If you'd known the distance, it wouldn't have made any difference. They would have just forced you into their trap," the man said. Then he paused for a moment and continued. "It actually might have been worse if you had resisted. You might not have survived."

The horses crested the hill and Farin saw the welcome sight of Hillside. Hope was restored as he realized that they had finished the first part of their journey. Then hope began to be replaced with an inkling of dread as the reality of what they'd been through sank in. If it almost killed them to get to Hillside, what would the rest of the journey be like? What were they going to do with no supplies? How long would they need to stay here for Kaz to walk again? Was the third stash undisturbed? How could they finish their journey? Did they want to finish the journey? With so many unanswered questions he remained silent as they approached the village.

CHAPTER 10

The group passed over a bridge that spanned the Hillside River, then entered the village. It was Kaz's first time in the larger town, and its location, on the side of a rather large, rolling hill, made the name make sense.

Farin and Garin had been to Hillside on occasion, so while they were looking around at all the buildings, Kaz just stared in disbelief at the size of this place. He had never seen so many people, buildings, or horses all in one place. They continued down the main street and off to first one side street, and then a second.

"Did you see that?" Kaz asked as he pointed to a building that was four stories high. "I didn't know they could make buildings that tall. Even the largest homes in Dungan only have two stories and a small attic."

"I told you," Farin reminded Kaz. "After my first trip here I tried to tell you the buildings were tall, but you said I needed to have my vision checked, remember?"

"Yeah, yeah, close your mouth for a minute, and let me enjoy this." Under his breath Kaz wondered aloud. "Why would you need a house so tall?"

In answer, Garin responded. "Dad told us that because of the population of the town, they need to build up when they run out of space to build out. It's a common thing to happen in populated areas."

Kaz stopped looking at the buildings, and scowled at the twins. "Between your analysis and Farin's sarcasm, this moment is officially ruined. Just keep quiet and let me enjoy this." The style of homes were similar to those in Dungan, only closer together. They were a mix of stone, brick and mortar, as well as some wooden houses of log cabin type construction. Most buildings had small shops on the main level with living quarters in the upper floors. The roofs were made with split cedar shingles or hardened clay tiles.

Just as Kaz thought he was getting used to the feel of the town, he was shocked by a new sight. Within the village limits there was a small pasture for horses. Only two or three horses were walking in the inadequate pasture while the rest were tied up in their stalls looking very restless. Kaz was used to seeing acres and acres of space for horses. When a Dungan horse was not being used for work in the fields or ridden, it was generally free to roam and graze. The pastures were enclosed by fieldstone walls or thick, thorny hedges to keep the horses from getting into gardens or crops, but they were never locked up like this. When they passed the small pasture, Commander Aldis pulled the reins.

"Here we are," he said as they stopped in front of the Hillside Inn.

"How can we ever repay you?" Kaz asked as he was gently placed on his feet to lean on his friends for support.

"There is no need," replied Commander Aldis. "Omer wants a peaceful realm; that's all the reward we need. Perhaps I can ask a couple of questions?"

"Absolutely!" Farin replied quickly.

"What did the bandits take from you?"

"Everything we had," Kaz replied quickly. He didn't think the officer needed to know about Garin's picture of Fenn.

"Can you be a bit more specific," he inquired further, "in case we find them we'll know what to return to you."

Kaz looked to the twins for help. He had packed some supplies, but mostly they had gotten things ready that morning.

"We had two packs filled mainly with food, two longbows, two gold coins, a hunting knife," Garin began.

"My sword," Farin cut in. "We also had some water skins and two quivers of arrows."

Commander Aldis nodded. "Are you sure there wasn't anything else, any jewelry or valuables?"

Garin laughed out loud. "There was one more thing," he said with a grin. "Kaz's necklace."

The commander did not smile, and Garin coughed to clear his throat and regain his composure a little. "Kaz had an old necklace that his Gran gave him. That was taken as well."

Kaz's face burned red as the soldier looked questioningly at the young man.

"We will continue to look for the thieves and let you know when we catch them. Stay at the inn so we'll know where to find you."

The three boys nodded their heads.

After a moment looking at the small band of young men, and as if reading their minds, the patrol leader tossed a small coin to Farin. "This will get you a warm meal and a roof over your heads for one night. Take care of your friend, and try to stay out of trouble," he said as he pointed at the entrance of the inn.

Kaz looked up and saw Bendar limping out to meet them. Bendar's lip was split open and his cheek was a dark purple color.

With that, the patrol officer turned and led his men back in the direction they had come. The thunder of the horses' hooves drowned out the calls of appreciation and thanks that the boys repeated until the horses were out of sight.

"How is everyone?" Garin asked as he looked at the other boys. Bendar nodded his head, and Kaz just grinned from ear to ear, happy to be safe, and finally in Hillside.

"Bendar, are you all right?" Garin asked.

Bendar moved his lips painstakingly, "I am just happy that you made it safely. I am so sorry I was not able to get back. It looks like you also met up with some trouble."

"I think we'll live," Farin answered. "Let's not spend too much time talking about what we lost. The first thing we need to do is find out what we do have."

"We'll get to that in short order, first we need to secure lodging and get Kaz off his feet."

Kaz was thrilled when Garin's suggestion was met with unanimous approval. Garin and Farin helped Kaz up the steps and into the tavern of the Hillside Inn.

Bendar pointed to a table near the back stairs. "Over there," he gestured as he moved ahead to pull out a chair for his friend. Kaz looked around the empty dining room that had nothing interesting except a small stage in front of the fireplace at the far end of an open room. It was not a room made for comfort and beauty, but a simple place for people to gather and meet with friends after a long day. It was still an hour until sunset, and the place was relatively empty.

"Can I help you?" the inn keeper said as they boys made their way to a table.

"It looks like we will be staying for a while," Bendar responded.

Farin pulled out the coin from Commander Aldis and handed it to the inn keeper. The large man looked down at the four boys.

"You'll be very cramped if this is all you can give me," he said pointing at the coin.

"Commander Aldis said it would be enough for a meal and a night here," Kaz responded as he took a seat at the table. "We were robbed on our way here, and they're going to find the robbers, then we can pay you some more. He told us to stay here for a while."

The man took the coin and rubbed his chin thoughtfully. "It'll pay for one night with dinner, or two nights without any food. Your choice."

"Thank you," Kaz responded. "Two nights will be great." He saw the look of despair on the twins' faces, but they also relented and began to nod.

The innkeeper pointed to the stairs. "Third door to the right," he said offhandedly, then he returned to polishing tables and preparing the room for other patrons.

When the inn keeper was gone, Kaz slumped down in his chair.

"When you came here with your dad did you meet anyone who might be able to help us out?" he asked Farin.

"You know we're not supposed to ask for handouts, and if we ask people Dad knows, it will definitely get back to him," Garin responded. He put his hands to his temples as if trying to massage away his problems.

"I wasn't talking about a handout. Do they need any workers?" Kaz clarified.

"I don't know, but I'm sure we can find out," Farin cut in enthusiastically. "When we came two summers back, the man who runs the coal mine was complaining about how hard it was to find good workers."

Kaz made a serious and disheartened face. "So they need *good* workers? We might be in trouble." With that said Kaz forced a smile and painstakingly shifted his weight in his chair.

"There have to be people needing help in their fields planting, clearing, or even harvesting wood," Garin added. "And I'm sure there are some housewives in town that could use some socks darned," he finished with a smile directed at Kaz.

"If only the town were in need of a smart mouth, then we'd have all the money we could carry." Kaz's comeback was ignored when Bendar quietly added some more bad news.

"We no longer have a horse here." He hung his head and took a deep breath before continuing. "I have convinced the stable owner to rent me one horse for a day so that I could go and get you, and recover what we left behind. He said that he is willing to accept some of the surplus materials as payment. It is a good thing his wife enjoys the taste of dried dram meat," he concluded with a half-smile.

"What we really need is some long-term work," Garin concluded. "Something that will pay for us staying here and eating."

Kaz raised his hand up and waved for the innkeeper. "Excuse me," he called out.

The man slowly made his way over to their table, while polishing a mug on his apron. "How can I help you?"

Kaz looked up at the man and tried to give a friendly smile.

"We're trying to find some work," Kaz began. The innkeeper didn't look very friendly, so he quickly added, "so we can get money to stay here, and eat the wonderful food we're smelling," the man seemed to soften slightly so Kaz continued. "Do you know of anyone looking for workers? Is Omer hiring anyone for the vineyards?" Kaz added as the thought came to him.

The portly man looked down at Kaz. "Omer never hires

anyone for the vineyards, I think he has private gardeners or something," he said with a shrug. "As for work here in Hillside, there is a group digging a ditch over on the east side of town, I think the project is almost done, but you could look into that. Any other work is posted in the town square. Just check it every morning and you might find ways to keep busy."

"Thanks," Kaz said, extending his hand. "My name is Kaz, it's nice to meet you."

The innkeeper shook his head slowly from side to side, but reached out and returned the friendly gesture.

"I'm Braden." He turned and left the group and returned to the counter to polish some other dishes.

"We've got some time to look for work before the sun goes down," Farin added. "Let's go see what we can find."

Bendar nodded his head.

"I will ask if Cam needs help in the stables. He seemed willing to help out with renting us the horse. Maybe there is work we can do for him."

"I don't think that's a good idea," Garin cut in. "Your limp is pretty bad. You two stay here, we'll go look for work. We'll let you know what we find." The twins stood up from the table, and left the inn.

"No point in staying down here," Kaz concluded, as he stood up and leaned heavily on the hand rail. He didn't like the idea of sitting in a small room, but the smell of food was making his stomach growl, and the thought of lying down was very enticing.

Despite his limp, Bendar put his shoulder under Kaz and helped him up the stairs. When they came to the door of their room and pushed it open, they looked at each other before stepping into the cramped space. The room had two cots and a small desk with a ladder-back chair. There was barely enough room for the four boys to fit in this space, let alone comfortably sleep. "Hopefully Farin's snoring tones down a little," Kaz said optimistically.

"And Garin's gas," Bendar added with a scrunched up nose.

Kaz laughed and patted Bendar on the back. "You're a

funny guy."

"I was not trying to make a joke," Bendar protested.

"I know," Kaz said as he lowered himself down onto one of the cots. "That's why you're so funny."

Bendar scrunched his eyebrows together, but did not respond to Kaz's remark. "Let me have a look at your leg," Bendar offered. Kaz turned over slowly and let out a small moan. Bendar removed the bandage, "Well," he began, "it could be worse."

"That's not comforting," Kaz said half into the rough straw pillow, while he strained his neck to see his leg.

"Just hold still," Bendar pushed Kaz back. "The scrapes are looking better, but the large cut bled some more today. In the morning I will need to go back for the supplies. We have to keep this wrapped and clean, and you need to rest."

Kaz covered his leg, then turned toward his friend. "You can't go back alone, what if they are on the road again?"

Bendar made a determined face, but Kaz could tell there was an underlying fear in his features. "Commander Aldis said he was going after them, so they will probably be in hiding for a while."

"What if they're not?" Kaz argued. "We can't risk you getting mugged again, and if you lose the supplies and the horse…"

Bendar held up his hand to stop Kaz, "They only caught us because it was a surprise attack. If I have a horse, I can outrun them and get back into town. Besides, with the supplies they took from us, they will need to sell them somewhere outside of Hillside or Dungan. Groups of bandits like that often move around to keep from getting caught. It is highly improbable that they will return for at least a couple of weeks, perhaps longer."

Kaz rested his head back on the pillow and looked up at the rough sawn roof boards. "I can't argue with your logic, Bendar, I never could. But if you want someone to go with you, we would all understand." From the corner of his eye, Kaz could see Bendar shaking his head from side to side. "That's up to you," Kaz relented. "I'm going to get some sleep."

As Kaz tried to fall asleep, his thoughts raced through all that had happened that day. In all the commotion, he hadn't had time to process the range of emotions he felt. The pain of his leg injury, the questioning of Bendar's loyalty, the relief at being helped which turned to horror, and the joy he felt when he saw Omer's soldiers. Most of all he felt a deep sadness and loss. When the bandits had threatened his friends, he had felt helpless and braced himself for their deaths. He had flashback memories of watching as a group of thieves killed his family. Kaz took deep breaths and tried to relax. He tried to tell himself he was safe now, and so were his friends, but a sense of disquiet kept creeping back into his heart. How could he have saved any of them? As his fatigue overcame him, Kaz fell into a restless sleep filled with dreams.

In the morning, Kaz moaned loudly as he rolled onto his side. He looked around the small room and saw that Garin and Farin were lying on the floor awkwardly scrunched so that they didn't touch each other. Kaz blinked his eyes hard, yawned and stretched his arms upward. With the day he had had, he wasn't surprised that he didn't hear them come into the room the previous night. As Kaz stretched he saw the twins begin to shuffle and wake up.

"Good morning," Kaz said in an overly cheerful way. "How did everyone sleep?"

Farin scowled at Kaz, "If you weren't an invalid, I'd make you sleep on the floor," he replied.

"I guess I could sleep on the floor," Kaz said looking at the twins, "but I think you two would need to snuggle up close to make room for me." Garin and Farin both sat up and scooted on the floor until they were sitting apart from each other. "So what's the plan for today?" Kaz asked.

Garin perked up and excitedly answered, "Last night we were able to start work digging the ditch." He began pulling his boots on as Farin continued.

"They will pay us each two coppers per day. If we show up early, and work hard, he said we might make a little bit more if the job gets done quickly."

Smiling, Kaz sank down onto a cot. "We're saved."

While Garin moved to the cot and surveyed Kaz's injury, Farin continued, "I wouldn't say that – they only need us for a few days. Bendar, has that brilliant brain of yours devised a plan for us?"

"Not yet, but I will be going to get the supplies today. Cam said he knew someone who might buy them, so if I can sell them by nightfall, I can start work tomorrow."

Garin looked questioningly at his friend, "Are you able to start working that quickly? You still look pretty beat up."

"I feel much better today," Bendar said unconvincingly through his split lip. But the boys needed all the money they could earn, so nobody objected.

After looking over Kaz's leg, Garin rewrapped the bandage. "You are definitely in better shape than this one. It'll be weeks before we can start our trip again. We're definitely going to need more work than just the ditch digging."

Kaz rolled over and propped himself up in the cot. "Give me a couple of days and I'll be up and ready to help."

"You are not going anywhere, Kaz," Bendar said with authority. "If you do not heal properly we will be here even longer, and if you get an infection that is not properly treated you could lose your leg." Bendar waited silently for a moment as if waiting for it to sink in.

Still stubbornly trying to be a helpful part of their team Kaz spoke up, "I wonder if anyone in the village needs someone to keep watch on the rooftops." Looking around and finding that nobody even considered this for a moment he added, "Come on guys, I'm just kidding around. I'll be good."

"What about trying to get our stuff back?" Farin interjected.

"Not this again," Garin said, but was quickly cut off.

"Why not? The bandits can't have gotten very far, perhaps they even come into the village at night. If we can find them…" Farin stopped speaking as he looked around the room. Garin and Bendar were both shaking their heads in disapproval.

Kaz propped himself up on one arm, and tried to speak some reason. "I know you want your sword back," he began.

"It's not just my sword," Farin cut in. "Our food, some gold, all of our weapons, even that necklace from Gran is worth something. Without supplies we're stuck here for at least a month, or worse, we'll be thrown out to survive in the streets."

In a surprising tone that almost resembled empathy, Bendar responded. "What you are saying makes sense. We need supplies, and we will need to purchase some of the things we have lost." Farin pointed at Bendar and nodded, looking grateful to have an ally, "However," Bendar continued with a look at the other two, "these men are experienced bandits. They are organized. And in my experience they are ruthless. If we met up with them again, I think we would not get our supplies back, and I fear we might have more incapacitated patients, or perhaps worse."

Crestfallen, Farin dropped his arms to his sides. "Fine, if you are all too scared to try," he said making a final jab at the others. "We'll just dig ditches and pray we make enough to not starve."

Kaz nodded, "That's exactly what we want to do, not starve." He leaned forward and stood up, testing some weight on his leg. It felt like fire shooting up his body. "I'm heading downstairs, I'd rather sit in a room of empty tables, than in this cramped space." Farin and Garin braced themselves under Kaz's arms and Bendar walked ahead of the group. His limp was noticeably less pronounced than before, which gave Kaz some hope for his friend's quick recovery. When Kaz came into the seating area, he instantly regretted it. He looked with envy at the greasy salted pork the boarders were having for breakfast, and the smell made his stomach groan loudly.

"We need to get going," Farin said as he longingly stared at a plate of food.

"Maybe we'll find some wild berries or mushrooms on our way to the ditch digging," Garin said hopefully. He avoided looking at the food as he and Farin exited the inn.

Bendar leaned down next to Kaz before leaving. "Even with us staying in the same tiny room, we can't live off the coppers they will earn if we want to eat. After I sell the supplies, we'll need me working if we want to stay here. I am worried that we might find ourselves without a place to live very quickly."

Kaz nodded and patted Bendar on the shoulder reassuringly, "I'm sure we'll find something for you. I'll ask everyone who steps through that door." He hoped he sounded more confident than he felt.

Kaz remained sitting at the table for a time after the others had left. The innkeeper wiped the table clean. "You boys are from Dungan, right?"

Kaz looked up, surprised that Braden was talking to him. "Yes sir. We're on our Troven."

"A foolish tradition if you ask me," he shot back. "Boys your age could get killed out there on your own." Kaz sat silently, not knowing how to respond to the man. "What happened to your leg?" he asked.

"A dram attack, it started bleeding again yesterday when a group of bandits threw us from their carriage."

The man shook his head in earnest. "See what I mean? It's not safe for you out there. Things are getting worse and worse. Bandits are filling these parts. They come into the village at night sometimes. You be sure to have your friends in early every night." Kaz nodded, not sure how else to respond. After the previous night, he was surprised that the inn keeper seemed to care. Braden's face creased with fatherly concern, but as Kaz met his eyes he had a grin that for a brief moment looked almost like pride. "So you survived a dram attack? That's pretty impressive. I bet some folks would pay a penny to hear that tale." With that he left to clear another table.

CHAPTER 11

In the open fields on the outskirts of Kinstock, Mylot rode his battle horse, Gapol. The pair had worked together for years, and they rode as though they knew each other's thoughts. Mylot tightened his knees, and Gapol quickened his pace. He then braced to make a jump over a large, fallen log. Largely using his knees and feet, Mylot directed the horse to make a hairpin turn, then charge back in the direction they had come. This was a challenging maneuver in the best of conditions, but Mylot insisted on always practicing in full armor, which made it unheard of.

"Good boy," he whispered to Gapol, as they finished their practice for the morning. "Nobody will stand a chance against us at the tournament." Gapol threw back his head and whinnied in agreement.

Mylot trotted back home to the Tran Estate. Despite the distance he had ridden with Gapol, he was still technically on his family's land. As Mylot crested a small hill, in the distance he could see the elaborately manicured gardens that led to the massive stone manor. The large horse easily made his way down the hill and onto the packed dirt road that led home.

Mylot's mind was so preoccupied with the tournament that was still months away, that he did not notice anything else around him. The servants shuffled out of his way and some rushed ahead of him to bring news of his arrival. The gardeners ducked behind bushes to remain unnoticed as the lord approached the estate. All Mylot saw was a path leading to the place where he would rest, eat, and then prepare for his sword lesson.

When Mylot arrived in the courtyard he was met by five servants. One escorted Gapol to the stables while the other four helped Mylot remove his armor. "Be sure to polish it," he reminded the man taking his shield, "Sir Rodnik will not be pleased if it is not shining."

As he removed pieces of his armor, there was a noticeable stir in the courtyard. All the women stopped what they were doing to watch Mylot, some more conspicuously than others. Mylot was a level five strongarm who had spent his life training. The constant training regimen had toned his body to perfection. His layered blond hair hung down to the nape of his neck, barely brushing his broad shoulders when he turned his head. But the feature that drew the most attention were his piercing grey eyes.

"Yes, Milord," came the automatic response, though Mylot was not looking, nor listening to his servant. He was smiling back at Lady Genene, who was shamelessly waving in his direction.

He walked up the stairs to his chamber where a hot bath was drawn and waiting. With a wave of his hand he dismissed the servants. He stepped down into the hot water and relaxed his tense and sore muscles. Almost immediately a young, light haired, servant entered the room wearing a formal black suit. At his collar and wrists he had small tufts of white silk. "Lord Mylot," he began with a bow, "I bring important news."

"It can wait," Mylot replied and continued sitting lazily in his bath.

"My Lord," the timid servant continued, "I was told it was urgent."

Mylot turned to look at the servant, surprised that he was still there. "It can wait," he repeated more firmly.

"Yes, Milord," the man said, and then he bowed and backed out the door.

After several minutes the water began to become lukewarm and Mylot rang a small silver bell that sat on a table next to his bath. Immediately, an elderly servant with a grim face that was creased with wrinkles came into the room. She closed the door firmly and scowled at the young serving girls who had ventured to peek in. She crossed the room and pulled the cast iron bucket from the fire. She slowly added the hot water into the tub, then left without a word. When the water temperature dropped a second time Mylot rang again. The second ring brought a middle-aged man who brought Mylot's robe and escorted him into his dressing chamber.

Although it was a warm day, the fire was lit in the dressing quarters to ensure comfort while changing. Sturdy leather pants, a cotton shirt and soft leather gloves were laid out for his sword practice with Sir Rodnik. Turning to leave the room, he saw the young, light haired servant standing in front of the door.

"Lord Mylot," he began, "you have a guest: Sir Theodore."

"Sir Theodore!" Mylot bellowed. "Why didn't you inform me sooner?"

"I'm sorry, My Lord," the servant said in his most humble tone while bowing deeply.

"That is not good enough! You kept Sir Theodore waiting. Get out of my sight!" With this said, Mylot grabbed the young man and half pushed, half threw him out the door. The terrified servant disappeared down the hall. "Somebody find out who that was and see he never steps foot on the property again."

Mylot drew himself up, then speaking to nobody in particular, announced, "I will meet Sir Theodore in the practice yard." Then he quickly walked out of the room and down the long corridor that led outside.

When he reached the door, he pushed it open and stepped outside, giving time for his eyes to adjust to the bright afternoon sun. Standing next to the fence, Sir Theodore was waiting. The large man had dark red hair that hung to his shoulders, and he was wearing a chainmail coat over his wool shirt. On his left shoulder he had a small plate-metal shoulder guard with alternating blue and white squares, the crest of the King's personal guards. Mylot looked longingly at that crest.

"Hello, Sir Theodore," was Mylot's friendly greeting. "What brings you out this far from the capitol?"

"I came to visit with your father, and speak with you," he added.

"It means the world to him when people come to visit," Mylot responded. "With his failing health he hasn't been able to go out and visit as he would like."

Sir Theodore shook his head, "It was my pleasure to come out here. We had a pleasant visit. He is a great man."

Mylot nodded solemnly. He knew that although Sir Theodore didn't say it outright, this trip was a final farewell. His father was dying, and many of the men and women who had served with him in the King's army had come to make similar visits.

"Yes he is," Mylot agreed. "I only hope I can one day be greater."

"Well that's the wish of every parent," Sir Theodore concluded. "Speaking of such things, have you decided if you will accept the appointment of Baron over this region? Your father managed to keep peace here for many years. Now that his health is failing I know the king wants to ensure a smooth transition in leadership."

Mylot shook his head. "I have things I need to do before I settle down."

Sir Theodore scoffed slightly, "Things that are more important than the safety of the people in this realm?"

"I thought you wanted me on the king's guard?" he asked. Mylot was surprised at how the conversation turned. He had thought Sir Theodore was going to try to recruit him for the king's guard again, and now he seemed put out that Mylot would not settle down as a baron.

"I would be a fool not to ask you, but now it seems you can do an even greater service to your kingdom," he argued.

Mylot shook his head, determined not to be swayed from his plans. "I will first prove that I am fit for the rank of baron. I will win at the tournament, and see where the winnings take me; perhaps join with the king's guard. Then when I have earned the necessary prestige, maybe I will settle down."

"Prestige?" Sir Theodore asked with his head tilted. "I'm not sure you need prestige to be a good ruler. Besides," he added, "I'm only looking for the best. If you do not win at the Lexingar tournament, I might find someone better for the king's guard, and the king might give the appointment of baron to someone else." Sir Theodore gave no indication that he was joking.

"I'll win at the tournament, and then I'll *consider* your offer," He countered confidently. Mylot knew that having won the Lexingar tournament in only two categories the previous year, he was one of the best soldiers in Denall, but this year he was going to prove he was Denall's champion.

Sir Theodore shook his head in disappointment, "That's up to you, son, but you know that the offer will not always be on the table. There are people lining up just for the chance to train for the king's guard."

"I know," Mylot said.

Sir Theodore then smiled at the younger man. "Now, I'm sure there was a reason that you had me meet you out in the practice yard. Why don't you show me what you've got?"

Without needing any more encouragement, Mylot picked up his wooden practice sword and stalked out into the yard to work with Sir Rodnik. He moved with the sword as though it was an extension of his body. Every stance was perfect and flowed seamlessly to the next. Sir Rodnik called out commands and Mylot obeyed instantly. He faced three opponents with practice swords, and with a single motion moved between the two attacking men, knocking them to the ground while maintaining his momentum and grip on the sword to lunge at the final man.

After watching Mylot run through drills and practices Sir Theodore called out. "Want to try that out on an old man?"

Mylot grinned from ear to ear. "Yes, sir!"

Sir Theodore stepped out into the practice ring and hefted a long practice sword. Looking down at it in disgust he called out. "I don't fight with clubs."

While Mylot retrieved his long sword, Sir Rodnik quickly leaned over and spoke into Sir Theodore's ear. "You might get seriously hurt. Did you not see what he did to the others?" The man looked at the practice opponents who were still rubbing bruises.

"You may not know this, but I've used one of these before," Sir Theodore said, holding the sword up.

"Yes, of course." The trainer bowed and retreated several paces to watch the match.

Mylot looked at Sir Theodore as he stood casually with his sword drawn. Mylot raised his sword to his forehead, then brought it down to the side, a sign that he was ready for the fight to begin. Sir Theodore returned the sign and then stood in place with his sword by his side. *What is he doing? He's just standing there; he can't defend or attack when he stands like that. Well, I don't want to kill him. Maybe I'll just go easy on him for a bit.*

With this last thought, Mylot approached Sir Theodore with a halfhearted overhand. Before he realized what was happening, Sir Theodore had ducked under his swing and moved behind Mylot. With Mylot recovering from over swinging, Sir Theodore was easily able to send him forward with a sharp kick in the bottom. Mylot fell forward, piercing his sword into the ground for support from falling flat. "So, young friend, are we going to have a real attack this time?"

Mylot advanced more seriously with overheads, side swings, backhands, and even some forward stabs that, if successful, would have killed Sir Theodore. Each time Sir Theodore was able to counter and block the attacks. After several failed attacks, Sir Theodore shifted his weight almost imperceptibly as he moved to the offensive. While Mylot was well-trained, he still had much to learn, and within moments of the offensive, it was clear that Sir Theodore was in control of this match. After driving Mylot back to the edge of the practice ring, Sir Theodore stopped suddenly and placed his sword on his forehead, then brought it down. The match was over.

Both men, now out of breath, walked back to the place where they had begun the match. "That was very impressive," Sir Theodore commented. "Can I give you a piece of advice?"

"Yes, sir," Mylot replied.

"I think you need to focus on one event. The most practical skill you will have in real battles is using your sword. I can tell by that match we had, that you have been neglecting your sword training for riding. If you want to start training for the king's guard, I advise you to drop out of the joust."

Mylot protested, "I'm already stronger than anyone else at the tournament, I don't need to work as much with the sword. It's the jousting that I need to win this year."

Sir Theodore handed his sword to Mylot's trainer and took a step out of the training arena. "That's up to you. Just remember that there is a difference between fighting for fame and fighting for your life." Sir Theodore held Mylot's gaze for a moment, then shook his head. "I think we both know you're going to ignore my advice, so I'll let you in on a secret. If you meet someone who matches your skills, defend for a time until you can feel the pattern of his movements."

"What do you mean, pattern of movements? Is that like the stances they use?" Mylot asked.

Sir Theodore looked at Mylot's trainer with a quizzical look, but found no help there. "The rhythm in which he is moving is the regular pattern that he changes attacks or stances." Still not understanding, Mylot shrugged his shoulders. "If you practice, you will start to see what I mean. When you face an opponent, match his attacks with defensive moves, follow his movements, then you will begin to feel patterns in his movements. When you do, you need to move just slightly faster than he does, and that will put him off balance. Then you can back him into a corner, or into a tree, or off a cliff. In battle, moving your opponent where you want him to go can often replace needing to strike the deathblow yourself."

"After I win the tournament, you'll have to show me that trick."

Shaking his head, Sir Theodore replied, "If you don't practice it, you might not be coming with me to Norwell, but if you do win, we can consider this a piece of early training. There are several things that you would have to learn from our trainers, like how to properly use that strength of yours." Smiling, he bid Mylot farewell.

CHAPTER 12

Farin set his pick in the pile of tools, then stepped out of the way to let Bendar put down his shovel. It was nice having some extra income from three people working in the trench instead of just two, but now that the trench was finished, they were out of work. "What are we going to do?" he asked Bendar. They had sold some supplies to pay for a doctor to properly clean and treat Kaz's leg, and on his recommendation, had traded with a travelling medicine vendor for something that would speed the healing process, but they wanted to keep as much as possible for their continued journey. The trench digging earned them enough to eat and stay at the inn for a few more days, but they needed to find something more long term until Kaz was fully healed.

"We will need to find something else while Garin is helping Will."

Farin nodded, then looked over to his brother. Garin had made friends with a man named Will who was building a house for his growing family. Although Garin tried to get work for Farin and Bendar, Will had said that he could not afford to pay three people to dig a foundation and put framing up. Also, due to the location of the cabin, Garin would be staying with Will for at least two weeks, and Farin was not willing to leave Kaz alone during the crucial stage of recovery. "I actually saw a posting today in the square for some work as a scribe. The merchant wants someone to help with getting his ledger in order and do some odds and ends."

Bendar looked up quickly. "That would be a perfect job for me! I have worked with my father for years doing similar things."

Farin nodded his head reluctantly. He knew Bendar was the logical choice for the job, and reading, writing, and keeping meticulous notes were not among Farin's strengths. While it made sense for Bendar to go after that job, Farin felt frustrated at being inadequate for the task. "It's right over there," Farin said, pointing down the street.

Bendar reached into his pocket. "Bring this back to Kaz," he said as he placed two coppers into Farin's hand. Farin looked down at the money, smiled, and shook his head as he watched Bendar trot down the street. He felt strange holding Bendar's money. What felt even stranger was how quickly Bendar dropped it into his hand as if he didn't give it a second thought. Despite any of Garin's doubts, he felt confident Bendar was fully invested in the success of their group.

Farin put the money in his pocket with his own payment for the day. The money was dwindling, and now he was the only one, besides Kaz, who didn't have any prospects for work. From their supply stashes they had kept their tent, some cloth for making bandages, one hunting knife, two longbows and some food. The rest of the material was sold in town for a small sum. Each day they gave the inn keeper some coins and watched as their meager pile of coins diminished. When Garin was finished talking with Will, the brothers walked back toward the inn. "What are you going to do?" Garin asked.

"I'll figure something out," Farin replied. "As much as I hate doing it, I know just about everything about farm work. I can help with animals, or any late summer planting if there are local people who need help."

Garin patted his shoulder. "Take care of everything while I'm gone. Kaz'll try to get moving before he's fully healed, and…"

"Yes, mother," Farin replied sarcastically. As they arrived at the inn, Farin stopped walking, and in a more serious tone added, "Take care of yourself too."

"I will."

"Hey, Kaz," Farin said as he entered the dining area of the inn. Kaz seemed to always be in that room when they got off work. Farin didn't blame him. Despite the bland decorations, it was much better than spending the day in the small room upstairs. "How's the leg doing?"

"It's feeling good. I was actually able to walk up and down the stairs a couple of times today, and I didn't even need to use the handrail." Kaz moved to stand up, but Garin waved for him to stay seated.

"That's great. Hopefully we'll be up for moving on in a couple of weeks. If our coppers can stretch a little farther that is." Kaz nodded. He looked like he was about to say something but stayed silent. "What's going on?"

"It's nothing. I just wish I could help, that's all."

"You need to focus on getting better," Farin said, not wanting to let Kaz have time to feel bad about himself. "And if I come back here and find that you've broken open your leg wound again because you were too stubborn to use the handrail, I'll leave you behind when we head east."

Kaz scrunched his face up, "Like you could survive the trip without me. It would be way too boring." Kaz sat up straight trying to look dignified, then in his best Bendar voice he continued, "Garin, you ate two and a half apples, the ration is for only two."

Garin couldn't help but crack a smile. The voice impression was terrible, but it sounded like something Bendar would say.

"Speaking of Bendar," Garin said pointing to the door of the inn.

Bendar came and sat at the table with a wide smile on his face. "I have obtained employment."

Farin felt like jumping and cheering. "That's great news!"

Kaz nodded, "Is it enough?"

"It is almost enough to cover the cost of the room and food. When Garin returns with the money he earns, and if Farin can find work to do we will have enough."

"Speaking of which," Garin said as he reached down to pick up his pack, "I'd better get going. I'm meeting Will at the lumber yard."

Watching his brother leave, Farin was filled with a mixture of guilt and frustration, but he was determined to contribute to their group in any way he could.

"I'm going out to check the town square again," he said as he left the inn.

"That's fine," Kaz called out, "but make sure to be back before dark, I have a surprise for you guys here in the tavern."

Farin stepped out into the road. He was certain Kaz's surprise was that he had convinced the inn keeper to give them an extra roll with dinner. They had spent quite a bit of time together, and the man was treating them a little better. Despite the offer of a surprise, Farin was more concerned with finding some kind of way he could help the group.

The streets were fairly active as he walked to the center of town. In the week they had been in Hillside he had become comfortable with the layout of the town and could easily find his way around. He recognized some of the villagers who had worked on the ditch digging, and the general store owner waved at him as he passed.

"Are you needing any help?" he asked.

"We've got all the help we need here with my four sons," he responded, "But I'm happy to buy some more supplies from you if you are short on money."

"Thanks," Farin responded. He knew the man was trying to help, but if he did sell their tent, or hunting knives, or any more travel supplies to this man, they would just need to buy them back in a couple of weeks when Garin returned. They already had a list of things they would need before they could leave, there was no sense making the list bigger.

He made his way to the town square and checked the board for any available work. It was empty, as he expected, but he hoped that each day would bring something, even something small, that he could do to earn some money.

Farin wandered in a large circle around the town as the sun set and darkness began to cover the buildings. He passed by the town square one final time before making his way back to the inn. It was only when he got to the front door of the tavern that he remembered about Kaz's surprise. When he pushed open the door, nothing could have prepared him for the shock of what he saw.

On the stage at the front of the tavern, Kaz was leaning on a bar stool while juggling an apple, onion and potato. As he threw them in an intricate pattern, he took a bite out of the apple, then kept juggling. "You never said you'd eat it!" Braden shouted above the crowd of guests, which caused the gathered men to cheer and laugh.

"What was that?" Kaz asked when he had swallowed the bite of apple. He kept spinning the food in the air, and in his distraction he took a bite of onion. The crowd laughed even harder.

Kaz stopped juggling the food, and Braden stalked to the front and took the potato from him. "I'll take this before you start eating it raw too!" he gave Kaz a half-hearted scowl but it was clear he was enjoying the show, and was pleased by the number of patrons who were enjoying themselves. Farin found a seat next to Bendar and watched as the show continued.

Kaz finished eating the apple, then held his finger to his mouth as if he wanted to tell everyone gathered a secret. "Have you ever seen a hound?" he asked. The people looked to each other, then back to Kaz. "Seriously, have you ever seen a hound?" he repeated.

Some people started shaking their heads, and many people replied by shouting, "No."

At Farin's table one man leaned over to a woman and Farin strained his ears to hear the man whisper, "Doesn't that man who sells herbs have a nose mark?" But it was too quiet for Kaz to hear.

At the front Kaz threw his arms up in the air, "I've never seen one. My friend, Bendar, lives half the year in Pike Point, and he's never seen one. On our way here from Dungan, Bendar told me the gift might be extinct, and that got me thinking. If a gift goes extinct, what happens? Is that just the end, or does a new gift rise up to replace the old one? I can think of a couple of gifts I'd love to have," Kaz turned to look up at the roof as if plucking some ideas from the air. "How about the gift of eating," he suggested. "I could eat what I want all the time and never worry about getting sick or getting overweight."

From the crowd a man called out, "Better guard your onions Braden!" The innkeeper jokingly wrapped his arms around a pile of vegetables, and everyone began laughing.

"How about the gift of charm," Kaz mused. "I would

always say just the right thing to that special girl." He looked around as if trying to be suave. "Oh wait, I already have that gift!" He turned around on the bar stool, then began scratching his chin as if in deep thought. "If there really is going to be a new sixth gift, and I had any say in it, I'd actually cast a vote on what it should *not* be. I'm serious, can you imagine having a child who has the gift of enhanced taste? If my friend Fenn ever had a child, that poor kid would probably starve to death. She can't boil water without burning it!"

Farin cringed at Kaz's joke and was thankful Garin was not here, but the crowd seemed to love his jokes. Kaz continued to muse about different gifts that he would not want people having and the gathered people ordered drinks and had a great time. When Kaz was finished he bowed deeply, wished them all a good night, and made his way up the stairs. Farin joined his friend and helped supported him under his arm. "Thanks," Kaz said when Farin took some weight off his leg. "I think I overdid it a bit back there."

"So that was your big surprise?" Bendar asked. "You made fun of us in front of a crowd of people?"

Kaz didn't turn around, "I didn't make fun of you," he argued. "I made fun of Braden and I definitely made fun of Fenn, but I didn't pick on you. Besides, that's not the surprise." He paused at the top of the stair case and instead of turning to go to their small room at the end of the hall, he went left and opened the door to a large room with two beds and two cots. "This is the surprise."

"Are you serious?" Farin asked in complete shock.

"Braden said it was a slow season and if I could bring more people in by telling stories and jokes he would let us have a larger room, and a discount."

Farin grabbed Kaz in a hug, "I can't believe it. I've never been so happy for a cot in my whole life."

CHAPTER 13

Dune sat uncomfortably on a small cart that meandered down the main road to Norwell. He shrugged against the uncomfortable wool poncho that Kire had insisted he wear. He appreciated Kire traveling with him for the past week, but he was actually starting to agree with the older man—he needed a new travel partner. "My turn is just up ahead," Kire said as if reading Dune's mind. "From here I'm going straight north, and I again recommend that you do the same. Or go south, or west. We've already had a couple of close calls this week, and from what your group of seekers near Eaton was discussing, and what we have seen of the seekers that were out and about this week, they are definitely heading toward Lexingar."

"Lexingar! Are you sure?" Dune asked, surprised by the surety of Kire's statement. Lexingar still lay many weeks' journey to the north, and there were numerous roads which led away from Norwell. As far as Dune was concerned, he would be tracking for several weeks before determining where the seekers were ultimately headed.

Kire merely raised his eyebrow in response as he observed Dune. Dune nodded his head with a sigh. After all these years it was true that there was no need to question whether Kire was sure about an observation. When Kire vocalized a determination based on the information he had, he was never wrong.

"I know you worry about my safety," Dune began, "but if I can thwart Mordyar's stone seekers, I can do something important to stop him."

Kire nodded thoughtfully. "I'm worried about more than just your safety," he began. "What if the prophecies are being fulfilled?"

"Are you talking about The Changing again?" Dune asked with a half smirk. "You don't think it sounds just a little too fantastic for the earth to shake and split open, making new continents and destroying the ones we know?"

"I wouldn't be so certain. Many scholars fail to understand what the Stones of Power are, or that they have already started gathering," he said, poking Dune's cloak for emphasis. "We have already seen changes in weather patterns, diseases rising up, and if Mordyar has his eye on Denall, war will come. These are all things that precede The Changing. They are all things that are happening now."

"That's another good reason to stop Mordyar," Dune argued.

"The only thing that can stop him is the one thing he's seeking. The thing you have hidden in your cloak. The thing you are bringing right to the seekers."

Dune pulled off the poncho, folded it and placed it in the back of Kire's cart. "I will be as cautious as possible, and when I know their plans, I will use all you have taught me to decide on the best way to," he paused, searching for the right word, "address the situation."

Kire pulled on the reins, bringing the cart to a stop. He sat sideways in his seat and looked right at Dune. "I am not surprised that this is your decision, but this is where our paths must split. When you find that you are in over your head, you know where to find me. Though I plan to pursue other methods, I am equally committed to stopping Mordyar."

Dune reached out and put a hand on Kire's shoulder. "I've never doubted that, not even for a second. I really do appreciate you coming this far with me," Dune said as he jumped down from the cart and untied his horse from the back of Kire's cart.

"It was on my way," Kire said with a grin. "Always happy to give a lift to another lonely traveler."

Dune jumped up into the saddle, and walked the horse to stand even with Kire. "I'm sure our paths will cross again, my friend."

"I feel certain that is true," Kire responded with a knowing look. With one last look of farewell and a raised hand, Kire whipped the mule and pulled on the reins, and the small cart turned up a horse path leading north.

Dune watched his mentor and friend trundle down the road for a moment, then kicked his horse into motion down the road east toward Norwell, following the tracks of the stone seekers.

Traveling with Kire had slowed Dune down a little, but he was quickly able to make up time, and the tracks of the seekers became more and more fresh. As he followed the seekers, he thought about what Kire had said, and he considered the danger of following them.

If the group of seekers all worked together, he could be overpowered and captured. Slowing his horse to a walk, he shuddered slightly at the thought of being a prisoner again, and he looked down at his calloused hands and slowly pulled up his sleeve to look down at an old scar on his arm. He knew what it was like to be a captive—to be forced to use his magic like a slave, but he also knew what he was fighting for.

He dropped his sleeve down again to cover his arm and looked up the road. As he cantered down the hard-packed road, he reassured himself that chasing down Mordyar's stone seekers was worth taking the risk of being captured again; it was worth any sacrifice. But he had also reasoned that being captured was a nearly non-existent possibility. They were not gathering to set up a trap for him, and he had learned, from painful experience, how to avoid being betrayed.

Three days after he parted ways with Kire, Dune found himself crouched low behind a tree, sneaking up on the seekers' campsite. He could hardly believe his luck when he discovered that this time they had not set any magical traps.

Dune padded his feet with a cushion of magic to avoid making any sound as he made his way close to their camp. On the perimeter, Edgar was sitting on a log with his arms crossed over his chest. He was leaning against a tree and softly snoring. *Not the best sentry.* The other seekers were also sleeping soundly, presumably having fully trusted Edgar's ability to stay awake and alert them to any dangers.

The magician reached out with his magic and touched the small vial that hung from Edgar's belt. While he could sense that what was inside had been created with magic, it also felt filthy and unnatural. In his years following the seekers, he had learned a little bit about the elixir they had with them at all times. All seekers took an oath to serve Mordyar and seek the Stones of Power. When they did, they were poisoned. The poison deformed their bodies, allowing them to see magical items, but eventually the effects of the transformation would kill them. Until then, the elixir they drank helped keep them alive, and they guarded it fiercely.

Dune watched Edgar for a moment. He did want to know where the seekers were going, but he didn't need them all alive. He also didn't want to alert the other seekers to the fact that they were being tracked. *What would Kire do?* He continued to puzzle out a plan as he stood just a few yards away from Edgar, then an idea hit him. *I wonder what Edgar will do if he runs out of that elixir?* Dune made a sharp point of hardened air that was hair thin, and he punctured the base of Edgar's vial with an imperceptible hole. When he released the magic, he waited several minutes until he heard a single drop of the liquid hit the ground. He then backed away into the thick darkness of the woods, and back to his campsite.

In the morning, Dune took his time getting up and ready. Despite being disguised in farmer's clothing, he didn't want to come upon the seekers face to face on the road, especially right around the time when Edgar discovered his empty vial. After a lengthy breakfast, he started walking his horse down the main road toward Norwell.

When he passed the place where the seekers had camped, he looked around for any signs of them, and found some tracks indicating that they had all left together from the camp. *Maybe they all shared their elixir supplies with Edgar.*

Dune urged his horse into a trot to make up some lost time. He was disappointed that his plan didn't seem to be working, but he kept moving, hoping that eventually they might run out. Through the late morning and into the early afternoon Dune continued to follow the road, checking from time to time for the seekers' tracks. As the evening began to settle in, he passed the place where they had stopped for a meal. Being a couple of hours behind them was a safe distance, so he was about to stop for the night when he heard a slight rustling in the woods. He gripped his staff and moved forward more cautiously. The sound was too clumsy for an animal, and too large to have been caused by the wind. As he approached, the female seeker jumped out of the bushes and landed on the road next to him. He pushed against her with magic, shoving her backward away from himself and his horse.

She screamed out. "Where did that come from? What's going on?"

Dune leapt to the ground with his staff in hand and some spells ready to release at her. As he approached, she didn't attack, but instead wandered in a circle with her hands outstretched. Dune sent out a locator spell into the woods looking for the other seekers. If she was a decoy, he was not going to be fooled. He felt through the magic of his locator spell that they were alone. He moved forward cautiously. "Where are the others?" Dune asked as he came closer to the seeker.

"Who are you?" she asked, looking around. Her eyes passed over him without noticing he was there, even though she had looked directly at him, Dune saw that her eyes were glossed over in an opaque white. The woman held her hands in front of her in fists. "Where are you?" She swung her arms out trying to strike at Dune, but she found only air.

"Calm down, I'm not going to hurt you," Dune began, "Where is Edgar?"

"That rotten snake!" she shouted. "He did this to me!"

Dune came close and spoke soothingly. "What did he do?" he asked softly, then he reached out and touched one of her hands that was still a fist.

She flinched and backed away, still not dropping her fists. "He stole something from me!" she spat out, "Something very important." She moved from side to side as if looking for the direction of an attack.

"I'm not going to hurt you," Dune reassured. "I live near Eaton, Edgar has stolen something from me too."

"Who are you?" she asked.

Dune didn't know how much of Edgar's affairs were known to this other seeker, so he didn't know if he could get away with making a name up.

"I used to be his friend, then he double crossed me and left town." Dune replied, hoping this evasive answer would stop her line of questioning. "I'm going after him and I intend to get my money back."

The woman dropped her arms to her sides and slumped to the ground. "Your money is gone," she replied. "If you chase him he'll slit your throat. It's better to just go home."

Dune sat on the ground next to her, then patted her on the shoulder. "What about you?" Dune asked, "What did he take from you?"

She scrunched her eyebrows together and hesitated for a moment before answering. "He took my medicine, I'm blind without it."

Dune shook his head. He should have known Edgar would never try to share the elixir. He would rather turn on his friends than risk not having enough for himself. For a moment, Dune almost forgot that the woman sitting on the ground in front of him was also a stone seeker, and he began to have pity for her. "I'm really sorry," he responded. "I guess we've both lost something important to Edgar."

She turned away and dropped her face to the ground. "Yes, I guess we have."

While he felt bad for the woman, he also knew that she might be able to help him. "If I catch him, I can bring back your medicine," he offered. "Where was he going?"

"I told you before, he'll kill you before he gives you back anything that he took. He wears some magical jewelry that protects him. You can't sneak up on him or he'll know. If you want to live, you should just go home."

"What about you? Why don't you go after him?" Dune asked.

"I'm as good as dead. Without my medicine I'll lose my mind and be dead in a week," she responded in a dejected tone. "There's no hope for me."

"Let me avenge you," Dune offered. If he could win her trust, even enough to let him bring her revenge to Edgar, perhaps she would share some additional information. "I'm a very hard man to kill. I'll find him, and I'll deliver a message of revenge for both of us." He let her consider that for a moment, waiting to see how receptive she might be to helping him in some way.

"His Han'Or," she murmured.

"What was that?"

"His Han'Or, his medicine. Take it from him. Let *him* know what it feels like to lose his sight and understand that he has only days left before his mind betrays him. Take his Han'Or."

"And if I take this Han'Or, will he lose his sight right away?"

"We have been on half rations for a long time, all of us except Edgar. My sight is gone because I have not had enough for many days. But Edgar always seems to find a way to keep himself properly stocked. It will take a few days before he loses his sight once you have taken his, but you must also make sure he cannot resupply from the others at the gathering. And the others will fight you as well…" she trailed off as she seemed to be looking around for something now.

"What cause are they fighting for? Maybe I can help."

Just then the woman's white eyes stopped their roving and lay upon the place in Dune's cloak where he kept the Magic Stone. The woman lifted her blind gaze toward Dune's face and he felt a chill as if she could actually see him. "They are preparing for our master to return."

Dune was filled with fear as he considered the next question. He knew that the seekers served Mordyar, and they all felt he would eventually come to visit them and reward their loyalty, but he had never heard of a group gathering to prepare for him. "When is he coming?"

The woman started laughing and it turned into an eerie cackle. "You'll never know until it's too late, stone holder."

CHAPTER 14

According to Dunkan's plan, each crew member came at the appointed time to the small room in the basement of a local tavern. P liked the location, as they were arriving in the early hours of the day; anyone in the tavern that early would be too inebriated to understand or hinder their plans. She watched through a small hole in the wall as Com was the first to arrive. He came in and sat down at a table across from Dunkan.

"Everything seems to be in place," he said as he leaned back in his chair. "Today's shipment is smaller than expected, but worthwhile."

Dunkan smiled at this news.

"Remember your orders. When we have the shipment loaded you take out Stash and Derft. They should be in the cart, so that shouldn't be a problem from your position. Then the two of us will drive the cart away."

Com rocked the chair back to four legs, stood up, and took a few steps toward the door. Before leaving he paused, turned around, stepped close to Dunkan, and spoke in a whisper. "If you have any plans to double cross me, just remember that I see everything." With this final pronouncement Com left the basement and passed by Flick and Scar who were just arriving.

"Hey, why are you leaving?" Scar asked, clearly confused.

Com continued walking as Flick gestured for Scar to shut his mouth.

Flick began to speak as they were walking across the small room. "When the shipment leaves the keep we'll intercept and deliver it to Stash and Derft." When they reached the table, he rested his hand on the table but did not stop to sit down. Scar rounded the table and sat down next to Dunkan and looked at him with a stupid grin. "We'll meet you back at Deadman Falls tomorrow just after noon." Then a pause. "Will that be enough time for you to get rid of Com and the others?"

Dunkan nodded. Then, looking at Flick he added, "Make sure that nobody suspects anything. One misspoken word to the wrong person and we won't live to enjoy our treasure." Flick nodded in response and gestured for Scar to get up out of his seat and follow him back out of the tavern.

Before leaving, Scar turned around to face Dunkan. “Flick says we need to watch you close, so I'm watching you close.” Flick shot Scar a look that would have silenced any half-intelligent person. Scar continued, “So you keep your word or we'll know you're a liar who didn't keep your word.” Scar was no intellect, but he was ruthless and as strong as three men, so he was an invaluable part of the plan.

“I will see you at the falls tomorrow,” was all Dunkan said.

The next to arrive were Stash and Derft. “How is the head?” Dunkan asked as Derft came into sight.

The large strongarm stopped rubbing his head and snarled. “It'll be a lot better when I'm away from here with all my money.” He smiled hopefully at Dunkan. “Are you sure I can't just kill the girl? I think I owe her that much.”

Dunkan remained seated, while the two strongarms stood behind chairs at the table. He gestured for them to sit down but they waved their hands in refusal. “It's too risky. You know what she did last night. We need to leave her behind and get out with the money. That is our best chance for success. She'll take the fall, we take the gold.”

“Yeah, I know, but I really want to get her back for this headache.”

“When you rub your head, think of it as a second chance at life. Not everyone else was that lucky,” Dunkan reminded him.

Bringing them back to the plan Stash interjected. “So after we kill the idiot and his thin friend, why do we need you?”

Dunkan slowly rose from his seat and walked up to stand toe to toe with Stash. “You are lucky I chose you to be one of three to take the treasure. Don't ever forget that.” Then as he pointed to the map laid out on the table he continued. “There are three roads that lead from our interception point out of Kinstock. All three have guards at the gate, one set of guards will let me through with no questions asked. Two of the roads will have some mutual friends on them,” Dunkan did not need to name the 'mutual friends' as members of their band he intended to double cross.

"Sounds good to me," Stash answered taking a step back away from Dunkan. P was impressed at how a level two intellect was able to intimidate such a large strongarm. "Thanks, by the way."

Dunkan returned to his seat, and looked down at his map. He ignored the two strongarms until they got the message and found their own way out. "I'm glad they are not going to be alive to enjoy the gold," he said softly as he looked over to the small crack in the wall. "I'll see you when everything is done."

Dunkan rose to his feet, rolled up the map and left the small room. When he was clear of the building P emerged from her hiding place. The plan was starting to come together, but it also hinged on a group of dishonest criminals following directions and trusting the man she had chosen to lead the heist. After doing an audio scan of the building, she left as she had come; unnoticed and alone.

* * * * *

The shining armor of the patrol of forty-eight guards entering the keep drew little attention this early in the morning. They were lost among the crowd of soldiers arriving for duty, changing guard, and performing routine training drills. The keep in Kinstock was no more than a small stronghold. The large stone structure was home to the Kinstock barracks, the political meetinghouse, and the mint. Despite the dwarfed size of the structure it looked like it was prepared to stop a full frontal assault of the King's army. Starting at ten feet from the ground the stone wall had rows of tall narrow arrow slits. On the inside of the walls there was scaffolding so that archers could quickly scale to their posts and fire hundreds of arrows from the safety provided by the thick stone wall. It was built to protect the large stores of gold that came from the mine.

The soldiers' duty was completed as the carriage loaded down with gold bars entered the keep. Exactly two hours later, as Dunkan had said, an old wooden cart left the keep through the same iron-reinforced door. It would be foolish to think the treasure was completely unprotected at that time, but the two visors sitting on the back of the cart with longbows, and the listener, who was driving, were hardly a match for the two well-trained thieves waiting for them in the woods.

Flick and Scar had taken up a concealed position behind the tree line at the side of the rarely used, packed dirt road, beyond what they suspected would be the listener's neutral hearing distance. Scar squatted behind some bushes, holding a live rabbit he had caught earlier that day. On the other side of the road was a pile of carrots and lettuce that Scar had shown to the rabbit several times. When the cart was about to cross their path he released the rabbit and, as expected, the rabbit ran for the hidden food. Scar raced after the rabbit, and, seeing the guards in the cart with drawn bows, he pointed to the rabbit and yelled, "Shoot it!"

The guards laughed at the foolish strongarm chasing a rabbit on foot, but turned their attention toward the rabbit, firing their arrows at the unfortunate decoy. With all of their attention on the rabbit, they didn't have time to react when Flick appeared from behind a tree with an armed bow, and Scar drew his concealed short hammer. Scar abruptly turned from running after the rabbit and smashed the two visors with his hammer. The driver of the cart had already fallen over, an arrow protruding from his back.

After wiping off his war hammer and replacing it in the leather loop of his belt, Scar held up a finger to Flick, indicating he should wait for a moment.

"What are you doing?" Flick asked, confused about what could possibly be important enough to draw attention away from a cart full of gold.

"I'm getting the rabbit."

"I can't believe it," Flick said, shaking his head.

"I know," Scar interrupted. "They actually got him. They're much better than the last crew. Good thing they weren't aiming at us."

"Not the rabbit. I can't believe you," said Flick as he pulled the driver off the cart and slid him behind a small mound and into a hole they had already dug. "We're stealing an entire cart of gold and you're worried about getting a rabbit."

"No need to leave a perfectly good meal to waste," Scar replied as he removed the arrow from the rabbit and deposited his lunch into the back of the wagon with the gold. Then he dragged both men from the back of the cart into the same hole in which Flick had hidden the driver. The two quickly covered the bodies with dirt and jogged back to the horse-drawn cart.

Flick moved to the driver's seat and turned back to look at his friend who had also removed the satchel of provisions the lead visor had been carrying. Gesturing to the rabbit and the bag of food with an ironic expression on his face, he hopped onto the back of the cart.

"That's why you're the brains of the operation." Flick said with a shake of his head. The two men chuckled as they moved the cart to the next destination.

Flick pulled up slightly on the reins when they arrived at a curve in the road that ended in a steep hill. He pressed the brake down and locked it in place, then got down out of the driver's seat and started unhitching the horse.

"We're a little behind schedule," he said to Scar. "We need to get moving." Flick made his best hawk call and waited for the response. A much more convincing hawk call was returned. "Good, they're here." Flick began to saddle the horse while Stash and Derft appeared from their concealed place in the trees. They were leading one mare for Flick and half a dozen pack horses for the Gold. "Did you count the gold bars?"

Scar looked at his feet. "I tried, but every time I got past eleventy I ran out of fingers, and then we hit a bump or the bars shifted, so I lost count." Then he looked up happily and continued, "But I did count ten bars at least fifteen times so that means we have at least thirty-six bars."

Cutting in before either Stash or Derft could overcome their amazement enough to comment on Scar's stupidity, Flick made an announcement. "The horse is saddled…"

"Yippee!" Scar shouted. He ran to the horse, jumped on its back, and took off at a gallop before anyone could stop him.

Shaking his head, Flick began to help unload the gold from the cart onto the pack animals. After a couple of minutes he also jumped on his horse. "I'm just worried he'll get lost or say something to the wrong person. I'll give you some of my share for doing all the loading." Then he was off as well.

"Wait!" Derft shouted, but his voice was drowned out by the galloping horse. Then to Stash, "What are we going to do now? We were supposed to wait till they helped us load the gold, then roll the cart down this hill with their bodies in it."

"I know the plan. We'll just tell Dunkan that they're dead. He'll never know the difference, and we'll kill him as soon as we're safely past the edge of town anyway, so it won't matter." The men quickly loaded the pack horses down with the gold and filled the cart with some heavy rocks. They then rolled the cart down the hill where it made some clear, deep tracks before disappearing off the edge of the cliff.

The two strongarms led the line of horses as quickly as they could to Dunkan, knowing that they were getting farther behind schedule.

Hiding up in a tree, P watched the men working and scheming. After they had moved out of sight and hearing, P lowered herself to her waiting mount and rode back down the path to keep an eye on her gold.

Dunkan was pounding down the grass as he paced back and forth by the side of a cart. Stash and Derft arrived and quickly jumped off their horses. Derft was the first to speak. "We were delayed in getting everything done."

"I can see that," Dunkan replied. "Is it all taken care of?"

"The cart fell on the rocks just like you said it would," Stash said with a nod. Dunkan's eyes narrowed almost imperceptibly, as if he noticed how the men avoided directly answering the question, but he quickly recovered a straight face.

"Good. Let's get this loaded and get out of here before anyone figures out what we've done. By now someone has surely noticed that the gold is missing." With that, Dunkan dismounted and began helping the two men load the cart with gold. When the gold was in the cart, they grabbed their shovels and covered it with a foot of soil. "Let's go!" Dunkan sat in the driver's seat with Derft at his side and Stash riding in the back. "Stash, keep your eyes open for anything unusual."

When they began to move, a solid thud sounded as an arrow stuck squarely into the side of the cart.

"Ambush!" Stash called out.

Dunkan silently cursed under his breath. Instead of urging the horses into action, he pulled his knife from its sheath and jammed it into Derft's heart while the large strongarm was turned around searching for the archer who had attacked them.

"What's going on?" Stash asked. Dunkan ignored him and just shoved Derft from the cart. Stash would never know the answer to his question as the second arrow from the woods found its target. "Get in, Com! We're running very late." Dunkan emphasized his words by waving his arm. Com jumped down from a tree and sat next to Dunkan on the front of the cart.

The two travelers, dressed in farmer's clothing, drew no attention as they passed through Kinstock, moving toward the gate at the far west side of town. They slipped a gold coin to the guard and passed through with no question. As they trotted passed the guard outpost building and around a bend, they shared a smile.

Two miles outside of town, Dunkan brought the cart to a halt and looked back.

"Did you hear something?" Com asked, scanning the surroundings with his enhanced vision. While Com was focusing a distance down the empty road, Dunkan's blade flashed. This time it did not find its mark so easily. Com dodged the blade and stabbed back with a dagger of his own. The two men lunged and dodged in a savage duel to the death. In a moment that was as much luck as it was skill, Com found an opening in Dunkan's defense and plunged his dagger home. Com had suffered a few surface wounds and one deep gash in his right arm, but that was a small price to pay for this much gold.

Com kicked Dunkan's corpse off the cart. P emerged from the woods and clapped her hands. “Nicely done!” She joined Com seated on the front of the wagon and he urged the horses to start moving. Although she was surprised that Com had won the duel, it made no difference to her who she split the money with, and she had made deals with both men.

Com and P rode for several miles before either spoke.

“Any plans to finish me off?” Com asked now that he had finished bandaging his wounds.

“Our team has shrunk enough,” P said, then she smiled at Com as she returned the reins to him. “For one day.” She realized that this joke was not well accepted as Com looked concerned and suspiciously fingered his weapon. “It was a joke.”

With a cold look Com sternly replied. “Keep those jokes to yourself.” He kept his hand on the hilt as the pair continued. He remained tense and alert for almost two hours while he moved off the main road and traversed down some smaller side roads and dirt trails, then he unexpectedly slumped over in his seat with an arrow in his heart.

On the road in front of the now driverless horse-drawn cart stood Flick and Scar.

“We thought it would be you and Dunkan,” Scar said. At first P was confused. She had never heard Scar say anything without his thick accent. “We want to thank you for making it so much easier to get rid of the crew. Couldn't have done it without you.”

She thought she had planned for every variable, considered all obstacles, but she had overlooked the fool right in front of her.

Flick looked to Scar, and for a brief moment P thought he was looking for approval to speak.

“To thank you, we're going to leave you alive. You'll probably be caught. The evidence we've left behind will certainly lead to a conviction and life in prison, but that's more of a life than you wanted to leave us. Maybe your dad will come find you and take you back home.”

"What do you know about my father?" she demanded with a death glare.

Flick laughed out loud at her question. "He's the man we work for. He needs some extra money for a supply caravan, we needed some favors, and here we are." He accentuated his words by pointing to himself and Scar. "It didn't take us very long to figure out who you are, Pentra. But lucky for you, we're not being paid to bring you in. You are free to go." He hesitated and grinned wickedly. "You can thank us at any time."

P began to speak, but there was no hint of thanks in her voice, "How did you do it?"

Scar stepped closer to the cart to answer her question. His proximity to P made Flick clearly nervous and he half drew his bow. Scar continued to move close to P, and in response to her question he removed his bandana. This faded piece of cloth had concealed three dots on his forehead. P gaped in obvious confusion.

"I love that look," Scar said, half to P and half to Flick "When people realize for the first time that it is possible to be a powerful intellect and strongarm."

P had heard of people who had been born with multiple gifts, but in all the cases she had ever heard of, the person was a level one for both gifts, making them rather weak. The double markings were considered a curse that nobody wanted, but also a curse so uncommon that people rarely, if ever, gave it any consideration. Part of her was enraged that her plan was foiled, and her mind raced as she realized that her plan to rescue the people of Hess was going to require an entirely new tactic now that she would be without the means to hire mercenaries or other professionals. Another part of her was somewhat appeased however, knowing that it had taken a person with this kind of gift to pull off such an elaborate scheme. Then she came to herself and realized that if she didn't do something quickly she would be left to whatever fate they had in mind.

She stood and hopped down from the cart, making a motion for the two men to take their place leading the horses.

"Well done," She said, and then she simply walked off the

road and into the woods.

"Aren't we going to do something?" Flick asked as P continued to walk unconcernedly farther into the woods.

Scar silently contemplated for a moment before answering. "Just let her go." Then, despite the distance she had put between them, he continued to speak in a normal tone as though P were standing close to him. "If I ever see you again, Pentra, I will turn you over to your father."

She heard him loud and clear. She knew what she would have to do next. She needed to find an assassin.

CHAPTER 15

The sharply dressed servant rushed outside to the training arena, "Sir Mylot, your father requests your presence."

"One moment," Mylot said as he pulled hard on Gapol's reins and his horse made a pinwheel turn. He squeezed his heels and charged down the field with his lance leveled at a target the size of his hand. He waited until he was in range, then drove his lance forward, smashing the exact center of the target, obliterating it with the force of the blow. He slowed Gapol to a walk and leapt off his tall war horse as he approached Sir Rodnik for a critique.

"Sir Mylot," the servant insisted, "you must come quickly." Mylot was not used to servants telling him what to do. He turned around angrily, but in the servant's eyes he could see urgency. "There's not much time." Mylot dropped his lance and began throwing down his armor as he ran past the servant and into the house. His father had been bedridden for many months, but within the past two weeks he had lost his sight, and his health was failing quickly.

Since he had gone blind, Mylot spent time each day by his father's side learning about all he would need to do to take over their estate. It was the most time he could remember spending with his father on a regular basis in his entire life. His father's career in the king's army had taken him away a lot. When Mylot was young, his mother died and he was always watched by nurses and housekeepers. Then, when his father retired from the military, he had been awarded the Barony of Tran, and was gone long hours each day with affairs of the local villages. Before his illness, Mylot would sometimes go months without talking with his father. Now he found himself running down a hall to see a man he had just spoken with an hour before.

As he approached his father's chambers, Mylot slowed slightly in order to catch his breath. When he arrived, a servant pushed the large doors open, admitting Mylot to the room. The massive room was filled with lavish paintings, tapestries, and statues. The natural light in the room came through a large, stained glass window depicting his father in full armor. Mylot went straight to the man lying in his oversized mahogany bed.

"Son, come close." Mylot's father whispered so softly he could barely hear him.

As Mylot approached, his step-mother and two step-sisters, who had been kneeling by the bedside, parted to make space for him.

"I'm here, Father."

His father blindly reached out his hand in the wrong direction and Mylot grabbed it, pulling it to himself as he knelt down.

"I need a moment alone with the new master of the house." The servants opened the doors, and quickly evacuated the space. Mylot came to his feet and helped his step-mother get up. She dabbed her tears and gripped tightly to her two daughters as she slowly left the room. When they were out in the hall, a servant closed the door with a solid thudding sound.

"Son, are we alone?"

"Yes Father," Mylot replied, not knowing what secret he was about to learn. He had never ordered the room cleared for his instruction before.

"I don't have much time, so I'm going to get to the point," his father began. Then he paused with a fit of coughing.

"I'll get the healer." Mylot stood to leave.

Shaking his head, his father regained control of his breathing. In a low voice he spoke, "No. I need to tell you something. Each year I have sent support to a family from town, a single mother and her daughter." He stopped talking and closed his eyes for a moment before taking a shallow breath and continuing. "Two years ago the mother died, and the girl has refused any help from me."

"Well, if she refuses help, what else can be done?" Mylot asked.

"Son, I have tried my entire life to think of others before myself. I served my country, I served my estate, I served the northern region, and I feel I have failed in one area. I have not been a good father. You have much to learn about compassion, and that is my fault," his father responded with a shallow smile. He coughed again before continuing. "I have something that belongs to her… it's hers… I don't have the strength…" Each word he spoke seemed an overwhelming effort. Mylot placed his strong hand on his father's shoulder.

"Whatever it is, I'll get it to her." Mylot said.

"In my library… My Maggie. Find that book. Go to the tournament." The last few words were barely a whisper.

"The tournament. Of course father, I will go to the tournament and ride with our family banners. I will proudly win for the house of Tran."

His father was silent for a moment, then he shook his head. "My Maggie," he repeated.

"The girl with the birthmark who used to play here when she was a child?" Mylot asked.

He spoke softly and Mylot leaned his ear next to his father's mouth so he could make out what he was saying. When he heard his father's secret, his eyes open wide in surprise.

"I promise I will find that book and deliver it, and I will win the tournament for you," Mylot vowed.

His father smiled and a single tear rolled down his cheek, the only tear Mylot had ever seen his father shed. After this final exertion, his body sagged, and instantly Mylot knew that life had left his father.

Mylot stood up from the polished hardwood floor and took a step away from the bed. He looked down at his father's body and softly spoke, "You were a good father."

The next two weeks were filled with a flurry of activity around the estate. The town officials from Kinstock, and people from each of the small, northern villages located within the barony came to pay their respects, and the manor house was filled with guests who had traveled longer distances to visit. Although it frustrated him to no end that he could not properly train, Mylot spent his days entertaining and reading condolence notes that came to the estate. He even received a note from his late mother's brother, Uncle King Robert, wishing him the best in this difficult time.

While Mylot was reading the note from the king, his step-mother entered his study with a bow. On her heels his step-sisters followed.

"My Lord Mylot," she began.

He cut her off, "Come in, please." He rose to his feet and waved for them to enter.

She bowed her head and approached him, "Mylot, what will you have us do?" she asked humbly. Although he hadn't put much thought into it, as the master of the house, he did now have control over their lives and future.

"You will stay as long as you like," he replied quickly. "You will keep your servants and your title." He paused for a moment and looked down at his step-family, the only family he had left. "You have been my mother for as long as I can remember. This is your home." He turned to his step-sisters and added, "All of you." He stepped forward and embraced his step-mother. "You are family."

"Thank you, My Lord," she answered. "You will be a great leader, like your father was before you."

"I don't know if I will ever make the impact that he did," Mylot replied, pointing at the pile of notices on his desk, "but I will try to make him proud."

"He always was proud of you," she said with a smile. "Would you like some help replying to these notes?"

Mylot gestured for them to join him closer to the table, "That would be wonderful."

He was pleased to see what a great impact his father had had on the lives of so many people, but he was also happy when the funeral was finished, the notes stopped coming, and the house cleared so he could resume his training and also fulfill his promise to his father. Each day after practice, he searched his father's library for the mysterious book titled *My Maggie.* Although this process was merely to retrieve each book off the shelf and open it to the front page to seek for a title, it took considerable time to go shelf by shelf through the extensive library.

One afternoon, after a particularly challenging jousting practice, Mylot found the book. Although it had no title, he knew it was the right book immediately. When he opened the book and saw the first page he stared in complete surprise. It was a hand drawn picture of Maggie, the strange girl with the dark birthmark covering half of her face.

When she was very young, she and her mother had lived on the estate. When Mylot was old enough to begin training with the combat instructors as well as the tutors, Maggie and her mother had moved into Lexingar, and he had not seen her again until the first year she had won the archery tournament. Mylot remembered how her appearance had changed each of the last few times he had seen her briefly at the tournament; the obvious signs of a life of poverty and neglect showing in her tattered clothes and dirty appearance.

When he turned the first page of the book, he realized that the book had no other pages. It was not a book at all, but a hollowed out box, concealing a miniature jewelry chest. The small golden chest had a keyhole on the front, and when Mylot shook the chest he could hear a small, hard object rattling inside. *How am I to find this girl? I've never heard where she lives, and from the way she has appeared at the last several tournaments, she seems not to even have a home.* He considered his options for a moment, and then realized, *The tournament! Of course. This will be easier than I thought. I'll just bring the chest along and give it to her at the tournament before my first sword match, then I'll be done with this business…*

CHAPTER 16

Farin walked slowly back toward Hillside Inn. During the weeks they had stayed in Hillside, Bendar worked as a clerk, Kaz put on a show for a group of patrons every couple of days, and he wandered the streets looking for any kind of job he could find. Today he was returning from a farm on the outskirts of the village that had needed some fence posts set. He hadn't had that kind of workout since he was on the farm back home.

As he approached the inn, he saw Commander Aldis standing out front. He waved at Omer's soldier.

"Hi," he called out as he came close. He hadn't seen Aldis since they came to Hillside. "What brings you back this way? Have you caught the crooks who stole our stuff?"

Commander Aldis smiled in a friendly way, then reached out a hand and gave Farin a formal handshake.

"I think they have moved on. We haven't seen a trace of them. I'm actually here on other business," he said. "I have heard that there is a young man telling stories about special, magical stones."

Farin pointed at the inn door. "You heard right. Kaz tells all kinds of stories. He's even told them about how you saved us from the bandits. When he tells the story you came in with sword drawn, chasing down the thieves single handedly."

Aldis cracked the slightest smile. "So his stories are all made up?" He sounded a little disappointed.

"Not all of them," Farin said as he pushed open the door for the soldier. "Most of his material actually comes from Bendar," he explained, pointing out his friend. "Bendar studies everything. Just last week he came across some old records where he works as a clerk. The records were about some boring trade dispute between landowners in Oakdale," Farin said as he stuck his tongue out in disgust. "Kaz turned Bendar's boring research into a grandiose tale of feuding families that nearly tore the kingdom apart."

Aldis pointed at Bendar. "What about the stories of the magical stones? Are those also made up?"

Farin shrugged. "Mostly. You'd have to ask Bendar if you want to separate fact from fiction. But be prepared to be bored." Farin led Commander Aldis to Bendar's table.

"Bendar," Aldis said, addressing the intellect. "Can we speak for a moment please?"

Bendar looked up from a book he was reading and seemed surprised to notice he wasn't alone at the table. "Y-yes," he stammered. "Yes, of course, Sir. It's good to see you again."

When he had Bendar's attention, the soldier turned to Farin, "Would you mind giving us a minute?" he asked.

A little surprised by Commander Aldis' dismissal, but happy to not have to hear Bendar's history lesson, Farin quickly agreed and left to watch Kaz sharing his tale of how he had bravely fought a pack of drams. The story was funny, and Kaz had the audience completely engaged, but after having heard it retold and changed a couple of times, Farin was more interested in finding out what other gossip might be traded at the other tables in the inn tonight. Perhaps he would get a lead on a new job. The marks on his ears flared red as, table by table, he turned his attention toward the back of the room. After a few minutes of shifting his focus from conversation to conversation, he realized he had arrived at Bendar's table.

Bendar was speaking quickly, so it seemed he was excited about whatever they were discussing, "...logical to conclude that there are indeed magical stones. Several books agree that they did exist at some time, and then were scattered to various places. Their current location is, of course, a mystery, but I doubt they would just disappear."

"Is their location *truly* a mystery? Have you never seen such a stone?" The question was met with stunned silence. Commander Aldis continued assertively, "You seem to know quite a bit about magical items. Perhaps you could come with me to Omer's keep and speak with him. He has a keen interest in the subject, and he's actually looking for someone to fill a vacancy in the keep."

Farin listened intently for a response. From the way the commander addressed Bendar, it seemed that his invitation was more of a command than an optional trip. "I have some important work to complete here in town, but that should only take a couple of days, then I would be happy to meet with Omer, though I can't stay for too long."

"I will return in two days to escort you to Omer's keep," Commander Aldis replied. "Be sure you have finished whatever important work needs to be done. I feel that after you meet Omer, you might *decide* you want to stay on at the keep." Commander Aldis said this with some significance, and the tone made Farin's skin crawl.

Farin turned around and watched as Aldis stood up from the table and strode out of the inn. Farin joined Bendar at the table, "What was that all about?" he asked. It was clear that his friend was shaken up.

"I am not entirely sure," Bendar said while he watched the door through which Aldis had left. "Kaz seems to have made a bit of a stir with his tales."

Farin looked at Kaz and around the room. The people were laughing and enjoying the show, but they couldn't actually believe Kaz was any kind of authority on magical history, could they? "They're just stories," he commented with bewilderment as he turned back to Bendar.

"I know," Bendar agreed. "But some people seem to think…" he stopped speaking and deliberately turned to look down at the table while placing his hand up to block his face.

Farin turned around to look at the door, but Bendar reached out and grabbed his arm. "What?" Farin asked, still craning his neck to look at the door.

"Look at me!" Bendar said in a hushed but insistent tone. Farin looked at his friend. "The coach driver just walked in the room."

Farin tilted his head down so he could subtly look over his shoulder. The thin man walked into the room and sat down at a table as he watched Kaz telling his tale. "We have to get Aldis!" Farin said.

"I don't think that's an option," Bendar replied, softly. He moved his head slightly, pointing at the driver.

Farin turned around and the thin man was looking right at him. He waved at the pair, then spoke in a whisper that Farin could barely hear. "Nice to see you again."

Farin stood up and was about to cross the room when Bendar grabbed his arm. "Not now," he said, urging his friend to sit back down. "We'll lose everything if we start a bar fight."

While glaring at the coach driver, Farin reluctantly took his seat in silence. He scratched a small note on the table with his fingernail, and Bendar looked down to see the word, 'listener'. He nodded and the two watched Kaz in silence until the show was over and Kaz had made his now habitual, dramatic exit, then quickly retired to their room, and locked the door behind them.

"What's going on?" Kaz asked, surprised by their sudden appearance. Farin held his finger to his lips and they all sat down on the bed in the corner of the room.

"Speak only in whispers and talk into the pillows as much as possible," Farin said as he beckoned to his friends to lean their heads in close together, and demonstrated how to hold a couple of pillows near their faces to dampen the sound of their discussion. "It should keep our conversation more private."

Kaz grabbed a pillow and held it up near his mouth. "Is someone going to tell me what is going on?"

"You've had your last performance," Bendar said. "We need to leave, tonight."

"What?" Farin and Kaz asked in unison.

Farin looked around the room, "We don't have the supplies we need yet, Garin hasn't returned, and you haven't collected the payment for your clerical work."

Bendar drew his eyebrows together and his marks flared maroon. Kaz held up his hand between the two other boys. "Would someone like to let me know why we're whispering into pillows and talking about leaving?" he asked, looking between Bendar and Farin.

Farin took a calming breath, "Sorry, Kaz. We saw the stage coach driver in the crowd tonight. He recognized us."

Kaz looked questioningly at Bendar and Farin, then dropped his pillow. He spoke in a loud voice, "It's a good thing

Omer's guards make regular patrols through Hillside," he announced. "We'll report any bandit we see and that'll be the end of it. Maybe we'll even get our stuff back."

Bendar shook his head, and pulled Kaz back down into their huddle. "It's not that simple. Commander Aldis also came back today too. He heard your stories about magical stones, and he's coming back in two days to take me to Omer's keep for what sounds like a lengthy internship."

"Hmmm," Kaz said softly. "That does complicate things."

"It certainly does," Farin agreed. "We can't leave because the bandits are back and will be on the roads."

Bendar cut in, "We can't stay because we'll be prolonged at Omer's keep. And," he added, "if we report the bandits, they'll probably just take us to the 'safety' of his keep sooner."

Kaz looked at Bendar with confusion on his face, "What's wrong with that? Wouldn't it be nice to be in the safety of Omer's keep?"

Bendar shook his head back and forth, "No, it would not. The way Aldis talked, I don't think I would easily be able to leave if he let me leave at all," Bendar took in a deep breath, seemingly looking for the right way to explain something. "In some of the texts I have read about these Stones of Power, they have stirred up some powerful disputes as people have sought for them. If Omer believes in the stones, a man with his power and influence could be a dangerous person to anger, especially if he thinks that we somehow have knowledge of where to find one of these stones for him. If we want to get to our destinations, we need to get moving." In Bendar's agitation over the situation, he threw down the pillow he had been holding and stood up to pace the room for a moment. Farin waved him back over.

"What are we going to do?" Farin whispered to his friends when they were huddled close together.

The three boys were silent for a time. Farin tried to think of anything that would help them get out of the situation. The people in Hillside had come to know that they were in the inn and that they were daily looking for work. They loved listening to Kaz's stories, and some of the people he had met had even suggested that they stay in Hillside for the duration of their Troven. They would notice very quickly if the boys just left. Kaz had also pretty much told everyone that their plans were to go to Norwell, so the first place people would look for them would be on the main road. "Is there another road to Norwell?" Farin asked.

"Not any well-travelled roads," Bendar answered. "There are some horse paths and hiking trails, but they are mainly through the rocky, northern forests. Not much lives in there."

"That sounds perfect," Kaz said a little more loudly than he anticipated. Startled by the sound of his own voice, he grabbed a pillow and pulled it over his mouth. "Fff muliv domurren a--" Farin yanked the pillow down from his mouth and dramatically mimed how to hold it near, but not on his mouth. Kaz smiled sheepishly and started again, "If we leave tomorrow morning at the normal time, nobody will think anything is amiss. We'll go our separate ways, then meet on the north side of town and head up to where Garin is working, pick him up, and start our trip through the Northern Forest."

Bendar shook his head almost as soon as Kaz started talking. "That kind of trip requires a lot more planning. We need almost completely different supplies than what we have been collecting," he said, pointing at the pile of materials in their room. "I'm planning for us to be able to collect food on our way, harvest berries, set up snares, maybe even trade with other travelers. If we go north, we'll need to carry all of the food we'll eat."

"Fine," Kaz relented, "We'll get more food, no big deal."

"It is a big deal," Bendar argued.

Farin placed a calming hand on each of the boys' shoulders. "It sounds like it will be a big change," he agreed, "But you won't have to do it alone. Unless you can think of another way, we need to move north, and we need to leave soon."

Bendar pulled out a piece of paper and began scribbling out a supply list. He then tore the paper into three pieces and handed one to Farin and one to Kaz.

"I am not happy with this plan," Bendar grumbled. "But if

we can get everything on this list, we can make it work."

Kaz patted him on the back. "Okay, so that's settled. Let's get some sleep. Tomorrow is going to be an adventure."

The boys carefully prepared their travel packs, trying to fit everything they had into them. After several weeks in Hillside, they still had lots of room in their packs for the supplies Bendar had put on their shopping lists.

Farin looked carefully at his list. It was amazing how quickly Bendar was able to make mental calculations and come up with exactly what they would need. Farin's list consisted mostly of dried food. Although one piece of jerky was light, he knew a pack filled with the stuff would be heavy. He didn't mind hard work, and was actually a little excited to get traveling again, but the more he thought of leaving behind any hope of recovering their stolen items, the more agitated he became. If they were going to strike off on their own again, he wanted his sword, not to mention the items his father had given to him and Garin from his own Troven. Especially remembering the smug look on that coach driver's face as he had taunted them below in the tavern earlier got his blood boiling. Farin decided he had one more thing he needed to do before they left town.

After Bendar and Kaz were soundly sleeping, Farin quietly slipped from their room. Without his brother in the room listening, he was easily able to get out of the room without waking either of them. Downstairs, some of the inn tables had patrons, but for the most part the tavern was empty. Farin walked out the swinging doors and into the dark streets. Other than returning to the inn at dusk, he had not ventured out much into the streets of Hillside in the dark, and he had never gone alone. Ignoring the warnings of the inn keeper, and everything his friends had said, he pushed down his nervousness and moved forward.

He started on the main street, making his way back the way they had come when they had arrived, then turned down some poorly lit side streets on the far west side of town. Down the dark street Farin could hear some hushed voices, and he decided this was where he would start searching for the thieves, and hopefully retrieve some of their stolen supplies. Now that the driver was back in town, this was his last chance.

He put his back to the wall of the building on his right and slipped down to squat near the ground. Keeping to the shadows, he shifted farther down the alleyway until he could make out the conversation with his enhanced hearing.

"I don't care where it came from," came the voice of a man who sounded ragged and desperate, "we need to kill it."

Farin held his breath, making sure to not make a sound. The marks on his ears flared up as he continued to listen, trying to figure out what was happening in the darkness.

"It's disgusting! Barely worth the effort," came the reply. Then without another word, there was a squeal, then it was silenced by a thudding sound. Farin released his breath as he recognized the sounds. On his farm he routinely killed rats that were in the grain room. These were not organized thieves, but the voices of desperate people reduced to hunting rats for food. Although he felt bad for them, there was nothing he could do to help. He moved back out of the alley and closer to the outskirts of town.

As Farin searched through the night, he found that most dark streets were empty in this area of town, and the people he did encounter seemed to crouch and cower when he came close. As the night continued, he became increasingly more confident that there was little or nothing to fear in the quiet, empty town. When he exited the residential quarter that was characterized by tiny homes with little garden plots along the outskirts of Hillside, he continued down the road toward Dungan. He wanted to see the bridge they had crossed on entering town before he made his way back to the inn. Before he could see the bridge, he heard some hushed voices in the distance. He strained his hearing and the small dots on his ears flared a dark shade of red. The voices came from under the bridge, and from his angle the sound of flowing water obscured most of what they were saying. He circled wide, moving off the road until he was in a direct line of the people and could hear them more clearly.

"How long will they stay?" asked a man, whose voice was

filled with fear.

"I don't know," a woman responded, "but each day I've checked them and there is no sign of it." Farin stood silently in the shadow of a tree, straining his ears to better hear their quiet exchange.

"The intellect insisted that they had it when they left, and Melna's informant told her that one of the boys had flaunted it at him as they left, mocking him for not having found it when he searched the kid. Where could it be?"

"I told you, I don't know. Maybe they keep it hidden in their room all the time. If I had something worth that much gold, I wouldn't carry it around with me to work in the fields."

"If you had something worth that much gold, you wouldn't be staying in such a small room either."

"Listen to me! If we don't find a way to get that stone we're as good as dead!"

"Don't you think I know that? I've been looking every day!"

"Maybe we need to be more direct," The talking stopped, and there was some shuffled movement from under the bridge. Farin couldn't see what was happening from his hiding place, and they had stopped talking. He wondered who they might have been talking about, or what stone could be worth so much gold. He looked back at the buildings on the outskirts of the village. The excitement of being out at night in a village that was big enough to have dark alleys and homeless people was quickly being replaced by the fear that something really bad was about to happen, and he didn't want to get caught up in it. Whatever these people were looking for, it had nothing to do with him finding his sword.

He stepped out from next to the tree and began slowly moving back to the road that led into the village. When he was out from under the dark shadow of the tree, two people came running from under the bridge.

"There he is! I knew I saw something."

Farin turned and slipped on some slick leaves, falling down to the ground. He clawed at the ground and pulled himself to his feet, then darted for the village. Behind him he could hear the people chasing him practically on his heels. He looked over his shoulder just as an unseen blast threw him to the ground, knocking the wind out of him. Rough hands turned him over until he was face to face with a middle aged couple. "How nice of you to come find us. It saved us some trouble."

The man pulled out a knife in one hand and dragged Farin with the other hand deeper into the woods. When the light of the village was obscured by a wall of trees, the man pushed Farin to the ground, and the woman who was with him tilted her head to the side, scrutinizing every inch of him. She reached forward and patted down his pockets, and when he pushed her hand away, the man kicked him in the ribs. Wincing in pain and holding his bruised ribs, Farin stayed still for the duration of the body search.

"Where is it?" the woman said while licking her lips.

Farin looked to the man and back at the woman who was standing over him. Their features were shaded by the darkness, but he could make out the knife in the man's hand, and a bottle in the other, perhaps a potion bottle he had used to blast Farin to the ground. Farin also noticed that the woman had a similar bottle dangling from her belt. "I don't know what you're talking about," he answered honestly.

The man brought his knife down close to Farin and spoke in a harsh whisper. "Bendar told us you had the stone! Where is it?"

"Bendar?" Farin repeated, trying to piece together what was happening. "I've never had any kind of stone. I don't know what you're talking about."

"The necklace, you fool. What happened to the necklace?" The woman said, practically spitting out the words.

"Gran's necklace?" he asked in confusion. "It was taken along with everything else."

The woman slapped him across the face so hard that stars appeared. Farin blinked his eyes, trying to clear his head.

"He's of no use to us," she said to her partner. "Let's dispose of him and be done with it!"

Although his vision had not fully returned, he kicked out at the couple. He aimed his foot at the man, trying to kick where he thought the knife was, but instead he connected with the bottle, which cracked as he kicked it out into the dark forest. Farin kicked out again at the woman and felt his foot connect solidly with her abdomen. She grunted and fell to the ground, and then Farin could hear the man moving in the woods to retrieve the bottle. Farin scrambled to his feet and began to run. He held his hands in front of himself as he crashed through the trees out into the open. Despite his lightheadedness, Farin was able to see the village, and continued running toward it.

When he was back on the road going into the village, he pumped his arms for as much speed as he could, confident he could outrun the older couple as long as they didn't hit him with magic again. Out of breath, covered with small cuts from the tree limbs, and scared out of his wits, Farin pushed through the inn doors into the now-empty tavern. He stopped for a moment, leaning on a table as he gulped in ragged breaths.

When his breathing was normal, Farin made his way up the stairs to their room, opened it without trying to be quiet, then pushed it closed deliberately hard, waking both Bendar and Kaz.

"What's that all about?" Kaz asked as he rolled over in the cot.

Farin didn't answer, but lit a candle. "We need to talk."

"I think it would be better if we waited until the morning," Bendar chimed in.

Farin reached down and pointed his finger in Bendar's face. "Wrong! We need to talk right now!"

Kaz pushed himself up to sitting and reached his arms between Farin and Bendar. "What's going on?" As Kaz looked at Farin's face, his own features softened. "What happened to you?"

Farin ran his fingers through his hair, and glared at Bendar. "I'll tell you what happened," Farin began. "I was nearly abducted by a man and woman who knew who I was. They asked me about Gran's necklace and said that Bendar told them I had it." He pointed at the intellect again to punctuate his words.

Bendar sat up slightly, and the look of fear and annoyance was replaced by a look of confusion. "Were they an older couple?" Bendar asked. "Thin, but in good shape, gray hair, they both have an odd kind of bottle hanging from their belts?"

"Yes, that's them!" Farin said in an accusing tone. "So you did tell them."

"Please sit down," Bendar requested, his brows drawn together. Farin hesitantly sat down, and the tension in the room started to dissolve. "They work with the merchant in town. They seemed like really nice people. Frankie used to live in Pike Point, so he has been very interesting to speak to."

"Yes, they are very kind," Farin replied sarcastically as he pointed at his scratched up arms and hands.

Bendar's eyes widened as he saw what had happened to his friend. He continued, "As I have been going through old records we often talk. When I told them about our Troven, they insisted on knowing everything, I guess they had heard one of Kaz's stories about the dram attack. I told them about everything we had stolen from us, Gran's necklace was just another item on the list. I'm not sure why they would think we still have it."

"Well they do," Farin cut in, "And they want it, bad enough to kill for it."

Farin stopped talking and turned his head to the side, and the marks on his ears activated. "Plans have changed. Grab your stuff. We need to go, now!"

CHAPTER 17

Trusting Farin's ears, the boys grabbed their travel packs, bows, and hunting knives, then left the room. In the hallway they could hear a commotion in the tavern below. "Are you renting a room for the night?" Braden asked. "If not, then I'm afraid you can't go up there."

Not waiting to hear any more of the conversation, Kaz led the group down to the end of the hall. He pushed on the window and it swung open.

"Let's go," he said, turning to his friends.

Bendar looked incredulously at Kaz, "Are you seriously going to jump out of a window? Do you want to injure yourself again?"

"No time for argument," Farin interjected. "They're paying for a room." He sat on the edge of the window ledge, turned around, and held on with his hands while dangling down. He let go of the edge and fell to the ground. "Come on," he called up to them.

Kaz lowered himself to hanging, then dropped down, landing on the ground. His leg flared in pain, but he tried to hide it.

"It's not bad," he called up to Bendar.

From the ground, Kaz watched Bendar make his way slowly out of the window.

"Hurry up!" Farin called up to him. As he turned around and tried to slowly lower himself to hanging, his fingers slipped and he began to fall. Kaz and Farin both reached out their arms under their friend to break his fall. Bendar landed hard on Farin, knocking him to the ground, while he almost entirely missed Kaz.

Looking down on the two boys who were groaning and lying on top of each other, Kaz couldn't help but laugh.

"Come on," he said, pulling them up to standing. "No time to take a nap." The three boys left the inn behind them and quickly moved through the dark, empty streets of Hillside.

When they came to the north side of town they began the

hike uphill through a seldom used dirt path toward Will's home where Garin was working. Kaz strained his eyes to see out into the night. His enhanced sight helped him see a little better than the other two boys, but he still felt like every other step was a guess more than anything else. Behind him, Bendar was quietly grumbling about how they didn't have the supplies they needed, and Farin simply walked in silence.

They walked through the night and into the early hours of the morning heading slowly north. Every time an animal moved in the woods, Farin raised his arm and had everyone stop until he was certain they were not being followed. As the night wore on, Kaz worried about Braden, and wondered what would happen in the morning when people realized they were gone. Would they go east on the main road, or would they send someone up here after Garin? Either way, they needed to get Garin and move on as quickly as possible.

After another hour of walking, Kaz pointed out into the distance.

"I think I see Garin." In the light of the early morning, he could see a house. It was one of the only houses along this path, and it had a freshly built addition. A young man was walking away from the house leading a horse. "Yup, that's definitely him," he said.

The boys moved a little quicker as they closed in on their friend.

"Garin," his brother called up to him. Garin waved and hurried to embrace his brother.

"It's good to see you," he said. "What's going on, why did you come out here?"

"We've actually got some bad news," Farin answered as he looked over his shoulder back down the path. "We need to get moving now, the bandits are back and there are some other complications."

"Are you serious?" Garin asked. Then he looked at the three boys. "Of course you are!" He patted the horse next to him gently. "And you've ruined my surprise," he said, pointing at the horse, "What do you think of her?" he asked his friends.

"You didn't steal her, did you?" Farin asked. Garin looked genuinely offended that that had been his first reaction.

"I'm just kidding," he reassured his brother. He stepped next to the animal and began a quick examination. The short, broad, brown mare stood still as Farin rubbed her nose. "She's built for work, not speed, and she's slightly past her prime, but overall, she looks very sturdy. She'll be a wonderful help," Farin concluded.

"This is quite a hefty payment for helping a man do a little digging and framing," Bendar said with some suspicion in his tone.

"Oh no," he said, as he threw a small coin pouch to Bendar. "That's my payment for the construction. Baby here is a loaner. Will wanted her delivered to his niece in Lexingar. When I said we were headed to Norwell, he made me an offer. If we take a small detour through Lexingar, we can use her to help carry our supplies if we get her there in good condition for his niece."

"I think our luck is starting to change," Farin said as he absently brushed the mare's flanks. Baby reared up and whinnied loudly, causing Farin to jump back out of hoof range.

"I also should mention that Baby doesn't like people touching her left side," Garin explained quickly, as he reached for her bridle and got her under control. "She was whipped as a foal. If anyone is on her left side, she wants to be able to see them at all times. Otherwise, gentle as a kitten."

"Thanks for the warning," Farin remarked.

"So, where are we headed?" Garin asked, looking at his companions.

Farin and Kaz turned to Bendar who closed his eyes, and the marks on his forehead came to life. While his eyes were still closed he started talking, "We need to keep moving north on this road, and then we should see a path leading east." He opened his eyes and looked a little frustrated. "I can't possibly know how far we have travelled, so I'm not sure how much longer it will be to get to the path."

"Do you mean that trail right there?" Garin asked, pointing to a small break in the road that could easily have been overlooked. "We use that path to get firewood. It leads deep into the woods. Will told me it gets a bit rocky and steep farther along."

Bendar nodded enthusiastically. "Perfect, let's get moving."

The morning was cool, but quickly warmed up as the sun rose high in the sky.

"Kaz, time to give that leg of yours a rest." Garin insisted as they stopped to get a drink from a small creek that ran next to the path.

"No argument here," Kaz replied. During their trip, each boy had a turn riding the horse, but Kaz took an extra turn from time to time as his leg was starting to throb with the exertion of the extra travel.

Through the rest of the day the boys kept moving, not wanting to lose time for any unnecessary stops, and not knowing if anyone had started tracking them. When the sun began to set, they set up camp off the horse trail in a sheltered section of woods. Kaz searched for some worn rabbit trails and set up some snares. They quietly ate a meal of dried meat, bread, and some wild apples they had picked off a summer apple tree near the road. As darkness began to fall, the boys hid themselves, and their horse, behind a thick wall of briars, and crouched close together for the night.

* * * * *

While Farin slept, holding onto his strung bow, his ears picked up the sounds of the night. An owl hooting in the distance, crickets chirping, and the breeze as it rustled through the forest. Then a twig snapped. Farin opened his eyes and slowly reached over to his brother.

Before he could touch Garin's sleeping body, he moved. *He must have heard it too.* Farin waited in complete silence for any other sign of what had made the sound. Nothing came. He strained his heightened hearing, and through the bushes and trees he could hear shallow breathing. There was definitely at least one person out in the distance who did not want to be found. The person stayed still for several long moments, probably trying to see, hear, smell, or detect the group in some way. Farin barely let himself breath.

"Nothing, let's keep moving." Farin recognized the male voice from his encounter near the Hillside Bridge.

"I don't see any fire," his companion observed. "They must know they're being followed. Either that or we've only picked up tracks from a local farmer's trips to gather firewood. We should recruit some help."

"Maybe tomorrow." With that said, the two people moved down the horse path a short distance and stopped again. Their search was very thorough. After nearly an hour of waiting in silence, the couple returned, walking back down the path. This time they did not sneak stealthily, but instead tromped through the woods. The woman cursed loudly as she tripped on a root or rock, and fell to the ground.

"We lost a lot of time today! If we don't find something solid to deliver to Melna, she might not hand over our supply of Han'Or for the summer. You heard about Carla, didn't you? They found her half way to Norwell, already blind and crazy, and she's not the first one who has run out of Han'Or. When we get back to Hillside, we'll let the others know the boys are gone. If we are all searching we'll find them soon enough. They can't have gotten too far."

Hearing her words, Farin reached over and poked his brother.

Garin didn't turn over, but whispered quietly so only Farin could hear. "Try to get some sleep. It'll be safer for us to get moving in the morning."

In the morning Farin sat up and stretched. His body was not accustomed to sleeping on the hard ground, and he twisted his body sideways, allowing his back to crack several times before he rose to his feet.

"Garin, Kaz, Bendar, time to wake up," Farin whispered loudly enough for everyone to hear.

Kaz moaned an objection, but before he could spout out a witty remark, Garin put his hand over Kaz's mouth, and motioned for him to remain silent. Kaz seemed to recognize the urgency in Garin's eyes as he nodded his understanding.

"What's going on?" he whispered softly.

Garin and Bendar sat up together. "Last night we had some visitors," Garin explained.

"Same ones that jumped me," Farin added. "They are definitely looking for us, and they have gone back to Hillside to get some help. For now we are ahead of them, so we need to keep moving.

"Any other cheerful news?" Kaz asked as he twisted his body, releasing an enormous crack from his back.

"We also need to avoid making fire at night, because that will be like a beacon to them." Farin added.

Bendar took a small stick and began drawing lines in the sand.

"This is Hillside," he said, pointing to the ground. "If my calculations are correct, we are about here," he pointed to a faint line. "The main road is the fastest way to get to Norwell," he pointed to their final destination, "but if we keep moving east through the woods, we'll eventually hit the North road that leads where we are going through Lexingar to Norwell. It will take longer, but I can't imagine anyone following us."

"Looks good to me," Farin said after examining the 'map' carefully. "I just wish we had already traveled more than a hand span away from the people who are trying to catch us."

"I'll check the snares," Kaz put in, "then we can get moving."

"We'll pack the supplies, and we'll eat while we're moving." Bendar said as he quickly began to roll up his blanket and stuffed it into a saddle bag. As he did so, Farin gestured to Garin, and the twins retrieved some food they could eat while they were walking and filled up their water skins from the nearby stream. When Kaz returned with the snares he had one scrawny rabbit that he quickly cleaned and hung from his backpack so they could begin their trek into the woods.

After two days of traveling, they left the relatively fertile woods and began walking on bare rocks. Farin had never seen any place that looked so gray. Although some moss and grass patches peppered the large rock terrain, and some trees had managed to get roots in the cracks of the rocks, it was still very barren. He didn't like how exposed they felt, but it also meant they were leaving no tracks behind.

After three days' moving and sleeping on rock, and Kaz returning each day with empty snares, Bendar began voicing concerns about their supplies. Within ten days they were living on half rations, making slow progress through the rocky forest. On the fifteenth day, they reduced their food to quarter rations, and their slow progress came to an almost complete stop.

"Bendar, are we going to die?" Garin asked as they stopped to make camp for the eighteenth time. They stopped before dark on a small patch of grass where a large tree had fallen that they could use as fuel if they needed a fire. A crystal brook had carved a crevice in the rocks, making a small creek they used for drinking water.

"I feel like it is a possibility," he responded as he dropped a medium sized log. He bent to pick it up again and found it difficult to hold the wood in his shaking fingers. "But before we starve to death, I will kill that horse over there."

"That sounds like a great plan," Kaz added. He had just returned from setting up some snares near the camp. "Let's eat Baby right now."

"Don't you dare!" Garin said in a threatening tone. "If it's a choice between us dying or the horse, then we'll kill her, but that is the very last resort."

"Should we stay here and try hunting and trapping for longer than just one night?" Farin asked. "Maybe we would have a better chance of getting something."

"I could use a break from all this walking," Kaz said, his wound on his leg was healed and he spent his share of the time walking, but it was still stiff and sore.

"I don't know if it'll make any difference," said Garin. "There don't seem to be any live animals around here, and I can't live off of dandelion leaves," he said as he popped one of the tart greens into his mouth. The lack of wildlife was frustrating at times, but it also was probably the reason they had been safe from any predators like drams, so he didn't want to complain too much.

"Well, it's decided then," Kaz said with a smile. "If it doesn't make any difference, let's just stay here for a while. With any luck we'll catch something, but at least I won't have to walk tomorrow. That'll be something to look forward to."

In the morning Kaz came back empty handed from surveying the snares, but he had shot a squirrel out of an oak tree and was pleased to bring back some meat. Bendar discovered some edible plants, including a large keenroot. The keenroot was often given to children as a punishment for not eating their dinner, but today it was savored as the boys' bodies utilized every ounce of nourishment they could from this disgusting tuber. Stopping for the day proved to be rejuvenating physically, but also frustrating as there was not much to do but wander around looking for more keenroot and listen to Farin complaining.

"Where are we?" Kaz asked before he went to sleep.

Bendar blinked his eyes several times before he answered. It looked as if the lack of food was impacting his mind. "By my calculations we should have already passed some kind of road. I think we have been angling toward the main road, so if we do not pass a trail or path of some kind we will hit that road eventually.

"Eventually?" Garin blurted out. "If we don't starve to death first."

"That is correct," Bendar responded.

"Stop talking like that," Kaz interjected. "We got some meat today, we've filled up on clean water and keenroot. The woods look thicker up ahead, so we'll probably see the end of these rocks in not too long. We just need to get some rest and we'll be fine."

The boys stopped talking and settled down for another night sleeping on a thin patch of grass that covered a hard rock bed.

Farin was woken up early the next morning by the sound of a hawk screeching in the distance. The hawk soared high above his bow range. He watched as it disappeared out of view, then he noticed something else that made him anxious, hopeful, and fearful all at once. In the sky not far to the southeast there was a trail of smoke.

"That smoke is not just from a campfire," Bendar observed. Farin hadn't noticed that the intellect was awake until he spoke.

"Kaz, wake up!" He called out. "Can you see anything we can't?"

"I can see that you don't like sleep," Kaz said as he rolled over. Then, with his eyes fixed to the smoke Kaz asked. "What could have caused that much smoke? I can't see anything that will help us know."

"It's out of our hearing range," Farin concluded, after his dots brightened to show his concentration.

"We have nothing to lose by going to see what is causing that fire," Kaz pointed out. "You guys have already decided that we're going to eat that horse, then die out here."

With that the boys quickly cleaned up the empty snares and the campsite, loaded up Baby, and nocked their bows, preparing for whatever was causing that smoke.

CHAPTER 18

Rejuvenated from having had some food and rest, it didn't take long for the boys to hike through the woods to a small hill that had been hidden by the thickening forest and crest the hill to get their first glimpse of what was causing the smoke. When Kaz looked down at the scene, he froze in horror. A group of travelers watched in dismay as a band of thieves rummaged through their wagons for anything of value. One of the wagons was burning, causing great billows of black smoke to rise into the air. Because of their proximity it didn't take Kaz's eyes to see that there were bodies on the ground from a recent skirmish. Kaz backed Baby up and they all knelt back below the hill's crest.

Farin was the first to speak. "What are we going to do?"

In his logical tone Bendar answered, "There are well over a dozen men that I can see, and more moving inside the camp. We have two longbows and a hunting knife. If Kaz uses his walking stick as a short staff we would still be completely outmatched."

"I'm not leaving them alone," Garin blurted out. "I can't believe you are even considering letting them kill those people. We need to do what we can to help. Don't you remember your oaths?"

"He's right," Farin said, gesturing to his brother. "We need to do what we can."

"I would like to clarify," Bendar added, "that I did not make any conclusions, simply observations. We are outnumbered and outmatched. Those are the facts."

"You can stay here, but I'm going down there to help," Garin declared. He snatched up a quiver from Baby's back and stalked boldly toward the crest of the hill.

Kaz hurried to step in front of him, his open hands held up, "Let's take another look. If all the fighting is done, then maybe they're no longer in danger. If they need our help, we'll do what we can."

The boys inched up to the crest of the hill and saw that the work of death was not nearly done. The thieves were pulling the surviving men and one woman from the huddled group of travelers. They were being lined up in front of a group of thugs while a burly man with a spiked mace in his hands directed other bandits to return to ransacking the camp. One man resisted being taken from his family and he was killed right in front of his children.

Not waiting for any more debate or logical input, Kaz nocked an arrow and strained his sight. He drew back the bow and zoomed even further. Kaz was not going to stand by as children became orphans as he had. He was focused on the center of the chest of the man who seemed to be leading the robbers.

Kaz drew the bowstring, and in a smooth motion released. Before the arrow even reached its target, he had a second arrow pulled to his cheek. By the time the bandits realized what had happened, two of them were down with arrows in their chests. They searched frantically for the hidden archers, and a visor in their group pointed toward the boys. He was the next to fall.

Without a leader and with no direction, the thieves loosed a misdirected volley of arrows toward the boys and began a hasty return to their horses. It was much more challenging for Kaz to hit the moving targets. One villain fell to the ground with an arrow in his shoulder, and another ran more quickly to his horse as an arrow grazed his leg. The disorder and new allies seemed to give the captives from the caravan some courage. They began to tackle and grab some of the retreating foes. They were able to take down several men as they tried to escape, but the majority of the bandits mounted and began a charge right at the four boys. Three of the bandits had bows at the ready, while the other eight had an assortment of weapons.

Bendar tapped Garin on the shoulder, "Can you hit them at this range?"

Garin drew an arrow back and loosed it in a high arch. It was caught in a slight wind current, and fell to the ground harmlessly. "I guess not."

"Better try again," Farin encouraged. He stood with his hunting knife in both hands, ready for an attack. "I wish I had my sword!"

While Garin shot another arrow into the field, Kaz continued to hit the incoming men. With the men on the move and the mounted archers firing back, he ducked behind a tree, then stepped out into the open as he had another arrow ready. Within a few moments, Kaz had loosed four arrows. Two of the mounted archers and one other bandit slumped in their saddles, but with the element of surprise eliminated, and the horses quickly closing the gap, the outlook was grim. Kaz began to shake slightly as this realization sank in. Bendar was right! He hit one man's shoulder and then he missed two shots in a row. Garin continued to get closer to the riders, but had not yet found his mark.

The riders continued to close in and Garin nocked another arrow, turned to face his foes, released, and quickly rolled behind a tree. When Garin was behind the tree, Kaz stepped out and saw that the remaining mounted archer had an arrow drawn and was aiming at the tree where Garin was hiding. "Wait!" Kaz shouted as he pulled back on his bow, but, his warning was too late. Garin rolled from behind a tall maple and released an arrow into an approaching bandit, hitting his horse. Then his eyes went wide with realization. The last mounted archer released his bowstring, hitting Garin in the right shoulder. Kaz released his arrow and the last mounted archer fell from the saddle.

Garin collapsed to the ground. His bow and quiver tumbled down the hill, spilling his arrows on the ground. Farin and Bendar both ran to Garin. Farin grabbed his brother and Bendar grabbed the bow and scrambled on the ground to retrieve some arrows.

With the mounted archers all eliminated, Kaz stood in the open where he could clearly see the remaining six riders, two of whom he recognized with a shock as bandits from the fake coach. Motivated by anger and a desire to avenge his friend, Kaz drew and released two arrows more quickly than he thought possible, but before he could shoot again, the men were on top of them. With no time to think or aim, Kaz shot his last arrow into the horse of the lead rider, ducked behind a tree, and ran for cover. The horse reared and fell backward, landing with a sickening crunch, squarely on the unfortunate rider.

The three remaining bandits jumped from their horses as they entered the dense forest in pursuit of Kaz. Two bandits held long swords and the third a mace. Bendar was crouched next to the twins and had retrieved some arrows. His position was no secret, as Garin's loud groans of pain and gasps for air could not be stifled. He drew his arrow back and shot one of the sword-carrying assailants. The remaining bandits immediately turned on the trio, weapons raised.

Bendar did not have time to draw a second arrow, but raised his longbow to block the strike of the mace as it fell. The mace broke through Bendar's upheld bow with ease and landed a solid hit on his right hand and forearm, crushing the bones and sending Bendar sprawling with a cry of agony to the ground.

The bandit raised his weapon again and swung it at Farin. Farin closed his eyes and gritted his teeth anticipating the impact, but the impact never came. Instead there was the sound of metal pounding into flesh. Garin, fighting past the agony of his arrow wound, had thrown himself in the path of the mace. With no protection, his body took the full force of the blow. Farin lunged at the bandit with his hunting knife held firmly in front of him. The knife met some resistance as it hit the man's leather armor, but with all of Farin's forward momentum, the knife sliced through the leather and into the man's chest. Farin stood up from on top of the fallen bandit and pulled the knife out of his chest. He stood holding up the small hunting knife defensively as the last man cautiously circled the three boys.

"Nice little toy you've got there," he said with an evil smirk.

"You're very brave—facing two injured boys and another with a hunting knife," Kaz called out from his hidden place in the woods.

The bandit turned around and looked into the trees. "Why don't you come out where I can see you and we'll see who is brave."

Not interested in having a standoff with the thief, or continuing their banter, Kaz stayed hidden and called out. "I'll put an arrow in your heart if you take another step toward my friends. I've killed enough for today, get out now if you want to live."

The man began backing away from Bendar and the twins while his eyes darted around, looking through the forest. When he was near the tree line, he leapt behind some thick brush, rushed for his horse, and rode away at a gallop. Kaz lowered his empty bow, glad that his bluff had worked, and ran to join his friends.

Farin, not seeming to care what was happening around him anymore, was completely consumed with taking care of his twin. "Garin, you'll be ok. Come on, just hold in there. We'll get you out of here."

Turning to face Kaz, Farin continued in desperation. "I don't know what to do! Garin is the one who takes care of us."

"He is still breathing," Bendar observed through gritted teeth, "but he's losing blood fast." He was cradling his right arm that had already begun completely turning black and blue.

"I need to…" Garin tried to speak, but his words were jumbled and hard to understand.

"You don't need to do anything," Farin insisted. "You saved those travelers. *You* led us in to save those people. You saved me. You are a hero."

With great effort Garin shook his head then tried to speak again. "Dad?"

"What about Dad?" Farin asked, clearly confused. "Should we take you home?" Farin turned to Kaz with tears in his eyes. "I always know how to finish his sentences. I don't know what he wants." Farin looked back at his brother. "Just tell me what to do. Anything, I'll do it!"

Garin reached his hand up and took Farin's hand. He tried to speak some more, but all that came was a gurgling noise.

Farin tried desperately to bring Garin back to consciousness. "We're here, Garin. Talk to me. Garin, you can't leave me. Garin, Garin!" Looking around for help from Bendar and Kaz, Farin called out. "Kaz, help me, we'll get him to the caravan. Come on, Bendar. Someone help me."

Kaz leaned down next to Farin and put his arms around his friend. "He's gone, Farin. He's gone."

"No, he's not! Help me get him up!" Farin said while pushing his friend's arm away. He continued to pull at his brother's lifeless body, trying to get him to wake up. "We'll get him some help." Farin reached under Garin's arms and began dragging him out of the woods. It took all his strength to drag his brother, and when Garin's boot was caught in a root, they both fell to the ground. Farin leaned over his brother and sobbed into his chest.

Kaz knelt down next to Farin, and tenderly placed a comforting hand on his back. He knew from personal experience that there were no words that could help, but he wanted his friend to know he was there. Farin's back was rocking back and forth in sobs.

"What's happening?" Farin asked, looking over his shoulder at Kaz. He closed his eyes tightly for a moment, then opened them and looked around as if he had forgotten where he was.

Kaz looked to Bendar questioningly. Bendar shrugged his shoulders. Then, gritting his teeth against the pain in his arm, he reasoned, "He is in shock."

Kaz pulled Farin close and held him tight. "It's going to be okay," he reassured. "We'll get help from the caravan."

"Okay," Farin said as he looked around in a confused, disoriented way. "Can you quit yelling?" Farin added. He put his hands over his ears with a pained expression. "You're hurting my ears."

"I'm sorry," Kaz whispered softly.

"Let me look at him," a deep voice cut in. Farin picked up the hunting knife he had dropped to the ground, and spun to face the newcomer. Kaz also held up his bow with both hands, ready to use it like a staff. He knew as soon as he looked at the man that he was not one of the bandits. He had gray hair, a short-cut beard, and was approaching with open hands and a look of sincere concern for what was happening. The man looked at Bendar first.

"This is serious," he said with a grim look on his face, then he turned to speak to several men who were trailing behind him. "Get in here, we have some injured men." After briefly examining Garin, the man gently brushed Garin's eyes closed. He shook his head slowly. "I'm sorry." With a companion he carried Garin's body out of the woods, Farin by his side, still looking around like he was disoriented and covering his ears.

Kaz slumped against the tree behind which Garin had been hiding, and sank to the ground, head in his hands. As people came and led Bendar to where he could get some help, Kaz felt shock and numbness wash over him, and he watched his friends being led away as though he were watching a dream play out. A sudden ill feeling caught at him. Although the boys had shared all of the responsibilities in camp, while traveling and hunting, Kaz felt responsible for his friends. Bendar was their planner, but the twins were here because they had chosen to follow Kaz. He was responsible for their safety, and he had failed his friends today. He wished he could take Garin's or Bendar's place. He replayed every shot in his mind; the shots that missed, and the times it took two arrows to take down a foe. If he had been more focused he could have saved Garin. While these events played through his mind he was brought from his thoughts by a sudden jab in his arm.

Startled, he looked up with a shake of his head to see the jab had come from the end of a cane. Looking down at him was a kindly woman with tears in her eyes.

"Come with me, young man." She took his hands and he stood up, nearly collapsing as his knees buckled when his eyes lighted upon the body of one of the bandits he had killed. The woman was much stronger than she looked. Kaz's stumble did not faze her, and she led him out of the woods. In the clearing, Kaz was still preoccupied with his thoughts and looking down at his feet.

"You need to look up," the woman said as she gestured toward a group of people who had gathered nearby. "It is always better to look at the good you have done and not focus on things out of your control. It's always better to look up." Kaz slowly raised his head and saw for the first time that a group of people was approaching. The throng crowded close and showered Kaz with praise and thanks. It was nice to see that he had helped do some good, but that did not take away the pain and horror that was beginning to register with him, and the responsibility he felt for the welfare of his friends.

Kaz was led by the grandmotherly woman to a large tent where Farin was sitting outside.

"How are you doing?" Kaz asked. Farin flinched slightly, and Kaz continued speaking in a quiet voice. "What's happening?"

"Bendar is inside," Farin said slightly above a whisper. "And they are cleaning up Garin's body," he paused for a moment, taking in a deep breath before he continued, "they are cleaning him up so I can prepare the body."

Kaz hugged his friend, "You won't have to do it alone."

CHAPTER 19

After sitting with Farin for a few minutes, Kaz was greeted by the same gray-haired man who had first approached them up on the hill. A tall, solid man with a sincere smile, he made Kaz feel comfortable. "I can't begin to express my remorse at the loss of your brother," he said, addressing Farin.

As he spoke, Farin flinched slightly as if in pain, then nodded his head. "Is the body ready?"

"Not yet," the man replied. "It might take some time to get him ready to be seen, but until then, I would like for you to come with me." He gestured for Farin and Kaz to stand up.

Kaz looked to his friend. He would go if Farin did, but he was not leaving his friend alone. Slowly, Farin stood up.

"I want to know when the body is ready," he said to the man.

"Absolutely," he quickly agreed. "My name is Odon. While we are rounding up some medical supplies and converting some family members' tents into medical stations, I would like you to meet some of the people who were saved by your bravery," he paused for a moment, overcome with emotion, "and sacrifice."

"I don't feel like meeting new friends," Farin protested, turning around to sit back down.

Kaz spun his friend around, "It'll be good to walk for a bit. You don't need to talk to anyone, just take a walk away from the medical tent."

Farin nodded his head and began following Kaz and Odon.

On the grass in front of an orange and green striped wagon, an elderly woman was sitting on a rocking chair watching as a group of people worked to disassemble the pieces of a wagon which had been burned beyond repair.

"This is Naida, she is one of the weavers we have here in Algernon's Caravan. She does some sewing and knitting, but her woven blankets are famous all over Denall."

When Odon came close she struggled to rise to her feet, but Odon hurried to her side to keep her from exerting herself, and motioned for the boys to come a bit faster. He quickly produced two stools for them to sit on.

"Here are my heroes," she said, holding her arms out. Farin took one of her hands and Kaz took the other. "My dear, sweet boys," she said as she squeezed their hands. With emotion in her voice she quietly continued, "I have something I want you to see."

She released their hands, pushed open a door on the side of her wagon, reached in, and retrieved a large, beautifully woven blanket. The colors were a bright and vibrant mix of yellows, pinks and purples.

"It's beautiful," Kaz responded as he looked at the superb craftsmanship. "My Gran does lots of knitting and sewing, and a little weaving, but nothing quite like this. It really is amazing! I can see why it's famous."

"Thank you," she responded. "It's a gift for your friend."

"Friend?" Kaz asked, not sure who she was talking about.

She nodded, then clarified, "Tomorrow we will have a ceremony to honor the lives of our family members who have passed on to the after-life. We usually wrap them in some kind of clothing or blanket."

"A journey blanket," Farin said as he understood what she was offering. "To help him comfortably get to his final destination. We have the same tradition in our village." For a moment he was choked with emotion, unable to reply. "It would be an honor to have this blanket for my brother."

"Oh no," Naida said, tears instantly in her eyes. "I'm so sorry. I had no idea it was your brother." She reached out and took Farin's hand in hers and squeezed tightly. "I'm the one who is honored." She tenderly placed the blanket into Farin's arms and patted him on the cheek. "Tomorrow at the ceremony, will you be sharing a few words about him?"

Farin looked to Odon and the older man gave a nod. "It's entirely up to you, Farin. We'd love for you to pay your respects to him in whatever way you would like."

"I would like that very much," Farin replied.

Naida seemed pleased with his answer and pulled on his hand as she moved forward to the edge of her chair. "I will be right by your side through the entire thing," she added.

"That means a lot, thank you." Kaz could tell by Farin's reaction that he was deeply touched by Naida's compassion. It seemed the older woman had a way of reaching Farin through all his grief. He felt a sense of relief as he realized that there were caring, able adults around to help his friend through this. He would be there to support Farin, but he wouldn't have to do it alone.

Odon quietly gestured to Kaz to follow him, and leaned over to Naida, touching her gently on the arm as he asked, "Do you think you could keep our young friend company while the healers finish preparing his brother's body?" She patted his hand and looked to Farin, who nodded his head in agreement.

Odon led Kaz through the camp where members of the caravan were busy tending to the wounded, repairing damage, and putting items away that had been strewn all about the camp by the bandits. As they approached a bright red wagon with a picture of a cow painted on the side, Odon tilted his head toward Kaz.

"We have another grateful family member here who has asked to meet you. Haylan!" Odon called out when he reached the wagon. He knocked on the side and called again, "Haylan, come on out here."

A man dressed in a long apron stepped out of the back of the wagon and jumped nimbly to the ground.

"Hello! Welcome to Algernon's Caravan," he greeted Kaz. He walked right up to Kaz and grabbed him in a hug. Kaz was shocked by the forwardness and looked at Odon in confusion.

"Haylan's a hugger," Odon explained.

"I can see that," Kaz said over the man's shoulder. "It's nice to meet you," Kaz said when he was released.

"We," Haylan opened his arms wide in a way that took in everything around them, "cannot express our gratitude for the help you and your friends were to us today. I, myself, was afraid that our little group would not see another day by the time those bandits were finished with us. We've encountered plenty of thieves and bandits in our travels, but this was really something else. Our caravan was started by a man named Algernon, and when he passed away we asked Odon to lead us, and in all that time we have never met a problem we weren't able to handle..." Haylan paused for a moment, puffing his cheeks for a moment as he held in a breath and then letting it out in a burst, looking around at the mess and damage done to their camp. "Well, today, that still held true, as the universe has sent you to us! My butcher's shop is open to you any time you should ever be hungry."

Odon indicated the picture on the side of Haylan's wagon. "He raises cattle, sheep, chickens, and pretty much anything that can be eaten."

"Indeed!" Haylan rubbed his hands together enthusiastically. "You can find my wagon in this caravan most easily! As a butcher, I think of beautiful, fresh, red meat. So I chose to paint my wagon red. Come to think of it, you can really find any of us easily if you know what to look for. I'll bet you can figure out our system pretty easily. Look over there," he said, pointing out across the group of wagons. "The blue wagon belongs to Raven, she deals mainly with foreign and rare items. Items that come from…" he paused in anticipation, waiting for Kaz to answer.

"Across the sea?" Kaz said in more of a question than an answer.

"Yes, exactly! And over there, the bright green wagon, can you guess what he does?"

Kaz shrugged his shoulders and looked back to Odon, hoping he would supply the answer for him to end this game. Finally he ventured, "Green is like grass, or trees. Does that person sell plants?"

"Very close," Haylan answered. "His family actually works together in their portable cooper shop."

"What does barrel making have to do with the color green?" Kaz asked.

Haylan smiled from ear to ear and chuckled a little, "Nothing at all, his wife just loves the color green." He slapped Kaz on the back and started to laugh.

Despite the intense emotions of the day, he was feeling a certain appreciation for Haylan's friendly manner.

Odon cut in before Haylan could continue the guessing game any longer, "When people come to trade or purchase items, it makes it easier for us to direct them if each wagon is a different color. Some of the colors are connected to the trades, while others are not."

"What are these boys doing for supper?" Haylan asked Oden.

Kaz was startled for a moment. He hadn't given a thought at all to what they would do for the evening meal, or to fill any other practical needs for that matter, and again Kaz felt relief and gratitude wash over him as Odon replied, "That's why we are here, Haylan, I thought you might have some ideas."

"Tonight you will eat with me," Haylan pointed at the small herd of animals he had out behind the wagon. "There's always extra at mealtime, and I'm happy to share. Especially today. Those crooks killed half a dozen animals, and I need to get them slaughtered properly or we'll lose all that meat. We'll probably lose some of the meat anyway."

"Do you need any help?" Odon offered.

Haylan leapt up to the entrance of his wagon. "I've got a couple of Taylon's older boys on their way soon. I might need some more help later on if you find anyone who's hungry. Just send them here around supper." He then turned to Kaz before re-entering his wagon, and stated in a more serious tone, "You are part of our family," he said, pointing around at the other carts. "Family is always welcome around our fires." Haylan nodded emphatically to drive the idea home, and then ducked back in the cart.

Odon began leading them to the next wagon. "He's a good man. He's almost always busy doing something, but he'll stop at a moment's notice to help a friend in need."

"He seems very friendly," Kaz remarked, remembering his hug.

Odon chuckled, "Yes, he is."

On their way back to Naida's wagon, Kaz saw a blacksmith

setting up a temporary forge in front of a wagon that was painted black, preparing to repair some of the pieces that had been salvaged from the burned wagon, while his well-built apprentice hefted the anvil onto a level spot. Several other people were scattering into the woods and returning with greens or lumber. A fairly large group was gathering the bodies of the bandits who had attacked, and some had already begun digging holes for graves.

Farin looked up as they approached and hastily rubbed some tears from his eyes. Naida patted his cheek gently, and indicated to Odon with her head, telling him to go see to his brother.

"Who is that?" Farin asked suddenly as he joined Odon and Kaz. He was pointing across the camp at a man who was holding a longsword, standing in front of two brown wagons.

"That's Blade," Odon answered. "Would you like to meet him? He makes weapons that we sell along our way. He works closely with our blacksmith, Rhett. Rhett makes the metal parts and Blade carves the handles, fletches the arrows, and does the leather work for the armor. Their wares sell like crazy around tournament time in Lexingar." Odon had already started walking toward Blade, but Farin put his hand out and caught Odon's arm.

"I actually don't want to meet him," Farin replied, surprising both Kaz and Odon. "I just wondered why he didn't do anything to protect you if he has a sword and other weapons."

Odon stopped at the edge of the open field that lay inside the circle of wagons, and turned to Farin with a serious look. Kaz thought at first that he would react with anger, or at least frustration at Farin's blunt comment, but instead the older man's answer came in a calm voice.

"Today's attack was a tragedy of misunderstandings and greed."

Farin flinched and covered his ears, "You don't have to yell!"

Odon raised a quizzical eyebrow, "You have very sensitive ears," he said in a whisper. "Maybe we'll look into that later. For now I think it is important that you know what happened. Around twenty well-armed bandits stopped the caravan. They came out from the woods, over there," he pointed at the thick trees to the north. "They were calling threats and talking nonsense. Before we could respond, Gefion, a new member of our group, decided that he would be a hero. He began fighting with one of the bandits and was able to wrestle the bandit to the ground and take his club. Gefion then killed the bandit using his own club. The mounted archers quickly killed Gefion." Odon stopped speaking, clearly upset.

"I'm sorry for your loss," Kaz said.

"So am I," Odon replied. "What Gefion never understood is what I hope you and your friend can understand while you are here—I would rather give all my possessions than lose the life of a family member." He stopped talking and looked around the wagons. "These people are all my family. You saved them, so you too are my family."

"So why wasn't anyone doing anything to protect your family?" Farin asked. This time his question was not in a tone of defiance, but confusion.

Kaz winced slightly, hoping Odon was not offended by the remark, and looked apologetically up at the caravan leader.

"I'm sorry," he mouthed at the older man.

"There's no reason to apologize," he answered. "I actually did step forward with my close friend, Blade, over there," he pointed again to the man with the sword who seemed to be taking reports from other caravan members and directing their clean-up efforts. "We showed that we were unarmed and wanted to speak."

"Weren't you scared?" Kaz asked.

"Yes, Kaz, I was terrified," Odon answered. "But I knew if I did not move to stop them, it would only escalate into a bloodbath."

"I asked what they wanted and tried to calm them down. They said that they knew we were hiding a magical stone somewhere in the camp. We denied it. They said they would kill us all, one family at a time, until whoever had it gave up the stone."

"A magical stone worth killing for?" Farin repeated, looking to Kaz knowingly. "Who are these people?"

Odon shrugged and shook his head, "I don't know who they are, or why they thought we had anything that belonged to them."

"What did you do?" Kaz asked.

"We told them we would show them all we had, insisting that we wanted no violence." Odon turned away from the open field and began to lead the boys back through the camp as he related what had happened. "They tied Blade and me up over there," he pointed, "and went into one of my wagons. They tore it apart, then after finding nothing, they set it on fire. They continued to search in other families' wagons, throwing everything out, damaging what property they could, killing some livestock, and threatening people while Blade and I were unable to do anything. Some of their men were lining up families while others were searching wagons. They had Bodd's family lined up outside his wagon," at this he pointed to the far end of the camp where Kaz had seen the man killed in front of his family, "He fought with the villains to keep them out of his home and they killed him on the spot. After that, more people started resisting, and a man who seemed to be leading the bandits began yelling a threat to kill us all, whether they found the stone or not. At that point I knew it was a mistake to let them tie us up, but it was too late. That is the very moment when you arrived."

Farin looked at the ground, seemingly trying to process all that he had learned, while Kaz took a deep breath.

"I'm so sorry,"

Odon smiled at Kaz, "There is no need for apologies among family."

"I think there is," Kaz corrected. "I saw it happening and I hesitated. I could have saved Bodd if only I had listened to Garin. I waited too long and I…"

By now they had arrived back at the make-shift medical tent where Garin and Bendar had been taken. Odon stopped walking and turned to face Kaz. He grabbed the young man in his arms and held him tight. Kaz was surprised by the man's actions, until he whispered in Kaz's ear, "The person they were threatening to kill next was my wife. She was being dragged away when you started shooting." He pulled Kaz away from his body and held him at arm's length. The older man's eyes were filled with tears. "I am one person to whom you will never need to apologize. You saved everything for me, and I promise if there is ever anything you need, you will have it."

"But you lost your home. How can you say I've saved everything?"

"The more time you spend with me, the more you will learn; I don't place value on trinkets and toys. I value life above all else." He turned to Farin. "Which is why I feel so terrible about what happened to your brother. He gave his life to protect us, and we will never forget that."

After a long, silent moment, Odon gestured to the entrance of the medical tent, but just as he was about to go inside, Farin pointed at a line of men tied up, being led to another nearby tent.

"What's that?"

"Those are the bandits who survived the attack," Odon replied. "We were able to grab a couple before they reached their horses, and some sustained minor arrow wounds. We got the man with the long blonde hair when he fell off his horse. It's a shame, that one," Odon remarked with a shake of his head. "We'll have to put him down." Kaz looked up to Odon with some alarm. "The horse," Odon clarified with a smile. "We're going to have to kill the horse."

Kaz gasped, "What are you going to do with the thieves? You're not going to kill them are you?"

"Why not?" Farin asked with a dangerous look in his eyes.

Odon rubbed his forehead next to his three intellect marks. "What do you think we should do with them? They attacked our people, killed your friend, tried to kill you, and if we let them go, they will probably come back with more men. In our tradition, a person who is assaulted has the right to declare his attacker's fate. According to the laws of Denall, attacking our caravan is a crime, punishable by death."

Kaz thought for a moment and shook his head. "I guess you're right, but it still seems so… wrong."

"How about you?" he asked Farin. "Do you want to go over there and finish the job on those men?"

Farin glared at them and flexed his arms. Kaz could see the anger in his eyes, but he also saw after only a short moment that the anger subsided and his features softened.

"I'm not a murderer,"

Odon was smiling. "I'm glad to hear it. You're good lads." Odon clapped Kaz and Farin on the backs. "These men are not murderers either," Odon clarified. "You brought justice to the man who killed Garin," he reminded, "and Kaz took out the men who killed Gefion and Bodd. Denall's law requires that anyone who murders another must be turned in to the authorities, but these hesitated just enough at the commander's orders that we were able to overpower them. I think there is still hope for these men."

"What do you mean?" Kaz asked.

"From time to time a bandit group will come. They usually are looking for food, and that we give them willingly. If they come violently, we defend our homes and families and usually we take a captive or two. When that happens, we make them work for us. That group will probably start out pulling a wagon, or hauling boxes. When they are far enough from home and feeling humble they usually agree to peacefully join with us. We have a pretty big group, but we can always use a couple more strong backs to help with the heavy lifting."

"Then what do you do?" Kaz was very interested.

"We take off their bonds."

"Don't they run away?" Farin asked.

"Sometimes, but for the most part they find that our way of life is better than thieving. You see, most people don't like to rob and cause violence. They do it out of desperation. When they have another choice, they take it. They end up being some of our best defenses against robbers. Just last year a group of thugs came to rob us and they recognized Bill over there," Odon gestured to a large man working on fixing a wagon wheel. "Instead of having a fight, we had a small reunion and went peacefully on our way." Odon was chuckling while he told this story.

"I think I understand," Kaz said, though some confusion still swirled inside of him.

"It's a lot to learn, but you'll see. Living at peace with others is the only way to find peace with yourself. Hopefully those bandits will also learn that lesson. In the meantime, let us properly honor our fallen. There will be plenty of time to deal with these men afterward."

Frustrated and confused, Farin entered the medical tent, ready to begin preparing his brother's body for the funeral the next day.

* * * * *

After assisting Farin to dress Garin's body with clean clothing that was brought to them by a group of women from the caravan, and sitting with his friend, letting tears freely fall between the two of them, Kaz left Farin in the care of the older of the two healers, Razer, who assured him they would take good care of him. Ever since the skirmish, Farin had been complaining of his head swimming, and winced whenever people spoke above a whisper. Before leading Kaz through the partition to visit Bendar, the younger of the healers had suggested that Farin must be in shock, and they both promised to make sure Farin would get some rest.

Bendar was sitting dejectedly next to a table covered with clean cloth and medical instruments.

"How are you doing, Bendar?" Kaz asked, uncertain what exactly to say.

For a moment, Bendar could only shake his head, and then he held up his wrapped hand and said hollowly, "They told me I may never use my hand again. Every bone was broken or crushed. Syd here has made a splint and wrapped it to help it to heal in the shape of a hand, but…" he trailed off.

"Bendar, I'm so sorry," Kaz said, taking a seat next to him. Bendar looked up as though he was confused to hear these words. "I did this." He said, as though annoyed that he would have to explain this to Kaz.

"What are you talking about?"

"I was the one who decided to travel this way. This was my plan…"

"No," Kaz said firmly, "This was all the fault of those bandits. We had to come this way because they wanted to do us harm. This is the fault of people looking for that stupid magical stone. If Omer and those two people who attacked Farin in hillside hadn't been so eager to find out about a magical stone, we wouldn't have had to take this route either. And, the bandits who attacked the caravan and killed Garin and smashed up your hand, they were looking for a stone too. This is on their heads, not on yours!"

"What?" Bendar said, sitting up straight and wincing as it causing his hand to shift position, "They were looking for a Stone of Power?"

"Odon, the leader of this caravan, told us that when the bandits showed up, they claimed that someone in the caravan had a magical stone."

Just then, Farin burst into that section of the tent from the outside, Razer close behind him.

"You're right! It is their fault!" Farin blurted out.

"What?" Kaz and Bendar asked together, exchanging bewildered glances.

"Kaz, you are right, this is the fault of those bandits. Some of them were with that group that grabbed us on the way to Hillside, and now that I think about it, someone else looked familiar." With that, Farin turned around just as suddenly as he had come and went hurrying out of the tent. Kaz and Bendar exchanged one more startled glance and then hurried after him. Razer went with them, apologetically explaining that he had been taking Farin to rest in a spare tent Odon had prepared for him, when suddenly Farin had asked why Bendar was speaking so loudly, then had stopped, and suddenly started hurrying back to them.

In a moment the group was inside the second medical tent where the captured bandits were being treated. The bandits lay in beds with leather straps holding them down. Some pushed and pulled against their restraints, while others laid still. As Farin looked across the patients in the tent, his eyes came to rest upon a well-built man with a week's worth of a beard and blood covering half of his face. The other two boys realized after only a moment what Farin had brought them to see. Commander Aldis was tied down on the bed at the end of the tent. Farin ran across the tent and slammed Aldis in the face with his elbow.

"What are you doing?" the girl who had been helping to bandage the bandits demanded.

Farin ignored her and threw fierce punches at the man's face, breaking his nose and splitting his lip open. When he pulled his arm back for another hit, Kaz was quick to leap forward, grabbing at him from behind, pulling him off of Aldis. Farin struggled to get free and was able to lash out with a wild kick that hit Aldis in the ribs and made him groan in pain.

"Farin, calm down," Bendar hurried in to address him. "I know you are upset, but you cannot do this." Bendar pointed at Aldis' restraints and said, "He can't defend himself. You can't attack a prisoner. Our new friends have things under control." Then, when Farin finally looked at him, still breathing heavily, Bendar said more quietly, "Please trust me. I will speak with Odon and we will sort this out. Something is clearly going on here, but you need to rest." Farin struggled to free himself from Kaz's grip once more, but Bendar said, "Please, let me handle this. Let me do something that can help to take away my agony over my part in bringing us here." Bendar's eyes were pleading. Farin's anger seemed to melt away and he finally relaxed. Kaz slowly released him, ready to grab his friend again if necessary. By now a small crowd had gathered inside of the tent, including Odon and Blade.

"May I have a few minutes to speak a word or two with this man?" Bendar addressed the caravan men who were tensely watching the exchange between the two friends. Blade and

Razer looked to Odon who looked back and forth from Aldis to Bendar several times before answering.

"You have ten minutes. All of these prisoners must be in good condition when I return. Is that understood?

As the group stepped outside the tent, leaving Bendar to interrogate Aldis, Kaz turned to Farin. "You heard mine and Bendar's conversation from halfway across the camp?"

Farin looked at him with surprise and then a look of befuddlement as the likelihood of that dawned on him.

"That's not so uncommon for a level four listener though," Razer put in as he carefully began guiding Farin toward the tent that had been prepared for the boys.

"Level four? I'm only a level two," Farin said with even more confusion.

Razer and Odon exchanged looks of amazement, and then Razer began to look around, finally pointing at Blade's sword.

"May I borrow that for a minute?" he asked. Blade looked surprised, but removed his sword from its scabbard and handed it to Razer, who in turn handed it to Farin.

"Turn it so you can see your left ear."

Farin looked at himself and was surprised at what he saw. Since he had left the inn in Hillside he hadn't seen himself. Even in the uneven surface of the blade he could see that he was thin and his eyes had large bags under them. He even had the startings of a beard.

"I look scary," Farin said out loud. Remembering then why he was given the mirror, he twisted it and leaned it back so he could see his left ear. What he saw on his ear shocked him even more than his current scruffy state. In place of two ear marks, he now had four. "What happened to me?" he asked, almost dropping the sword to the ground, then he took another look to make sure he wasn't seeing things.

"I've only once heard a rumor of this happening before," Razer answered, "but it seems that when Garin died, you got his gift. Perhaps there was a special connection between you as brothers."

"He was so much more than my brother," Farin said,

letting the tip of the sword drop to the dirt. "Garin was my twin, and my best friend. Did you know that he was the one who told us to save you?" Then, with emotion filling his voice he continued. "He has a girl and a dream, his life is all planned out. He didn't even need to have a Troven, he already knew who he was and what he wanted to do. He's the good one. I should have died -- not him." Farin sat down on the ground, clearly overcome at last by the demands of the day, and hid his face in his hands.

Odon sat down next to Farin. "It sounds like your brother was a wonderful man." After a few moments of silence Odon continued. "I have found that when some people survive and others do not, it is not always the best people who stay here. It seems to me that the people who stay here still have work to do and things to learn." With that Odon patted Farin on the shoulder.

Farin stood up and glared at Odon. "What am I supposed to learn?"

Odon nodded his head once as he also stood on his feet, "I can't answer that for you, but I can tell you something."

"What's that?" Farin asked, looking up to the older man.

"Garin left you a very special gift to help you along the way," he said as he touched Farin's left ear.

* * * * *

With Farin finally settled for some rest, and Bendar back at the medical tent, Kaz wandered about the camp for a few minutes, wondering what he could do to keep himself distracted. He borrowed a shovel from one of the caravan members and made his way across the camp to help the travelers dig a common grave for the bodies of the assailants. When he got to the edge of the camp where they were digging, one man looked up to him and shook his head.

"You really don't need to do anything," he began as he wiped sweat off his forehead. "You've helped us so much today." He climbed out of the hole in the ground and held out his hand. "My name is Strazar, but most people around here just call me String."

Kaz took his hand and shook it. "String. It's nice to meet you. I really could use something to keep me busy. If I could help a little, I'd really appreciate the distraction."

String looked in the hole, then back out. "I think this is almost done, and it's pretty crowded in there, if you really want to do something, you can help Vernand over there with the bodies."

Kaz paled slightly, and String jumped in, "Never mind, you don't need to help there. Really, we're fine, just go sit by a fire. We'll be starting to prepare supper in not too long. My wagon is the one over there painted white. It actually looks almost gray now," he said half to himself. "Anyway, you're welcome to join our fire for supper."

Kaz looked over at the white wagon and considered taking String up on his offer, but the idea of just sitting around didn't sound too appealing.

"I'll go see if Vernand needs a hand," Kaz offered. "It was nice to meet you."

Kaz picked up the borrowed shovel and made his way to Vernand. The group of people with Vernand were stripping the corpses of anything valuable, and then the bodies were dragged and piled next to the common grave. The weapons and armor were placed in a pile to be traded. The horses were turned out to graze.

"Hi," Kaz said to the man who seemed like he was in charge. "Where can I help?"

Before he looked up from his work Vernand pointed over his shoulder, "Just go over there and pick a body. We have half a dozen left to clean."

"Okay," Kaz responded. He went to the pile of bodies. This wasn't how he had expected to occupy himself, but he was determined to make himself useful. He looked at the bodies, noticing that most of the bandits had been level one and two strongarms. The body that caught Kaz's attention was a level three with larger arms than most. Kaz was not interested in the marks on the man's arm but the familiar dram tooth that hung from his arm guard. Kaz recognized him as one of the men from the coach that had assaulted and robbed them just before they reached Hillside; he was the one who had searched Garin. Kaz took the dram necklace off the thief and put it in his pocket. *I think Farin will be happy to have this.* Kaz pulled off the man's thick leather coat and skull cap and put them in a pile of armor. Then he began removing the thief's hard leather leggings when he noticed a small lump in the ankle of his pants

The bandit had a hidden pocket that was completely covered by his boots and leggings. The man was a thief among thieves; he had this safe place to hide some small, valuable trinket. Wondering what this treasure might be, Kaz lifted the man's pant leg and found something unexpected: the necklace he had received from Gran. Garin had said that it looked expensive, this thief must have shared that feeling. Placing the necklace carefully into his pocket, he thought out loud.

"I guess Gran was right, that thing really is trying to find me."

Kaz continued to help with the work for almost an hour until everything of value had been removed from the bandits, the bodies had all been laid in the common grave, and the sun began to set. The fires around the caravan's campsite were lit and people started to gather with their families. Kaz surveyed the scene with amazement, almost not recognizing it as the campsite they had first been led into following the skirmish. Everything had been cleaned up, and even Odon's burned out wagon had already been completely dismantled, and work on a new one had begun using the reclaimed parts.

CHAPTER 20

On their way to join a growing group of caravan members at the fire near Haylan's wagon, the three friends were preparing to eat their first warm, full meal since leaving Hillside. Despite the emotions of the day, they were all very much looking forward to it. Razer had fitted Farin with a wrapping to cover his ears while he adjusted to his newly elevated gift.

Farin pulled the material back to show Bendar his left ear.

"Take a close look," he offered to his friend, who had only joined them in the last half hour, and still had not heard about Farin's new markings.

Bendar leaned in close and released an audible gasp, "Farin, what is this!"

"I guess it is a parting gift from Garin."

"I have read before of a sibling absorbing the gift of a departed brother, but I thought it was a myth. This is extraordinary!"

Kaz playfully punched Farin's arm, "I guess that means I'll have to let you in our exclusive level four club. When we get back to Dungan it'll be me, you, and that strongarm fieldworker your dad hired."

"I think I'll decline your generous offer," Farin said with a slight grin. It was good to see Farin smile after the day they had had.

Thinking about Garin, Kaz reached into his pocket. "That reminds me," he pulled Garin's dram tooth out. "I found this on one of the bandits,"

"Is this what I think it is?" Farin said, taking the tooth from Kaz.

In answer, Kaz held up Gran's necklace. "It was definitely Garin's dram tooth. I know because this was also on the body," the sight of Gran's necklace produced another gasp from Bendar. Kaz put the necklace on and tucked it under his shirt. He thought about how Garin was willing to wear the jewelry for him. It was just one of the many ways Garin showed he was a true friend. Farin was also putting the dram tooth necklace over his head. Bendar took in a sharp breath, apparently ready to ask a question when suddenly they were greeted loudly.

"Hello!" Haylan called out though they were still several yards away from his fire. "A seat for our guests of honor," he called out as he pointed to three ladder-back chairs that were empty. "What would you like?" Haylan asked as they found their seats. "We have some beef, chicken and lamb." Kaz looked around the fire and saw Blade, Razer, Odon and some other members of the caravan whose names he had already forgotten. They all had food and were in friendly conversation.

"I'm starving," Kaz answered.

"Then you can start with a little of everything!" Haylan filled up a plate from the grill and brought it over to Kaz. After getting food for Bendar and Farin, he took his seat. For a while, Kaz quietly ate his food while looking around the fire. This evening was unlike anything he had ever experienced in the sheltered village where he had grown up. The people around the fire had different hair, clothing, skin color, and spoke with varied accents, but they all acted like a large family as they laughed and ate together. He loved the diversity and richness he felt in their presence.

Kaz took a bite of beef from his plate and could barely contain his excitement. The spices on it were like nothing he had ever tasted before, and the flavors came alive as the meat practically melted in his mouth.

"This is amazing!" he called out to Haylan.

"Don't mention it!" the friendly man replied. "Seriously, if you can stop eating long enough to tell me you liked it, then it's not good enough." He laughed as he threw another piece of meat on Kaz's plate.

Kaz began devouring the food, but couldn't fully enjoy it as he watched Farin poking at the food on his plate, not eating much. Kaz could tell his friend was hurting terribly. As he was putting his own plate down so he could move next to Farin, Odon walked around the circle of people who surrounded the fire and patted Kaz on the shoulder as he passed.

"Hello again to you, my young friend. As you have surely

seen, word of your archery skill has flown through the camp like a wild fire. One of our family has expressed a particular interest in meeting you. When he was younger he was one of the best archers I've ever seen."

"He's an archer?" Kaz asked, now more interested in meeting him.

"I thought it might be good for the two of you to get acquainted."

Odon lifted his arm to beckon someone, and a moment later a large, level three strongarm emerged from a group on the other side of the fire. Kaz guessed he was in his fifties or sixties, and a little out of shape, but he still looked very strong. Odon stepped forward to meet him as he approached, and introduced Kaz.

"Boon, this young man is Kaz, he is the bowman from the woods."

"That was some amazing shooting!" Boon said. "I haven't seen anything like that in years."

"Thank you." Was all Kaz could think to say.

"Do you think you could do that again?" Boon asked.

"What do you mean?"

"Shoot like that, you know targets that far away."

"Targets are not a problem," Kaz said with a tap to his left eye. "I can hit just about anything I can see." The response seemed to please both men and they looked at each other and nodded, though Kaz had no idea what he had said that would cause such a reaction.

"I have something that just might be for you," Boon said as he walked over to a large parcel he had stashed beyond the ring of chairs. "Just wait here a minute."

Kaz turned to Odon. "What's going on?"

"Just wait."

At least this new exchange seemed to be taking Farin's mind off of his troubles, as he interestedly watched what was happening, and slowly began to eat. After a short wait, Boon returned carrying a black re-curve bow with a quiver of black-shafted arrows.

"Take a look at this," Boon said as he handed Kaz the bow. It was lighter than it looked, Kaz noted, as he took it from Boon. "This is a special weapon. It was a gift from years ago when I was living on Sephra Island. It's made of the best iron ash." As Boon said this he looked to Kaz expectantly.

"It's really curvy," Kaz responded, not sure what else to say. The bow looked interesting, and different, but he wasn't sure what might be so special about it that would get these two grown men so excited.

"It's the best kind of bow in the world." Boon said in a slightly miffed sort of way. "It can shoot…" Boon turned to Odon as if to ask if he was wasting his time.

Bendar leaned over to Kaz and whispered, "You should really act a bit more impressed. Any foreign made weapon of rare materials has a chance of being… special!"

"Kaz, if you've had enough food for a moment, why don't you step over here and give that bow a try for a moment," Odon suggested genially. Several people from the gathering at Haylan's wagon were now watching them with interest.

"Give it a try," Odon said to Kaz when he had joined him a few paces away. "Pick any target you can see."

Kaz tested the tension of the bow. It was strong, but he was used to pulling a full-sized longbow, so he felt that this would never match that range. He smoothly drew one of two dark feathered arrows from the quiver when Boon jumped forward.

"Wait!" Boon said. "Only use the white feathered arrows, the black feathers will be a little unpredictable."

"Are they magic?" Kaz asked expectantly.

"Yes, but we don't know what they do, so only use them in a case of extreme emergency. In fact, let me take those back," Boon said as he pulled the second shaft from the quiver. "Better safe than sorry."

Kaz drew a white feathered arrow, glanced around in the waning twilight for a good target, and then aimed for a damaged wagon wheel about fifty paces away that was leaning against a rock. He released the bowstring and the arrow flew several feet above the wheel.

"That was amazing!"

"But you completely missed," Odon said, somewhat confused. Now it was Kaz and Boon who shared a knowing look.

Kaz drew a second arrow and took careful aim, this time directly at the wheel, giving no compensation for arrow drop. He released, and the arrow struck a half-hand below his intended mark. "How can this be?" Kaz asked as he turned to Boon.

"Not now, son. Try something farther away. How about that tree?" Kaz gasped as he saw how far Boon was pointing. The distance was easily fifty paces farther than his longbow could shoot.

"I don't think it will go that far," Kaz said

"Just give it a try," Boon replied.

Kaz drew the bow full length and aimed far above his desired target.

"A little lower or we'll never get that arrow back," Boon directed.

Skeptically Kaz lowered his aim a few degrees.

"Little lower," Boon repeated.

Kaz lowered the bow while looking at Boon.

"That ought to do it."

At this point Kaz was aiming no higher than the top of the tree to make a five hundred yard shot. Sure that the arrow would hit the ground, Kaz felt for a lull in the wind and released. As though by magic, the arrow flew in an almost flat arc and hit the base of the tree.

"Good shot!" Boon said while clapping. "Did it hit the tree?"

Kaz, initially surprised that Boon couldn't see for himself, and then mildly more surprised as he realized how far he was seeing in the near dark to give the answer, responded, "Just at the base of the stump, a little off to the right."

There was some excited murmuring from the crowd of onlookers who had now abandoned other conversations entirely, and were gathering to watch Kaz shoot.

"I think you finally found someone worthy of that bow,"

Odon laughed as he patted Boon on the back. "Boon has been auditioning archers all across Denall since he found that thing," he said to Kaz, though loudly enough to keep the crowd informed.

"Is it magic?" Kaz asked.

"Sure is," Boon said with a shrug. "But I'm not sure of its full enchantment. This much I do know, when I pull it back it always outshoots me and I've never hit a single target."

"It would take some practice to be perfect with it," Kaz noted, "but this is amazing."

Boon clapped Kaz on the shoulder. "I'm willing to let you practice with it if you're willing to take some training. If you really can master that bow, it will be yours."

Kaz didn't know what to say. He looked at the bow in amazement, reverently rubbing the beautiful iron ash. He handed it back to Boon when he extended his hand for it, and then returned to sit with his friends. After returning the bow to its case, Boon also joined the boys at the fire side. He reached out to Bendar.

"So you are another of our heroes? It's wonderful to meet you," Boon patted him gently on his good shoulder. "And Farin, I am so sorry for your loss," he spoke reverently, "If you ever need anything, you come and find me," he pointed at a bright yellow wagon not far from where they all sat.

"Thanks," Farin responded. "Actually, I'm a bit tired."

"Oh, of course," Boon said, standing quickly and extending a hand to help Farin to his feet. He tapped his head as though it was something he had forgotten.

"Thanks," Farin said. He put the plate down with some food still on it, then he left the light of the fire and retired to the tent that had been provided for him and his friends.

When Farin had retired, Boon pointed at Kaz's plate. "You'd better eat up or you might hurt Haylan's feelings."

"Haylan told me that some of the wagons are painted a color that helps to show what their trade is." Kaz began as he watched Farin walk away, rubbing his face. "What is it that you do? Catch sunlight in bottles?"

"He is a bit of a free spirit, this one," Odon said as he circled back to their group. "He collects things he finds interesting, then trades them for other stuff. When he opens his wagon for business it's a mystery what he'll have."

"And this is why I have the most interesting things to sell from the whole caravan!" Boon declared enthusiastically. He and Odon continued on with some spirited bantering about the nature of Boon's trade choices. Half listening with amusement, Kaz sat silently eating the delicious food and wondering what their adventure would bring next. *Would they continue on? Would Farin go back and tell his parents what happened? Was there a doctor in a nearby city who could help with Bendar's arm?* There were so many questions, and Kaz hadn't even begun to think about what he wanted for himself. But for this moment, sitting watching the caravan members in their 'family' made him think of Gran. He tapped his shirt and felt Gran's necklace against his skin. It was the only thing he had from home, and now it seemed to bring him some comfort. He pulled the necklace off his neck and held it out to look at it by the light of the fire.

Boon reached out and grabbed the necklace from Kaz unexpectedly. He held it close to his chest and looked around the fire to see if anyone else had noticed it, then he whispered quietly to Kaz. "Do you have any idea what this is?"

"Yes, I do," Kaz said, curious as to why Boon was acting so strangely. "It's a piece of woman's jewelry that has found its way back to me again." For Kaz the necklace was now not only a gift from Gran, but also a memory of Garin, and he felt odd having it taken away from him. "Can I have it back please?"

"Yes, certainly," Boon said quickly, handing it back to Kaz. "I'd keep it to yourself if I were you. You do remember that the bandits came looking for a magical stone, right?" Kaz nodded. "If you start flashing that thing around, it could mean trouble."

Bendar cut in, "How can you be so certain this truly is a magical stone?"

Boon leaned close and whispered so only Bendar and Kaz could hear. "In all my life, and in all my travels I have seen its like once, on the Isle of Sephra, just off the coast from Pike

Point. That was the reason I went into caravan trading. I have searched my whole life for another one."

"What's so special about this necklace?" Kaz said, still not understanding.

"Not the necklace," Boon said shaking his head. "Don't you know what stone you hold?"

"My Gran said it was special, and that it chose me. Bendar thought it might be magical, but I don't know much about that sort of thing."

Boon held out his hand, "Can I hold it for a minute? I just want to do a quick test."

Kaz hesitantly handed over the stone, and Boon gripped the side of his chair. His arm muscled bulged, but nothing else happened. "Nope, not the Strength Stone."

"What are you doing?" Kaz asked, somewhat exasperated at the odd behavior.

"Have you checked it with your sight?"

Kaz shook his head, and held out his hand for Boon to return the necklace. "I really don't understand what you're talking about," Kaz answered.

Bendar looked at Kaz and back at Boon. "Are you saying this is one of the Stones of Power?"

"I can't be certain," Boon answered, "but it looks just like the Intellect Stone. That almost metallic, polished finish is not something you see very often." Bendar looked down in awe, then he turned to Boon.

"You said you saw one before?"

"Yes, the Intellect Stone was on Sephra Island, several decades ago."

Bendar leaned back a little in his chair and rubbed his chin. "That is very interesting," he remarked. "How can we tell for sure if this is one of the Stones of Power?"

"If Kaz uses his enhanced sight while touching it, we'll know if it is the Sight Stone." Boon answered.

Kaz put the necklace back on, and tucked it under his shirt. "I'm not sure how this is supposed to work, but I'll give it a try." Kaz looked over at Boon's wagon that was about fifty paces off to the left. Kaz could normally see most of the details of an object at that distance. The yellow painted side of the wagon could be seen clearly, then Kaz tried something more challenging, but within his normal abilities -- he concentrated on one specific wagon wheel. At this distance, making out the details of such a small object was the extent of his natural capacity, but he felt he could keep going. He focused in closer and closer, one spoke of the wagon wheel, one small crack in the spoke, one particle of sand in the crack, and then he stopped and turned to look at Bendar, then to Boon. *Bendar's stories were true!*

"This is what they've been after! This stupid rock has caused nothing but trouble!" Kaz grabbed at his shirt where it covered the necklace.

"Calm down," Boon placed his hand over Kaz's.

Kaz turned on him, and glared. "If this is what they want, they can have it! I don't want this cursed thing anymore!"

Bendar grabbed Kaz by the shirt and pulled him up to standing. He bowed slightly to the people around the fire, and pulled Kaz to walk away in the direction of their tent. Boon stood up and followed.

"You do not seem to understand," Bendar said as he walked across the empty field with Kaz. "You cannot give it away."

Boon caught up to them and nodded his agreement. "Your friend is right. The Stone chose you. You need to keep it safe and learn how it works."

Kaz stopped walking and looked at Boon and Bendar.

"If I keep it," he began, then he looked at the wagons that bordered the edge of the large clearing, "then we are all in danger. Look at what has happened to us so far. It's all because of this," he hit his chest.

Bendar shook his head, "Everything that has happened is because of evil men, not because of that. Aldis told me that one of the men from this group, probably the one who had the stone hidden away, had told him that he had seen us trade it to a travelling medicine man. They have been tracking every regular trade caravan that comes through Hillside this time of year.

Does it not seem significant that the bandit with the stone was assigned to the raiding party that just happened to catch a caravan that was right on our very winding, unpredictable route? That stone was meant to come back to you. The Stones of Power are more than just some gift-magnifying trinkets. They are talked about in many of the prophecies of The Changing. It does not say exactly how, but they are a powerful defense against evil. If they fall into the wrong hands, it could spell disaster."

Kaz put his hands to his head and released a frustrated sigh. "I don't know what to do!"

Bendar took Kaz by the arm and pulled him along toward their tent. "You do not need to do anything. I think I have a plan to keep us safe. Just make sure you keep the Stone close to you."

Kaz reluctantly nodded.

"And try to keep it hidden," Boon added.

CHAPTER 21

Farin hardly slept that night, and early in the morning, he left their tent, feeling that he needed to be moving or he would lose his mind. Many others in the camp were also stirring, kindling fires, preparing meals, and setting up chairs and stools in the field at the center of the camp in preparation for the funeral.

Farin made his way to a large stone under a broad, leafy tree. He concentrated on blocking out all sound as he looked down in his hand. When Garin was dying, he had reached out and not only grabbed Farin's hand, but placed in it Garin's most prized possession, and Farin's heaviest weight -- a picture of Fenn.

How was he going to tell Fenn about Garin's death? More importantly, how was he ever going to be able to face his parents again? Garin, the one who was going to go back to live on the farm, had given up his life to save the son who was leaving.

What words could he speak at the funeral today that would do Garin justice? Farin looked down at the picture of Fenn and tears streamed down his cheeks.

* * * * *

"Hello," Boon greeted Kaz with a solemn countenance as he emerged from the tent he had shared with Farin and Bendar the night before.

"Good morning," he replied. "Is something wrong?"

Boon shook his head. "It's mourning day. The day we give reverence and respect to those who passed away." He pointed out into the field where three graves had been dug, and the three bodies were wrapped in blankets. "Their graves will be marked so we will always remember them as we travel past this region."

Kaz nodded numbly.

Boon stepped up to Kaz and put an arm around him. "He is family. You are family." Boon guided Kaz through the field where the other caravan members were gathered. They stood next to Bendar near the outskirts of the group.

"Where's Farin?" Kaz asked.

Bendar pointed at the front of their gathered group. Naida was seated next to him, holding on to his arm. Although Farin seemed distant and closed off from the other caravan members, he seemed to have made a connection with the grandmotherly woman.

When Kaz and Boon joined the group, Odon stood up to address the crowd. Kaz looked around and saw that everyone was here.

"Gefion has not been part of our family for long, but we have all been recipients of his service. He was a hard worker, strong as an ox, and sometimes just as stubborn," Odon added with a smile. This comment made the crowd ripple with grins and light laughter.

As Odon continued to speak, sharing stories of Gefion, Bendar's marks flared red.

"What's going on?" Kaz asked in a whisper.

"I am just thinking something through, nothing to worry about." Then, as if it were an oversight, Bendar lightly smacked his head. "I forgot something in our tent. I will back soon."

Kaz didn't know what could possibly be important enough for Bendar to leave now, but he had learned not to argue with the intellect.

"Hurry back," Kaz encouraged. "You don't want to miss Farin's part."

Bendar slowly moved toward their tent, and Kaz turned back to listen to Odon. The caravan leader had just finished speaking about Gefion, and was now addressing Bodd's family.

"You were always his top priority. When Bodd first brought you into our group, I asked him why he wanted to leave his successful fiber mill to join a wandering caravan. He told me that he worked so many hours in the mill that he was missing watching his children grow up. He wanted to make a change so that he could work with you each day. He said he wanted to be a dad, not just a provider." Odon stopped speaking, and with tears in his eyes he looked at Bodd's family.

"He was a great example to us all."

The audience murmured some words of agreement, and Boon patted Kaz on the shoulder.

"I really don't think I've ever seen a more dedicated father."

"He sounds wonderful," Kaz agreed.

Odon wiped his eyes and made his way over to Farin.

"Now we will hear a word or two from Farin. He would like to share with us a little about his twin brother who gave his life to protect us in the tragic attack yesterday."

Farin stood up in front of the gathered people. He looked from left to right until he locked eyes with Kaz. Kaz nodded encouragingly, but he also felt a pit in his stomach. He knew what it was like to lose family and he couldn't imagine the pressure Farin was feeling at that moment.

"When we were kids, Garin and I used to get in trouble together a lot. I got us into the trouble, and we both got blamed and punished together," Farin began. He looked up into the air as if reliving some of the moments. "I put the saddle on the goat; he got caught riding the thing. I left the sheep gate open; he helped me gather them up again. And when my parents came outside looking for us and found us getting the last sheep back into the sheep yard, we both were lectured for letting them get out. No matter what I put him through, he was always there for me. He was the best person I've ever known. Just before his death, he was thinking about helping all of you, and his final act was to literally take a hit for me. He gave of himself for all of us. I don't know what I'm going to do without him," Farin paused and took several calming breaths before he emotionally concluded, "but I do know that I will never go wrong if I try to become like him."

Farin took a step toward his seat, and Odon intercepted him. He pulled Farin into a hug and led him to his chair. Odon nodded, and a group of people lowered the three bodies down into the graves.

"It is now time to pay your last respects."

Farin and the families moved up to the edge of the graves and stood for some time with their heads bowed. When they were finished, they moved to the side and the gathered group began to trickle past the graves in single file, giving time for each person to say their final farewell. As Kaz watched the caravan members talking together and greeting Farin, Kaz looked over his shoulder and noticed that Bendar had still not returned.

"Did you see Bendar come back?" he asked Boon.

Boon searched around for a bit, "Nope," he responded simply. "He must be somewhere in the group, or just going off to over-think things again."

"You're probably right," Kaz agreed. He knew it would be rude to leave and go looking for Bendar instead of paying his respect to the deceased, but he couldn't help but feel that something was wrong. He ignored the feeling and slowly moved with the group closer to the graves. Having each member of the caravan take time to share their thoughts took over two hours, and by the time Kaz was standing near the graves, Farin looked emotionally spent. Kaz bowed politely at Gefion and Bodd, then he came to the hole in the ground that belonged to Garin.

Kaz looked down at the body that was carefully wrapped in an exquisite blanket. The body of his friend. He couldn't think of anything to say, but he felt like he needed to just stand and honor Garin with a moment of silence before he made his way over to his friend.

"How you doing?"

Farin looked up as if seeing Kaz for the first time, and rose to his feet to hug his friend.

"My goodness, I need to get away for a bit. These people are all very nice, but I just need some down time."

"Is that why you took off by yourself this morning?" Kaz asked. He motioned for Farin to sit back down, which his friend gratefully did.

"Yeah, had a bit of time this morning, then Odon came and we talked about what was going to happen today. It's actually sounding like a pretty great day," Farin remarked. "After this is done," he said pointing around at the burial service, "then it's just eating, relaxing and socializing. I think I'm going to take them up on the eating and relaxing part, and then I'll take a nap."

Kaz nodded, "I'm with you on that one, but I might do

some socializing. There was this one girl..." Farin crossed his arms over his chest and shook his head in disbelief. "What?" he asked defensively, "Don't tell me you didn't notice the one with the dark brown hair; she's gorgeous. Don't worry," Kaz said with a reassuring pat on his friend's arm. "I'm sure she has a friend for you, and perhaps another for Bendar.

"Where is Bendar?" Farin asked, bringing Kaz back to his previous worry.

Kaz looked over his shoulder and saw that the crowd was beginning to disperse to their wagons.

"I haven't seen him since the ceremony started. I'll go check in the tent."

"I think I'll go with you," Farin responded. "I'll walk Naida back home, then I'll be right there."

Kaz began walking back to his tent when he saw the dark-haired girl standing in the field. He diverted to the right so he would pass by her.

"Hi," he said with a charming smile. "I'm Kaz. I don't think we met yesterday."

"No, we didn't," she answered matter-of-factly while politely shaking his hand. She was very pretty, but she was also almost crushing his hand in a death grip that seemed like no effort for her at all. Before he could start a conversation with the strongarm, her sparkling green eyes looked past him. He followed her gaze over his shoulder and saw Farin escorting the elderly woman back to her wagon while carrying her rocking chair in one hand. She released his hand and looked back at him briefly as if she had already forgotten he was there.

"It was nice to meet you," she paused for an awkward second.

"Kaz," he filled in for her while he rubbed his hand.

"Yes, Kaz. I'm sorry," she apologized quickly. "Didn't mean to hurt you." She said looking down at his hand with a faint smirk. She turned and walked away toward a group of brown caravan wagons.

Kaz shook his hand to get the circulation back and resumed his walk to their tent. He threw open the flap.

"Bendar," he called as he entered, but it was empty. He looked at their pile of supplies and immediately knew something was wrong. Bendar's pack was gone.

Kaz ran across the camp and headed toward the framed outline of Odon's new wagon. The ribbing that had been fitted into the wagon base had been covered with some tent canvas to provide Odon and his wife a shelter for the evening. Kaz had no idea where Bendar was, but if anyone had answers, perhaps it was the caravan leader. As he passed the medical tent, Razer threw open the front of the tent, and joined with Kaz running.

"What's going on?" Kaz asked as they both closed in on Odon's wagon.

Razer didn't answer, but instead banged his hand on the side of the wagon where a framing rib was outlined under the canvas, "Odon, are you here?"

Odon stuck his head out of the make-shift wagon covering, "What's wrong?"

"They're gone," Razer answered. He looked at Kaz as if annoyed at having an eavesdropper.

Odon stepped out of the wagon and dropped to the ground, "Who are you talking about? What's going on?"

Razer leaned in close, "The bandits from the raid are gone. They took medical supplies and left. I don't know when they left, or how they escaped, but they are gone."

Odon's eyes opened in shock and he looked over at the tent.

"Bendar's gone too," Kaz added. "During the service he left, and when I went to find him, his pack was missing from our tent."

The marks on Odon's forehead darkened for an instant. "They'd need horses if they plan to get away," Odon said to Razer. "Go make sure the horses are secure, check with Ramond." Razer began jogging, and Odon called out, "Be cautious." Razer turned back and nodded.

When Razer was out of earshot Odon turned to Kaz, "What would motivate Bendar to help them get away?"

Kaz looked around in confusion. "Nothing," he responded quickly. "I just saw that Bendar's pack was gone and I came to find out if you knew anything. Why would he help them?"

Odon looked again at the tent and back to the burial site. "They couldn't have done it on their own, and the plan to go during the burial ceremony when the thieves were not being watched was pretty clever. Bendar could easily have planned and helped with their escape, and if his pack is gone, what does that tell you?"

Kaz raised his hand to his head. "Oh my goodness," he said when understanding began to dawn on him. "That's what he was talking about."

Odon leaned close, "What's going on Kaz? Are my people in danger?"

"I don't think so," Kaz answered, then in a more confident tone he corrected himself. "No. Of course not. Bendar isn't going to do anything that would hurt us. He told me that he had a plan. Something that would keep us safe."

"What was his plan?" Odon asked. He looked slightly alarmed.

"I don't know. He didn't say." Kaz tried to think back to the conversation he had with Bendar. Bendar told him to keep the Sight Stone safe and a secret. He told him to keep it with the caravan. But he hadn't mentioned anything about what he was planning to do, and now Kaz felt like a fool for not asking.

Odon held his hands together and blew a long, loud whistle that sounded through the entire camp.

"Bendar might not mean to bring harm to us," he said with a slight tone of skepticism, "but those thieves cannot be trusted. We need to get moving." Odon took a step away from Kaz and began walking to the center of the camp to where a member from each wagon was moving to meet with him.

"What about Bendar?" Kaz demanded. "If those men are dangerous, he might be in danger."

Odon clenched his jaw and motioned for Kaz to follow him. They walked to the middle of the field, and Odon began talking as soon as he saw most of the caravan representatives were within hearing.

"The bandits from the raid yesterday have escaped. Bendar,

one of the young men who saved us, might be with them," he added with a sympathetic look to Kaz. "We need to pack up camp and prepare for departure, and I'd like to send a group of scouts to track the bandits and find out where they are headed. When we have more information we'll decide if we need to leave right away or not. For now, prepare your families for a quick departure."

"I'll track them," Blade answered, stepping forward.

"I'd like to go too," Farin added from the far side of the group. Odon and Blade both began shaking their heads, but before they could speak he continued, "If Bendar is in danger, I'm going. I can easily hear what they're saying from a hundred yards away through the woods. I can help."

Odon nodded, "Blade, can you get him a horse?" Blade nodded and motioned for Farin to join with him. "Everyone else, pack up and get things together."

The small group dispersed and Kaz made his way to his friend. "I'm going with you too," Kaz said as he approached Farin and Blade.

The older man shook his head, "We're just tracking them to see which direction they went. It goes faster with two riders. We'll bring back news as soon as we know anything."

Kaz wanted to argue, but Blade didn't wait around to hear what he was going to say, he just started walking toward the horse line. As Farin passed his friend, he stopped.

"Can you help Naida? Make sure her things are packed up? We'll be back soon." Without waiting for a response, Farin jogged away to catch up with Blade.

* * * * *

Farin and Blade galloped down the main road leading west. The tall, slim caravan member was dressed in casual, woolen work clothing that was a stark contrast to the sword that was strapped to his horse. The way he rode, and even the way he moved, seemed more like a well-trained soldier than a leather worker.

"They have a two hour lead on us," Blade said as he rode next to Farin, "but when they left they did it quietly, and they have some injured men, so we can probably catch up to them when they stop to rest."

Farin nodded and leaned down on his horse, urging it forward. They continued down the road, easily following the tracks of the men who had escaped. He kept his ears sharp for any sounds down the road, and also listened passively to the woods in case some of the escapees had hidden themselves to watch for pursuers. His heightened hearing seemed to work not only better than it ever had before, but he could also do more things at once with it. He smiled as he thought of the wonderful final gift his brother had given him.

As they charged down the road, Farin heard some rustling, and he motioned for Blade to slow down.

"Up ahead," Farin whispered. He pointed out to their right in the woods. "Something is moving in the trees."

Blade nodded and then dismounted, silently pulling his sword from his saddle sheath. Farin was amazed at his stealth as Blade walked smoothly through the woods, silently leaping from rocks to open spaces, never once snapping a twig or brushing leaves. Farin tried to copy his movements, but was not nearly as good.

"Shhh!" Blade whispered back to Farin as he stepped on a dried leaf that cracked in half. The sound would not be noticed by the strongarm thieves, but that was not good enough for Blade. The older man stopped and knelt down to the ground. "Remember," he cautioned, "we are here to find out their plans."

"What if Bendar is their prisoner?" Farin argued softly.

"Then we'll go back for support," Blade answered. "If we attack and get ourselves killed, we put the entire caravan at risk. Do you understand?" Farin nodded. "Can you hear them yet?"

Farin shook his head. "There is a lot of motion in the forest that direction," he responded, pointing out into the trees, "but I can't make out any words."

Blade stood back up and continued moving between the

trees, silently creeping up on the bandits. As they closed in, Farin began to hear indistinct chatter, then he began to make out the words they were speaking. He patted Blade on the back and they both stopped and crouched down to the ground.

"There are two men talking now. They are arguing about who is going to start the fire." Farin continued to passively listen to the unimportant conversation. "Can we move closer?" he felt silly asking Blade for permission, but it had been very clear from the moment they left that he was in charge.

"Why?"

"If we could see them, we'd know exactly what's going on with Bendar."

Blade shook his head back and forth. "If we can see them, they can see us."

Reluctantly, Farin nodded.

"I heard a ripping sound, like they are tearing fabric, and one of them is moaning softly."

"They're probably replacing his bandages," Blade remarked absently. "Anything else?"

Farin focused his heightened hearing and scanned through the woods toward the bandit camp. He tuned out all the ambient noises and became excited when he found Bendar's voice. "Bendar is whispering," Farin said in a mix of confusion and happiness.

"What's he saying?"

Fain began repeating what he heard from his friend, "… has nothing. The Algernons are too busy traveling and trading to study."

Aldis responded in a voice just above a whisper. "What does studying have to do with this?"

"They don't know anything about the Stones," Bendar responded. "Why would they try to collect them if they don't know their use or their worth? They travel light. Why carry rocks with them?"

There was a silence for a moment, then Aldis spoke again. "If you don't have it, and they don't have it, then what good are you?"

Bendar's voice seemed to have some fear behind it as he responded to the threat. "The Algernons don't have one, but I know where to find one, and I can help get it safely to Omer."

"We're not going to Omer's keep yet," Aldis argued. "First we need to recruit some help and go after that caravan."

"That's enough," Blade said as he tapped Farin's back. "We need to get back now and we need to get moving east."

"Wait!" Farin said, almost forgetting to whisper. "We can't leave now. We don't know anything for sure."

Blade put his hand on Farin's shoulder, "We need to get back," he said. For the first time in their trip his voice was soft and almost compassionate. "We know that they do want to come back after us, and we know that Bendar isn't being held against his will."

"Didn't you hear what I said? That bandit threatened him," Farin argued.

"Yes I did hear that," Blade responded. "And I know how difficult it is to lose a brother and a friend within a couple of days, but you need to think about what's happening over there. When the bandit asked what Bendar was useful for, Bendar responded by trying to convince him to keep Bendar with them. I don't understand why, but it seems your friend wants them to take him to Omer's keep."

"Maybe that's to lead them away from the caravan, to keep you all safe."

Blade nodded, "That's true, it might be to keep us safe, and they might listen to him, but it could also be for any number of other reasons, and they might not take him east. Either way it seems your friend is safe, for now, but the caravan is not."

Blade looked at Farin for a long moment, and although the older man could simply command Farin to go back or leave him behind, it seemed to Farin that he did care what Farin thought and wanted him to see it was the only way. Farin thought about Bendar in the camp surrounded by the thieves. He knew that if Bendar was there, he had helped them escape. He didn't understand why Bendar would do that, or what his plans were, but he did know that the intellect would not have gotten into that situation without thinking through every angle. Bendar was in their camp under their rule, but in some measure Farin felt sure Bendar was in control. He also knew that if he didn't return to the caravan, he would be risking the safety of Naida and all the other Algernons.

"You're right. We need to go."

CHAPTER 22

Farin woke early in the morning and pushed open the flap of his tent.

"Come on!" Kaz moaned as the first rays of sun filtered through the opening. "We're staying here for at least a couple of weeks. I want to sleep in till at least lunchtime." For almost two weeks the caravan had been on the move. From the time Blade and Farin had returned with the news that they might be under attack, they had moved out early each morning heading southeast. Each day after an early signal that woke the whole caravan, they would strike camp and move as far as they could before setting up for the night. Kaz and Farin traveled with the Algernons and were given some work to do each day.

"Don't you want to explore?" Farin asked as he held the tent flap open even further. Kaz didn't respond, but instead threw his blanket over his face.

Farin dropped the tent flap closed and stepped out into the quiet morning. He looked around at the colorful wagons and tents that were set up around the edges of a clearing. He walked past the outskirts of the wagons and followed a brook. Farin jumped out onto a large boulder and watched as the shallow stream parted around him before it emptied into a medium-sized lake.

Farin sat and quietly listened to the water running down the stream and the distant sound of some people opening their tents and greeting the day with exaggerated yawns. He looked out over the lake and into the nearby woods and he could quickly see several good fishing holes and some chipmunks, birds and other small game. It was a good spot to stop and resupply.

With his enhanced ears Farin heard some footfalls and knew that someone was coming down the path toward the stream. After a couple of steps he knew it was Angela. The distinct way she walked with a light but solid step was easy to pick out. She slowed down, and her steps became more quiet, and Farin knew she was trying to sneak up on him.

"Hi Angela," he called out without turning around.

"One of these days I'll get past your super sensitive ears," she promised. She finished coming down the path and stopped on the shore across from the rock. "Scoot over," she called out as she braced herself to jump over to the large rock.

Farin moved a little and patted the rock. Angela easily leapt over the water and sat down next to him. There weren't many people his age in the caravan, and he found himself spending a lot of his down time chatting with her.

"I thought you'd be sleeping in today after all the work you've been doing these past couple of weeks."

"It's been hard on everyone," he responded dismissively. "I'm just glad to have something to do. You know, keep my mind distracted." Some days were harder than others to wake up and not have Garin around. They sat for a moment in silence as Farin looked down at the rock and tried to not be overcome by the feeling of loss.

Angela stood up and jumped back onto the bank.

"Come on," she beckoned. "Let's check this place out."

Happy for the distraction, Farin dusted off his trousers, rose to his feet and joined her on the grass. As they walked along the shore of the lake, Farin picked up a flat stone and threw it out over the water. The stone skipped two times before sinking below the water.

"What was that?" Angela asked with a raised eyebrow.

"That's called skipping a stone. Do you want me to show you how?" he asked as he picked out another stone.

Angela picked up her own smooth stone and touched the edges. "This one looks pretty good."

"Yeah," Farin agreed. "That'll do nicely, now you lean back and…"

Before he could say anything, Angela put her hands on her hips and tilted her head to the side, "I think you misunderstood," she interrupted. "I know what skipping a stone is, I was just wondering what you just did." She threw the stone out and it bounced off the surface of the water, skipping seven times before it finally stopped about half-way across the lake.

"Alright, strongarm," Farin teased as he picked up another

rock and attempted to outdo her display. His next rock skipped farther than his first, but still didn't come close to Angela's throw.

"I didn't even use my gift," she said pointing at her arm.

Farin picked up a third and fourth rock tossing them out over the water. "Ouch," he said when he threw a fifth stone. He grabbed his shoulder.

Angela laughed loudly at him. "You should probably stop before you hurt yourself too badly," she teased. "Although it would be a great excuse for losing a sparring match, I'd hate to have you injured on your first day of training."

"Training? Are you serious?" he said with delight.

Angela gave him one of her infectious smiles. "Last night my dad mentioned that he was impressed by how much work you and Kaz were doing around the camp. Now that we're stopped for a while and Kaz will be working on his archery with Boon, he said he'd be willing to talk to you about doing some sword training."

Farin rolled his shoulders around and then bobbed his head from side to side as if he was ready to start the training that very minute. Each day of their journey Angela jogged next to the caravan company in full armor carrying her sword. When they stopped for breaks Farin often saw her doing sword forms. Some he had been taught, but most of them were far more advanced than anything he had ever seen. "That's fantastic! I'll go talk with him right now. Is he up?"

Angela smirked at him. "He's awake, but if you go talk to him you really need to stop bobbing up and down like a jackrabbit." She placed her hands on his shoulders and pushed him down as if the motion would make his excitement more grounded. "Be respectful and enthusiastic, but not giddy."

"Got it," Farin agreed. "This'll be so great! I've always wanted to learn more with the sword, and it'll be fun to spend some more time with you."

Angela slapped him across the face. Before he could even think to rub his reddening cheek, she stuck her finger inches from his nose. "If you even hint that you are doing this to spend time with me, my dad will tie you to the front of our wagon and you'll be pulling it for the rest of the season," she said seriously. "Besides," she added, placing her hands back on her hips, "if you do get in the practice ring with me, I'm not going to go easy on you, so I don't think it'll be much fun. Well, not for you at least."

Farin backed away from her and held his hands up, ready to block any incoming attacks she might throw. He couldn't believe she hit him, and by the continued sting on his cheek he was pretty sure she didn't hold back. "I'm going to go talk with your dad now," he said as he continued to back up. "And by the way, you are a very scary person," he added with a friendly grin.

"I'm not scary at all compared to my overprotective single father. If you want to see scary, and feel real pain, just tell him you want to train so you can flirt with me. The reason he left the king's guard and joined the caravan when my mother died was to keep me away from the soldiers and the barracks. That little tap I gave you is nothing, believe me."

Farin looked over his shoulder up the path to the caravan campground.

"Maybe I'll just take knitting lessons from Naida. It seems like that might be the safer thing to do."

Angela walked up to him, turned him around by his shoulders and they walked up the path together.

"Since when were you interested in doing things the safe way? Just get up there, follow my advice, and you'll be fine." She continued up the path and Farin followed.

When they arrived at their wagons, which were set up to form the sides of a three sided practice ring, Blade was seated on the back of one of their wagons punching rivets in a piece of soft leather.

"Hello," he greeted as Farin approached.

"Hi," Farin responded. Up until this point he hadn't had a lot of conversations with Blade and he didn't know whether to call him Blade or sir. "What are you doing there?" he asked pointing at the leather.

"This'll be some leather leggings, but I'm pretty sure that's not what you're here to talk about, is it?" he asked as he put down the leather and stepped off the wagon.

Farin shook his head, but was unsure what to say. He stood still as Blade walked around him, inspecting him carefully.

"Angela tells me that you are interested in training with us." He continued to circle slowly around Farin as he spoke aloud his assessment, "You have good build. You're a hard worker. I've seen you swinging some twigs and sticks as we've been walking, so I know you've handled a sword before." He stopped in front of Farin and looked down at him. "The main question, young man, is what your intention is?"

Farin tried to swallow but his throat was suddenly completely dry. "What do you mean?" he asked. He wanted to look to Angela for guidance, but he didn't dare.

Blade smirked a little as if he had some kind of private joke. "I haven't heard much about your plans. How long are you planning on staying with Algernon's Caravan?"

Farin released a breath he didn't realize he was holding, "Oh, my intentions for staying with the caravan, yes. Kaz and I were actually just talking about that yesterday. We're going to Norwell, and you are headed to Lexingar so we thought we'd stay with you at least until we get there. That is if it is all right with Odon. We haven't really talked to him about it yet."

Blade nodded. "Odon has already told you that you are welcome to stay, so that means that as long as you are pulling your weight, which it is obvious you are willing to do, you can stay. It is up to you, but if you do train with me, as long as you are with the caravan you must keep our rule in regards to defense of the group: 'bruised or dead.' You will need to learn to fight well, and to execute clean attacks. We only kill when absolutely necessary to defend life, otherwise your skill should be such that you leave your opponents bruised, but otherwise unharmed. Odon takes life very seriously, and the chance to redeem a life has proven to hinge upon the mark being left with minimal injury."

Farin looked back over his shoulder at his tent, and the wagons that were set up. "I'd like to stay, at least until we get to

Lexingar, perhaps longer depending on where you are headed."

Blade rubbed his chin thoughtfully and walked over to a small shelf where he retrieved a practice sword. "Here you go," he tossed the sword, wooden blade first, at the young man. Farin dodged to the left and grabbed the hilt of the sword with his right hand and spun it around to point back at Blade. The older man nodded approvingly, "Good catch. Footwork needs some work, but overall, that was well done."

"Thank you," Farin responded.

Blade walked back to him and circled around him again. Farin wondered what he could possibly learn from his endless circles but he remained standing during the inspection. When he was again standing in front of Farin, he held his hand over his mouth and tapped his forefinger on his upper lip several times before he spoke. "Three months isn't much time, but I think you have great potential."

"Three months?" Farin asked in surprise. "I thought the trip to Lexingar was only a month, or six weeks at the most."

Blade dropped both hands to his side, "We're not like a stage coach," he began with a smile. "These past two weeks have been very different as we've been on the run. Usually our trip will take us up through some smaller villages where we'll be stopping to trade, and from time to time we'll set up camp and work on making our wares. We're not planning to get to Lexingar until the tournament season." He stopped talking and gave Farin a penetrating gaze. "Does that change your plans?"

Farin didn't want to make any decisions without consulting Kaz, but he also didn't want to turn down the chance for some real sword training. "Three months of training sounds great," he responded. "When do we start?"

Blade's grin widened into a full smile. "It started two weeks ago in the woods when you chose to follow me back to our group. Your sword training will start after your morning run."

"Morning run?" Farin asked scrunching his eyebrows together in confusion.

Blade patted him on the back. "Try to keep up with Angela, and whatever happens, don't drop your sword."

Farin's eyes lit up, "I get a sword?"

"Of course you do," Blade responded. "How else can we do training?" Much to Farin's dismay, Blade reached down and touched the wooden practice sword. "It's right here. We'll start with this, then move on to the real thing when you're ready."

Angela walked up next to Blade and gave him a kiss on the cheek. "We'll be back in an hour. Love you, Dad." As she passed Farin she reached out and slapped his practice sword to the ground, then began running out past the caravan wagons.

Farin bent over and grabbed the sword, holding the grip tight in his hand, determined to not drop it again. He started running without looking back at Blade, worried he'd get a disapproving look for failing to obey his first instruction.

*****

Despite his claim that he wanted to sleep in all day, Kaz left the tent shortly after Farin woke him up. Each day of their travels, he had gotten more and more comfortable with the magical bow Boon had shown him, and now that they were stopped for a while, he wanted to see what he could really do with it.

"Are you up yet?" Kaz asked quietly outside Boon's tent.

"I'm up here," Boon answered from inside the bright yellow wagon. "I bet I know why you're here."

Kaz smiled when Boon came out with his bow.

"Thanks," Kaz said as he reached out and took the weapon.

Boon stepped close and whispered, "Are you wearing the Stone?" Kaz nodded. "Good, I want to see what you're capable of with this bow and enhanced sight."

Kaz grabbed his quiver from the side of the wagon and slung it over his shoulder. "I'm ready when you are."

"Hold on for a minute, I'm not going anywhere on an empty stomach." Boon threw some twigs on the coals of last night's fire, and while they were slowly catching, he filled a pot from his water barrel.

"You don't need to make that much, I'll just eat when we

get back. I'm planning to get some small game while we're out."

Boon stuck out his tongue. "Meat for breakfast? Yuck!" He built up the fire and hung the pot on his tripod.

"I don't want to be a burden."

Boon waved his hands dismissively, "Nonsense. You've been nothing but a help since the moment you showed up, I honestly can't ever imagine you being a burden."

Kaz smiled and took a seat on a log next to Boon's growing fire. "I'm happy to help. In fact I wanted to talk with you about staying around for a while. Maybe until Lexingar if that's okay."

"Of course," Boon answered absently. "Stay as long as you like, we can always use hard workers like you and Farin." He scooped out some milled grain for porridge.

"That's great," he said enthusiastically. Traveling with the caravan had been the best traveling arrangements they'd had since leaving Dungan. "Now that we're stopped, is there something I can do to earn my keep?"

Boon nodded. "There's always something to be done. We do quite a bit of hunting and fishing while we're camped. When you do get some of that small game you were talking about, Haylan can cure the meat, Blade works with the skins, and even the bones can be used for jewelry. I'm sure they'd be happy to have your help."

Kaz was thrilled at the news that his archery practice could also be a way for him to do some work around the camp.

"Now keep in mind," Boon added, "That they can only use so much meat and skins. You don't want to put anything to waste. So just ask them what they need before you go out."

"You sound like my father," Kaz said with a smile.

"He sounds like a smart guy," Boon responded with a slight laugh. He stood up and poured the mixture into the pot and began stirring it. "I'll have to tell him what a great help you were while you've been here."

Kaz got quiet for a moment and Boon's smile changed into a concerned look. "He actually was killed by thieves several years ago."

"I'm so sorry," Boon began instantly.

"It's fine. It's been a long time," Kaz answered, looking away, "He's the one who taught me to use a bow, and ride a horse. I just think he would like to hear about what we did to help, you know?"

Boon stopped stirring the food and turned to face Kaz. "I'm not sure about many things in this ever-changing world, but there are two things I feel very certain about. The people who have passed on are watching over us, and I know your father would be very proud of what you've accomplished."

Kaz smiled and a tear ran down his cheek and he wiped it away. "Thanks, Boon. You know, my parents' death, it's the reason I couldn't stand by and let those bandits attack you."

The older man patted Kaz on the back, and stood up to get two clay bowls and a jar of honey from his wagon. "It's a sad truth that sometimes bad men need to be killed to save innocent people. I wish it wasn't the case, but as long as there are evil people, the world needs men like you who will stand up for those who cannot defend themselves." He dumped the steaming porridge into the bowls and put in a spoonful of honey.

Kaz stirred a spoonful of honey into his porridge and set it down on the ground to cool. He didn't know what kind of 'man' he was, but it was nice for Boon to suggest that he was heroic. "So what ideas do you have for target practice today?"

"I wanted to do some distance tests on stationary objects. When you mentioned doing some hunting that got me thinking about birds and smaller animals. Even larger animals could be a challenge if they were moving, or if you aimed for the eye. So basically, we have lots of options." Boon took a large bite of his porridge. "Eat up and we can get going." He stood up and went back to the wagon and retrieved a full quiver. "Also we'll be using these for our target practice. It would be a shame to lose or break the iron ash arrows shooting at trees."

Kaz finished his food, switched out the quivers and they walked into the woods. "There's not much moving out here," he commented when he noticed the stillness of the forest.

"That's not a surprise. Whenever we stop, Blade always has Angela doing laps around the place in the morning before she does her sword drills. She runs through the woods making a racket. I imagine it'll be even worse when Farin joins with her. But don't worry, they stay close to camp, so once we get a little distance between us and the wagons we'll start to see some wildlife."

"It's probably safer that way anyway," Kaz remarked as he stepped over a fallen tree. "We don't want a stray arrow getting anywhere close to anyone."

Boon nodded, "Another lesson from your father?" Kaz nodded. "Sounds like a smart and cautious man."

After walking for several minutes Boon came to a stop in a part of the forest where the trees were larger and more spread out. "We'll do some target training here, then we can move a little deeper into the woods for hunting. Wait here for a minute," Boon walked out into the woods and picked up some leaves and pinecones as he went. He stopped at a large tree about forty yards from Kaz and wedged the stem of a leaf into a crevice in the bark. "Do you see this?" he called.

Kaz waved in reply. Boon moved to several other trees and set up some objects of varying sizes, each time calling out to Kaz to make sure he could see them. After he had a dozen targets set up he made his way back to Kaz.

"Let's begin. First I want you to…"

Kaz drew an arrow, and shot it at the leaf Boon had placed first. Just as the arrow landed, Kaz drew again, hitting the next target. Then the third. He hit each target Boon had set up in the order he had placed them. After less than a minute, all twelve targets had arrows protruding from them.

"Very impressive," Boon said. "Now what I'd like you to do is to actually knock down each of those items."

"Knock them down?" Kaz asked in surprise. "How can I make a leaf with an arrow through it fall?"

Boon shrugged. "I don't know. Why didn't you wait for instructions?"

Kaz dropped his shoulders, a little deflated, "I just thought you'd want me to hit them."

The older man motioned for Kaz to join him as he went to

retrieve the arrows. "I know you can hit an oak leaf from forty paces with that enchanted bow. That's not a challenge for you. What I want is to see you push your limits. Try to hit the stem of the leaf, or the piece of bark that is holding it in place. That's a challenge. That's how you'll get better. Use your Sight Stone to focus in on the small details, then try to hit something so small I can't even see it." He pulled the closest arrow from the tree and handed it back to Kaz.

Kaz replaced it in the quiver and followed him to the next tree. "I see what you're saying. When I hunt, I always aim for the eyes. I don't have to, but it's more of a challenge, it helps me get better."

"That's exactly it. You have a great gift, and you've already used it to help save people. Imagine what you could do if you hone that skill to perfection. Especially now that you have the right tools." He touched the bow.

Kaz pulled the next arrow from the tree and smiled. He started to feel a new excitement well up inside of him at the thought of journeying with the caravan. He looked forward to this chance to focus on archery and master the use of the Sight Stone, and he felt confident that with the magic bow, the Sight Stone, and Boon's tutelage, he could do anything.

CHAPTER 23

The capitol city of Norwell was located in the center of Denall. It was a majestic city with a thriving population. The central feature of the city was the large castle which comprised the southern side of the city wall. The entire structure was built using large blocks of white marble that were polished and hardened by magic. On the four corners of the castle, turrets extended up into the air, and in the middle of the square structure, a massive tower rose higher than them all. On the top of each tower, four guards stood and valiantly searched the horizon for any sign of danger. These men wore light armor, and on their belts hung bull horns that they used to sound an alarm should they see any sign of danger. Although Denall had known peace for many years, the king was a cautious man and would not allow his soldiers to become relaxed in their duties.

Throughout the city there were several training grounds for the army, and today was a day of special anticipation. Each year, a group of recruits were accepted into the training program for the army. Hundreds of young men came and signed up for service. Over the next several weeks they would be assessed and sent to the most appropriate field. Most would be foot soldiers, many would become archers, some would be sent to train for riding, and a handful would be selected to train to become knights on the King's personal guard. It was a day of excitement and activity in the training yards.

From across the street, Trae watched longingly as the lines of young men signing up to join the army were processed. Since the time he was young he had always dreamed of being a soldier, but now, at the age of twenty-three, he had accepted that this would never be a reality. He grew up watching soldiers train using swords, axes, spears, lances, maces, and bows. He had helped build many of the weapons they used each day, and when work was slow, he even mimicked their movements and the drills he had seen so many times. Unfortunately, Trae's experience and skill as a blacksmith made him more valuable working at the forge than fighting in the battlefield.

"Trae! Break's over. We have horses to shoe and armor to mend." Trae dishearteddly joined his father next to an anvil and pulled a piece of steel from the furnace, ready to work the red hot metal.

Trae was a level four strongarm with solid muscles that came from years of hefting and hammering metal. He had inherited his thick, curly brown hair from his mother and his bulk from his father, Noch. He wore a leather apron with a loop for his hammer and hard leather boots. Unencumbered by the thick clothing, he was able to work the metal into precise shapes and patterns that would fit together perfectly. He held a steel sheet in some solid iron tongs and worked it around the anvil with definitive strokes from his large blacksmith hammer.

Trae had worked as a blacksmith next to his father for as long as he could remember. His father was well known for being one of the best blacksmiths in the kingdom. More important than his skill on the anvil was his reputation for being a completely honest man. As his former apprentice and now business partner, Trae worked with his father and shared in the profits. They had recently been commissioned to make shoes for all the horses in the Norwell army, though right now Trae was completing a suit of plate armor for a wealthy baron.

Trae concentrated halfheartedly on the sheet of steel he was curving into a cylinder that would soon be a shin guard. As he finished the piece and placed it into some water to cool and harden, the army commander stepped quickly into the smith shop.

"Noch, how are those horseshoes coming along?" he asked before he stopped walking. The commander was a short man, but firmly muscled. Under his red cape, his chainmail made a low, metallic rubbing sound as he walked to Noch.

"Commander Pang, we were not expecting you so soon," Noch said as he crossed the shop to greet his guest. "We have finished half of the horseshoes and we are on schedule to finish the rest as we discussed."

Commander Pang nodded his head firmly, then continued. "We need to add to that order, and we need to expedite the delivery." Noch's eyes widened somewhat as he considered how he could accomplish all the work. "We need one thousand arrowheads: five-hundred broad head and five-hundred bodkins."

Noch whistled through his teeth at the pronouncement, "And you want these done in ten days?"

"In five," the commander corrected.

"I can't do that for you," Noch said, head shaking. "Even if Trae and I had an assistant we couldn't do that much in such a short time."

Commander Pang scowled, not liking this answer, then after a moment of contemplating he asked, "How quickly can you have them done?"

Noch looked around for a quill and moved to a table at the end of the shop. He made some quick scratches on a piece of parchment, then looked up, satisfied. "I think if we put everyone else on hold, we can finish both orders in eight days."

"That will have to do then. Make a delivery each night of what you have finished," Commander Pang said, and then he turned and briskly left the shop.

When he was out of the shop, Noch turned to Trae, "I guess we'll be burning the fires all night for a while." Trae nodded, and Noch continued, "Check the store room, and then go to the smelters. We'll need more supplies to make this order."

"Can't we work with what we have and get supplies tomorrow?" Trae asked.

"Son, is the army leaving on an expedition?"

Furrowing his brow in confusion, Trae shook his head.

"Is there an army waiting outside the castle gates?"

"Not that I know of," Trae answered, still confused.

"Then why does the army need one thousand arrowheads?" Noch asked.

"I guess they want them to put on the end of one thousand arrows," Trae answered.

Noch shook his head and put down his hammer. He took Trae by the shoulder and turned him to look out of their small shop.

"Look out there in the streets." Trae saw Commander Pang exit the barrel maker's shop, then move down the street to the fletcher's. "It's like I keep telling you, you need to think about the bigger picture. This kind of rushed order, during a time of peace, serves one of two purposes. Either it is to stock up for some expedition, or a wise king is testing to see what we can do under pressure."

"I see," Trae replied. "So you think this is some kind of test?"

"I don't know, Son. All I can say is that if we are not the first to buy the wrought iron bars, there might not be enough to meet our needs, and we won't make our deadline."

Nodding with understanding, Trae stoked the fire, checked the store room, and then headed to the smelter's for supplies. Down the streets of Norwell, late into the night the shops had lights in their windows as the craftsman worked all evening to fill the demands of the King's army.

Noch retired shortly after midnight, and Trae continued until the early hours of the morning. He knew he needed sleep when he pulled the iron bar from the fire and stared at it while it cooled from yellow to orange, then back to black without striking it with his hammer. Despite his superhuman endurance, Trae's mind needed rest. He made his way through the house, grabbing a loaf of bread that he ate while he changed for bed. He massaged his right arm, pressing deeply on a knot in his bicep. The final thought he had before falling asleep was the dread of seven more days of this brutal schedule.

After three days of getting up at the crack of dawn and staying up into the early morning, the pair was making significant progress toward having the arrow heads completed.

"I'm going to call it a day," Noch said to Trae shortly after the sun had set. "You've earned a break too. Come on up to the house and get some real rest."

Trae gratefully accepted the offer and went with his father upstairs to their small apartment.

"Hi Mom," Trae called out as they reached the top of the stairs. "Wow! That smells wonderful!" he commented as he noticed the aroma of dinner.

"There's my long lost son." She smiled as she opened her arms to embrace Trae. "Whoa! You don't smell wonderful!" She took a step back, "I'm your mother, and I love you dearly, but there is no way I am getting any closer to you until you've cleaned up."

"Come now, Mother, we can't boil water this late at night, we'll be up for hours," Noch protested as he entered their home.

Holding her nose she pushed them both back down the stairs. "Then go jump in the river for a quick rinse, or you'll spend the night in the shop."

The two men descended the stairs and left the shop. In the streets they noticed that some craftsmen were busy, but many had also retired for the night. As they walked, Trae thought he saw something move in the darkness.

"Did you see that, Dad?" he whispered.

"Sure did, Son," he replied. "Keep your eyes sharp." The two men continued down the street, but their casual walk changed into a stiff, suspicious trot as they quickly moved their heads from side to side scanning their surroundings.

When they came to the Rathan Blacksmith shop, Noch spat on the ground. He had never liked the Rathans. They had the skill to be good blacksmiths, but they lacked the integrity. While it was well known that they often cut corners on their work, they saved enough by producing low quality products that they were able to undercut the other blacksmiths in the area.

"Dry throat, Noch?" The sudden noise from the ally beside the blacksmith shop startled Trae and Noch, and they both jumped and turned toward the sound.

"No," Noch curtly replied.

"Hey, boy," Mr. Rathan called out when they had passed him, "did I see you hauling a cart filled with iron from the smelter's three days back?"

Trae didn't turn to look at Rathan or respond to his question, they just continued walking down the road to the creek where they quickly cleaned up, then headed back home for a well-earned break.

In the morning, Trae woke early and headed out with his cart to pick up a pile of firewood. Collecting firewood from the forest was often uneventful, but he still always kept a strung bow over his shoulder and quiver of arrows hung from his belt. He not only carried the bow for protection, but also to hunt small game he saw while gathering wood. He circled around behind his home and walked past the barracks. Although it wasn't the most direct route, he always liked seeing the knights and apprentices practicing. He stopped and watched for a time, then headed out into the woods.

The sun was just coming up and the dew still hung from the leaves as Trae made his way through the woods. He gathered some fallen brush and chopped a fallen tree into small sections. In short order, his cart was loaded with logs and he was ready to return home. Before turning back for home, he drew an arrow from his quiver and slowly took aim at a light patch of bark in a distant cherry tree. He inhaled deeply, then released the string, sending the arrow sailing directly into the chosen spot.

When the work slowed down at his father's shop he liked to spend time in the woods practicing with his bow. Although he knew he would never be an archer, or soldier, he thought that knowing how to use a bow would be a good defense if he ever needed it. He drew another arrow and turned quickly to shoot it into a tree about thirty paces to his left. Then he drew a third and fourth, sending them into their desired targets. After emptying his quiver and retrieving the arrows, he turned the cart around and headed back home.

As he approached the blacksmith shop he immediately knew that something was not right. His father was rushing around frantically. When he came into view, his father made some wild motions with his hands.

"Drop that wood and get over here!" he yelled. "We've been robbed!"

Trae quickened his pace, but continued to push the cart home. There was no point in losing a load of wood along with whatever had been stolen. When he entered the shop he questioned his father.

"What was stolen?"

"The iron. All our iron bars are gone." Frantic, Noch rushed around the shop looking in every nook and cranny, searching for the iron.

Trae approached his father and placed his hands calmly on the older man's shoulders, "Do you hear that?"

Noch stopped searching for the iron and stood up. The sound he heard was the consistent clanging sound of metal on metal. What made his face burn with anger was that it was coming from down the street at the Rathan blacksmith shop.

"That good-for-nothing scoundrel!" Before Trae could stop him, Noch was running down the street to the other blacksmith.

"Stop! Dad, stop!" Trae called after his father. Despite his calls, Noch reached the Rathan shop and burst open the door.

"Morning neighbor," Rathan said with a friendly smile.

"None of that! Give us back what you took and I won't report you," Noch replied firmly.

"I don't know what you are talking about," Rathan countered. "You're lucky I don't kick you out of my shop right now for such an accusation." With this said he placed his iron back into the coals and raised his hammer up. His three muscled sons gathered in around him. "We got our iron from the smelter this morning, it was the last he had in stock, go down and ask him yourself."

With a small smile on his face Noch looked Rathan in the eyes. "Bullying me isn't going to change anything," then he added, "I never said that you took my iron."

In a moment of shock, Rathan's eyes opened slightly in surprise, but he quickly recovered. "Everyone knows that it is in short supply. Besides, we've all seen that boy of yours," he said pointing at Trae, who had joined his father, "working through the entire night. It's obvious that you just ran out."

"Rathan, you are a dirty scoundrel and one day you will pay for it."

Rathan walked slowly forward, gripping his heavy hammer. "I can overlook you interrupting my work, I can overlook your accusations, but that sounded a lot to me like a threat. Nobody comes into my shop and threatens me!" His sons fanned out to his sides. His oldest son was only seventeen, but they were all well built from blacksmith work, and they were armed with their hammers.

Noch took a step backward and raised his open hands. "I wasn't making a threat," he replied. "I was just saying that you need to watch how you do business, because one day you will need to answer for it." With this said, Noch stepped out of the shop and turned back to his house.

"Dad, I really think we could have held our own against them. I've always wanted the chance to teach them a lesson."

Shaking his head, Noch turned to his son slowly. "I'm sorry I got hot-headed back at our shop. Some lost iron is not worth getting killed over. You know better than anyone that I would never hurt a fly. I just wish there was a way we could prove that iron is ours. Now we owe the smelter for the iron, and we're going to miss our deadline with Commander Pang."

"Couldn't we talk to the smelter and at least check if Rathan is telling the truth?"

"No point in doing that," Noch replied. "I asked the smelter yesterday if he had any more, and he told me the last five bars were set aside for the Rathans."

"That was way more than five bars in their shop," Trae argued.

"I know, but there is no way for us to prove they stole them. I just wish there was some way to deal with that bully that wouldn't end with me in the ground."

"Well, at least we delivered what we finished each day, and that didn't get stolen," Trae said, trying to be optimistic about the situation. "Let's go home and figure this out."

The next morning, Trae was awake before sunrise. He ate some dried meat with some cheese and a thick slice of bread, dressed for a day of hard labor, and then went downstairs into the blacksmith shop. The entire previous day had been spent trying to find a solution to their predicament. In the end it was agreed that Trae would work mining ore for the smelter for three days. For his work he would be forgiven the debt for the stolen iron and given a significant discount on his next purchase. This deal was the best they could get at this point, and although it would leave them only one day to complete the order, it was the best chance they had. When he entered the workshop, he stopped short and stared in shock.

"Hi Trae," came the familiar voice. "Glad you got up early. It's time for us to go."

CHAPTER 24

Trae didn't think he would ever see Dune again after their last encounter, but it seemed he had survived and, as promised those years ago, he had returned.

"What are you doing here?" Trae asked as he walked across the room to his friend.

"I'm here on important business, and I need your help. You will need to come with me," Dune answered, so matter-of-factly that Trae stopped half way across the room, rethinking his desire to embrace him.

"It's wonderful to see you again, but now is a really bad time. I need to get going to the mines, then I'll be at the anvil for two weeks getting caught up, and then I have to…"

Dune cut him off with a wave of his hand. Trae was completely silent, knowing that when a magician waved his hand there was no telling what might happen.

"It has been taken care of. Come with me."

Dune walked outside and stood in front of the workshop. He turned to see that Trae was still standing in the shop. He motioned for Trae to follow him out into the dark, empty street. "You will meet me at the north gate in two hours. I will be there with all the supplies we need. Begin by walking down this road. When you…"

Trae cut him off, "Didn't you hear me? I can't go! My family is depending on me right now, and if I leave I could ruin our family's reputation. People are counting on me."

"I don't have a great deal of time, Trae. What we are doing is more important than some lost wrought iron and a couple of arrowheads."

"How did you know about that?"

"I told you everything is taken care of. I think that with all we've been through, you would have learned to trust me." Waiting to see Trae nod, Dune continued, "As I was saying, at the end of this road you will see the smelter. Wave at him. Then you will take a detour past the mines. Wave at the head miner. Then make your way directly to the north gate. If you pass

Commander Pang, be sure to wave at him as well. I have already packed your things, so there is no need to wait. You should begin walking now. We haven't much time." Without waiting for a reply, Dune vanished, leaving Trae alone in the road.

Trae looked around, completely shocked by what had just happened. He would have instantly dismissed the idea of following Dune, but because of his plans for working in the mines, he was already dressed in sturdy, comfortable clothing, and he was planning to go toward the mines. He decided to walk as far as the mines before determining what to do.

Trae walked down Smyth Street, passing the smelter's shop just as a lantern was lit. Feeling awkward and foolish, he walked up to the shop door and pushed it open slightly. He looked in and then waved at the smelter.

"Oh Trae, so glad to see you before you left. Good luck on your travels, and thank you so much for the help." The smelter then went back to work setting up shop for the day. Trae slowly closed the shop door and continued walking down the street, baffled by the strange turn of events.

Trae turned down a side street that would lead him to the mines. After walking about thirty paces, he saw three young men walking very slowly. When they came closer, Trae recognized the Rathan brothers. He wished that he had brought some kind of tool with him that he could use as a weapon. Finding these three in a dark side street was sure to end badly. Deciding to not delay the inevitable, Trae continued walking down the road, trying to look as confident as possible. He clenched his hand into a fist, flexing his biceps. If they wanted a fight, he wanted to be ready. When they came closer, he noticed that their clothing was covered in dust and dirt, they were walking hunched over, and the oldest was limping severely. The closer he came to them, the more he was certain they would not be in any shape to pick a fight.

"Are you all right?" Trae called out when they were ten paces away.

The three brothers jerked their heads up when they heard his voice. The oldest brother stood protectively in front of his younger siblings.

"Please," he begged, "Just let us go home." Then the boy began to sob uncontrollably. "Please! Please!"

Trae reached out to comfort his neighbor. He knew something was wrong if a Rathan used the word 'please'. He was surprised the boy knew that word.

"Of course I'll let you go home," he replied. "Is everything okay?"

Ignoring his final question, the three boys ran down the street in the opposite direction and quickly turned right. Trae looked around suspiciously, not knowing if there was some kind of strange joke he did not know about. He searched up and down the street for anything that would give him some understanding of what was happening. Not finding any answers, he continued down the street and out of town. As he passed by the mines he waved to the head miner, and much to his surprise, the man waved enthusiastically back.

"Thank you Trae, and have a wonderful trip."

"Thank you?" Trae replied tentatively. Then he stopped walking. "Can I ask you what it is that I did for you?"

The head miner furrowed his brow in confusion, "I don't understand."

"I just want to know why you thanked me. What is it that I did for you?"

The miner pointed at carts and barrels loaded full of ore. "You worked through the night and gave us all the ore we need to get caught up on our demands, just like it says in this note." Stepping forward, Trae reached out expectantly and the man handed Trae the note. "Are you feeling all right?"

Head Miner Jomal,

I regret to inform you that I will be unable to help in the mines as I am traveling today. I hope this will help supply the smelter with what he needs. In the morning I will pass by to bid you farewell.

~The Blacksmith

"Thank you," he said, ignoring the strange look from the

head miner, and put the paper into his pocket. He decided that at the absolute least, he would meet with Dune and get some answers about what was going on. He continued his trip to the north side of Norwell. *I just hope I don't pass Commander Pang. I don't think I can handle any more mysteries today.*

As he walked to the north side of the city, Trae could clearly see the large, northern gate. The gate had a steel reinforced drawbridge that crossed the dry moat. Two guards in shining armor stood watch, monitoring the people who came and went. Much to Trae's surprise, Dune was casually speaking with one of the guards. He was dressed in travel clothing, with a shirt that came to his wrists; he clearly did not want anyone to know he was a magician. At the sight of Dune, Trae began walking briskly. He closed the distance between them and just as he was about to call out to the magician, Dune turned to face Trae and waved him to come closer.

"Come on, I've been waiting for you," he called out. The guard and Dune stopped their conversation and looked expectantly toward Trae. Despite the desire to quickly run to the pair of men, Trae continued at a slow pace, forcing them to wait for him. It was a small victory, but for the first time this morning, he felt like he had some control over what was happening.

"This is the friend I was telling you about," Dune said to the guard.

The guard smiled broadly. "He's just as you described, walks slowly like you said too."

"Well it was a pleasure talking with you, but we need to be off." With this farewell, Dune mounted his tall, black stallion and handed the reins of a second animal to Trae. He waved to the guards, then kicked his horse into action and began a steady trot away from the city, leaving Trae standing next to his bay. Trae swung his leg over the horse and galloped to catch his friend, then matched his pace.

When he was down the road a distance so that he felt safe talking, Trae wheeled his horse in front of Dune's.

"When are you going to tell me what is going on?" he

demanded. "I've been living in a daze from the moment I woke up. My enemies are doing work for me, and my debtors are thanking me. I have no idea what my father is doing…"

Holding his hand up to stop Trae from saying anything else, Dune spoke softly. "I told you it's been taken care of. Your father has been restored what was rightfully his, your pleasant neighbors will leave your family alone, and I left a note for your father so he will be expecting you back in about three seasons when we return."

"Three seasons!" Trae repeated as he raked his hands through his thick hair. "Will you please tell me what we're doing and why, in the name of the King, it will take three seasons?"

"Certainly, my friend," Dune said casually as he urged his horse forward and Trae fell in beside him, "I thought you'd never ask."

Trae exhaled in exasperation. "I don't know where you think you got your sense of humor, but you are not funny."

"I think I'm hilarious," he countered, "and you would too if you saw the look on the faces of the Rathans when a terrible magician entered their sleeping chambers," Dune smiled.

"Well that does explain a lot," Trae admitted as he allowed himself to laugh lightly. "How did the old man react?"

"You know the rules, Trae. I never spook and tell."

"Come on Dune, you can't just leave it at that." Trae looked longingly at Dune. "Don't make me beg."

"Let's just put it this way, I think he will need to spend some of the day down at the stream doing some laundry."

Trae laughed out loud. "That serves him right, dirty thief."

"To set the record straight, he never stole from you," Dune corrected, "I stole your iron."

"What? Why would you do that?"

Dune slowly breathed out, "I needed to have the iron so that I could make the arrowheads for your father. He has probably already discovered the completed arrowheads, horseshoes, and armor in his storage room."

"Can't you just make arrow heads appear?"

Dune laughed, "I wish. Magic doesn't work quite like that.

I can't create something out of nothing, nobody can."

"I've seen you pull things from the air."

"Yes, I can take dust from the air and make it into something more solid, but that takes a great deal of energy, and making dust as sturdy as iron is no easy task. Shaping a metal is much easier than creating something from scratch."

"So, in one day you made as many arrowheads as two seasoned blacksmiths could make in three days?"

"Don't be silly, I had some help, but that is neither here nor there. Do you want to know why you are here?" Startled by the change in conversation, but happy to finally learn what was really going on, Trae nodded his head. "Good. Follow me." Dune increased pressure on the sides of his horse and galloped off the main road.

CHAPTER 25

Dune and Trae entered a small, abandoned, one room cabin off the main road. The door of the underwhelming wooden structure had long since rotted off its hinges, and Trae could see several patches of roof that were damaged or missing. The walls in the cabin were bare, and the floor was covered with a layer of dust and mouse droppings. It had a table that was covered in spider webs, and next to the table there were two chairs, one of which was turned over and lying on the floor.

"Wow, Dune," Trae began, "this is a really nice place you've got here."

Picking up the overturned chair, Dune sat at the table and motioned for Trae to join him. Trae stepped to the chair and dusted it off with his hand, then sat down carefully, not sure if the chair would sustain his weight. When Trae was seated, Dune looked across the table at him.

"I'm glad you like it." The tone of Dune's voice gave no indication that he noticed the sarcasm in Trae's comment. "We need to get started quickly, so I will not have time to give you a full tour." With that said, Dune let a smile cross his lips.

Trae laughed lightly and shook his head. "Seriously, what is this place?"

"It's just an old hunting cabin I use to store my supplies."

"Supplies?" Trae looked around the empty room, confused.

"We'll get to that later. Right now I need you to focus with me." Dune pulled out a small map and unrolled it onto the table. Trae reached to the floor and picked up some small stones. He placed a stone on each corner so that the map would lie flat. Dune rolled out his side of the map and ran his hands over the corners, smoothing it out flat on the table. Experimentally, Trae removed the stones and his side of the map rolled up. Replacing the stones, Trae looked up and saw that Dune was watching him impatiently.

"I can't believe you used magic to hold down the sides of a map," Trae said.

"I'm surprised that you picked up dried bear droppings to

hold down that side."

"Are you serious?" Trae asked, and then he rubbed his hands off on his shirt. "Why didn't you tell me? Or you could have flattened the entire map."

"This was much more fun." With a wave of his hand, Trae felt a gush of air and the bear droppings fell to the floor while the map remained flat.

"So, what is this all about?" Trae asked as he pointed over the map.

"Let's start with us. We are here," Dune said, pointing to the map, "just north of Norwell."

"And…"

"And I have been tracking some of Mordyar's stone seekers since Eaton," Dune said, indicating a small village in the Egtharnton Plains. "And now they are headed up to Lexingar." He moved his finger north up the map to point to another unlabeled dot.

"That is an awfully long trip. What do you suppose they're doing?" Trae asked.

Frustration creased Dune's brow. "I'm not exactly sure. I do have a theory, though, and I will need to make a slight detour here," he indicated a small fork in the road just south of Lexingar, "to make sure I am prepared in case my theory is correct."

"Why can't you just grab one of them and interrogate them? Can't magicians read minds?"

"You should know better than that after our previous… adventures. Though it is a rumor that has widely circulated, and frankly has been encouraged by others like myself, none of us actually has that ability. As for other interrogation methods, even though I could have stopped the seekers I was tracking, or caught them multiple times, they all clam up when they're in the dungeon. They are incredibly dedicated to their master, and most starve themselves to death when incarcerated. I've been following them, trying to learn their plans, find their leader, and stop them for good."

"And now this group is heading to Lexingar?"

"Not just this group. There are more of them on the move, and they are *all* headed for Lexingar. I've been chasing Mordyar's seekers for a long time, and I have never seen them take a road trip like this. Seekers seek. They blend in, earn people's trust, then subtly ask around for unusual talents, or pose as collectors of magical items. They don't trek most of the way across Denall, or compete for space."

"Wait, we are going to a place where there will be *groups* of seekers gathered? Why didn't you just say that in the first place?" Trae looked around the room exasperated. "Back in my blacksmith shop you could have said, 'Trae, I think all of the stone seekers in Denall are headed to a party, want to come crash it with me?' and I would have replied, 'No Dune, I have to help take care of my family.' Then we could have saved racing around the countryside."

Dune nodded. "There is more to it than just that."

"Okay, will you please tell me what this has to do with me? You can follow them to Lexingar, you can find out what is happening, and you can handle it with your super magic powers. Why did you bring *me* into this?"

In a very sincere tone Dune replied, "I need someone to watch my back. I need someone I can trust completely. My friend, you are the truest man I know. Without your help, I could still be wasting away in that slave camp. I need your help to make sure that others will escape a similar fate." For the first time since this trip had begun, Trae was sure that Dune was being serious with him. He sighed deeply as he sat back in his chair and rubbed his face for a moment.

"Have you ever thought that this might be a trap? The seekers are looking for the stones we carry. If there are dozens of seekers all in one place at one time, that's the place I don't want to be. I'd rather go home, wouldn't you? Let's go home and just forget about Mordyar's stone seekers."

"You may think you can forget about them, but they will always seek you," Dune said sadly. "I heard them talking one night when I was near Eaton. They spoke of a blacksmith who worked all night and didn't seem tired. "

"When did you hear that?" Trae asked.

"When I was leaving Eaton. I thought they were not interested in you, then the leader of their group peeled off and snuck into Norwell to watch you. I've been keeping watch on your shop since I got here, and I stole your iron so he couldn't see you working all night."

"Then you had the Rathan boys work all night in the mine," Trae added, understanding dawning.

Dune nodded. "It seemed a good way to keep him from suspecting you. But now this seeker of ours has turned his course north again at a breakneck pace. There must be something earth-shattering happening there. You need to stay away from your father's blacksmith shop, I need someone I trust, and the Stones of Power need to be protected."

"I guess we don't have much time to waste," Trae conceded.

"That's the spirit," Dune said, standing up. He waved his hands, and the back wall of the cabin slid to one side, revealing a hidden closet filled with curious objects. Trae stared with wide eyes at the collection of armor, weapons, potions, salves, and clothing.

Dune changed into the formal black robes that were traditional for master magicians to wear, and pulled a staff from the closet. The staff looked like any normal short staff, but Trae knew better. Most magicians carried a wooden staff that was enchanted in some way. Dune also pulled a longbow from the closet with a quiver of matching arrows. After retrieving his equipment, he looked at Trae. "Do you want to take anything?"

Trae walked to the small closet and surveyed the weapons and tools. He first reached for a large broadsword.

"I wouldn't use that one. It is cursed with a spell that will attack the user," Dune advised.

Next, Trae reached for a long sword and Dune shook his head. He looked down at the small short sword and then, without reaching for it, he looked to Dune, who was still shaking his head.

"You told me to get a weapon, and now you're telling me not to take any. Why don't you just tell me what you want me to take?"

"That's a great idea," Dune said. He reached into the closet and pulled out a longbow with a quiver. He handed them to Trae, then reached out for a one-handed mace and shield that had matching patterns on them. "That will go very nicely with your armor."

"What armor?"

Dune reached into the closet behind his robes and started pulling out pieces of armor. First the breastplate, then leggings, gauntlets and a helmet. Trae noticed immediately how skillfully the gleaming plate armor was crafted. He picked up a piece and also knew, by the weight, that it was magically enhanced.

"What is the enchantment on this armor?"

"It is stronger and harder than any natural metal, and it is light as a feather, you'll barely feel it," Dune replied. "Put it on and we'll get moving." As Dune left the small cabin, the map rolled up and disappeared, and the wall closed back over the closet.

In a short time, Trae emerged, fully clad in armor. He mounted his horse and hung his shield on the left side of his saddle. "Do you really think I need to wear this while we travel down the road? Won't it attract attention?"

"Not at all," Dune replied. "People will just think we are heading to Lexingar for the tournament. We'll be hiding right out in the open. Besides, you're traveling with a magician in a black robe. How often these days do you see a magician announcing himself with this get-up? I don't think many people will even notice you." The pair moved through the woods back to the main road, then headed north for Lexingar.

CHAPTER 26

"There it is again." Dune said as he pointed to the ground.

"I still don't see what you're pointing at."

"Just look down at the side of the road where it meets the soft sod."

"Okay, I see it now," Trae lied. Every time they passed a sign of the seeker Dune was chasing he tried to show Trae, but Trae was no tracker. He couldn't tell the difference between a horse track and a human track, and on the hard packed road, he couldn't make out any tracks at all.

"That track is about half a day old. You can see that the dirt is dried, and the grass off the edge of the road has been packed down after the print was made, which means we have made up some time today. At this rate, we will catch him before he reaches Lexingar, possibly as early as tomorrow, and hopefully we'll be able to get more information about what he plans to do there."

"I'll take your word for that," Trae commented in a tone that clearly showed he was not interested in any more tracking lessons.

"I'm just showing you because you might need to know how to track someone one day," Dune started. "I just hope my life never depends on you tracking me down."

"Well that makes two of us. How about you do the tracking, and I'll just stay focused on not getting separated?" Trae looked far down the road and sighed loudly while shaking his head.

"What is it?" Dune asked as he stopped looking for tracks and focused up the road. Instantly he had his answer. "Oh no, not another delay!"

A small group of travelers were stopped in front of the Gulpa Bridge while two men engaged in hand to hand combat. The thin bridge was blocked off by five men on either side so the two sparring were undisturbed.

"What are we going to do?" Trae asked.

"I guess we'll have to watch them. This should be fun."

"Can't you just..." Trae moved his hands around in swirling

patterns, "you know, move them out of the way?"

"That only gathers more attention, and makes our trip dangerous. I think it's best for us to just wait for the excitement to die down, and then move on." The two men slowed their horses as they neared the bridge.

On the bridge there was one man in full armor toying with his weaker opponent. The armored man was dodging wild swings and delivering controlled jabs to the other man's torso. He called out taunts and jeers, egging the other man on until the man, sensing his eminent defeat, just dropped his hands to his sides. The man wearing the armor swung a powerful backhand that sent the weaker man sprawling onto the ground where he lay in a heap.

"Who's next?" The man looked into the group of travelers on either side of the bridge. "I'll let you all pass once I've had a challenge. I need to keep warmed up for the tournament."

One of his thugs walked up and held his hands open to the crowd. "Who will be the next to face the powerful Rawley?"

Trae dismounted and a woman who was standing by the bridge, holding a young, crying child, turned to him.

"We've been here for an hour. I need to get home before the rain comes." With pleading in her eyes she looked at Trae. "Please, help us."

Trae pushed into the crowd, "I'll go have a talk with this Rawley."

"Do be careful," the woman warned, "he's a brute!"

Trae pushed through the crowd, making his way to the man who was bellowing out threats and challenges. When the crowd parted slightly, Trae saw the large, fully armored man clearly for the first time. He wore a deep scowl and glared at the audience while he drew his sword and swung it in intricate patterns.

"So I have a challenger!" Rawley said, pointing his sword at Trae.

"I'm just here to cross this bridge."

Ignoring Trae's response he continued. "Pick your weapon and we'll begin."

Trae turned to look at Dune, but he was several paces

behind, riding his horse through the crowd. Not entirely sure what to do, he stood and considered the man.

"What's the problem?" Rawley asked, "Is this warrior afraid of a fight?"

"I'm glad to see that you're excited about the upcoming tournament, but these people really need to get going. You've had your fun, now move on." Trae led his horse forward across the bridge.

"I see we've found a coward." The man mocked as Trae passed him. Trae had learned to ignore empty insults from men with empty heads. He leaned down and helped up the man who had fallen in the last challenge. He helped the man make his way over the bridge and through the thugs on the far side. They crossed completely, disregarding Rawley's comment and existence.

"Perhaps he is a coward, or perhaps he's wise enough to not waste his time and energy on fools." Trae turned to see that Dune had joined him at the edge of the barricade of thugs still seated on his horse.

The man was noticeably unsettled by the presence of a magician. "I was just having some fun, no harm done."

Dune looked down at the man. "What will it take to get you off this road and out of my way?"

"I'm just trying to practice, you know, for the tournament." His voice steadied as he continued. "If your friend can beat me, or at least give me a challenge, we'll be out of your way."

"What if my friend knocks you flat on your back, and breaks your nose and every other bone in your body? Then how will you prepare for this tournament?" Dune looked steadily at the man, not breaking his gaze.

"Can he do that?" the man asked, fear creeping into his voice.

"If you do not take your men and get out of the road, you'll soon find out." Dune spoke softly, but his voice easily carried over the silenced crowd.

The man began to back away and his friends joined him. Dune and Trae stood on one side of the bridge, and Rawley stood on the other. The crowd walked between them, thankful to be moving on.

Thanks and kind words were showered upon Dune and Trae as the crowd passed. On the other side of the road, the travelers were not as friendly. When most of the people had passed, a small boy with a mischievous look, ducked out from behind his mother and spat on Rawley. Rawley reached out with lightning speed and backhanded the small boy with a gauntleted fist, sending him sprawling and crying on the ground, blood streaming down his face.

Before anyone else could react, Trae stepped across the bridge and shoved hard against Rawley. The man, not anticipating Trae's strength, flew backward several feet and lay sprawled on the ground. Trae gently lifted the child.

"Are you all right?"

The mischievous look had been replaced with fear and pain as the boy sobbed. Dune took the boy from Trae's arms.

"I'll take a look at him." Dune tended to the child's needs and Trae turned his attention to Rawley and his band of miscreants.

"That was quite a shove," Rawley remarked. "Want to try that out on my sword?" The travelers spread out to give them space, and Rawley's men fanned out in a half circle.

As Rawley's men drew their weapons, Trae knew they had no intention of making this a fair fight. He felt almost naked as he compared his small mace with the larger swords the men brandished. Fortunately, he was also protected with a medium shield and the feather light armor that would allow him to move more freely than these men could ever manage.

Rawley and his gang crept forward until they were within striking distance. With an evil grin, Rawley made a motion with his sword that directed his men to make the first move. They had witnessed Trae's strength and heard the threats from Dune, so although they outnumbered him, they advanced cautiously and as a group.

Trae had experienced bullying before, and he had some experience with defending himself, but he knew it would take more than brute strength to get out of this mess. Before he could register what was happening, two men advanced on him from both sides. He brought up his mace to deflect the swing of the sword on his right as his shield was raised to block the attack from the left.

As if by its own volition, after blocking the sword strike, the mace turned a half circle and landed a crashing blow on the helmet of the man to his right and the man crumpled to the ground. Surprised by this turn of events, Trae turned his full attention to the fallen man. Seeing a moment of opportunity, the men to his left pressed forward in unison. Trae was struck by one sword in the left shoulder and an instant later he was pushed back by the force of a man who had run shoulder first into Trae's shield.

Focusing on the advancing group on his left, Trae widened his stance and pressed back against his shield. As soon as he moved his shield arm, the force from the left side was gone. Trae lowered his shield, and to his surprise, the man who had pushed against him was flat on his back. At that moment Trae realized that the weapons Dune had picked for him were magically enchanted too.

With an added level of confidence, Trae began to advance on the group. He tried to start at one side of the half circle of men, but within moments they had completely surrounded him. He swung his mace at the oncoming enemies. The mace skillfully deflected swords and counter attacked, striking arms, heads, and chests. Each time an enemy's attack was blocked by the shield, the weapon was not only deflected, but was thrown back with considerable force, often disarming the attacker. Three times men were able to strike Trae, but he did not feel their blows beneath his armor. Within a few short moments, the fight was over.

The only two men left standing from Rawley's crew were incompetent fighters who had lost their weapons while striking the shield. After retrieving their swords, the men thought better of attacking again. Rawley was among the fallen men. Blood gushed down his face from a broken nose and he was clutching his right arm, which was severely broken.

Without speaking a word, or giving them a second thought, Trae turned around.

"How is the boy?"

Dune nodded his head. "He's fine. As soon as he was healed, he kicked me in the shin and ran to his mother."

Trae couldn't stop from smiling. "I really like that kid."

Without another word, the pair mounted their horses and galloped down the road. When they had traveled a safe distance, Trae turned to his friend.

"So when did you intend to tell me about the weapons?"

"Oh yes, thank you for reminding me. Those weapons of yours, they are enchanted. Just be careful not to lose them."

CHAPTER 27

Kaz waited silently in the woods, scanning in all directions for any movements. There was a slight rustle in a tree to his right, but he was not interested in small game today. The caravan had stopped and set up camp for the last time before going into Lexingar for the tournaments. They were stocking up on supplies, and Kaz had become so expert using his bow that they almost expected that when he went into the woods, he'd come back with an animal that had only an arrow wound in its eye.

Caravan life had quickly become a welcome routine for Kaz. While they were stopped at a village for trading, or at a clearing near a lake to replenish their supplies, he completed archery training each day with Boon, then he went hunting.

When they were traveling between stops, he would get up at the crack of dawn, eat, then help strike camp, hitch up the wagons to horses, and then drive until about noon. The caravan only traveled for half days because they needed to hunt, gather, or trade. If they came to a village they would spend two or three days trading before resuming their trek. Most people rode in the wagons or on horseback. For Kaz, Farin, and Angela, the morning was spent walking, jogging or running to keep up with the caravan.

At first, he and Farin struggled to keep up, while Angela easily maintained pace with the moving wagons while wearing her armor and carrying a short sword at her side. Kaz had felt comforted to see he was not the only one bent over, gagging for air every time they slowed down or stopped, but that Farin was also struggling. Angela made it worse by never missing an opportunity to goad them. At least Kaz wasn't wearing armor like Blade made Farin do.

By the end of the first month with the caravan, he and Farin were already noticeably different, and now that nearly three months had passed, he could barely be recognized as the boy who had shot arrows from the woods to save the Algernons. He was eating healthy food each day, and his body was filling out with hard muscle. He was in much better shape, but it was nothing compared to Farin's transformation. Farin was no longer complaining about wearing armor during the morning runs, and looked like he was built to be a blacksmith.

Kaz saw a twitch in the distant woods that brought his thoughts back to his hunt. It could have been a rabbit or squirrel, but from his angle and distance it could also be a deer's ear or tail. He watched the spot and, within a few silent moments, the large buck stepped out from behind a dense row of trees. With a regular bow the deer would have been safe from even the best hunter, but Kaz was not a regular hunter, and his enchanted bow made him deadly at long distances.

He silently drew his bow back and raised it slowly up so he could sight down the shaft of the arrow. A slight breeze made the leaves shift in the woods and the animal perked its ears up. It was on heightened alert and Kaz knew that any sudden movements would mean he had missed this chance. As the wind stopped, he smoothly released the arrow and watched as it found its mark.

As Kaz dragged the buck out of the woods he looked to the row of wagons and saw Farin and Angela still practicing. Farin was working some forms that looked to Kaz like he was doing an elaborate dance with a longsword in his hand. Although he didn't understand much about using a sword, he was impressed at how smoothly Farin handled the weapon, and how quickly he had progressed from the wooden practice swords to using the real thing.

It was also fun for Kaz to watch Angela beat Farin in every match they had in the practice ring. He always came to Kaz with lame excuses about being distracted by her deep green eyes, or reminding Kaz that she was a strongarm, but after almost three months he wondered if Farin was holding back a little in their matches. She moved flawlessly from stance to stance, but despite her experience and strength, Farin seemed to have the advantage of speed.

"Haylan," Kaz called out when he came into the clearing.

Haylan waved at Kaz and rushed over with a small handcart.

"I know he's trying to get you into shape, but I think Boon

should let you get some help dragging the larger animals out of the woods."

"Thanks for the offer," Kaz replied as he hefted the animal into the cart. "But if I do get help before I come into the clearing, I'm sure he'd find some way to make me work out even harder. Besides, this one isn't that big."

Haylan looked down at the animal and then back to Kaz.

"It's pretty big," he countered. "Thanks!"

"Any time," he responded. "How much more do you need?"

"I don't know," he hesitated for a moment and looked over his animals. "Maybe one more in a day or two should do it. They take time to butcher, and we'll be leaving for Lexingar before we know it."

"Sounds like a plan," Kaz said as he grabbed the handle of the cart and helped Haylan take the animal the rest of the way to his wagon. "I'll check in with you in two days to see if you need anything."

"Perfect," Haylan replied. "I talked with Blade today, and he has some arrows for you, but he said they're the last ones he's fletching for you, so be careful with them."

Kaz grinned and headed off toward Blade's wagon. On his way through camp he passed the caravan families who had become his friends over the past months of traveling. They were mostly hard at work getting supplies and wares ready for the tournaments. Kaz had never been this far from Dungan, but even he had heard a little about the event where men and women from across Denall gathered to compete in events to win prizes and prestige. As the activity among the Algernons increased, so did his excitement and anticipation to attend this event.

When he arrived at Blade's wagon, Kaz lifted his chin in greeting.

"I heard you made some arrows for me," Kaz began, "Thank you."

"Actually, Farin made this batch," he answered. "They're not good enough for me to sell in Lexingar, so I figured I could let you have them."

"Thanks a lot," Kaz responded unenthusiastically. He looked over at his friend, still working through some stances. "He's a much better swordsman than he is a fletcher."

Blade nodded, "You've got that right. But he is getting better," he added. Kaz looked down at the arrows, and they did look pretty good. "Besides, I don't want you shattering the shafts of my arrows while you show off."

Kaz held his hand to his chest pretending to be offended. "Show off? I just do what Boon tells me to do."

"Right," Blade responded unconvinced. "And you don't seem to mind at all when the girls gather to watch you do target practice."

Not liking the direction the conversation had taken, Kaz reached down and picked up the arrows. "Speaking of target practice, I think I'd better get going."

Kaz walked back out into the woods and sat down on a large, fallen tree. Although it had been a lot of work and it wasn't an easy way of life, he had enjoyed his time with the Algernon Caravan. The closer they got to Lexingar, the more he thought about what he wanted to do, and the more he realized that he didn't know.

He could easily see himself staying with the caravan traveling around, hunting and working, flirting with the girls and being Boon's apprentice. He could finish his Troven in safety and see a lot of the country, but for him it seemed like a bit of a cheat.

For Farin staying made sense, he had always wanted to travel the country and have sword training, and he was getting both of those things. And Blade was starting to train him in fletching, leather work, and repairing weapons. For Kaz it was just like being a kid back in Dungan. Doing chores for different families, helping out when he could, but never really having his own place. He felt like he was again in a rut, happily going on in life, but not really in control. He wanted to do something meaningful and lasting. He wanted to make a difference before he went back home, but he didn't know how.

CHAPTER 28

Dune and Trae rode through the drizzling rain on the road to Lexingar. The larger man, in full plate armor, hunched against the cold wind that magnified the chill of the rain. He shivered briefly and tried again to retain his heat by hugging himself. He turned to his right and saw, with frustration, that his tall companion rode, back straight, seemingly unaffected by the weather. The rain had left a sheet of water over the hard packed road that completely erased tracks. After several hours of plodding slowly north, they dismounted and pulled some fruit leather and hard tack from their saddlebags.

"How much farther will we be going today?" Trae asked as he pulled a bite off.

"Given the way our seeker left Norwell in such a hurry, and the fact that we haven't caught up to him, he must be in quite a hurry to get to Lexingar. If something significant is happening among the seeker population of Denall, I want to make sure we don't miss it. We'll travel all day and slow down if we happen to catch up to him tomorrow."

"What if he stops today to take shelter from this weather? Won't we pass him?"

Dune considered the possibility for a moment before responding. "You might be right, but arriving before he does wouldn't be so bad. It would provide an opportunity to look around, see what other seekers we can find. I'll wager good money, though, that he is still pushing forward."

"I guess that makes sense, but I can't imagine anyone crazy enough to travel hours on end in such depressing weather." Trae made eye contact with Dune to be sure he didn't miss the implication. Then he rubbed his arms to lessen the chill on his soaked body.

Finished with his meal, Dune replaced his things in the saddle bag, grabbed the pommel of the saddle, and easily swung up onto his horse.

"Looks like the rain will be stopping soon." Dune pointed to a clear blue patch through the clouds.

"That is something to be happy about," Trae replied as he climbed up into the saddle. He kicked his horse into action and they continued down the road, chasing the clear sky. They rode for another hour in the drizzling rain before they were at last bathed in sunlight.

When the sun came through the clouds, Trae marveled at how beautiful the countryside was. On the horizon, a rainbow extended across the sky, arcing over the rolling landscape. There were some houses and small villages peppered along this well-traveled road, but mostly it was hills and open space.

From time to time a patch of trees gave variety to the otherwise cleared land. As they came out of a small forest, Trae motioned for Dune's attention.

"Do you see that pheasant?" He pointed at the bird.

Without any reply Dune pulled his bow from off his shoulder and nocked an arrow. "Looks like dinner to me."

Trae raised an eyebrow, then pulled on the reins, bringing his horse to a stop. "We must be seventy five paces from that bird. Are you sure you can make that shot?"

Dune released the pressure on his bow and turned to look at Trae. "Where would you like me to hit it?" he asked, voice filled with confidence.

Trae began to laugh lightly, "I think if you can hit the bird at all it will be a miracle."

Dune pulled his long bow to a full draw and released the bowstring, sending the arrow sailing at the plump bird. The sound of the bowstring and the arrow startled the bird. When alerted, the bird raised its head a few inches to listen for danger, not knowing that this small movement had saved its life. The arrow sailed through the air where the bird's head had been. The bird took flight far across the field and Trae's laughter filled the air.

"Do you think you can do better?" Dune asked, challenging his friend.

"I think we both know I could have hit that pheasant," Trae said with slight amusement as he urged his horse into motion. "I'm just impressed at how close you came to hitting it."

"Anyone could have hit the pheasant," Dune said, "I was aiming for its eye."

"Why would you ever need to hit something so small at this distance?" Trae asked, furrowing his brow.

"You might be surprised," Dune answered cryptically.

"I doubt it. It sounds to me like a pretty lame excuse for missing the bird." Trae looked ahead and urged his horse back into a walk.

"Could you hit a bird's head at seventy five paces?" Dune asked from two steps behind.

Trae looked over his shoulder at his friend. "I already told you, there's no need. I'd just make sure I hit the bird."

"So, are you saying it is too much of a challenge for you?"

Trae pulled his bow from the case and stopped his horse. "Pick a target."

Searching for just the right target, Dune carefully looked in the trees and bushes.

"The knot on the maple tree," Dune pointed, "right there, where the road begins to dip."

Trae pulled an arrow back, released his breath, and then shot the arrow at the tree. He had never used the bow before and he overestimated the pull weight. The arrow thudded into the tree an entire hand span lower than he anticipated.

"That would need to be one large pheasant." Dune commented.

"That tree is easily one hundred paces," Trae complained, "and it was my first time ever using your bow."

"Take another shot then," Dune encouraged, "Two if you need them."

Trae pulled a second arrow, drew it, and released. The second arrow struck just one hair to the left of the knot.

"That is too bad," Dune said. "Good thing I packed food for our trip or we would definitely go hungry."

"Why don't you make the shot," Trae retorted. "You can even have two shots if you need them."

Dune shook his head. "I will certainly not need a second shot." Pulling back his bowstring he released, and the arrow struck the tree right next to Trae's. After the first missed shot, he pulled a second arrow from his quiver, drew, and released, hitting the exact center of the knot. Not wanting to be outdone, Trae took a third shot at the tree and was able to get an arrow inside the knot. They kicked their horses into a canter and retrieved their arrows. Their friendly archery challenge continued through the afternoon, and by the time they were ready to stop for dinner, they had a fat pheasant that had been shot through the eye.

"This is delicious!" Trae commented as he took another bite of the succulent bird.

"That was a great shot." Then tapping his temple as though he had forgotten something Dune finished, "Remind me who shot that bird in the eye."

"You did," Trae conceded between bites, "but if it came to a real archery tournament, I'd definitely come out on top."

"Well, it's too bad we're not going to Lexingar to enter an archery tournament. I guess we'll never find out." Dune then wiped his mouth clean. "Are you ready for sleep?"

"Who's going to take the first watch?"

Shaking his head Dune turned around, "Well, you can take watch if you like, but I'm just going to sleep." Dune turned around and placed his hands in front of himself palms together. When he extended his hands downward a small movement happened in the soil directly in front of him. Then as he spread his hands, an opening appeared in the ground, just big enough for a person. "Do you want one?"

"Absolutely!" Trae said excitedly.

Dune created a small shelter for Trae, then motioned for Trae to enter. "I'll seal off and conceal the top so you'll be safe. I'll also set up something for the horses. Get some rest. You'll need it tomorrow."

* * * * *

"Here we are." Dune declared abruptly as he reigned in his horse.

"Here we are where?" Trae asked, confused as he looked around at the empty crossroads.

"You remember our little planning meeting at my stash house? I told you that I would need to take a detour to make sure I am prepared in case my theory about the seekers' meeting is correct."

"What about needing to get to Lexingar as soon as possible? Remember riding all day in the freezing rain?"

"It's true, we do need to make sure that we have eyes in Lexingar to make sure we don't miss any developments regarding the seekers' plans…"

Trae stopped his horse, "So, we need to split up."

"Are you sure?" Dune asked.

Trae nodded confidently. "I'll keep moving forward, slowly. If I pass the seeker, or if he passes me, we'll know where he is, I'll keep an eye on him until you get back. How long is your detour going to take you?"

"It's entirely possible I could catch up to you before you reach Lexingar, but I can't guarantee it. I need to gather some items, and it may take longer than anticipated."

"You can teleport! How long can it possibly take for you to grab what you need and meet back up with me? You'll definitely catch up to me before I reach Lexingar."

Dune shook his head with a chuckle, "You know I can't just vanish and appear at the crossroads, right? Teleporting has its limits. If I don't get back in time, report to Sir Theodore that I am on the trail of a mid-level seeker who may lead us to the head of the organization."

"Wait a minute!" Trae held up his hand to stop Dune from saying anything further. "You work for Sir Theodore?"

He shook his head and pressed his lips into a line. "No, I work *with* Sir Theodore." Dune said. "I just doubt you'd be able to get an audience with my direct superior."

"Are you serious? The King?" Trae asked in amazement.

"Please stay focused with me for a minute," Dune scolded, then continued. "If you beat me to Lexingar, go to Goldsmyth Lane and stay in the magic shop. If I haven't come in a day or two, report my progress to Sir Theodore. You can find him at the barracks beneath the stadium. I'll meet you there as soon as I possibly can."

"Wait, Goldsmyth Lane? What should I tell the owner?"

"Well I imagine Uncle Morgin will be happy to have company."

"Your Uncle Morgin? I doubt he will be very happy to see me." Trae was beginning to feel like the challenges of this little expedition were getting out of control.

"I'll get something worked out. If he gives you any trouble, tell him that I'll be arriving shortly."

"This sounds more and more like you'd better meet me before we get to Lexingar," Trae concluded, not liking the contingency plan.

"Then I'd best be off," Dune responded.

"Safe travels."

Dune inclined his head. "To you as well, my friend. Be cautious, the seekers can be anywhere. Probably best to travel as we did in Egtharnton." He then waved his hands in small circles in the air while looking directly at Trae. He then made a slight nod, "That will do."

"What was that?" Trae asked, but without saying another word, Dune handed the reins of his horse to Trae and vanished.

Walking slowly down the road waiting for Dune to gather some materials for a mysterious contingency didn't seem like a very dangerous part of the plan, but he would still follow Dune's advice to use caution. When he had first met Dune, and helped him escape from a magician work camp, they had gone by fake names, dressed in farmer's clothing, and pretended to have nose marks. He guessed that nobody would recognize him as a blacksmith while he was in a full suit of armor, especially if he called himself by his made up name from that summer several years ago, Trevor.

Trae continued north through that day and into the early afternoon. The rolling hills that he once considered so pretty were becoming so similar he wondered if he was making any headway. Although he had no idea what he was searching for, he continued to look at the ground from time to time for some kind of track, but all he saw were some wheel ruts from a horse-drawn cart. Throughout the day, Trae saw no sign of the seeker, but he did shoot a medium sized rabbit that he slung to his saddle.

As the sun set, Trae realized that there was no village or farmhouse in sight, and he searched for a small patch of trees or other safe place to rest his head for the night. In the distance he saw the orange glow of a fire and urged his horse toward it.

Years ago, when traveling with his father as an apprentice blacksmith, he had been taught how to travel safely. Fires in the woods at night were sometimes used as decoys to lure people into a trap, so they always needed to be approached with caution. Although Trae knew he needed to exercise caution, he also knew that there would be many travelers on this road, and most people making camp would welcome the company to share the night watches.

When closing in on the fire, Trae could see that it was small, not big enough to give heat to more than five or six people. He dismounted and made sure to make sufficient noise while approaching that it was no surprise when he emerged into the cleared camp site. As a measure of caution, his mace hung loosely by his side in case he needed to make a hasty escape. When he reached the light of the fire, he showed his empty hands clearly and addressed the group.

"Hello, gentlemen."

His greeting was not entirely accurate as there was a woman in the group, but with her size and her back being turned, it was an honest mistake. In addition to the woman, there were three men in this group. One man had an arrow nocked and ready to be drawn, and the other two nervously held their weapons. "What is your business here, warrior?"

"I'm just traveling north to the tournaments, looking for a place to rest. Is there room at your fire?" Trae turned his back on the group and untied the rabbit from his saddle. He knew turning his back left him completely exposed, but by the look of this group, they were not setting an ambush. Having retrieved the rabbit, Trae added, "I also need a place to cook this, and some friends to share it."

The woman nodded to the man sitting next to her, and then he motioned for Trae to join them. "My name's Wilbur, this is my wife, Melna."

"I'm Trevor," he reached forward to grasp Wilbur's hand, and was greeted with a firm handshake.

"Good to meet you, Trevor. I'll start getting that skinned," Wilbur said, motioning for the rabbit, which Trae handed over. "You can tie your horses up on the other side of camp with ours, then come join us."

After taking care of the horses, Trae took his place, sitting on the ground close to the fire. Wilbur was almost done getting the rabbit ready to cook, and the other men had resumed their previous conversation. A short, but rather large man was speaking.

"I know I won't win, but I'm hoping to get the right people's attention. Then maybe I can get some work escorting supplies, or guarding a noble's keep, or something like that."

"Have you thought of joining the army?" Trae asked.

"Haven't you been listening to anything I've been saying?" he said as he turned to see who had spoken. "No, I guess you haven't. Hi Trevor, I'm Rafe. Right now I'm not on the best of terms with the army."

"Oh, sorry to hear that," Trae said awkwardly.

The other man by the fire smiled broadly, then broke the silence.

"Don't worry, Trevor. We've just been sharing why we're going to Lexingar. Wilbur, Melna, and I are going in to do some trading. Each year we meet up on the road to Lexingar. They just picked me up yesterday."

"So that must be your wagon over by the horses."

"You bet. We specialize in woodworking. Lexingar tournament is our busiest time. It takes us almost two seasons to make the crafts we sell in just a few days." He looked around as if to search for unseen listeners, then continued. "My real passion is collecting unique magical items. Nothing big, mind you, just small trinkets and the like."

"He's obsessed!" Melna clicked her tongue as she cut Edgar off.

Waving his hand dismissively, he continued, "Do you have any magical items? I'll pay a fair price."

Shaking his head, Trae responded, "I'm sorry. I don't have any need to trade magical trinkets."

"Well that's too bad. If you do find any at the tournament, let me know. We'll be pitching a large, green tent just north of town to sell wares with some other craftsmen."

Wilbur rolled his eyes and waved the man to silence, "Enough with the sales pitch, Edgar. I want to hear his story. Can I guess by your armor and horse that you're going to try the joust?" he asked.

Trae groped for some good reason why he was headed in that direction.

"Uh, no, I'm just meeting a friend there. We like to watch the action."

Edgar nodded. "Of course he's not going to compete. That armor and those weapons of his would disqualify him immediately." Everybody's attention was turned on Edgar, and he looked directly into Trae's surprised eyes. "I told you, I specialize in magical items."

Caught completely off guard and locked in a penetrating stare from Edgar, Trae was beginning to feel cornered.

"You can never be too careful," he said, "lots of thugs and bandits around lately."

Edgar broke eye contact and looked around casually, "You are absolutely right. You can never be too careful. That's why I'm looking for magical items. They can mean the difference between life and death if you should ever get in a pinch."

"Here we go again. When have you ever been in a pinch?" Wilbur said, but he was cut off by Edgar.

"That armor was enchanted within the last year by a very powerful circle of magicians. If you could just tell me where you got it, I would be greatly indebted to you."

Shaking his head, Trae exhaled slowly, choosing his words

very carefully. “I’m sorry, I can’t help you. This was given to me as a gift. A friend of mine gave it to me as thanks for help protecting his goods on a recent business trip.”

“That is a friend indeed,” Edgar replied, then looked up to everyone around the campfire. “I’m sorry to dominate the party. I just get a little crazy about magical things.” He then smiled at Trae. “If your friend ever has trade business down south, send him to my shop. I run a small woodworking shop just north of Eaton.” At the mention of Eaton, Trae started to connect all the dots. Dune had lost the seeker’s tracks right around the time Edgar said he had started riding on the cart with Wilbur and Melna. Edgar was asking for small, magical trinkets. Trae’s mouth went dry as he realized he had found the stone seeker, the very stone seeker who might recognize him as the blacksmith from Norwell. He wondered how close Edgar had gotten to his shop. Had he gotten a clear look at his face?

Forcing the words to come, he responded, trying to keep his voice level. “I’ll keep that in mind. If he mentions such a trip, I will be sure to send him your way.” He watched Edgar for a reaction, but the other man did not seem to know who he was. He hadn’t acted like he recognized Trae when he first came to their fire. Maybe the suit of armor and fake name were enough to keep him safe, but either way Trae felt very vulnerable. He subtly pulled some of his hair down over his face, hoping it would help maintain his cover.

“If you ever see him again will you send him *my* way?” Rafe cut in. All the men around the fire laughed – all but Rafe.

The fire sizzled as some juice from the rabbit dropped off the spit. “This shouldn’t take too much longer. It’ll be nice to have some fresh meat,” Wilbur commented. “Trevor, would you mind turning this for a bit, I need to take my medicine.” Wilbur moved aside to allow Trae to take a turn at the spit, then removed a strange bottle from his belt and took a drink.

“Do you want to join us tomorrow? We’re all going to Lexingar. It’s much safer to travel as a group, and you seem like a good man,” Melna offered suddenly. It struck him then that the way Melna and Wilbur kept returning their eyes to his magical armor was much the same as Edgar. If it was true that Edgar met up with them yearly to trade together, perhaps it was because they all shared the same true profession.

"I don't know," Trae said, "I usually leave very early." He tried to think of another way to find out more about Edgar's friends as Wilbur took back control of the spit. Then an idea came to him. "Actually, I have to get there soon enough to meet up with my friend. When he last wrote to me, he said he had some special stones he wanted to trade before the tournament, but was concerned about security. We are meeting up to conduct some business, and then will enjoy the festivities."

It was subtle, but at the mention of "special stones," Wilbur, Melna, and Edgar all startled noticeably. Rafe simply went on picking at his fingernails.

"I am interested in trading for magical stones. I'm actually sort of an expert on stones. Do you think you might be able to persuade your friend to give me a chance to bid on some of his merchandise?"

"I will speak with him when I see him in Lexingar." Trae's heart was beating quickly now that he knew he would be sharing a campsite tonight with not one, but three seekers. He didn't trust them, and the less time he spent with them, the less likely they would be to learn more about him or the Strength Stone he carried. However, he also knew that staying with them might be his best chance to learn more about their plans in Lexingar. He would need some time to think.

"We're up pretty early each morning, so do feel free to join us. You can stay with us as long as you like, though we don't want to slow you down." Wilbur then turned his attention back to the rabbit, making sure to keep the spit turning.

CHAPTER 29

After a pleasant summer trading season, the caravan had arrived at Lexingar a week and a half before the tournaments. They had set up outside the city with the wagons in a circular formation, and the tents set up inside the ring of wagons. In Lexingar they were able to trade for goods from many different places, and after their journey, they had supplies and were ready for a longer-term stay. On the first day at their new home, Kaz and Farin had gone into Lexingar to deliver Baby.

It was especially difficult for Farin as he said goodbye to the horse Garin had procured for them. Giving the horse back was like parting with something that connected him to his brother. The remainder of that trip into Lexingar, Farin had been very quiet and went straight to their tent when they returned to the caravan.

On their walk through the large city the next day, Farin seemed back to his usual self, and as they walked, Kaz realized that for the first time in a long time, despite the crowds, they were largely alone.

"So Kaz," Farin began. "What are you planning on doing now that we're safely here?"

"I don't know. Part of me wants to go back to check on Bendar, part of me wants to just join the archers in the army and never turn back. I've also thought of going to Norwell like we planned, but with all that has changed, that just doesn't seem right." Then with a shake of his head he continued. "But the biggest part of me just wants to take Angela and run off into the sunset." With that last comment Kaz earned a sturdy punch from his friend. Kaz often teased Farin about his close friendship with Angela. "What? The way she looks at me when I'm practicing is like; well I guess it's like all the other girls."

"Yeah, she wants to laugh and then run the other way like all the other girls."

Then he spoke in a sarcastically serious tone. "Farin, you don't have to make fun, I can't help it that I'm so much better than you in every way…" With that Farin just shook his head and shoved Kaz. Unfortunately for Kaz, the shove carried him out into the cobblestone street and in front of a carriage.

The two laughed as Kaz gave an over exaggerated bow of apology to the patrons of the carriage and resumed walking off to the side of the street.

"Seriously Kaz, what do you think Bendar is doing?"

"I don't know. Bendar left us, which makes me think he has some kind of. . . you know. . . maybe he had a plan that we would only ruin if we showed up. Maybe he got away and is headed down south to the universities like he wanted, or maybe he is back in Hillside, or back out west on a sailing ship, trading in the islands. We have no way of knowing." At this point Kaz was shaking his head.

Farin interjected. "I've been giving it a lot of thought lately, and I can't think of any good outcome for us going back for him."

Kaz looked over his shoulder, then back at Farin. "What do you mean?"

"If he didn't get to Omer's keep, then we'd feel completely foolish showing up there asking about him. If he's with Omer and in prison, we'd be caught too. If he's there and alive, he gave himself up so we could go free, and having us go there would negate what he did for us. No matter what, if we show up, Aldis will want to have a word with us. If he's dead, we might be putting ourselves in the same danger."

"Stop right there!" Kaz cut him off.

"I know we said we wouldn't consider that, but we have to be realistic. What good can we possibly do for him?"

The minutes dragged on as Kaz searched for some answer, but in the end conceded. "I guess you're right, I just don't want to leave him if he needs us. If he is in prison, I want to go in and do anything in my power to get him out." Again Kaz looked over his shoulder.

Farin followed Kaz's gaze, but saw nothing in the crowd.

"Did you see something? You keep looking back there."

"I'm sure it was nothing. What were you saying?"

"Blade said that the caravan is planning on staying here for a month, two at the most, then heading up the Gulpa River and cutting across to Kinstock, then heading back toward Hillside. If we stayed, we could keep training and take the entire caravan through to trade with Omer. We'd be safe through the winter, and in the spring when we got to Omer's vineyards, we'd get answers." Farin waited a minute to let his plan sink in. "And we could see some more of Denall before we settle down."

Kaz looked thoughtfully at Farin. "And you wouldn't have to leave Angela."

Trying to cover an obvious blush, Farin brushed off the remark. "Oh come on, seriously. That's not why… I'm just trying to make sense of everything."

"I know." Then, with a mischievous look Kaz added, "But it sure is fun to tease you about your new girl."

"I'm not going to explain this to you again." Then after a pause and an innocent look from Kaz he continued. "She's not my girl -- you know that. You're such a pain."

When he had stopped grinning at Farin's reaction, Kaz made one more serious comment.

"Your plan makes sense, but I'm just not sure it's the best plan for me. I don't know if I can leave him there until the spring. Either way, the caravan will be here for at least a couple of weeks, so we have some time to think it through." Their conversation trailed off as they left Lexingar through the main gate and headed back to the caravan.

A slim figure inconspicuously slipped down a side alley, a slight grin of satisfaction on her face, confident that she had found the one she was looking for.

Returning to the caravan, Farin and Kaz came upon Angela, who was crouching behind some water barrels.

"What are you doing?" Kaz asked in a louder than needed voice.

"Shhh!" Angela gestured for them to get down with her. "They're talking about us."

While both Kaz and Farin waited in anticipation, Angela did not add anything.

"What are they saying?" Farin finally asked.

"I don't know," Angela said pointing to her left arm. "For some reason, being a strongarm doesn't help me hear what they are saying." Then turning to Kaz Angela asked, "Kaz, do you know anyone who could possibly help us *hear* what is happening in there?"

Responding to this obvious plea for help, the marks on Farin's ear lobe darkened and he shared the conversation that he heard.

"How do you think they'll do?" Odon asked the trainers.

Blade was the first to answer. "He's good, but I wish I had another year with him, or two. If he goes out into the real world, he could very well get himself killed before he ever realizes his potential."

Boon was shaking his head. "Kaz is very different," the larger man said with a frown. "He already far exceeds my greatest expectations. I'm encouraging him to move on. With the bow, I don't know if he could find a teacher; he's the best I've ever seen. He is pretty good with the staff, but with that bow in hand he'll never have to use it."

"I've talked to both of them and tried to get them to stay," Odon said. "They are very hard to convince."

"They've been through a lot," Blade said.

"And they feel the pressure from their village tradition to do everything on their own," Boon added. "I wish there was a way to help push them to seek some help in getting better."

"Why not sign them up to compete in the annual tournament," Boon suggested.

"I don't know," Odon replied at this suggestion. "It might give them the boost they need to seek more help, but we don't want them getting hurt."

"It can't kill them, and it may bring them the humility they need," Boon countered.

Blade's voice was filled with concern as he asked, "What if they win?"

Odon whistled. "Maybe you need to learn some humility too. They're young, never been in a tournament, and they would be facing nobles who train their whole lives for this. I don't think they'll win."

Boon nodded, but not to Odon. "Odon, I know we're pretty disconnected from what happens in the world, but I've never seen anyone shoot a bow like Kaz."

"Blade, do you really believe Farin could win? Has he ever won a match?" Odon asked. "Also, the tournaments require that the contestants can't use magical equipment. Can Kaz make those shots with a regular longbow?"

"We have nothing to lose by having them compete," Boon finally said. "If they win, they may realize what a benefit it has been to have been able to train with us, and they may want to stay for more, if they lose they may especially feel the need to pursue further training to become better. We have faith in our apprentices, and there doesn't seem to be a downside."

Blade added, "Odon, I know that you are proud of them, just as we are. I think this is a great opportunity for them to gain some experience and hopefully see some of their hard work pay off."

"We'll do it!" Farin said, bursting into the tent.

"Farin, how many times have I told you not to listen in on conversations?" Blade halfheartedly scolded. Then his look turned grim when he realized Angela was with them. "Young lady, the answer is definitely no!"

"But Daddy, if I don't go, who's going to win? Farin's going to get experience losing--why can't I go to actually win?" Ignoring Farin's mock-offended face and looking only at her dad, Angela made a pleading face that only a teenage girl can make.

The three contestants were entered into the Lexingar annual tournament; Kaz for archery, and Farin and Angela for the sword. That was the last trip into the city for the young men. The next morning, training changed drastically, as the trainers prepared their students for competition instead of survival.

CHAPTER 30

In the morning, Trae tied his pack horse to the small horse-drawn cart before the group headed north together. The previous night's conversation had been friendly enough, but after realizing he was sharing a fire with at least three seekers, Trae was on alert for any clue they might give about their plans after the tournament, or the real reason for their gathering. He also felt scrutiny behind Edgar's questions or sidelong glances, making him choose his words very carefully. He wanted to be away from the seekers, and especially Edgar who might eventually recognize him, but he also understood that the best way to know what they were doing and where they were going was to travel with them.

The group stayed together through the next days as they plodded along toward Lexingar. During their final day of being together, three more companions joined their traveling group: one couple who lived two days' travel south of Lexingar, and who would be selling their pottery under the great, green tent Melna was bringing into Lexingar packed on her large, horse-drawn wagon next to several large barrels of what Trae had guessed was some sort of liquor, and another lone traveler who was going as a spectator. Trae watched Edgar interrogate the man about magical items while Wilbur and Melna waited for the man to respond, then silenced Edgar and made the man feel more at ease. They worked together so well that Trae would have never have suspected them to be working together if he didn't already know to look for the tell-tale sign of obsession with magical items. He also noticed that they never questioned the potters, which gave him some clues about the green tent.

After eight days of traveling, a distance that should have taken six, they arrived at Lexingar. They said goodbye, wished each other luck, and Edgar gave a final reminder to visit the green tent if they ever found any unique magical trinkets, jewelry, or stones. When everyone had parted to go their separate ways, Trae silently moved to a side street to think things through.

It was difficult to find a place to stop with his two horses in the crowded streets. The tournament was starting the next day, and already the population had swelled. When he found a place to stop, Trae watched the crowd for someone who looked local. After a few moments, he was able to pick out an elderly man who was not following any of the knights or running in and out of the shops. He guessed this man was not from out of town. "Excuse me, sir. Can you tell me how to get to…Smyth Street?"

"Well lad, there is no Smyth Street that I know of, but there is a Blacksmyth, Goldsmyth, and Rosesmyth. Not sure how that last one got its name. It's an odd name for a road, Rosesmyth. But all the same, where are you headed?"

"Goldsmyth, that was the name."

"You'll continue down this road to the end, then take a right. In three blocks, you'll find Goldsmyth. It's a long road, what kind of shop are you looking for?"

"Nothing in particular, just heard it was a good street to do some shopping."

"Aye, it's a great street for that sort of thing. You'll probably want to stable those horses before going down that way, it's very crowded. There's a stable on Rosesmyth Street that has some space. That's down there, second road to the left. Odd name for a street – Rosesmyth. Don't you think?"

"Yes it is rather odd."

"That's what I've been telling Maybell all these years. Why did we move to a city that would up and name a road Rosesmyth?"

"Thank you very much!" Trae said when the man took a breath. He was beginning to think this man might not be the most reliable source for getting directions. "I appreciate the help. Enjoy the tournament."

"Oh yes, the tournament. I'll probably lock myself in my blacksmith shop while my wife sells some of our wares. Have you ever seen a piece of wrought iron turned into a rose?"

"I don't think I ever have," Trae responded. "Thanks again for the help."

"Well if you ever want to see one, go down this road, and

take your second left. We live above the shop, so we're always home."

"Okay, thank you again." Trae led his horses behind him as he moved down the road. The man waved kindly. Trae determined to avoid talking to anyone as long as he could. He walked down to the end of the small side street and turned right onto Goldsmyth Street. Despite the man's warnings, it was not overly crowded, and Trae continued walking, keeping a watch out for magic shops.

Trae looked at each building as he passed down the street. There was a mix of houses, inns, and shops. After several blocks he was beginning to think he should turn around and try the other direction. He had already seen three jewelry shops and two armorers. Trae tugged on the reins and led his horses down the road, deciding whether to keep walking or to return the way he came, he heard a familiar whistle. He perked his head up and looked for the source of the sound. He heard it again, and headed to the empty alley between two buildings. Once out of the main street and in the shadows, he heard the whistle again from farther in the darkness. Trae reached up to his saddle and retrieved his mace while he cautiously proceeded down the alley.

The whistle came again, and Trae knew that it was Dune making the sound, but he didn't understand why he was not showing himself or why was he luring Trae down this alley.

"I'm here," Trae called. "Come on out into the light." In response, he heard a faint whisper that he could not make out. "What was that?"

This time, slightly louder, he heard his friend, "Get back here and keep quiet."

Trae looked behind himself to see if he had attracted any attention, then he walked farther into the alley, following the sound of his friend's voice. Without any warning, Trae felt air compress around his body, stopping him from being able to move or speak. Dune stepped out of the shadows and quickly waved his arms in spiraling patterns as he walked beside the horses. After walking the full length of the horses on both sides, he repeated the hand movements around Trae, and then he nodded.

"It appears that you are safe." With this pronouncement, Trae found himself released from the air.

"What was all of that?" he demanded, throwing his arms up in the air in frustration.

"I was checking for any curses, or spells, but like I said, you're safe. Come with me." Dune turned and walked down the alley and sat down on a small crate. "So, what did you learn from our seeker friends?"

"Wait just one minute," Trae said, holding his hand up. "How did you know about them?"

Dune looked at his friend innocently. "I've been following you for a couple of days. I acquired what I needed as quickly as could have been hoped," he held up a small, green bottle of liquid, "and then caught up with you well before you reached Lexingar." Trae's mouth dropped open in surprise and annoyance. "So what did you learn from them?" Dune asked before Trae could have another outburst.

"I don't know where to start," Trae began, scratching his head. "They are meeting in a green tent on the north side of the city. They're posing as craftsmen selling their wares."

"A green tent, that's very interesting. Did they say how many would be there?" Dune asked, he pulled out a small notebook.

"No, but I think I was traveling with five."

Dune raised his hand to cover his mouth, then lowered it to his chin, as if in contemplation. He then scribbled some notes on a piece of paper. "Five seekers in one place, that was risky for you. It's a good thing you are in disguise."

"What? Do you mean dressing up like a knight in all this armor?" Trae asked, pointing at the breastplate. "You never did explain how to take it off."

"I was actually referring to your face, but the armor also had its purpose," Dune replied, voice filled with amusement.

Trae stopped searching for the opening on his armor.

"My face?" Trae asked, touching his cheek, "What is wrong with my face?"

Dune looked down the alley and saw a small rain barrel. "This will be fun. Come on over here." He stood beside the large, wooden barrel. "Take a look."

Trae slowly leaned over the barrel, not knowing what to expect. In the reflection, he saw dark hair, green eyes, and a rather large, unshapely nose. He suppressed the urge to scream out and looked sternly at Dune. "Take it off."

Dune raised his pointer finger and spoke as a teacher addressing a student. "Listen, Trevor, it was for your own protection."

"Take it off!" Trae repeated more loudly.

Dune took a step backward. "Calm down. It'll only last another week."

"Another week!" Trae burst out. "I'm going to look like this for another week? Is there anything else you haven't told me?"

Dune smiled broadly, "I suggest you continue to go by Trevor."

"Gladly. I don't want to taint my good name with this ugly mug." Trae's words came out in a flurry.

"And one more thing," Dune added, as though he had just thought of it.

"Really? More? Did you make me have a pot belly and a furry chest under this armor?" Trae was getting restless and started pulling at his armor to get it off.

"Oh yeah, there's a bit of a trick to that. You need to press up in here." As he said this he reached up to the small of Trae's back, and with a clicking sound the armor opened easily. Once free of the armor, Trae threw it to the ground and ran back to the barrel. Dune spoke from behind him while Trae scrubbed his face ferociously. "It's actually about your stone."

"What about my stone?" Trae asked, still annoyed at his friend.

"The seekers can see magical items. When you use a magical item, it is especially easy to spot." Trae stood up, turned around and looked to his friend. "The armor covers your body, but more importantly, it covers the stone."

"I haven't used the stone in the last eight days. I haven't

needed to."

"That's good. Those stones are powerful, so if you had, they might have seen it even through your armor," Dune replied.

Trae was still frustrated that his friend hadn't told him about the disguise or the power of the seekers, but he was happy for the protection.

"How can they see magic?"

"Magicians can cast a simple spell to detect magical items, or see what magical items can do, but not even magicians can see magic like seekers." Dune looked down the alley before continuing in a softer voice. "When they become seekers, they make a vow to seek the Stones of Power till they die. They drink an elixir that helps them see magic."

Trae nodded. "That sounds pretty good. Do you have any of it?"

Dune shook his head in disgust. "It's not that simple. The elixir changes them so that they crave magical items. In time, they become blind to everything else. The elixir is a poison."

"So you're saying that magical items are all they think about?" Trae asked, confusion showing on all his magically altered features.

"No, it's much worse than that. In time, magical items are all that they can see. They literally give up their sight, and they also give up their sanity, though that takes a little longer."

Trae scrunched his face in concentration for a moment. "How long does it take till they, you know, go blind and crazy?"

"That is a mystery," Dune said with a shrug, "but they do slow down the process using another potion. Did you notice their bottles?" Dune asked, tapping his belt.

"Now that you mention it, they each had the same kinds of bottles in leather cords tied around their waists. They drank from the bottles every few hours or so. I just thought it was a different way to carry water."

"That was no water," Dune said in a dark tone. "Those bottles are what help them keep their sight and their grasp on reality."

"Well, that makes our job pretty easy," Trae jumped in. "All we need to do is get those bottles from them."

Dune shook his head. "That's easier said than done. They always keep the bottles with them, and they seem to have an inexhaustible supply of the stuff."

"So, can we poison it?" Trae asked, and then Dune looked up at him with a broad smile. "If we know they'll drink it and only give it to seekers, we could use that to our advantage," Trae continued.

Dune had begun to nod excitedly, but suddenly brought his finger to his mouth, and peered down toward the alley's entrance. "Put your armor back on, and wait here, we can't have any of the seekers seeing us together. Whatever happens, you stay down." Dune pulled out his staff and urged his horse forward.

Trae moved silently into the shadows and grabbed at his armor. As he carefully dressed in his armor, he watched his friend.

Taking full advantage of the intimidating prospect it should be to encounter a master magician, Dune threw back his cloak, showing off his long, dark robe and leapt atop his battle horse, his staff outstretched.

"What business brings you here?" He bellowed.

If the man approaching him felt any uneasiness, his steady pace masked it perfectly. He carried a large cudgel in his right hand. His face was deformed with scars and a crooked nose, which had obviously been broken more than once. He was wearing hard, studded leather armor, and Dune noticed that a small, familiar bottle hung from his belt. When he came closer, Dune could see that there was an animal by his side; a large, wolf-like dog. It growled loudly and crouched, ready to pounce. The gray and white hair on the animal's back stood on end. The man continued to advance and did nothing to calm the animal.

"I warn you -- do not take another step," Dune declared.

The man continued to walk.

Without saying another word, Dune moved his right hand in a sweeping motion in front of his body. Trae did not know what he had done, but the magic seemed to have no effect on the approaching man. As he got closer, the man picked up speed until he was at a full run, weapon raised. Dune threw a small ball of fire at the man. The ball flew at him, and just before scorching him, it shrank and disappeared.

"Get him!" At this command from his master the dog lunged forward. Dune's horse was well trained and dodged the wild dog's sharp teeth. Dune swung his staff. The magically enhanced staff struck the dog with powerful force and knocked it to the ground, yelping in pain.

Before he could confront the man, Dune was thrown off his horse by a powerful, unseen force. He flew backward through the air and pounded into the wall of the alley, falling in a heap on the ground, far from his staff. Trae gripped his mace and braced himself to attack. He was not going to let the man kill his friend.

"You warn *me* not to take a step?" The man let out a raspy laugh.

As Trae was rising to his feet, Dune rolled onto his side and held his hands out in front of him. He made a slight motion with his hand and a stone from the ground flew at his attacker. An instant before the stone could hit, the man deftly raised his cudgel, which met with the stone, breaking it into a spray of sand. With this moment of distraction, Dune levitated his staff and drew it into his hand.

Dune moved forward and began a series of spinning attacks with his staff. The staff whirled effortlessly in Dune's skilled hands. He attacked with such speed and fury that the man was hopelessly outmatched, and if it were not for the cudgel, that seemed to be magically throwing the man's arms around defensively, and his armor, he would have been quickly killed.

Dune continued to advance, but the cudgel, more than the man, moved quickly to block his attacks, and when he was able to strike the man, he seemed to not notice. The way the man reacted to the attacks, it seemed that his armor was magically enchanted like the armor Trae was wearing.

While still pressing the man back using his staff, Dune also hurled some more rocks. The cudgel moved with lightning speed to stop most of the attacks, but it could not stop everything from getting through.

Dune slowed his attack with the staff while at the same time picking up two stones on opposite sides of the man. In one motion, Dune thrust with his staff and simultaneously threw the rocks. The cudgel first blocked Dune's attack, then it moved to deflect the larger of the two stones. The smaller stone struck the man's helmet with no effect, and fell to the ground.

Dune stopped his attack and the man backed up a pace. "So, now that you see you can't defeat me. What shall I do to you?" The man smiled wickedly and raised his weapon, ready to attack.

Trae tightened his grip on his mace. He was not going to stay hidden while his friend lost a fight in a dark alleyway. That man's magical cudgel and armor couldn't possibly keep up with two attackers at once. From the corner of his eye, Trae saw the wolf-dog moving. Dune was focused on the man in front of him and didn't seem to notice the dog. The animal lurched back on its hind legs, positioned to attack. As the dog began to move, Trae came out from behind the water barrel, running to intercept the dog. The animal jumped forward, but Trae caught it in mid-air, smashing it to the ground with his mace.

At that moment, Dune raised both hands. Three stones from behind the man rose from the ground at the same time.

"You fool!" the man bellowed. "Have you learned nothing? I'll beat you and your friend here, and there's nothing you can do about it." Trae advanced on the man, holding his mace in the air. While three large stones were floating in the air, there was also a tiny, almost imperceptible red fleck that was hovering above Dune's shoulder. Before Trae could move in on the attacker, the three stones hurtled toward him. His weapon made an arched sweep that smashed them to powder. In that same instant, the small, seemingly harmless, grain of sand launched directly from Dune's shoulder into the man's eye. Before the magical cudgel could defend him, the man fell to the ground.

Dune knelt next to the corpse "He had an awful lot of magical defense items," Dune remarked as he made a pile of jewelry, armor, and weapons. When all the magical items were removed, he grabbed a leather sack from his saddle bag, and placed the items in it. He then removed the leather pouch with the seeker's elixir and placed it with the other items. Dune raised his right hand and the sack rose into the air. When he closed his hand, it disappeared.

After the items were gone, he rubbed his hands together three times, then opened his hands palms down toward the man. A white hot flame appeared, encompassing the body. After a short moment, Dune lowered his hands and the flames died down, leaving only a small oval of ash. He mounted his horse and turned back to Trae.

"Thank you. If you go down the street two blocks you'll find the magician's shop. I'll send word to you there." Without waiting for Trae to respond, he kicked his horse into motion and rode out into the street as if nothing out of the ordinary had happened.

After Dune left the alley, Trae silently thanked his friend for the protection offered by the armor and disguise, then he threw his leg up over the saddle and made his way to the magic shop.

CHAPTER 31

The thin, wooden door creaked loudly as Trae pushed his way into the small magic shop. After leaving the alley, Trae had walked down the street and circled back to make sure he wasn't being followed, then he headed for the shop. Morgin was standing behind the counter, smiling when Trae arrived. He had more gray in his long beard than when Trae had last seen him at the magician work camp, but otherwise he looked like Trae remembered him. When first seeing Morgin, Trae unconsciously glared. He had no love for the tall, lanky magician. Seeing Morgin's look of confusion, Trae remembered that the man did not recognize him, so he softened and returned a weak smile.

"Hello, I am looking for a place to stay. Do you know where I can stable my horse for the night?"

"Oh yes." Morgin walked quickly from behind the wooden counter. "I've been expecting you. I'll be right there." He joined Trae on the street outside his shop and directed him to the small stable behind the shop. "That is where the horse can stay, I'll have him fed and brushed each day, as instructed."

Trae was not sure what kind of arrangements Dune had made, but decided it best to play along. "Good, and where will I be staying?"

"Right up the stairs, Sir…" Morgin paused and raised his eyebrows questioningly.

"Trevor," Trae said. "You can call me Trevor."

"Wonderful, Sir Trevor. I'll get your horse in the stable. Just go up there and your room is on the right." Trae nodded and made his way up the narrow staircase and ducked through the low door as he entered a cramped room. He looked around and was grateful to see that it had one small window to break the monotony of the otherwise bare walls. In the corner there was a modest bed and a sturdy stool. He reached up to the latch on his armor and unclipped it. It felt good to finally have the armor off for a time. While he pulled off his boots, Morgin knocked on the door.

"Come in," Trae answered.

"How is everything?" the older magician asked.

"This will do nicely. Thank you."

"I don't have a dining hall, but you are welcome to join me for supper at my table down the corridor."

"That sounds nice," Trae responded.

"We will be eating in about two hours, after I close up the shop. You can also look in the shop for any magical items that may interest you. I have some that would make wonderful gifts…"

"Tomorrow, perhaps," Trae interrupted. "Now I think I will rest from a long ride."

"Of course, of course." Morgin bowed slightly as he exited the room. Trae had never seen Morgin act so humbly toward anyone. *What had Dune told him? What had Dune offered to pay him?* Shaking his head, he dismissed these unimportant questions and laid down for an overdue rest.

It seemed only moments since his head had touched the thin pillow when there was an urgent knocking at the door.

"Sirrrr Trevorrrrr," Morgin tentatively pushed the door open holding a small wooden box. His other hand was viciously scratching his body and his voice sounded like a sheep bleating. "This came forrrr yoouu. Urrrgent business."

"Is everything all right?" Trae asked as he tilted his head to see the magician.

"Pleeeaseee, take it." Morgin said holding it out to Trae.

Moaning, Trae rolled off the bed and reached out for the package.

Morgin stepped into the room, handed Trae the box, then retreated.

"Thank you." Morgin's voice had returned to normal and his scratching had stopped. He promptly closed the door behind himself and left the room. Puzzled, Trae waited, listening as Morgin's footsteps moved down the stairs back to his shop.

Trae slid the top of the box back. In the box was a scrap of paper that had been folded and sealed with melted wax, a small white pebble, and a green bottle containing some liquid. Trae removed the seal from the message using his small boot knife and read:

Sir Trevor,

When convenient, walk to the green tent and put this liquid in the barrels behind the table. If you are stopped, tell them you came to trade this stone with Edgar and you'll meet him at the archery tournament. Best to not use your stone.

If anyone other than you tries to open the box, they may feel somewhat sheepish until they have returned it to you.

Trae moaned about his lost sleep, and then chuckled thinking of Uncle Morgin. After stretching his arms out wide, he quickly dressed in his full armor and exited the magic shop. Walking through Lexingar was slow going. The city was filled with people, and with the tournaments beginning tomorrow, all the contestants were strutting around, some of the more notable ones followed by small crowds.

Down the main street, Trae was amazed at the musicians, storytellers, and jesters entertaining large groups. On one block, the crowd was so thick that Trae needed to hop up onto the steps of a small soap shop to make his way through. From the height of the porch he saw what was making all the commotion. A fire eater was billowing smoke and fire from his mouth. He continued to watch the show over his shoulder as he edged around the crowd until he bumped into a small table he had not seen.

"You look like a strapping young man. What can I put you down for?"

Trae looked up to see that he had run into a sign-up table for the tournament.

"Oh, sorry. I'm not signing up for any events."

"It's a great chance to win some extra coins." Trae hesitated and the thin man with oily, slick hair began his sales pitch. "Single sword combat is only five pieces of gold, and the winner takes home fifty. All you need to do is win five rounds."

"Not today."

"Archery is three pieces of gold. You compete against fifty

people. If you hit just two direct bull's eyes you could win the entire thing. Fifty gold pieces for the winner, I'm sure you can hit two bull's eyes."

"I really do need to be going." Trae moved away from the table with the man's offers following him. He did glance back to see the fire eater, but through the throng, he could not make out anything that was happening.

The sun was setting by the time Trae reached the north end of town. His rumbling stomach reminded him that he had not eaten since breakfast. Feeling the grumbling in his belly, he thought that it might have been better to wait at the magic shop until after supper, but the longer he was out, the more he realized that waiting longer for the crowds to dissipate would be futile. It was the day before the tournaments were to begin, so the streets were getting more crowded, and by the sounds of the people, they would be up all night long.

Trae left the city through the north gate and immediately saw the large, green tent. The tent was situated along the road with the opening facing the road so that anyone passing could peer in and look at the supplies. Looking for the barrels, Trae walked down the main road out of town and past the large tent. He saw tables and stands set up with various items for sale ranging from wooden toys to leather clothing. The owners were haggling with customers, while also engaging in polite conversation. Trae noticed, in a quick glance over the people in the tent, that the owners all had bottles hanging from their belts. He also noticed that as he passed by, many of them looked up at him. He remembered that the armor he was wearing was drawing their gazes like manure draws flies.

"Hello!" Trae cringed when he heard the familiar voice.

"Hi, Edgar."

"So, did you find anything valuable to trade?"

Trae took a deep breath, readying himself to keep one step ahead of Edgar. All he wanted to do was get out to the tent, dump the liquid into the barrels, and go back to the shop for rest. However, he was almost certain Edgar wouldn't leave his side. He searched for the right words to explain why he had come out to the tent, and as he did, his hand rubbed the white stone that was in his pocket next to the small bottle.

"My friend has left some of his merchandise in my care, and I thought you or your friends might be able to offer a good price on one of the items."

"Really?" Edgar was sincerely interested. "What sort of item? Anything magical?"

"He had a stone that he gave me, but I'm not sure what it does." Edgar's eyes opened wide, and Trae thought he might fall over. He recovered quickly however, and seemed to be calculating as he swept his gaze around, making eye contact with a couple of other venders.

"As we only just arrived, I have mostly only got merchandise available for barter. Would you consider a trade for some of my best work?" he indicated the tables full of wooden items just inside the large, green tent.

Trae turned away and began to walk back toward the city. "I don't know. He said it was special. I think we would only be interested in coin."

"Did he say anything else?" Edgar quickly said, trying to keep Trae from walking away.

Trae turned back to Edgar with an evasive face. "Not really. He is a very mysterious person."

"Well, if you want, I can look at the stone, and then I can tell you what the stone can do. Magical items can be dangerous; it's best to know what they do." Edgar reached his hand out expectantly.

"You might be right, but perhaps it would be best to have a professional magician evaluate it," Trae said. He hoped that by stringing Edgar along for a short while, he could get a look at the barrels. "Perhaps arrangements could be made for a sale after you have had some time to trade and accumulate some coin. Why don't you show me around the tent?"

Eagerly, Edgar led the way into the tent. "This is Sareena; she sells rugs, mats, blankets, and fine woven clothing. It is of the highest quality." The woman behind the table smiled and inclined her head, but she kept her eye on Trae's hand where he held the stone. The table was covered with an assortment of materials with wild patterns and colors. Trae picked up one shirt that was the brightest yellow he had ever seen. It seemed to glow when he held it up in the lantern light. After a few moments examining some items, Trae moved to the back of the tent, passing a table filled with clay pottery.

As they walked past several venders, Trae kept moving toward the back of the tent, always looking for some barrels containing the strange seeker elixir. When he reached the back table, he saw Melna. "Hello, Melna. It seems you were able to get everything set up."

Melna nodded. "I see that you found something magical, otherwise Edgar wouldn't be following you like a lost puppy." She clicked her tongue and glared at Edgar.

Trae turned to see the hurt look on Edgar's face at this comment, then he looked back to the woman.

"Yes, I was hoping to help my friend sell a magical stone." Melna's eyes widened almost imperceptibly which, on her otherwise stone face, spoke as loudly as if a normal person had smiled from ear to ear and danced. "I'm looking around to see if it is worthwhile to recommend a trade for the stone, otherwise I'm sure to find someone in the city who can tell me what this stone can do."

"I'm sure Edgar here will find something for you, he is very interested in magical items." Melna spoke with an uninterested tone, though it sounded somewhat forced.

"Well, there is one thing I could use." Trae started looking around behind the table until he spotted two large barrels. "That," he pointed to the containers that he felt sure held the seekers' elixir.

When he pointed at the barrels there was a sudden tension in the tent. With his peripheral vision, he could see Edgar putting his hand on the hilt of his hunting knife, and other seekers in the tent dropped all pretense of being merchants as they watched Melna. At this moment Trae realized two things: first, he had found the elixir, and second, it was Melna who was the head seeker. Melna gave Trae a level look. "What do you want with that?"

"I'm so thirsty! I skipped supper tonight, and I could really use a drink." Trae could feel the tension in the tent dissipate. Edgar dropped his hands to his sides and the other seekers went back to their business.

"Those barrels, sadly, have spoiled," Melna answered with a sickly smile. "Unfortunately, all we have is a rain barrel at the front of the tent." Melna motioned in the direction of the barrel and Edgar jumped to action.

"I guess that will have to do," Trae responded with forced disappointment.

"Come with me and quench your thirst," Edgar said, pulling on Trae's arm.

Trae stood his ground for long enough to incline his head. "Thank you, Edgar. Melna, it was a pleasure seeing you again."

The pair walked quickly to the rain barrel and Trae took a deep, refreshing swallow.

"So," Edgar began, not wanting to miss an opportunity, "let's have a quick look at this stone."

Trae handed Edgar the small, white stone. For a moment, Edgar silently stared at the stone. At first, he simply stood, but after a few moments, large beads of sweat formed on his forehead. Without warning, he looked up at Trae.

"I'll give you three gold pieces for the stone. It's magical, but not powerful."

"Edgar, I am no fool," Trae said, grabbing the stone from Edgar's hand. "I can see in your eyes that you would give me everything in this tent for this stone."

"No, wait. I'm sorry," Edgar pleaded. "You're right, the stone is worth more than three gold pieces." He held his hands together in a pathetic beg.

"What does the stone do?" Trae asked, giving the small man a level look.

Edgar could barely take his eyes from Trae's hand to look up at his face. "I don't know."

"Our business is done here." Trae walked away from the tent with Edgar in tow, talking so fast, Trae could barely make out the words.

"It's the truth. That is what intrigues me about this stone. I swear." Trae stopped and turned, giving Edgar a this-is-your-last-chance look. "It is powerfully enchanted, more powerfully than almost anything I have ever seen, but I don't know what it does. I swear that is the truth, on the life of the king!" Trae knew that even Edgar wouldn't lightly make that oath, which meant, for now, he hadn't figured out that the white stone was a fake.

"Now that you've had a good look at this stone, can you give me a better estimate of its worth?"

"It would be much easier if I could keep it for a while." He reached out his hands.

"That's definitely not going to happen." Edgar closed his hands and dropped them to his sides. "I'll meet you at the archery tournament tomorrow, and I'll trade a fair price for this stone. I'm going to visit some magic shops in the city and see if anyone else can find out what this stone is worth."

"I don't think we need to wait till tomorrow. If you just let me look at it again…" Edgar pleaded.

"I'll see you tomorrow at the archery tournament." Trae turned and walked out of the tent.

When Trae returned to the magic shop, it was well past dark, and the lanterns in the shop were all extinguished. He experimentally pushed on the door and found that it was locked, so he knocked quietly at first, then increased the intensity of his knock until Morgin appeared.

"It's rather late, Sir Trevor."

"I am truly sorry. I tried to rush back, but the streets are packed."

"Yes, they get that way this time of year." Morgin inhaled deeply. "Come this way and get your rest, you need to be at your best tomorrow." Trae tilted his head and raised an eyebrow. "You know, for the tournament," Morgin said, answering the unvoiced question.

"Yes, the tournament will be quite a spectacle," Trae replied, then moved toward the stairs.

"The ranges are open early for contestants to practice, so I will have your breakfast ready at dawn."

Trae did not know how to respond to this. After a silent moment he simply said, "Thank you." Morgin retired to his room, and Trae made his way down the hall to the guest bedroom.

Trae opened the door and entered the room. He could sense the presence of a person behind the door, but did not want to give that fact away until he knew he had a tactical advantage. In a smooth motion, he slammed the door fully open, jamming the intruder between the wall and the door. He unsheathed his dagger and circled around the edge of the door while using his enhanced strength to crush the man to the wall. He quickly sheathed the dagger and released pressure on the door when he saw Dune behind it.

"How kind of you to greet an old friend in such a manner," Dune said while rubbing his ribs.

Trae closed the door. "What are you doing?" he demanded in a harsh whisper.

"I thought to myself, where can I go to get myself crushed to death? Then it came to me, sneak up on Trae, so here I am."

"Seriously, why are you here?" Trae asked as he removed his armor and sat on the side of the bed.

"Well, for starters, you didn't poison the seeker's juice."

"I was in a tent filled with two dozen seekers, what could I have done? I thought we were going to meet at the green tent. I could have used some help back there."

"You did get some help back there, and two other times between the tent and the shop." To give meaning to his words, Dune threw three seeker bottles on Trae's bed, sat on a small stool, and leaned close. "They are hunting you to get that magical stone you have. They care about nothing but seeking magic, especially stones."

Trae stood up and looked out the small window, then pulled the shades tightly closed. "Do they know I'm here?"

"No, you're safe here tonight. That's one of the reasons I picked this shop as our base of operations, it is filled with magical items, so it's a perfect hiding place for us."

"And our stones."

"Exactly."

Getting overwhelmed by all that was happening, Trae blurted out, "So what do we do next?"

"You have arranged for Edgar to meet you at the archery tournament, so we'll start there. We know there will be a large crowd, so that will provide relative safety. We can also guess that most of the seekers will come into town during the tournament to search for any stone holders."

"So that is when you'll slip the poison into those barrels," Trae concluded.

"Well, it's not quite that easy." Dune slowly responded.

"What do you mean?"

"I'm a magician. Seekers are very suspicious around magicians. I wouldn't get within a hundred yards of that barrel without being followed."

"Why don't you disguise yourself or dress in normal clothing?"

"They see magic!" Dune exclaimed throwing his hands in the air, exasperated. "Don't you listen to anything I say?"

"Well, maybe if you'd just speak clearly, it would be a lot easier to figure out what you're trying to say!" Trae countered, going right up to Dune's face.

"I'll try to use small words for you. We need one decoy and one person to drop the poison." Dune made a long pause, then patronizingly nodded his head, "Are you with me so far?"

"Just get on with it," Trae said in annoyance, backing away.

Dune continued at his normal speaking pace. "So, I'll get to the final round of the archery tournament, and then I'll use my stone. It will be like a beacon for all nearby seekers."

"Wait a minute. You're going to be competing in the archery tournament?" he asked, facing Dune again.

"Yes, and so are you." Dune responded, pointing at his friend.

"What? That makes no sense. How can I poison the barrels if I'm in the tournament?"

"If you would listen for a minute, I'll explain. We need to

have as many seekers gathered as possible, that means we need you to have an excuse to stand up in front of a large crowd for a prolonged period of time with a magical stone."

"Well, I guess that makes sense." Trae replied in a tone that said he clearly did not think it made any sense.

"As I was saying," Dune continued, ignoring Trae's confusion, "when you are eliminated from the tournament, you will go with Edgar. I will use my real stone in a dramatic, tie-breaking final round, and all the nearby seekers will see that I have a magical item, and they'll stay. Then you can go with Edgar, knock him out or kill him, and then poison the seeker juice."

"You make it sound so simple. I remember watching you with that seeker in the alley. What if he has magical protection?"

Dune shook his head, "Edgar is not a fighter; he is here to trade, plain and simple. Just hit him really hard when he's unarmed and not suspecting it."

"Fine. What will you do?"

"Well, I guess I'll have to hide or run away. Not much else I can do with thirty seekers on my tail. You just need to make sure your part is done. Any more questions?" Dune stood back up and walked to the small window.

"One thing is bothering me about this plan," Trae began. He spun around and leaned on the wall. "It all hinges on your ability to force a tie breaker in the archery tournament."

Dune smiled at Trae and then opened the window to exit. "Don't lose sleep over that part." With that said, he vanished out into the night.

CHAPTER 32

Kaz walked down the streets of Dungan taking in the fresh spring breeze with its thousand familiar smells. Each breath was inhaled slowly and savored as the scents carried with them memories of a happier time. The flowers planted next to the town hall, the baker's bread, the smoke from the blacksmith shop, even the unique smell of the market that could never be called good was welcome to his nose today.

While the smells filled his senses, he strolled slowly down Main Street with nothing on his mind but enjoying the moment. He saw some familiar friends waving and greeting him. Garin and Farin almost bumped into him, being so engulfed in their banter that they were not watching where they walked. It was good to see his friends. As he continued down the street, he began to hear a soft hammering sound that was steady and methodical. At first he looked to the blacksmith shop, but the sound did not fit, then he was by the bakery, but there were no sounds that would cause this beating. It did not come from the general store or the inn, and was not caused by a rug being beaten to remove the dust. Thinking it might be a horse hoof, he checked the stables, but all he found there were some empty stalls.

Trying to ignore the sound was becoming more and more difficult as it became louder, so Kaz went in search of the one person he could always count on to figure out mysteries. He knocked and slowly opened the door to Bendar's home. Welcomed by Bendar's parents, Kaz asked after their son and was directed upstairs. Kaz found Bendar sitting at a desk studying some books on philosophy. "What's causing that sound?" Kaz asked his friend.

Bendar turned to look at Kaz, and Kaz immediately realized something was very wrong. Bendar was wearing thick makeup that obscured not only his natural skin tone, but it also made it impossible to see some of his facial features. His cheeks looked puffy and his lips looked fake.

"Come on Bendar," Kaz insisted. "Take that off so we can

talk."

Bendar slowly reached for a rag and wiped the thick, white paint off his face, revealing something Kaz had not expected. It was not Bendar's face at all but a familiar face he could not place. The features of the older man were smooth but strong. He looked sternly at Kaz but said nothing.

Confused and scared, Kaz ran out of the house. He ran past Bendar's parents, down the main street, and to the one place he felt he could call home. As he ran, the drumming continued and increased until the pounding was unbearable. Just as the noise became so all-consuming he felt it would crush him, Kaz crashed into Gran's house and shut the door tightly.

Safely behind the door, Kaz stopped to catch his breath.

"You can stay here if you like," Gran's familiar voice said.

Resting his weight against the door, Kaz looked up to see Gran.

"I don't understand," Kaz began. "What's happening? What is that noise?"

"That noise is your destiny, and you can choose to go to it, or you can choose to stay here." Gran looked at Kaz in a loving, but expectant way. He knew he needed to make a choice.

"What will I find if I go out there?"

"It will be hard. You will find pain. Friends will be dead again."

Hearing the word *again* made Kaz begin to remember some far distant reality where friends had died, or been hurt and lost.

"Why would I ever want to go out there?" Kaz asked.

"That is your road to being a man," Gran said.

"So I have to go out there to become a man?" Kaz asked, still confused.

"That is the way you must go if you want to reach manhood, but it is your choice. It will be the most difficult thing you have ever done, but in the end it will make you a man like no other."

Kaz looked frantically around the room. "I don't understand. What is this place? Am I dead? If I'm dead, where is my family? Why did Bendar's face change?"

"Settle down, son," Gran said in an all too familiar, calming tone. "You can't have all the answers now or you could never grow from making a choice. If you stay here, you will be safe, but you will never grow. If you want to grow, you must face adversity and make decisions without having all the answers." Then, after giving Kaz a moment to digest what she had said, she continued. "You need to decide."

Looking to Gran, he asked one more question. "What do you think I should do?"

"Kaz, I love you like a son. I am proud of who you are. The question is not what *I* think, but what do *you* think? Are *you* proud of who you are and what you have become, or do you want to be more?"

"I don't really know what I have become. I don't remember…"

"Now is the time to decide, follow your feelings and choose."

Kaz stood up and looked back and forth between the door and Gran.

"I know what I need to do." He clasped Gran in a tight hug, then walked over to the door and stepped out.

* * * * *

The city was a mass of excitement long before the sun came up. Throngs of people crowded around the roped-off rings that would soon have contestants. Small children wedged between legs to get a better view, and everywhere people cheered and applauded when a contestant would make his or her way to a fighting ring.

Inside his quarters, Mylot tuned out all the bustling and cheering from outside as he sat meditating on the floor. He had been trained to ignore the unimportant and focus within. *Breath in, breath out.* Slowly his chest rose and fell as he focused inward. After several minutes of complete silence, Mylot struck his hands against the floor.

"I need to take care of this!" he burst out, pointing to the jewelry chest on the table.

Sir Rodnik calmly replied, "My Lord, now is not the time to think of trinkets, it is the time to think of your upcoming match, your movements, and find the calm you need." He moved his hands down in a calming gesture.

Mylot got up and threw his arms in the air. "I know it's a small thing, but it's like a thorn to me. Once I get it taken care of, I'll be fine. I just need to at least have a plan to deliver this." He reached down and grabbed the chest from the table. "I made a promise."

"Can't one of the servants do it?" Sir Rodnik begged.

"No. This is something I need to deliver personally."

Seeing that he would not compromise, Sir Rodnik conceded. "Your first event is hand-to-hand combat. You will win the first round quickly. There will be time between your matches to visit the archery tournament."

Mylot cut him off. "I want to be rid of this before I start fighting. I will go to the archery stage first, then come back and fight." Mylot glared at Sir Rodnik, daring him to make a counter offer.

Sir Rodnik exhaled in frustration. "Both events begin at the same time, and the streets are packed full of people, even if we left right now…"

"Fine," Mylot relented, "If it is too crowded, and we are delayed, we will deliver it after the first match. But, I will at least try to get it to her before I begin fighting, then my mind will be fully calm." Mylot walked to the door and motioned for a servant to open it. With his final declaration the matter was decided and he expected obedience.

"My armor," he commanded.

"Yes, Milord."

*****

The chubby man taking names at the registration table was rushing quickly from one task to another, and his face was red with exhaustion.

"What's your name?"

"Sir Trevor."

Without looking up from his paper he continued to speak. "Very good." Pointing to the side he continued. "Get your regulation bow and arrows from there, then make your way to the platform."

Trae moved to the side, then turned back. "Thank you."

Surprised, the man looked up. "What was that?"

"I just said thank you," Trae replied.

"Oh," the man said, then after a short pause the man smiled slightly. "You are welcome, young man. Good luck today."

"Thanks!" Trae repeated with a smile, and then proceeded to try out the pull weight of some long bows. The first bow he tried was too long and awkward. He tried the bow one size smaller, it was sturdy, and felt more natural in his hands, he selected this bow and the arrows that matched it. He turned and almost ran into a tall figure in a long, dark robe.

"Wasn't that a nice scene back there?" Dune said sarcastically.

"What are you talking about?" Trae asked in confusion.

Dune leaned in and spoke in a whisper. "You were being too nice to the registration clerk. You need to remember you are a knight, Sir Trevor. You have to act aloof and above those of lesser class. Just think cocky and arrogant."

Trae tilted his head to the side and smiled. "So basically you want me to act like you?"

If he was amused by this comeback Dune did not show it. He walked past Trae and tested a bow. He spoke softly to his companion, though his back was facing him. "Just try not to draw too much attention to yourself, and remember we want to force a tie."

In character, Trae turned away from Dune, raised his head and walked confidently to the center of the stage where he set down his arrows. He had arrived early for the event, and he had much of the stage to himself. There were two other archers taking practice shots down the row, and soon Dune would pick a bow and join them on the platform.

*****

At first light, Kaz, Farin and Angela made their way through the crowded streets of Lexingar to their events. Farin and Angela had full armor on while Kaz was wearing comfortable clothing that allowed for complete movement. His only armor was the leather arm guard on his left forearm to protect from the snap of the bowstring. The three entered the city for the first time in weeks and they were amazed. The entire city had turned out to see the tournament. The streets were packed, filled with people waving banners of all kinds. Some of the clothing, hair styles and makeup were unlike anything Kaz and Farin had ever seen. Angela had to answer their unending questions about the different-looking people from all over Denall. The only people with horses in town today were those competing in the equestrian events and the nobles of high enough rank to have been approved entrance for their carriages.

No amount of vision practice could have prepared Kaz for this scene. Boon had him doing practice exercises, surveying vast areas to help him pick out details. As Kaz scanned, everything changed so quickly, and there were so many details, that it made him dizzy. He just stuck to following Boon through the crowded streets to the archery area. Kaz wished Farin and Angela luck as they parted for their separate events.

"I think I made a mistake," Kaz said to Boon as they approached the archery range.

"What mistake was that?" Boon asked.

"I thought it would be an unfair advantage if I used my stone, so I left it with the caravan," he replied.

Boon stopped and patted Kaz on the back, and with a proud smile on his face he addressed the young man.

"You're a good lad. It wasn't a mistake. You'll do just fine without any magical help."

Kaz nodded, feeling a little better, but still feeling a little lost without his magical stone. At the archery range, Kaz registered for the event and stepped over to select a regulation bow.

"Wait a minute," the man at the registration booth stopped him. "You just wrote Kaz as your name. Don't you have some kind of a stage name or title?"

Kaz looked to Boon a little confused and the shrug that Boon gave him did not help.

"Just Kaz is fine."

"I guess I can introduce you as 'Just Kaz', but it's a little boring. I think you'll need to add something," the man insisted.

"Back home they called me 'Eagle Eye'." This made the man smile as he wrote the name down on the paper and waved for Kaz to pick out a regulation bow and arrows and move to the range. After pulling back on three or four bows, Kaz found one that he liked. He picked up the bow and the arrows that matched it.

Boon leaned in close to Kaz. "Remember everything your father taught you." Kaz nodded, feeling both nervous and excited.

"I will. I feel like something big is going to happen for me today, like I'm standing on the edge of my future somehow. That probably sounds silly, but I had this really intense dream last night, and now I feel ready to move forward with whatever comes."

Boon squeezed his arm and nodded, "I'm proud of you no matter what happens," he dropped his hand and gave Kaz a sly smile, "but if you don't win, I'll never hear the end of it from Blade, so don't let me down." With that said, he waved Kaz away, and the young man moved forward for his first look at the archery range and his competitors.

There were targets ranging from as close as twenty paces to about seventy paces. At the close end of the range there was a wooden stage on which all the competitors stood. Behind each firing position was a number nailed to a post. The numbers were being replaced by stage names as contestants signed in. A man had just nailed a board with the name "Kaz the Eagle Eye" on the post next to Kaz. Each contestant was in a group of five archers who shared targets down range. Kaz moved from his post to stand close to the front edge of the stage to begin his practice session.

There were at least fifty archers lining up and firing practice shots at their targets. Kaz took careful note of how many shots were hitting direct bull's eyes. He took some of the regulation arrows, and with his first shot, he hit the outside wood of the target.

"Wow, we've got a challenge here in this one," said the strongarm standing three people away from Kaz. The smirk on his face made Kaz want to shoot the nock off the next arrow that he fired, but he took a deep breath and continued to do as Boon had instructed. He missed the bull's eyes constantly, but he was honing in on what he wanted to hit. First the line between the yellow and white circle, and then the knot on the wooden target stand, then the feather of an arrow that was way off target. After hitting all the targets he selected, he also aimed at some pieces of wood, or arrows in the ground much farther down range. This helped Kaz get a feel for the bow at all distances.

After two dozen practice shots Kaz was completely comfortable with how the regulation arrows flew using this bow. He continued to shoot arrows, but from this point on he watched his competitors closely. The smart mouth three people down, whose name Kaz had learned from the recently placed placard was Sir Trevor, was actually very good with his bow. He was wearing full armor, but was able to shoot quickly and accurately despite the extra weight. There was a man down near the end that also hit most of his targets. Kaz couldn't see his name posted behind him, and his face was hidden by the hood of the long, black robe he was wearing. People around him gave him a little more space than he needed. Although Kaz had never seen a magician before, for some reason it surprised him to see the man in an archery tournament. He hit bull's eye after bull's eye; it seemed this competitor was, ironically, not playing any tricks. There was a young lady in red next to Kaz. Although she was inconsistent with hitting the targets, when she did hit a bull's eye, it was dead center. Kaz thought perhaps she was playing the same game that he was. He didn't mind keeping an extra close eye on her as she was very easy on the eyes.

Then he saw a contestant who was not shooting any practice arrows. She had arrived after Kaz and just stood there. This girl had matted hair that looked like it hadn't been washed in ages. Her clothing was dirty and hung loosely on her skeletal frame. She had a dark brown birthmark that extended down the length of the right side of her face. Kaz noticed that some members of the crowd were making fun of her and calling her "Mangy Dog".

Although she didn't seem to notice their jeers, it bothered Kaz to see this behavior. In an effort to distract her from her tormenters, Kaz boldly walked over to her.

"Hi," he began, extending his hand and standing between the audience and the frail young lady. "I'm Kaz, from Dungan." After a long pause, with no response, he continued. "I see your name is Maggie," he said, gesturing toward her placard. "Don't you want to try some practice shots?"

Maggie stepped close to him and Kaz involuntarily stepped back. She smelled as bad as she looked. "They look the same as last year. I don't need the practice." Then she turned away and stood silently by her placard.

"All right," Kaz said, still trying to be friendly. "So, do you have a stage name, or title they're going to post for you, or is it just 'Maggie'?"

Maggie turned back to him and then looked down the line of people. "I'm not here to put on a show for them," she replied pointing out to the crowd. "I just want to win and get this over with."

The person next to Maggie stopped taking practice shots and tapped Kaz on the shoulder.

"Hi, Kaz, was it?"

"Yes, what's your name?" Kaz replied to the friendly competitor who greeted him.

"My name is Gorgal," The man in his mid-thirties then gestured toward Maggie. "She likes to be left alone."

"Oh, I wasn't trying to bother her; I just didn't like how they were treating her," Kaz said as he pointed at the audience, who had quieted slightly since he had approached.

"Well, she'll win again this year, take the money and leave -

- like she does every year." He said it so matter-of-factly that Kaz froze.

"She won last year?"

"She wins every year. We're shooting for second place, boy." With that, the man picked up an arrow and shot at the closest target. If his stance, grip and shot were any indication, he wouldn't be getting that second place prize.

Looking back at Maggie, Kaz saw a look of deep sadness. He watched her face for several moments, wondering what kind of life had led to her being here like this. As she turned and looked into the crowd, Kaz thought he saw a glimpse of fear in her eyes. Following her line of sight, he saw a man a few years older than himself coming toward her. He was parting the crowd as he made his way to the archery firing line. The man looked to be in his twenties, with the build of a warrior, and he was wearing full, gleaming, plate armor. Kaz slipped through a small space in the fence and fearlessly walked directly up to the man, determined to keep him from Maggie.

"Hi," Kaz said in his most casual tone.

"I don't have time to speak with you right now. I am not interested in any offer you have to make," the man said, then tried to push Kaz aside.

Kaz looked at the man, confusion all over his face, and asked, "Why on earth do you think I would want to make you an offer? Do you owe me money?"

Pride bruised, the man stopped. "Do I owe you money?" he repeated, clearly offended. "How dare you insult me!" The man walked up to Kaz and stood within inches of him. The crowd around them parted into a small, tight circle.

This question had the desired effect. The man was completely distracted from his prior fixation on Maggie, and all his attention was on Kaz. Unfortunately, Kaz was beginning to feel that he did not want this man's full attention.

"I meant no offense, big guy. I was just saying hello." Kaz gave the man an innocent smile.

"You're not stopping me to hire my blade?" When Kaz shook his head he tried to push on, holding a small, jeweled box in his hands.

"Why would I want to hire you?" Kaz asked.

"I really don't have time for this," he said, turning his back on Kaz.

Kaz, knowing that his chances to delay the man were slipping, tried a different approach. "I'm only interested in hiring winners."

This stopped the man in his tracks again. He stepped over, looking squarely into Kaz's eyes.

"I am Mylot of the house of Tran." Seeing that this meant nothing to Kaz, he continued. "I am not only going to win today, I'm going to win the single handed sword fighting, the double handed swords, and the jousting."

Kaz then looked over at the sword ring where Farin and Angela were getting registered. "I bet that girl over there can beat you. Hopefully, you don't have to face her today. However, if you want to have any *hope* of winning, you'd better get back over there. It looks like they are calling out the contestants for the first match."

With this last comment, Mylot shoved Kaz out of the way, made one final look over to where Maggie was standing, and briskly strode back to the fighting ring. Kaz breathed a sigh of relief and returned to the firing line. He looked over at Maggie, who didn't give him a look of thanks, but of confusion. Kaz simply shrugged his shoulders as the announcer began to give the archers instructions.

* * * * *

From the stage, Trae watched Kaz's interactions with Maggie and he made a quick conclusion: he liked the boy.

Trae had also spotted Edgar in the crowd. The seeker was looking for him and waved enthusiastically when he finally spotted him.

"Hello there!" Edgar called. Trae gave the slightest inclination of his head, just enough to acknowledge Edgar's existence, but not show any sign of friendship. Edgar tried to push his way to the stage, but before he could get far, the crowd shouldered him out and Trae turned his back on the man. Trae looked to his right, trying to make subtle eye contact with Dune, but Dune was still loosing practice arrows down range, not interested in anything but the tournament. Trae realized that he also needed to get into the right frame of mind. It was time to force a tie.

Trae was familiar with the rules for archery tournaments, so he only half listened as the announcer stood and spoke. Five rounds of shooting, five people shooting at each target, each person hitting the bull's eye earned a point per round. The closest arrow to the center of the bull's eye gained a second point each round. If an archer hits the exact center of the bull's eye, the other archers can aim at the colored feather of his arrow for an extra point. With this many archers he didn't know if there was anything he could do to help, but he wanted Dune to make it to a tie breaking round while he edged off the stage and got Edgar alone.

The announcer loudly bellowed, "We will now begin the first round at forty paces." Trae watched as the first archer in their group, a woman in green, not only missed the bull's eye, but almost missed the target completely. It was then his turn to shoot. Trae shot his arrow into the bull's eye pretty close to the center. He noticed that a small crowd cheered when it hit the target. Trae turned around and found that Edgar had made his way closer to the stage and had a small cheering section of faces Trae recognized from the green tent. Getting Edgar alone was going to be harder than he expected.

After Trae's shot, Kaz hit the bull's eye just inside of Trae's arrow. The boy definitely knew how to shoot. Trae checked the score after the first round of target shooting. He had one point, Dune had a single point and 'Bull's Eye Bebe', a woman down the row, had gained the second point for the first round, a fact which was loudly announced to a healthy round of applause once all the first-round contestants had completed their shots. Things were working out so far.

Round two began at forty-five paces. Trae hit the bull's eye again, and again Kaz landed his arrow right next to Trae's, only slightly closer to the center. Trae began to wonder if the young man was toying with him to make up for his earlier jeer. Trae also realized that if this boy could put his arrows so accurately on the target, it was just a matter of time before he started aiming for the center of the bull's eye and not for the inside of Trae's arrows. At the end of round two, Dune had earned the extra point, placing him in a tie for first place. Even greater applause met this announcement as the contestants were reshuffled ahead of round three.

The third round began with Kaz shooting, and almost missing the bull's eye because an unexpected gust of wind carried his arrow off course. Trae watched as other archers hit their marks down the range. Although not a visor, he could see that Dune was not going to gain the second point for this round, and he also knew that Dune would struggle as the distances increased. He was a good shot, but he was up against the best in Denall. Then the woman in red's arrow landed very close to the center of the bull's eye.

Trae tried to stay in character as an uninterested knight, while his eyes darted to the other targets to see if another archer would get closer to the bull's eye. While looking down the range he felt he was being watched, and slowly looked over his right shoulder at the other archers. Maggie, the girl with the matted hair and rags was looking directly at him. At first he was repulsed by her dirty appearance, but then he looked into her eyes and he was truly unsettled. She looked at him as though she could see right through the armor, arrogance, and act he was putting on. For a moment he paid attention to nothing but this girl. Then she smiled slightly and nodded.

Trae looked away, and his first inclination was to peek over his shoulder in the other direction to see who she was nodding at, but he knew it had been him. *What did she know? What did that smile mean? Most importantly, what had he missed while staring at her?*

It was Trae's turn to approach the shooting line. He looked at the other targets on the field and felt confident that Bull's Eye Bebe, the woman in red who had won the first round, would earn the extra point in round three. Not having full faith in Dune's ability to gain the extra point in the next round, Trae made a decision that he was sure Dune would not approve of. He aimed at the center of the bull's eye. Trae's arrow sailed into the target just right of the center of the bull's eye. He had earned the extra point for this round and moved into a three way tie for first place. While this was not part of Dune's plan, Trae had helped keep Dune in a tie for first place, which is what he wanted. He could always miss the target on the final round and let Dune move on. Still, he avoided looking down the line of archers toward Dune as the announcer tried to yell over the shouting crowd to officially declare the tie moving into round four.

In the fourth round, Kaz shot second. The boy did what Trae feared he would, he hit a direct center bull's eye. The boy had the ability to win the entire tournament, and now he had moved himself into a four way tie. Trae knew that if Kaz shot like that again, the tournament would be over. Unsettled and looking for advice on how to proceed, Trae instinctively looked toward Dune, but he found nothing there. Dune was focusing on his own shots and keeping himself separated from the other people in his group. He made no attempt to return a look to Trae. However, Maggie was looking at him again. Trae shot another bull's eye, keeping himself in a now increasing tie for first place with Dune, Bebe and now Kaz, a fact that was putting the crowd into a cheering, singing mass of excitement as the tied contestants were announced.

Before the fifth and final round began, Trae walked to retrieve his arrow. As he did, he made sure to walk in front of Kaz. After cutting Kaz off, he turned and looked down his nose at Kaz and sniffed loudly. Although he felt bad treating him poorly, he knew that the only hope for Dune to make it into the final round was for Kaz to be focusing on Trae's arrow, and not the center of the bull's eye. After snubbing Kaz, Trae turned to the audience and saw that Edgar's group had grown to include what had to be almost all the seekers from the green tent. Dune had been right about them, the prospect of getting a magical stone had drawn them in.

Trae shot his arrow into the bull's eye fairly far from the center and, as expected, Kaz landed his arrow just inside Trae's. If someone was able to get a shot closer to the center of the bull's eye, Kaz would not win the tournament this round. The unfortunate reality was that this meant a five way tie, and Trae was going to the final tie-breaker round with Dune. It wasn't exactly what they had planned on, but he felt like it was the only way to keep Dune tied for first place. In the final round, the judges took quite a bit of time deliberating before the announcer spoke.

"There will be a tie breaking round six." The roar of the crowd was deafening. "Maggie is our fifth contestant progressing to the final round," the man continued. "The target will be placed at one hundred paces. The archers will have no practice shots at this distance. Good luck to everyone."

Having no more reason to be a snob to Kaz, Trae decided it was time to give him a well-earned compliment.

"I'm impressed, farm boy," Trae began. "Win or lose, you sure put up a fight today."

Kaz was silent for a time, then returned a compliment. "I'm just glad that I shot after you for three rounds. All I was aiming for was to get inside your shots." The two nodded approval to each other and waited as the other leading contenders joined them on center stage for the final round.

* * * * *

Mylot had returned to the sword ring just as his name was announced. Since then it had been a long morning for him, winning sword matches, and trying to keep an eye on who his greatest competition would be. During his breaks between matches, he tried to get the chest delivered, but the crowd was too thick around the archery range as the competition there seemed to be progressing to ever-increasingly tight odds. Once he had heard the announcer's voice carry across the field, acclaiming three contestants tied for first place as they moved into their fourth round. It was the first time in years that Maggie didn't just win right away. Now that he was in the final match of sword fighting, he needed a quick victory. He handed Maggie's chest to Sir Rodnik and took his helmet. Mylot looked at his opponent for the final match, a young man named Farin.

While he had a good, natural stance, and he was well built, he was young, inexperienced, nervous, and seemed distracted by a young lady sitting anxiously by his trainer. Mylot recognized the girl. She had also been competing in the single-handed sword matches until the third round when she was eliminated for an excessive use of force on her opponent.

Fortunately, Farin was a listener, giving Mylot the advantage of strength, and no fear of being overpowered. He hoped to finish the final round quickly and get back to the archery ring, then he could concentrate fully on the other events for the day.

The head judge stood up from his elevated seat.

"The match will end when one contestant has three clean strikes on his opponent. We are looking for clean strikes, not deathblows; this is a tournament, not the battlefield." This comment was clearly directed at Mylot, who smiled and nodded at the judge. "Begin."

The fighting ring was made by sturdy posts set up in a large circle connected by a thick cord. The two fighters walked around the outside of the ring opposite each other as if assessing his opponent. Then, in an unexpected move, Farin was the first to advance on Mylot. He quickly darted across the ring with an overhand swing, and at the moment before it was easily blocked, he pulled back his sword and thrust forward. Mylot knew he had won a quick victory in some previous rounds by using feinting tactics, and quickly sidestepped, correctly anticipating a feint and making Farin momentarily lose his balance. Now it was time for Mylot's attack.

The experienced noble swung his long sword upward toward Farin's body armor. When that attack was deflected, he moved forward with a side swing, then an overhead, continuing on with a sequence of seven offensive movements that usually left his opponents battered and defeated. The young man was certainly quick, and had perfect footwork, but Mylot did not have time to continue this match. He needed a quick victory. Relying on his superior strength, Mylot swung fully at Farin's body with all his might. While this attack was an easy one to block, Mylot was confident it would overpower his younger opponent.

Instead of blocking the attack, Farin dropped to the ground just as the sword was about to strike him, leaving Mylot off balanced and confused. Dodging an attack was not something his sparring partners ever did. It was not something that people did in tournament fighting. It seemed more like what he had seen from Sir Theodore. From behind, Farin thrust, then slashed in a series of quick movements that kept Mylot parrying the onslaught and moving backward. Farin's attacks were systematic, but unpredictable, and he kept Mylot on the defensive as he backed close to a pole. As they approached the boundary, Farin pressed even harder, moving his sword more quickly, trying to find an opening in Mylot's defense. Mylot, out of instinct, kept Farin at bay while he also sought opportunity to strike a clean blow on his opponent.

After the time for the first round ended, the announcer loudly whistled for the two fighters to return to their trainers. The first round finished without any direct hits. Mylot returned to Sir Rodnik.

"What am I doing wrong?" he demanded of his trainer.

"You have executed every stance, defense, and attack perfectly," Sir Rodnik said while massaging Mylot's sword arm.

"I know that!" Mylot cut him off. "What do I need to do to beat him?"

"Just keep wearing him down, you have the advantage of strength, endurance, and experience, keep him constantly needing to change tactics, wait for him to make a mistake, then strike quickly and definitively."

"Where did this boy come from?" Mylot asked to no one in particular.

"I've been wondering the same thing. I've never seen him or his trainer here before. It is amazing to watch you both. Such different techniques! Both effective, yet very different."

Mylot turned his head slowly and raised an eyebrow at Rodnik.

"Well, I'm glad that you are enjoying the show. Just keep watching for a weakness, and keep a closer watch on that," Mylot picked up the jewelry chest from the wooden bench and placed it in Sir Rodnik's hand.

While they were resting, Mylot looked over to see Farin, the girl, and his trainer. Farin was talking with the girl, and his trainer was standing behind them, not giving any advice. Seeing that Farin would have no help from a mentor gave Mylot hope that the second round would turn to his advantage quickly.

The crowds swelled around the sword ring as word of the speed of the two swordsmen spread, and when the second round was ready to begin, Sir Rodnik had to shout for Mylot to hear him. "Remember what I told you. You have all the advantages, just keep in control of the round." Mylot nodded and returned to the ring.

For the second round, the two faced each other and wasted no time when the ring judge shouted the command to attack. In a fury of motion the two instantly advanced. Their swords moved in swoops and arcs, crashing together in a blur of motion mixed with the sound of steel on steel. The second round was not a time for holding back. For Mylot it was a time to win and move on. He was standing toe to toe with an unknown swordsman and he was not going to give an inch. There they stood for the duration of the second round in nearly the center of the fighting ring, avoiding the fenced edges.

For most attacks, Farin matched him stroke for stroke. However, when he made any kind of attack meant to overpower his opponent, Farin dodged, using speed to nullify Mylot's superior strength. When the ring judge whistled loudly, they both stepped back, slowly maintaining eye contact with the other, unaware of the wild cheers from the crowd or anything else but the opponent.

"They are delaying the next round." It took a moment for the words to sink in and for Sir Rodnik to fully capture Mylot's attention.

"Why? What's going on?" Mylot demanded.

"The king is coming," his trainer answered.

Mylot rolled his eyes. "Why are they bringing Robert?"

"King Robert," Sir Rodnik corrected, "The javelin throw has ended and his majesty is coming to see the final match. I know he's a relative, but in public you must call him King Robert."

"This can't be happening!" Mylot ran his fingers through his thick hair in frustration. "I need to get that chest to Maggie, and it seems all of Denall is getting in my way. There is still time," Mylot said as he looked over to the archery stage. "This next round must be the last."

"King Robert cannot see you fail," Sir Rodnik reminded.

"Fail?" Mylot cast a withering glare at his mentor. "It is not a matter of *if* I win, but *when* I will win."

Sir Rodnik nodded quickly. "I was merely suggesting…"

"Farin is fast, he's talented, but I am in control of the match, biding my time, waiting for a mistake or an opening where I can finish him."

"I know that…"

"Good." Mylot turned from the man and took a deep, calming breath. "Be sure you don't forget it."

A stir began in the crowd as people parted to make room for the royal procession. The King rode atop a large, white stallion surrounded by his personal guard. He wore a long, red cape, light but sturdy armor, and a simple, yet elegant golden crown masterfully etched with his crest. Sir Theodore was standing in the tight circle positioned behind the King. When King Robert arrived, the judge for the match moved from his elevated seat on center stage to allow the King the best view of the match. The guards stood closely around, making sure to not obscure his view of the fighting ring.

When he was seated, he made the slightest motion with his left hand and the judge stood to begin the round. At first his voice cracked, but he quickly regained his composure. "Take your positions, and begin!"

Mylot had already decided that this round would end quickly, so he advanced on his opponent. He began with swirling overhands interspersed with fast stabs aimed at his body. Mylot used his powerful wrists and arms to quickly change the direction of his attacks at the last moment. To all watching, it seemed a one sided fight with Mylot in command. Although it was clear that Farin was not an easy target, Mylot's offensive onslaught kept Farin constantly on the move.

Using this forward momentum, Mylot backed Farin up to a post and was about to deliver a final blow that would either push Farin out of the ring, or strike past his defenses. Just as he moved forward to make the attack, Farin pushed off the ground and slid on his knees while spinning with his sword poised in front of his body. This evasive move effectively dodged Mylot's swing while keeping his body protected. The even larger advantage was that when Farin came to his feet, he was inside the circle and Mylot was now backed up to the rope. Farin then began a series of fast attacks. While they were not as strong or quick as Mylot's initial assault, they kept him in place against the edge of the fighting ring for a time and earned a thunderous applause from the crowd.

After regaining his footing, Mylot advanced on Farin, backing him across the fighting ring in the opposite direction. Each time he thought that Farin was cornered, the speedy youth would dodge, jump, slide or sidestep, forcing Mylot to press him again. This pattern continued until he heard the loud whistle of the match judge announcing the end of the third round. Mylot felt like a complete failure.

He looked up at Sir Theodore, then to the king, and dropped his gaze to the hard packed ground. In the first event of the day in which Mylot would appear before the king, he had not only failed to quickly eliminate his opponent, but they had gone for three full rounds without Mylot even scoring a point. He wanted to throw his sword down in the ground, but decided better of it knowing Sir Theodore would not be impressed.

"Sir Mylot." Surprised to hear his name called out, he turned to see that it was the head judge addressing him. "Come sit on this bench while you await the final round." Mylot obeyed, taking his place next to Farin. He was pleased to note that Farin was almost gasping for breath.

*****

On center stage five archers gathered, ready to shoot for the championship. They sat on a large, wooden bench awaiting their turn. Dune was the first to attempt the one hundred yard shot. He took his place center stage, drew his bow, and quickly released. He turned around and sat down on the bench without even looking to see where the arrow had landed. The crowd applauded politely for the magician. Trae could see that the arrow struck into the target very close to the center. He was impressed by Dune's shot.

Trae was the next to take aim. He walked to center stage with questions filling his mind. He was supposed to be gone with Edgar, bartering for the fake stone while Dune was the on-stage distraction. With both men on stage surrounded by a group of seekers, their plan was quickly falling apart. Trae nocked and drew his arrow. He needed some time to think this through. How could they trade with Edgar and have the seekers stay away from the tent? Time was running out as he stood center stage holding the taught bowstring.

Just before he released his arrow to deliberately sail wide, an idea came to him. Trae flexed his muscles and tapped into the power of the Strength Stone. From behind him he could hear Dune's robe shifting as he moved in his seat. Trae continued to pull power from the stone, hoping that it was enough to attract the attention of every nearby seeker. Then, after holding the bow for much longer than was necessary, Trae sighted down the arrow and released a perfect shot.

As if on cue, and reading his thoughts, Dune stood to leave the stage.

"Good match, archer." He reached out and patted Trae on the shoulder at the same moment that Trae subtly handed him the small bottle of poison. Then, for the first time since they were on the stage, Dune briefly looked into Trae's eyes and gave a slight incline of his head and what Trae thought looked like a smile. Dune then disappeared off the stage and into the crowd. He hoped that by drawing the seekers' attention he had salvaged what he could of their plan.

While the announcer called for Dune to come back, and the archers on stage were all watching the hooded figure leave, Trae looked out into the crowd to see that the seekers had no interest in Dune. They were all looking intently at him. Apparently the stone had done its job. Trae smiled broadly and waved his hand slightly to the crowd, again playing the part of a noble contestant who was about to be announced winner of the archery tournament. He just needed to keep up this act long enough to ensure that Dune had the time he needed.

After the announcer calmed things down, Bull's Eye Bebe took her place on center stage. She looked nervously down range at the distance and drew her bow. Her bow was grossly underpowered for a one hundred yard shot, so she aimed in an elevated arc. When she released, the arrow soared and it stuck into the wooden edge of the target. As the arrow flew the crowd cheered, then as it hit the target, there was an audible, disappointed gasp. Bebe raised one hand to the crowd as she returned to sit on the bench with the other archers.

Kaz was next to shoot, and he confidently strode to the center of the stage. While most of Trae's attention was focused on what he would do with a mob of angry seekers, he was interested to see how this youth fared at this range. Kaz smoothly nocked his arrow and drew the bowstring, he raised it to the perfect elevation and released. Trae was surprised at how quickly he drew and released, knowing all the factors that he must be considering before making such a vital and challenging shot. Despite the quick release, the execution was flawless. Kaz's arrow hit the only place on the target where he could earn not one, but two extra points, his arrow had grazed the colored feather of Trae's perfect bull's eye. The audience went wild with excitement.

"Never in the history of this event has someone hit the

colored feather on the hundred yard shot," the announcer bellowed. "We have a new champion!" The crowd cheered and Kaz stood on the stage with his arms raised. He waved to the people and inclined his head to his competitors, and bowed to his trainer, but then he turned around and stopped his celebrating. Maggie was standing, ready to fire her final arrow.

The announcer chuckled slightly, then began to speak, "Don't you see…" as the announcer spoke, Maggie drew her bow and took aim. Before releasing her arrow she turned to look over her shoulder at the announcer. With a look of complete defiance in her eyes, she released the arrow while looking away from the target. She dropped her longbow, stalked across the stage, grabbed the prize money, and walked away, pushing her way through the crowd.

Trae was shocked by this display. *What was she thinking?* Then, from beside him he heard a whisper,

"She won." Kaz had spoken to himself in a voice so quiet that only Trae could hear.

"What was that?" Trae asked.

"Her arrow is touching my colored feather and yours as well. She just hit a spot that was hair thin in both directions from one hundred yards. I don't know how she did it, but she won."

Without knowing what else to do, Trae sat back down, allowing the judges to take all the time they needed to come to a decision. Once they announced Maggie as the winner, he began to clap his hands loudly.

"Bravo!" He continued to cheer for longer than was necessary, trying to extend the celebration and delay his meeting with Edgar.

* * * * *

After Mylot and Farin were sitting together on the wooden bench, the judge stood up in the ring and addressed the crowd. The presentation was unorthodox, but he seemed unable to resist the chance to stand and speak before the king.

"I present to you two young men who have proven their

great skill…" Mylot ignored the small speech and looked over his shoulder. When he turned he cringed. Standing by Farin's trainer was the tall boy who had stopped him from reaching Maggie. The young man smiled widely at Mylot while waving like a buffoon. If that farm boy was back, that meant the archery tournament was over. He hung his head and let out a groan, feeling the weight of failure pressing down on him.

"Are you all right?"

Mylot turned and looked in the direction of the unfamiliar voice. It belonged to his opponent, Farin. He sat up, took in a deep breath and replied, "I'm fine."

"Okay, you just looked like you lost something very important."

Mylot raised an eyebrow as he looked at Farin. Mylot was surprised, confused, and not sure how to respond.

"I … well … let's just say that hopefully I haven't lost it forever."

Farin smiled warmly, "I sincerely hope that too."

Mylot nodded to Farin. "Thank you."

He knew the feeling of people being nice because they were forced, or because they had something to gain, but this was different. Mylot felt sincerity from Farin.

Before he had time to consider this strange turn of events, the judge finished his speech and called them to the ring for the final round.

"This round has no time limit. You will face each other until there is a victor." Then, with a flourish and a dramatic pause, the judge announced loudly, "Begin."

Mylot and Farin met in the center of the stage with a crash of their steel blades as they began a fourth round. After the extended break they were both rejuvenated and moving more quickly than before. They attacked, parried, dodged, and moved perfectly from stance to stance. Mylot began forcing Farin backward, then Farin found an opportunity to press him back. When Farin was moving forward, Mylot defended automatically, and while he was moving backward he remembered what Sir Theodore had taught him at his estate several months ago.

Maneuvering an opponent into a vulnerable position was more important than making a deathblow. Up to this point in the match, Mylot had been trying to make a quick victory by hitting Farin with a powerful strike, and the younger man had successfully dodged his way through the match. Mylot stopped moving backward and stood his ground while Farin attacked.

He shifted from stance to stance, blocking Farin's regular attacks, until he finally understood something else Sir Theodore had taught him. He could feel Farin's rhythm. Strike, strike, strike, lunge. Strike, strike strike, lunge. He added a variety of attacks into this pattern, but it always ended with a strong forward, right side lunge. Mylot just needed to throw off his rhythm.

As Farin was moving to make another lunge forward, instead of parrying the attack and trying to make a counter attack, as he had done before, knowing the attack was coming, he twisted his body to the side, allowing the sword to slide harmlessly past him, and he struck out with the hilt of his sword in a quick jab that caught Farin in the chest. It was not a hard strike, but it jarred him enough that Mylot was able to make two more quick strikes that brought the match to a close. The audience ruptured in applause and Mylot looked past them up to Sir Theodore who inclined his head knowingly.

The announcer and judge stepped out into the ring and proclaimed Mylot the victor of the final match. In his previous years of fighting he had not given his opponents a second thought after defeating them, but this time was different. After being pronounced the winner, Mylot walked over to Farin and called his name. Farin reached up and took Mylot's outstretched hand. Mylot pulled Farin to his feet.

"I have competed in this tournament the last five years, and won the last three."

Farin nodded, but still looked sad. Mylot wondered what he could do to help the young man feel any better, then he saw the boy make a subtle glance at the girl sitting by his trainer. Mylot smiled inwardly as he realized the boy felt bad, partly because he was trying to impress this young woman. Mylot placed his arm to his chest in a sign of great honor and spoke loudly so everyone near the ring could hear.

"You are a very talented swordsman, one of the best I have faced." He then raised Farin's arms into the air and turned him to the crowd.

The crowd cheered loudly for Farin, and Mylot could see the boy filled with a sense of pride. Then he turned Farin to face King Robert. Mylot and Farin both fell to one knee before the king motioned for them to stand. King Robert then rose to his feet and applauded both fighters, nodding in approval. Mylot looked up at the King and inclined his head,

then winked and mouthed to him, "Thanks, Uncle Robbie."

CHAPTER 33

After leaving the archery tournament, Dune made his way quickly through the crowd to the southern gate. Dressed as he was in a full magician's robe, Dune easily passed through town as the people parted to give him space. Before exiting the south gate, he ducked into a secluded alley and quickly took off his robe to reveal a sturdy pair of woolen pants and a nondescript, rough wool shirt. He tucked his robe into his satchel, fastened a small falchion on his belt, and left through the gate on his way to the green tent.

The outskirts of town were very quiet and eerie compared with the boisterous crowds at the tournaments. While walking to the tent, Dune looked around and found that he was the only person traveling this road. Hopefully his luck would hold and he would find an abandoned tent. He continued to walk quickly down the main street out of town until he could clearly see his destination, then he began to walk more casually in case there were any unwanted eyes following him.

As he passed the opening of the tent he took a sideways look and was disappointed to see three women in it guarding the merchandise and the barrels. Dune continued to walk past the tent. When he was out of their line of sight, he ducked into the ditch beside the road and waited. He cautiously watched and listened until he was satisfied that nobody was following or watching him. He then silently transported himself from the ditch to directly behind the tent, right next to the barrels.

Standing outside the tent he could hear the women talking.

"That fool better come running right back here when he has it," spoke a first woman with an old, tired sounding voice.

"I think you scared him too much to do anything else," came a second voice, also old and ragged.

The third voice spoke with a smooth and young tone, "You will give him the Han'Or when he comes back, won't you?"

"Why should I?" Again, the first woman spoke. "He is far too aggressive, and threatens all that we are trying to do."

"He is very…forward, but he also gets answers when *some*

are too timid to ask."

"Some? What are you trying to say, Genea?" the second woman shot back quickly.

"Just that he is an asset; *he* at least tries to find the Stones of Power."

"I'll tear out your heart, you…" Although hidden behind the thick canvas, Dune could practically feel the tension between the women.

"Now girls, stop bickering." The first woman clicked her tongue at them before continuing, "We have much to do, and this petty behavior is not helping." A silence fell between the pair that stretched on. "If he comes back with a magical stone, then yes, I will give him some Han'Or."

"If we're keeping Edgar, then who will we eliminate? Mordyar didn't send enough elixir for everyone."

"We'll weed out those who are least productive; perhaps some of the older seekers can make room for the young." Dune could hear them clearly through the canvas as they discussed the strengths and weaknesses of several seekers. Although he suspected it was not made in Denall, it was a revelation to hear that this Han'Or came directly from Mordyar. He wondered what methods the sorcerer was using to import the elixir.

"We need to figure out something quickly," the young woman said. "Many of the seekers are down to their last drops of Han'Or. Some are losing their sight already. It won't be long before they begin to lose their connection with reality."

"Maybe it is best to see who runs out first," came a suggestion. "We'll see who has chosen to squander their gift."

"They have gathered here to refill their supplies," she argued.

"Wrong!" the older woman interrupted in a shout that silenced the argument. "They have gathered here to show who is most capable! It would be ludicrous to think that this tournament could proceed without attracting a single stone holder. The people of Denall are weak and vain. They desire the petty prestige of loosing an arrow at a colored target better than the next fool, or smashing an opponent off a horse with a stick.

I am certain that one, if not more stone holders will be tempted to use their enhanced gift to win some glory. These seekers are here to show me who among them is valuable and who is not. When they retrieve a Stone, I will reward them with a supply of Han'Or and present the Stone to Mordyar myself. Once a Stone is found, we won't need the others anymore. It doesn't matter what we do with the Han'Or or what we do with Edgar. The Stone is all that matters."

Although he was pleased that there was a general shortage of Han'Or, and therefore less for the seekers, he needed to focus on reducing it more drastically. With their magically enhanced jewelry and weapons he could not openly face three seekers alone, and he could not teleport the poison he had acquired on his detour into the barrels from his position unless he knew exactly where the barrels were. Without any better solution forthcoming he decided to do something very rash. He drew the falchion from its sheath and with a quick stroke of the curved blade he sliced cleanly through the green fabric to reveal three very surprised and angry seekers.

* * * * *

Trae stayed on stage as long as possible after the archery tournament was ended, but with Maggie gone, and Kaz running off toward the sword fighting, he could not avoid Edgar any longer. He collected his winnings from the third place award and walked down the stairs.

"Hello, Edgar."

"Sir Trevor," he began with an incline of his head and a flourish of his hand, "that was a magnificent display. A perfect bull's eye from one hundred yards. Simply stunning."

"Yes, thank you," Trae said in a condescending tone. "So where can we go to speak of this stone?"

"Anywhere you feel comfortable," Edgar replied, failing miserably at trying to not seem too anxious. "We could go to my tent, or perhaps a more secluded place where we can openly talk."

"I'll stay here in public, if that pleases you," Trae replied.

Edgar began to shake his head. "Well, it does not please me." Edgar dropped all polite pretenses as he motioned for his seeker friends to gather near. When they had formed a tight circle surrounding Trae, Edgar stood within inches of him. "I want that stone, and you're going to give it to me one way or another. I don't care if we have to drag you down an empty ally and hide your body later." As he spoke, Trae was almost overwhelmed by his foul breath and the crazed look in his eyes. "Or would you rather go to a more familiar place? Perhaps we could meet with you in the magic shop. I'm sure your magician friend would be more than accommodating to have us pay him a visit." Edgar let the implied threat hang in the air while he waited for a response.

Trae struggled to keep his voice steady as he addressed Edgar and fought to ignore the tight circle of seekers. "I suppose right here would be a fine place to conduct our business."

"Wonderful!" Edgar announced. "I did tell them you were a reasonable man," he said, pointing to his friends. The circle opened a little as the seekers backed up to give Trae some more space.

"I assume that *you* are also a reasonable man, and willing to offer a fair price." Edgar nodded at the implied question. "So what are you willing to offer for it?"

"I'll start with an offer of your life," Edgar smiled wickedly, "and I will also restate my offer from the other night: three gold pieces for the stone."

Despite being intimidated by the circle and Edgar's threat, Trae needed to act the part of a noble. "I doubt you would kill me here in front of all these people, so a threat on my life does not strengthen your position. As for the gold, if you recall, I have already refused that offer. I believe it is worth fifty gold pieces."

"That is a bold proposal, my friend, very bold, and don't be too sure what I will and will not do in public." Edgar gave a moment for his threat to sink in, then made his counter offer. "Ten gold pieces is a fair price. We don't even know what the stone can do."

"I like this stone. I think it helped me hit that direct bull's eye in the tournament. Perhaps it is a Luck-bringing Stone; they are very rare, and very valuable. Forty gold pieces for the chance at a Luck-bringing Stone is a bargain price."

"If this was a Luck-bringing Stone, it would be worth one hundred times that amount, but we both know that it is not."

"How can you be so sure?" Trae asked, trying to keep the seekers occupied for as long as possible.

"Because, Sir Trevor, if this stone brought luck, you wouldn't be here," Edgar gestured to the circle surrounding Trae, "would you?"

Despite the desperate situation, Trae smiled, "You have a solid point. I'll settle for thirty."

Edgar raised his hands in the air and let out an audible laugh, "I like your style! I think in another lifetime we could have been friends. I want to pay ten, you are offering thirty, let's say we meet in the middle. Fifteen gold pieces."

Trae made a questioning look, as if to ask if the man was joking. After no response he stated his concern outright, "Meeting in the middle would be twenty pieces of gold."

"Well, I'm not so good with math. Besides, I felt like rounding down. So what do you say?"

"I say twenty pieces of gold and a promise that I will never see you or any of these friends of yours again," Trae countered. He wanted to keep pushing Edgar, but the seeker seemed to want the negotiations to end quickly.

"Deal. After today you will never see any of us again," Edgar reached into a small leather purse and carefully counted out twenty pieces of gold.

Trae pulled the white stone from beneath his plate armor and placed it into Edgar's outstretched hand. Edgar quickly handed the gold to Trae, closed his hand around his treasure and dashed away into the crowd. Trae breathed a deep sigh of relief and watched closely as the seekers disappeared into the crowd, all moving in the general direction of the southern gate—all but one. One young seeker in a deep maroon tunic began heading south, then unexpectedly veered East. Suspicious, Trae followed at a distance to see what was more important to a seeker than the possibility of having found a Stone of Power.

* * * * *

The three women glared at Dune through the opening in the canvas tent, then quickly grabbed some weapons and lunged at him. He parried and dodged as quickly as he could, drawing the women away from the tent. It was clear that these women had little skill with the short swords they hefted, but the swords' magical enchantments were quickly making up for the bearers' ineptitudes.

The oldest of the women had a bright steel sword that unnaturally gleamed in the sunlight. She lunged forward ahead of the younger women and Dune sidestepped, moving his sword to intercept hers. Just as the weapons were about to meet, a brilliant beam of light reflected directly from the sword into his eyes, obscuring his vision. He jumped backward and moved to block another attack, and the same light momentarily blinded him. Each time their swords were about to meet, her sword sent out a blinding light into his eyes. It was a frustrating enchantment. Dune stepped back, trying to dodge rather than block the sword as he blinked his eyes back into focus.

The second woman had emerged from behind the leader. Dune dodged a wild swing and then shoved her, knocking her off balance. Dune lunged forward, and much to his surprise, the woman spun and her sword clashed with his, completely blocking the attack. He turned his blade quickly and attacked with an underhand. The sword, more than its owner, moved into another perfect defense. Dune smiled to himself as the sword jerked from side to side, blocking a series of attacks. He was sure that if he could continue striking at this woman, the sword, enchanted to defend her, would tear her shoulder from its socket. Unfortunately, he could not just focus on this woman as he had two others to deal with.

Dune dodged a wild swing from the older woman and struck her with a backhand that sent her sprawling onto the ground. He then turned to face the third. She approached with her sword held awkwardly in both hands and pointed it at him. She was no killer, her eyes told him that much. The sword shook as she approached.

"Why are you here?" she demanded.

"You must be Genea," Dune began kindly.

"How did you know my name?" she yelled angrily.

Dune put up his hands in a gesture of nonviolence and addressed the girl. "You don't have the look of a seeker. Have you made the oath yet?"

"Don't say a word!" The older woman had regained her footing, and the three seekers stood together in a line. "I don't know where you heard about us, but you will take your knowledge to the grave right now." With this declaration the three women advanced on Dune.

Dune was overwhelmed trying to avoid having his sword making contact with the older woman's sword, while keeping the second off balance, and he was not quite sure what to do with the youngest. He was retreating farther from the tent, leading the women away when a motion on the road caught his attention. Edgar was running full speed from the southern gate. Dune had run out of time.

He needed to end this fight quickly, so he turned his full attention to the oldest seeker and began advancing on her. He faked attacks, while ensuring that he avoided contact with her magically enchanted blade. While he tried to gain an advantage on her, she swung wildly to keep him at bay, and the two other seekers advanced from behind.

"Don't move!"

Dune could feel the tip of a sword pressed firmly into his back. He stood still and glared at the older woman in front of him.

"So you thought you could stand against us? You fool!" She raised her short sword in a high arc over her head, then swung it directly at Dune's head. At the moment when the blade was about to make contact, Dune vanished. Her sword passed directly through the air where he had been standing and toward the other seeker. The magical sword that had been previously held in Dune's back jerked upward in response and met the attack in a crash that temporarily blinded the seeker.

From inside the tent Dune could hear them argue and fight as they tried to figure out where he had gone. Now inside the tent he raised his falchion and drove it downward to destroy the first barrel of Han'Or. Expecting to receive little resistance from the old barrel, Dune was severely jarred as his sword came to a complete stop, not even scratching the surface of the wood. Destroying the mixture was not going to be easy.

Dune pulled at the lid of the barrel, but it didn't budge. He magically lifted it above his head and slammed it to the ground, he even shot some magic, but it did not break. Frantically, he swung his sword at each container, again trying to spill the contents, but nothing happened. After repeated failures, Dune stopped to think through the problem, but his time had run out. He heard the sound of Edgar's panting approaching the opening of the tent. Before Edgar could enter the tent, Dune ducked under the table and pulled a pile of hand woven blankets over his body.

"Melna! Melna!" Edgar called from inside the tent. Dune heard him run inside the tent, then the footsteps moved farther away. They would all be back soon and Dune needed to be far away.

He looked from under the blankets and he could see the barrels. It was so frustrating to be so close to the elixir, but unable to do anything to dump them out. He fingered the little green bottle of poison in his robe. If he could poison the liquid, he didn't have to destroy the barrels, but they were still sealed. Dune reached out with an imperceptible strand of magic and touched the closest barrel. He could feel the protective shield, but he could also feel that it was a physical shield only. It would protect the exterior of the barrel from any outside attack, but it did not protect the inside of the barrel.

By now, other seekers had arrived at the tent door. Dune could hear them approaching the table and talking in hushed whispers, waiting for Melna to return with Edgar.

"It's right here, I'm telling you we all saw it," Edgar was returning to the tent. "He used the stone to enhance his strength as he held the bowstring."

"This is not the Strength Stone," Melna replied curtly, throwing the stone to the ground. "If he used a stone to enhance his strength, then he still has it. Find Han, and then go pay our friend a visit. Don't come back without the stone." Dune heard footsteps scurrying quickly away.

"Genea, take three seekers and make sure the job is done."

"Yes, mother," the young woman answered. Dune was surprised by the pronouncement, as Genea looked nothing like the older seeker. Dune had no time to consider the exchange, as there was a flurry of motion, and the seekers rushed to obey their orders.

"The rest of you, there was a man here in his late thirties, a little taller than Edgar. He couldn't have gotten far. He has dark hair, dark eyes, and he carries a falchion. He is a magician. Kill him."

A rush of feet hurried in all directions searching for Dune while he silently waited just out of sight.

When the footsteps quieted, he slowly peered out from under the covers. There were two pairs of legs he could see from under the table -- Melna and the other older seeker he had fought with earlier.

Knowing the seekers' power for detecting magic, Dune had one chance to sabotage the elixir before they would know his location. He retrieved the poison and looked out at the barrels. He had teleported himself or small objects hundreds of times, but this was different. He needed to teleport half of the poison into each barrel simultaneously, then get out. He just hoped it would work. Dune reached out with his magic, splitting the contents of the poison and teleporting it into the center of each barrel.

The moment Dune touched magic, the two nearby seekers shrieked and grabbed their weapons. They turned the table on end, ready to strike the blankets. Before their swords could find him, Dune teleported again.

*****

Through the crowded streets of Lexingar Trae followed the seeker in the maroon shirt. After changing course three times, Trae was certain he knew who the seeker was following. A tall, slender woman with knee high leather boots, a leather tunic, and a long, flowing cape hanging down her back. Her long, dark hair hung perfectly braided down her back. She continued through the streets of Lexingar, stopping to peer into shops and speak to those she passed, unaware that she was in danger. Trae's first instinct was to jump the seeker and ensure the woman was safe, but, remembering his actual purpose here in Lexingar, he kept his distance from the seeker, watching to see what he was up to.

For half an hour the seeker kept following the woman up and down the main streets of Lexingar, and just as Trae was beginning to lose patience with the pursuit, the woman began to run. The seeker broke into a dash, followed by Trae. Trae pumped his arms and legs for more speed, determined to catch the seeker before he could reach the woman.

She turned down a side street and the seeker ran after her. When Trae arrived at the ally he skidded to a halt. He saw no signs of the woman or the seeker. He continued jogging down the street, looking in the shop windows and down smaller side alleys. After walking down this street for several minutes, Trae saw something maroon. He proceeded with caution down the muddy street. On the ground, lying lifelessly, he found the seeker, but the woman was gone. Trae looked up and down the alley searching for the woman. He wanted to call out to her, but he felt foolish calling without knowing her name. Under his breath he spoke,

"Thank goodness she's safe."

Trae looked around a final time before leaving the alley. On his return trip to the magic shop, he doubled back several times to ensure he wasn't being followed. When he reached the shop he was greeted by Morgin.

"Hello, welcome back. How did the tournament go?" the

old magician asked in an uninterested tone.

"It went very well. I was the second runner up," Trae responded. He had more important things to worry about than the tournament. He walked through the shop and toward the stairs.

"That is impressive for a warrior to also be so talented with the bow," Morgin reached for some arrow heads and he held them up, as if trying to sell them to Trae.

"Thank you," Trae cut him off. He walked past and found his way upstairs. When he stepped into his room he felt the presence of someone behind the door. Assuming it was Dune, he addressed the sneaky magician, "How did everything go?"

Before he realized what was happening, Trae was clubbed over the head, and everything went black.

* * * * *

Pain throbbed through his entire body as Trae began to regain consciousness. He did not know how much time had passed, but he looked around the room, and saw all his belongings spread on the floor.

"How does one remove that armor?" Trae looked up at the sound of the familiar voice and saw a crazed smile on Edgar's face. He tried to move, but his arms were tied securely to a chair, and his mind was still foggy.

"Edgar. What are you doing?" Trae asked in a slurred voice.

Edgar slapped Trae across the face. "How do I take off this plate armor?"

Trae shook his head, recovering from the blow. "Edgar, I don't understand. I thought you got what you wanted."

"It would be a lot easier on you to just answer my questions," Edgar pulled out a thin blade and moved closer to Trae.

"Wait. Edgar, please! What are you doing?"

"Trevor, I made a promise that you would never see me again. The only way I can be sure to keep my promise is if you can't see at all."

CHAPTER 34

Boon and Blade left their apprentices to explore Lexingar with a few words of caution, and the advice to stick together. The three started off with excitement, exploring all the great city had to offer.

"Look at that jewelry shop!" Angela exclaimed.

"Too bad you don't have any money," Farin reminded her. Not seeming to hear him, or perhaps not caring to listen, she grabbed his hand and pulled him into the shop.

"I'll be right here," Kaz said to the pair as he leaned on the door of the shop. For a while he watched with amusement as Angela led Farin from one display to the next. When he turned around to look at the streets, he was surprised to notice a woman standing right next to him, watching him intently.

"Hi, Kaz," she said in a friendly tone. "That was some amazing shooting today." She had a casual smile and friendly manner that set Kaz at ease.

"Thanks," he answered, not knowing what else to say. The crowd was fairly large at the archery range, but even with a large crowd, he thought he would have remembered seeing this woman. Her long black hair and dark eyes were mesmerizing, and when she smiled he felt like he was weak at the knees. It was probably a good thing he hadn't noticed her during the tournament.

"My name is Pentra, but everyone just calls me P," she said as she extended a delicate hand to him.

"I'm Kaz, nice to meet you, P," he replied as he took her hand and shook it. This response made her smirk and he realized that she had already called him Kaz, and she had seen him shoot, so of course she knew his name. Feeling rather stupid and knowing that his face was burning red, he tried to start a conversation with the woman.

"Are you from Lexingar?"

"I live here now," she answered, then she paused as though she were considering what to say next. "Have you ever heard of Baron Omer?" Kaz nodded. "What do you know of him?" she asked.

After a moment to consider his reply, Kaz cautiously answered, “Well, he has the best vineyards in Denall. By all reports he seems to be a fair lord to his people, keeps them protected with his soldiers.” She was nodding and looking at Kaz thoughtfully.

“It seems that you don't trust the reports,” she said in a very perceptive way.

“I don't know. I just think there may be more to him than he lets on. Good, bad, or otherwise I have no idea, there's just more…” With that, Kaz asked a question of his own. “Why are you interested in what I think of the baron?”

“It looks like your friends are done flirting in the jewelry shop. I'll stop by later today and we'll continue this conversation,” she waved her fingers as she stepped into the street and melted into the crowds. Kaz watched her until she was completely lost to sight.

“What you looking at?” Kaz was startled by Farin's question.

He turned and absently responded. “Nothing. Just the people.”

“Well, let's get going, there are lots of other people to see down that way,” Angela pointed as she led the way down the street that seemed most likely to have shops with soaps, lotions and jewelry. Kaz noticed that she had not released Farin's hand since she had dragged him into the shop, and Farin was not objecting.

Kaz walked behind the two feeling very out of place. After the third shop he interrupted her unending chatter to bring her down a notch.

“Wow, Angela, if you don't watch which stores you go into people are going to start noticing that you're a girl.”

“I'm sorry, Kaz, who is it that wears a lady's necklace?” she countered in a tone that was more harsh than playful.

“Calm down there, little girly. Your mood swings are just going to make everyone know you're female.” With a bit of a huff and a sour look she turned from Kaz and continued down the street to the nearest fabric shop and darted in with Farin in tow. It was unusual to see her interested in anything other than weapons and fighting.

Kaz spent the rest of the afternoon scanning the crowds for P, hoping he would see her again while he waited outside shops with jewelry, scarves, clothing, and of course swords and armor. Those two were a perfect match for each other.

While waiting outside an armory, Kaz spotted one shop that interested him quite a bit, and he convinced the other two to follow him for a change. He entered the magic shop and was surprised by the variety of materials that were for sale. There were weapons of every kind, armor, clothing, stones, and jewelry, but what made this shop interesting to Kaz was the fact that all the items were enchanted. First he looked at the arrow heads.

"What will these do?" he asked the man behind the long, wooden counter.

The man was tall and slender with a look of age and wisdom. His grey hair and beard were long and seemed to flow down and meld into the long grey robe he was wearing. On his left wrist Kaz could make out a red mark, but was unable to see the number of marks as the man was partially hidden by the counter.

"These are all fire tips," he answered in a raspy voice with a foreign accent. "They will burn hot like the sun as soon as they leave your bowstring. They will penetrate the strongest armor, but they can only be shot once." Then, looking at Kaz steadily, he added, "They are five gold pieces each." Looking down at the small box of arrowheads, Kaz carefully replaced the one he was holding, realizing what a treasure the enhanced weapons were.

"If I bring you an enchanted arrowhead, would you be able to tell me what it does?"

The man nodded thoughtfully. "Certainly, for a fee of course."

Kaz moved closer to the counter and saw some small stones and rings that looked fairly common.

"What are those?" he asked pointing to a set of rings.

"They are rings of fire and ice. They are a helpful pair to

have for traveling. If you are cold, the fire ring will warm you, if you are hot the ice ring will cool you down. They have also been used as weapons." Kaz looked confused. "Would you linger in a fist fight if your body had a sharp pain of frost or burning each time you were struck?"

"No, I guess not," Kaz admitted. "So, how do they work?"

"When you are feeling a chill, you press the fire ring against your body and the ring will give off heat. If you are feeling hot and want to cool down, do the same with the ice ring. The amount of heat or cold from the rings increases as you press the rings harder against your skin. Each ring will last almost a year if you use its power sparingly."

Kaz smiled and asked the cost of the rings. The store clerk explained that because of the size of the rings, and this common type of enchanting they had, and because the enchantment did not require too many days to create, the rings were only ten gold pieces each. Kaz reached into his pocket to retrieve the twenty-five gold pieces he had won from winning second place in the archery tournament and found that he only had thirteen pieces left. Cursing under his breath that he had let his guard down and been robbed, he turned back to the store clerk longingly. The man took Kaz's thirteen coins and handed him the pair of rings that looked identical.

"I'll give you this deal because I like your eyes; you seem like a good boy." Kaz put them on and tested their magic before leaving the shop.

* * * * *

Dressed in his dark cloak, Dune stood in the shadows outside his uncle's magic shop, watching as Edgar and another seeker entered, followed shortly by Trae. He had reached out with magic and quickly learned that both seekers were covered with magic jewelry and weapons. Before he faced these two foes he needed to create a magic block over the entire shop. Dune began to emerge from his hidden place to follow when a group of two boys and a girl opened the door and entered the building.

He ducked back. One of the boys was Kaz, the tall young man from the archery tournament. He watched them walk around the shop looking at items and talking with Morgin. As they were searching the shop, Genea walked past. She led three other seekers to an alley across the street from the shop. Once there, the four seekers waited and observed.

Dune watched as Kaz made a purchase and moved to exit the shop. He pulled the cowl of his cloak over his head and walked across the street to his uncle's shop just as Kaz reached for the door.

"I hope you didn't spend too much on those trinkets," Dune said, seeing the cold and heat rings in Kaz's hands. At that moment Dune had an idea. "They won't last you to the end of the week."

In defense of his merchandise Morgin bellowed, "Be silent."

Dune pulled down his hood and looked at his uncle. "Morgin, it has been too long." Morgin immediately fell silent.

Addressing the youth, Dune continued, "Give them here." He stretched out his hands and took the rings from Kaz. Heat and cold rings were a simple enchantment that required very little energy, but he intended to use this display as a decoy for weaving his magic block. He solidified some air under the rings and lifted them into the air, then infused them with some light so they would glow as if being forged. While he hung the rings in the air, he began skillfully weaving the magic block around the shop. Although he could still cast spells and create enchantments, all magical items within the store would not perform their functions. He worked as quickly as he could, not sure what was happening to Trae upstairs. When the magic block was finished, Dune infused the heat and cold rings with energy.

Dune gave the rings back to Kaz, and as he walked the young man to the door, he explained how they worked. Before Kaz could leave, Dune added,

"Great job today! That was truly amazing!"

"Thank you!" Kaz said. "You did great too!" Dune nodded, then opened the door for the trio to exit. He closed the door and latched it shut behind them.

* * * * *

"That was odd," Angela commented, looking back at the closed shop.

"I'm just glad he came and fixed your rings," Farin said to Kaz. "Do you even know how much money you just spent? That would feed the entire caravan for a week."

"I won that money from the tournament," Kaz countered, "and the caravan easily made that much selling the horses, armor and weapons from the robbers. Just let me enjoy this, okay?" He finished by giving Farin a sharp punch to the left shoulder, which caused a jolt of cold to run through his arm.

"Ouch! Watch it with that thing!" Kaz smiled and they continued down the street. "I bet you could have gotten both rings for five gold pieces," Farin commented as he quickly dodged Kaz swinging at him with the fire ring. "Next time let me do the talking."

Kaz noticed as he tested the rings that not only were they much more powerful than before Dune had 'charged' them, but they also fit much better. He continued to play with the rings for the rest of the afternoon and evening on their way back to the caravan. The most interesting discovery was that when he was wearing both rings on one hand, it gave the person being punched, usually Farin, quite a jolt as the cold and hot ran into him at the same time. After accidentally numbing Farin's arm for half an hour with an exceptionally hard punch, Kaz let him put on the rings to return the favor.

What Kaz did not expect was for Farin to put on both rings and punch him square in the face. Kaz was in a daze for several minutes. After getting over the initial shock of what had happened, he laughed with Farin about how funny it must have been to see. Angela wasn't overly impressed with their boyish games, but she also took a turn to warm herself as the evening breeze began to blow. Before they reached the wagons, when she thought nobody was watching, Kaz saw her experimentally punch herself in the arm.

CHAPTER 35

"What are you doing here?" Morgin demanded.

Not responding to him, Dune simply raised his hand and enclosed Morgin in an invisible cage of air, then dropped him to the floor.

"Stay there and you should be safe."

Dune rushed upstairs and kicked in the door to Trae's room. Trae was tied to a chair. Edgar leaned in at him with a thin, sharp knife while another seeker watched. Dune reached out and wrapped a string of air around the dagger, then pulled it from Edgar. With the dagger in hand he advanced on the two men. Confident in his magical objects more than his skills, the second seeker drew his sword and lunged. Dune sidestepped the attack and struck him on the back of the head with the butt of Edgar's knife.

Edgar quickly moved to attack with his sword. Despite losing his magical enchantments, the sword was much larger than Dune's stolen knife and it easily knocked the knife to the floor. Edgar lunged forward in a second attack and his sword stopped in the air inches from Dune.

While Edgar pulled against the invisible force that held his weapon, Dune attacked with his bare hands. He struck Edgar quickly in the gut, neck and face, knocking him out. Dune tied the two unconscious men in thin weaves of air, and with a movement of his hand threw them into the corner of the room.

Dune moved to his friend's side. "Are you all right?" he asked as he untied his arms and examined his head wound.

"A little groggy, but I'm doing a lot better now."

"Good, because we don't have a lot of…" Before Dune could explain, Genea joined them in the now crowded room, followed by her group of seekers.

Genea motioned to one of her companions who walked into the room and stood by Edgar and Han.

"I see Melna was right to send us."

"Genea, you are not like them, you don't need to do this." Dune looked pleadingly at the young woman.

"You don't understand anything!" she spat. She nodded at the seeker in the corner who quickly drew his sword, and in two quick slashes killed Edgar and Han. "I must obey." For the first time in their brief encounters Dune wondered if she was as crazed as the other seekers.

"Trevor, how's that head of yours?" Dune asked as the two men backed up against the wall. Without time to answer, Dune and Trae advanced on the four armed seekers. Trae slipped under the forward thrust of a long sword and drove his elbow hard under the man's chin. He twisted the sword from the attacker's hand and drove him to the ground with a solid front kick. With sword in hand he faced the next seeker.

Dune threw a ball of frozen air at one seeker while he lunged forward to grab Genea. To his complete surprise, he passed right through where Genea had been standing and landed hard on the floor. Spinning to stand up, he saw her moving her hands in a familiar pattern and mouthing some very dangerous words. Dune reacted instinctively, creating a protective barrier of water around himself as a fireball shot from her hands. The magic fire met the water in a fit of sizzling and popping, leaving the room a steam bath. Dune had never encountered or heard of a magician seeker. What could be the meaning of this? He wanted to take this seeker alive for questioning.

While the two magicians circled the room, waiting for the other to make a move, Trae had his hands full. Despite handling thousands of weapons in his work as a blacksmith, Trae had never received any formal training on using them. He was lucky to be facing seekers who relied so much on the magical enhancements of their weapons that they too were unskilled swordsmen. Trae moved forward with a wild swing and it was met with an equally untrained block. The two men swung their swords in wide arcs, uncontrolled stabs, and made shaky blocks with the weapons awkwardly held. Knowing of his inexperience, Trae relied on his gift as he pulled strength through the stone and swung with all his power at the man's torso. In that moment the seekers in the room were all distracted by the activation of the stone as if a flash of sunlight had just blinded them.

While the seekers focused on the flash, Trae's sword broke through the sword of his opponent and struck him, and Dune reached out with magic to bind Genea. He quickly cast a second spell to block her from touching magic, but it was too late. Just before the spell reached her she vanished. Dune knew that while she was skilled, her natural strength was relatively weak, she could not have teleported far with that spell, and although he regretted it, he had no time to pursue her.

In the room there were three dead seekers, one unconscious from the ice attack, and Trae's wounded opponent who was now looking up at Trae as he shakily held the sword inches from his face.

"We don't have much time," Dune said, addressing the seeker. "Why the new urgency to locate stones? Why is Melna leveraging you with Han'Or?"

The man on the floor coughed out a laugh. "Do you really think I'll tell you? You must be the greatest fool in all of Denall."

The seeker shook slightly as he began rising from the floor. His body spun so that he was held suspended in the air inches in front of Dune.

"Your trinkets won't help you here, and you've seen what I'm capable of. I'm going to ask you one more question. Is Mordyar coming to Denall?"

He stared silently into Dune's eyes, refusing to speak. He tried to spit, but it flew backward, soaking his own face. Unable to wipe it off, he just hung there in silent defiance. Trae stepped forward.

"Let's try a different approach." He pulled his stone from beneath his plate armor.

As soon as the seeker saw the stone he began struggling against his invisible prison. He frantically heaved his head back and forth, unable to move anything else.

"Give me that!"

Trae calmly placed the stone back beneath his armor and addressed the seeker. "You are a stone seeker, and now you've found the Strength Stone. How does it feel to come this close to your entire purpose in life and know that you will never have it?" The man's body began shaking violently, his eyes rolled back in his head and unexpectedly he went still.

The two men stood silently looking at the lifeless body, completely dumbfounded by what had happened. Dune lowered the corpse to the floor, then looked at his friend.

"Well that was a different tactic for interrogating."

Trae raised his hands innocently. "How was I supposed to know that would happen?"

"I don't know, but how about next time we find a seeker we don't show them our stones," Dune said, voice filled with frustration. He began stalking back and forth in the small room, trying to gather his thoughts.

"Good plan," Trae agreed, then pointing to the remaining seeker he asked, "What about this one?"

Dune looked over his shoulder at Trae as he walked past. "I know of a special place for him." Dune stopped and crouched next to the seeker and quickly removed all his jewelry and magical items. "Can you tie him up?"

Trae's face narrowed in confusion. "Why don't you just tie him up with magic like you did the others?"

Dune sat down on the small stool, his shoulders visibly slouched. "This has been an exhausting day. I need to conserve my energy."

While Dune sat for a time, recovering some strength, Trae grabbed some rope from the hallway and tied him up, then placed the unconscious seeker in a large grain sack he retrieved from the horse stall.

"I have plenty of energy left."

"Just be sure not to use your stone for extra strength," Dune cautioned.

As he tied the sack closed, Trae nodded so Dune could see. "Speaking of which, why could I use the Strength Stone here, but their magical items didn't work?"

Dune answered thoughtfully, "That's a really good question." Then after a long silence he replied. "I'll have to give that some thought later. For now we need to get moving." Dune stood up and led the way out of the small room.

In the magic shop Dune approached the counter and looked down at his uncle.

"Morgin, thank you for waiting." Dune waved his hand and Morgin was released from his invisible prison.

"What evil have you brought here?" he demanded, glaring fiercely at his nephew as he returned to his feet.

Ignoring his questions, Dune addressed the older man. "It is urgent that we leave right away. I have no doubt that you can dispose of the bodies upstairs." His words were laced with disdain. "We will also be needing funds for our journey."

"I can give you…"

"You will give me all the gold that you have without a word of argument, or I will leave the magic block on your shop." Dune's voice left no room for doubt. He was not negotiating, he was making a demand that Morgin would obey.

In the air next to Morgin a large bag of gold appeared and he reluctantly placed it on the counter. Hoping to gain some advantage from this exchange he spoke.

"Does this settle our scores?"

Dune looked at the man and shook his head, "You will never be welcome back."

Morgin shook a hand in the air. "No, I know that." Then he made a downcast glance. "I meant between us." He slowly looked up until he was looking Dune in the eye. His eyes brimmed with tears.

Dune narrowed his eyes and skeptically scrutinized the older magician. He could see that his uncle was sincere and there was true pain behind his eyes. Unsure whether he could speak any words of forgiveness, he simply nodded his head.

Morgin bobbed his head up and down in gratitude, "I know it's too late for this, but I am sorry for what happened."

Ignoring the apology, Dune continued on his business, "I have some magical items of varying quality and usefulness, which I cannot afford to carry any further." He held his hands out in the air and spread them apart. In the air a small opening appeared. From the opening fell the weapons, armor and jewelry from all the seekers they had encountered in Lexingar. "I'm sure you can find a place for these."

Morgin's face lit up with greed as he looked over the loot that was easily worth double the gold he had just turned over. Getting Morgin's attention Dune continued,

"Remember to dispose of the bodies. More people may come looking for us, so be wary."

Trae slung the large sack over his shoulder, trying as much as possible to make it look like grain.

"Where are we going now?" Trae asked.

"We need to deliver this seeker."

CHAPTER 36

After his victory over Farin in the one-handed sword competition, Mylot had returned to Sir Rodnik craning his neck to look into the crowd.

"She's gone," Sir Rodnik said as he patted Mylot on the shoulder.

"I know." He slammed his gauntlets down on the wooden bench. "It's so frustrating!"

"You need to focus on the tournaments, and we'll find her later."

"After the archery match she disappears. Nobody knows where she goes, or what she does. How can I find a ghost?"

Sir Rodnik took a slow, calming breath before addressing his overly excited trainee.

"Ghosts don't need gold. She comes to the tournaments each year to win some gold. She must spend it somewhere. We'll send out word, even offer a reward if needed. We will find the girl."

Nodding, Mylot replied. "You're right. She needs to come out of hiding some time. Nobody can magically change gold into food." Mylot patted his trainer on the back. "Good thinking."

"Now are you ready to go win this tournament?" Mylot made a determined face and nodded slightly. "Good, then stop playing around with these guys and finish them quickly. Conserve your energy for the other events."

"Yes, sir."

He returned with Sir Rodnik to their apartments to prepare.

In two handed sword fighting Mylot had a great advantage. For most warriors, wielding the large weapons was difficult, but as a level five strongarm Mylot could easily handle it. In battle the two-handed sword was effective because the momentum and power of each stroke was deadly. When a soldier swung a two-handed sword full strength, defense was futile. Any weapon raised in defense was cleaved in two or knocked to the ground by the sheer weight and force of the attack. For Mylot, however, he not only had the strength to make brutal offenses, but also the control to maneuver the weapon quickly and skillfully. He could wield the large blade in a single hand, parry an attack, and then counter with an unstoppable forehand or backhand. In two-handed combat he was invincible. Soon after the matches began, he was declared the champion of the two-handed sword combat.

The final event for the day was the jousting. Jousting took place in the large stadium on the western side of the city. The seats were filled with hundreds of people waiting to see the horses and riders charge with their ten-foot lances. King Robert sat on a large throne directly across from the center of the arena where the lances would strike. This year it was announced that the king would be presenting the award to the winner of the joust.

A large man with a booming voice called for attention to begin the competition. "The first contestants will be Gojor from Eaton and Yendys from Horspathe."

The riders took their places on either side of the arena, horses impatiently prancing as they awaited the sign for them to begin. The judge nodded his head and a squire moved out to the fence that ran the length of the arena which showed the horsemen the line they must ride.

The squire raised a flag above his head and the two riders lowered their lances. When the squire dropped his flag and dashed to get away from the center fence, the riders urged their horses to action.

Hooves pounded on the sod as the powerful warhorses galloped. The contestants held the horses' reins with their inside shield arm, and their lances in the other. As they closed in on each other, Yendys aimed her lance for Gojor's chest and Gojor chose the more challenging target of aiming for the head. Yendys drove her lance forward and ducked her head to the side. Yendys' arm shook with the full impact of the lance striking Gojor's chest. The lance broke in two and Gojor wobbled in the saddle, nearly losing his seat. Gojor was unable to recover from this strike and after two more passes, he was eliminated and Yendys advanced to the second round. The crowd cheered.

Mylot stood on the ground brushing Gapol's flanks. Despite the noise, excitement and anxiety, the well trained horse stood still. "I hate this part." The horse reared his head and whinnied as if to agree. "An hour of waiting for a moment of excitement."

"Better get used to that, boy." Sir Theodore walked to Mylot and placed a steadying hand on Gapol.

"It's wonderful to see you." Mylot continued to absently brush Gapol while he turned his attention to Sir Theodore.

The older man nodded. "You have been very impressive today. You attracted the attention of the King. If you win, he'll be sure to have you join his guard."

"Thank you." He inclined his head slightly.

Sir Theodore smiled. "Anytime. Anything to increase the pressure on you. I know you work best under pressure." Mylot shook his head. "You'd better saddle up, you're up against Thuey."

"Are you serious? He came back? I thought after his embarrassing display last year he'd give up." Mylot took a half step so he could look around Gapol. He looked out into the arena, trying to see any sign that Thuey was actually competing.

"You might be surprised." Sir Theodore kept a straight face as he helped Mylot up into the saddle.

"Still trying to increase my pressure?" Mylot asked with a grin.

"Smart kid." The knight slapped Gapol on the rump and he began walking out to the stadium.

"Mylot of Tran," the announcer shouted. Mylot was given a warm welcome as he rode to his starting position. Mylot grasped his lance in his right hand and lowered his helmet visor using his shield hand. Looking down the jousting line he saw that Thuey's horse was stamping its hooves nervously. Gapol stood completely still, waiting for direction from his rider. While waiting for the flag Mylot tested the weight of the lance. It had good balance, and despite the awkward length, he could manipulate it with ease.

The flag was raised and the lances lowered. When the flag

dropped, Mylot kicked Gapol into action. Within a few steps the horse had accelerated to full speed and they thundered toward Thuey. When they were about to cross paths Mylot drove his lance hard into Thuey's oversized upper body while Thuey's lance was easily deflected off Mylot's shield. Thuey bent backward in the saddle and dropped the reins of his horse. His arms flailed wildly to maintain balance as the horse continued to trot across the arena. When he reached the far side where he was to prepare for a second run, Thuey raised his hands in a sign of surrender. The match was ended.

Mylot watched Thuey's team help him get down off the horse and remove his dented armor. Mylot dismounted Gapol and shook his head as he walked past Sir Theodore. "Happy now?"

"That was jousting," Sir Theodore said while still clapping.

"Yeah, more like a slaughter." Mylot walked Gapol in a cool down lap around the paddock before leading him to his stall. "Do you think he'll come back next year?" Mylot looked back out at Thuey to ascertain his condition.

"Hopefully he's learned something," he replied. Then he pointed at Mylot, "And hopefully you have as well."

"What do you mean?" Mylot asked over his shoulder as he handed Gapol's reins to a stable hand so he could carry on a more direct conversation.

Sir Theodore placed his hands firmly on Mylot's shoulders. "Treat each opponent like he could be the one to kill you, give your best every time, don't hold back."

"But these men aren't trying to kill me," he countered. "It's just a tournament." He said, pointing at the injured man. "I think I really hurt him this time."

"I'm not talking about the tournament. Your training for the King's personal guard has officially begun, if you accept the post," Sir Theodore reached out his hand.

In his excitement to share the news Mylot looked around for Sir Rodnik, or anyone he might know. There was nobody. He turned to Sir Theodore and grasped his hand. "I accept."

"Good, then get Gapol out of that stall and let's get going,"

Sir Theodore turned to leave.

Mylot looked out at the cheering fans and the king, seated to watch the jousting, then back to Sir Theodore, wondering if he was serious.

"What about the tournament?"

"I'm sure someone else will be happy to win," he replied with a dismissive wave of his hand.

"I can't just leave, what about the people who have come to see me fight? What about Sir Rodnik and my servants? What about…"

Sir Theodore turned around and interrupted. "If you want to be part of the king's guard you need to learn some things. First, I give commands and you take them. Second, you are part of a team now. It's not about you, and your fans, and your servants, and your victories. It is about working with a team for the good of Denall. It's your choice. But I promise you one thing. This is your last chance to join with us." Sir Theodore continued to walk away.

Mylot massaged his temples with both hands as he looked to the crowd, the other men waiting to joust, and finally at Gapol. This tournament had been all consuming for him for so long he hated the thought of just leaving. If he followed Sir Theodore he would never know if he could have won and he would lose face to hundreds of people. Was the loss worth what he would gain? His time was running out, Sir Theodore continued to walk away.

* * * * *

When they were within sight of the caravan, Kaz held out a warning arm.

"Something is not right."

Farin, trusting Kaz's sight, stepped between Angela and the caravan in an overprotective gesture.

"What is it?"

"I'm not sure -- there is a large crowd at the wagons," Kaz said, indicating the direction with a movement of his head.

Angela pushed Farin aside with a scowl. "Let me see!" She stood up on her toes and put her hand over her eyes. She turned to Farin and quietly said in an annoyed tone, "You'd better not get all protective on me, or I'll never hold your hand again." Then to show him she was both serious and tough enough to handle herself, she gave him her hardest punch.

"Ouch!" Farin yelled, drawing curious heads from the tents that were set up around them.

Angela immediately grabbed his arm. "I'm so sorry! I forgot I was wearing the ring." She tried to comfort him while she nursed his injured arm. She took off the red ring and handed it back to Kaz who was grinning from ear to ear, trying not to laugh out loud at what was happening.

The three walked stealthily as they approached the wagons. When they were within Farin's hearing he began to listen.

"It's safe," he concluded after listening for several minutes.

"What's that supposed to mean?" Kaz asked.

"Well my, dim-witted friend, that means that there is no danger." Without another word of explanation Farin walked right to the circle of wagons.

"That's not what I meant," Kaz protested. "What did you hear?" Kaz followed Farin and Angela as they walked. When he caught up to his friend, he gave Farin a playful punch in his injured arm, this time with the ice ring.

"Wow!" Farin announced. "That actually made my arm feel a lot better, here, do that again." Kaz lightly pressed the ice ring to Farin's burned arm, stopping when Farin waved his other arm. "Those rings are amazing!" Farin concluded. Kaz made an I-told-you-so look and Farin conceded. "Fine, fine, it wasn't a waste of your money. Let's just get on with this and find out what is happening in there."

When the three came closer to the caravan, the attention of the crowd turned to them. Some people rushed up to them and shook their hands while others patted them on the shoulders, seeming happy just to touch them. The three slowly made their way through the throng toward Boon and Blade, who were speaking with some people who seemed to have some authority.

"Here they are," Blade said proudly. "I told you they'd return soon," then to Angela and Farin he said, "This is Sir Theodore, Blade Master of Norwell, and a recruiter for the king's guard."

Sir Theodore wore a chainmail shirt under a leather and on his left shoulder he had a solid steel shoulder guard with an alternating pattern of blue and white squares, the crest of the king. Farin and Angela shook hands with the man and then looked back to Blade for some kind of explanation.

Sir Theodore spoke to them both, "I train the sword at the battle barracks in the capitol. I was very impressed with your performances today and want to extend an offer for both of you to return with me to Norwell to train and compete for the honor of defending the king." His stance looked casual, but also somehow dangerous at the same time.

"I don't understand," Farin began. "We didn't win."

The tall knight smiled and responded, "That's true, and you, young lady, were disqualified for poor sportsmanship," Angela looked at her feet, "but you both showed the makings of blade masters, and I want to take what Blade has started and help you to reach your potential."

Angela and Farin looked at each other, then they looked at Blade. He motioned as if to tell them it was their choice.

"Can we have some time to think about this?" Angela asked. Several people in the crowd gasped in surprise that they did not immediately jump at his offer.

Sir Theodore nodded his head, "Of course you can. This is a big decision, and probably wasn't part of your plans. But I want to warn you that this opportunity may never present itself again. It is a great honor to be chosen to train for the king's guard."

"Thank you, Sir," Farin said.

"Thank you," Angela repeated.

"You obviously don't know what life in the barracks is like, or you wouldn't be thanking me. It is hard work. Long days and aches and pains in places you didn't know could hurt." Then Sir Theodore looked distantly into the sky and added, "But if you survive, it is the greatest training you could ever hope to receive." He returned his gaze to the two young students. "We leave for Norwell at first light. If you are there, we will gladly have you come with us. If not, I wish you the best in your future." Sir Theodore then placed his right hand on Blade's right shoulder and Blade returned the sign. Then without another word he turned and left, taking with him in his wake about two thirds of the crowd that had gathered around the wagons.

"You two have raised quite a bit of excitement with your matches today," another man was saying, as he emerged to meet Farin and Angela. "My name is Ngoo," he said as he extended his hand.

"How can we help you?" Farin asked, getting right to the point.

"I buy goods in Lexingar and trade them mainly in Kinstock. I also make some trips to Maplewood and other smaller villages."

"That's great," Farin said, clearly uninterested in hearing the details of his business.

"The problem is that I need some guards for my goods. I can't promise the prestige of being in the king's guard, but I can promise that the money is much better." With a smile that reeked of dishonesty and greed, the man quickly continued, "I'll pay you five gold pieces per successful trip to Kinstock and back. What do you say?"

"We'll need some time to think about it," Angela said flatly. "But for now I'm going to lean toward no."

"How about you, young man?" he said, turning to Farin.

"I'm not interested in being a body guard. But thank you for the offer."

Ngoo turned and left briskly. Kaz heard him mutter under his breath, "Spoiled brats! I need bigger guards anyway."

"Wow, I think we just avoided a terrible fate with that one," Farin said to the others.

The evening continued in this same way. Offer after offer was presented to Farin. Some also included an offer for Angela, but after his display in the sword ring, and the standing ovation from the King, he had become something of a celebrity. While the crowd thronged around Farin, Kaz was able to quietly sneak past unnoticed.

Kaz was anxious to get back to Boon's wagon. He did not like to be without the Sight Stone. Kaz crept into the wagon and reached under his bedroll to find the stone he had carefully hidden. Then he checked his bow. He liked competing at archery, but he was looking forward to using his iron ash bow again.

"Are you in there?" Boon's voice came from outside the wagon.

"Yeah, I'm here," Kaz replied, replacing his bow and stepping out of the wagon.

"I didn't get to talk with you much after the tournament. How did you think it went?"

Kaz had thought again and again about the woman he had met in Lexingar, but he realized that he really hadn't given much thought to his performance in the tournament.

"I don't know. I could have done better."

"I agree," Boon said, much to Kaz's surprise. "If you had shot on the first three rounds like you did in the fourth and the tie-breaker, you would have won without contest." Boon continued in a lighter tone,"But for your first tournament, in the expert category of archery, against the best in the kingdom, I'd say you did an amazing job." Then Boon let a smile crease his face as he brought Kaz in for a one-armed hug.

Kaz responded, smiling, "Yeah, I was pretty amazing today," then his brow furrowed and he asked his mentor a question, "Why are there no crowds seeking my attention?"

Boon looked thoughtful. "Archery is not a high demand talent. If you can hit a man from fifty paces, that's good enough for most traveling guards, and anybody can pick up a bow and within a couple of months be good enough to do that. Also," Boon added, "most fathers teach their sons how to use a bow from the time they learn to walk."

"I guess that makes sense," Kaz said with a downward glance. "I just thought that making an incredible shot like that would get me some kind of chance to get out of here." Realizing what he had said, he looked up to Boon. "Not that it's bad here, I've learned so much, I just…"

Boon interrupted him. "I understand. The traveling and trading life is not for everyone." Then he said in a lower tone, "There's really not much more I can teach you."

Kaz, seeing a strange look in Boon's eyes, asked him, "What is it?"

"I had a son once. He was gifted with the bow and staff, like you. I trained him until I couldn't teach him anything more. He joined the army and went to the islands in the west to help make peace and end the foreign disputes. He didn't come home," he paused and turned his head up to look Kaz in the eyes. "These past months I've gotten used to having you around, and I had some hope that you might want to stay, but I knew in my heart that was a selfish wish. You are destined for greatness, and I need to share you with the rest of the world."

"Not to worry," Kaz said, trying to lighten the mood. "I don't think the world has any desire to take me."

"That's not entirely true," Boon said, pointing to a distant figure standing outside the circle of wagons. Kaz was delighted to see that P was there looking right at him. When he looked at her she smiled and nodded. The way she reacted, he thought that maybe she was a visor; she seemed to see clearly that he had turned to look at her. But he didn't remember seeing a mark near her eyes. Now, as he thought back to their meeting, he hadn't noticed what mark she had.

Boon lowered his voice so that it was almost inaudible, "Kaz, I want to give you a piece of advice. There is only one job that will pay top dollar for sharp-shooting distance archers -- assassinations." The truth of this sank in to Kaz. "If you choose to go down that road it will be difficult to come back."

Kaz looked up to Boon. "What should I do?"

"Just be sure of your target. One shot from your bow could end the reign of a tyrannical leader, but it could also destroy a nation. Remember what you have learned." Then he added, "If you ever get into trouble, you can always come home." He pointed to the wagon and Kaz nodded.

"Thank you," was all Kaz could say as he hugged his mentor, then he turned to meet up with P.

CHAPTER 37

Normally, it would be harder to see while outside the ring of wagons as the fire from within cast long shadows of darkness, and Kaz marveled yet again at the power of the Sight Stone as he was able to see the uneven ground beneath his feet without giving much thought to the darkness. When he had closed the distance between himself and P, he heeded the advice of his mentor and proceeded with caution.

"Hi, it's good to see you again."

"That was some good advice he gave you," she said.

Shocked by her statement, he responded with a question. "You heard what he said from that far away?"

"Yes, and it wasn't much of a challenge." The way she said it told him she was not giving him a false sense of her abilities, nor was she bragging; just stating a fact. "So, we want you to kill a man for us. Do you have the stomach for the job or not?"

Kaz was again surprised by her forward question. He was hoping for some pleasant conversation, or at least to see that infectious smile of hers again, but instead he was being dealt a rather harsh reception.

"I'm not committing to anything until I have some information." P waited, clearly impatient. When she did not respond he continued. "Who is the target?"

"That I will not tell you yet. I can't have you running off to warn the target."

"All right then, what has this person done that makes him or her worthy of this end?"

"That's a great question, and one I can answer." P looked around, then stood silently, Kaz guessed she was scanning with her ears. "Let's go sit by my fire to talk." They walked for several hundred yards and sat down at a fire ring near some tents. The tents were in poor condition and seemed as though they would hardly provide much shelter on this early fall night. Kaz also noticed that there were no horses tied near the tents.

"You said you lived in Lexingar. Why do you have a fire?" Kaz said somewhat suspiciously.

P smiled and nodded. "Now you're starting to use your head. What else did you notice?"

Kaz, thinking that this was a test, began to look around, but he was stopped by P's hand moving over his eyes. "Not what *can* you notice, but what else *did* you notice?"

Kaz thought back through what he had seen coming up to the camp. He wished he had spent more time looking around and less time focused on looking at P.

"The tents are not fit for this weather. There are no horses nearby."

"Good," P said, as she uncovered his eyes. "So what do you think is happening here?"

Kaz was never good at these mind puzzles -- he would trust Bendar for this type of game.

"I don't know," he answered, and before he could stop her, P slapped him across the face. "What was that for?"

"That was you dying. The mission we're offering to you is of great importance. Paying attention and then drawing conclusions is vital to making it work. You can't say 'I don't know' and expect to survive." She paused for a moment, then calmly repeated her question, "What is happening here?"

Kaz, still rubbing his cheek answered, "Well, my best guess is..." His head started feeling like it was spinning as he was struck again. He thought that he had a fast hand, but P had lightning reflexes.

"Try again, and this time with confidence."

"Either you set up this camp to secure some space so that you could beat on me, or there are some very poor people who travelled a long way with no horses." Kaz focused on making sure that he didn't make this statement seem too much like a question.

"Please make a decision, think of all you know about me and all you have learned since you have been here. What is going on here?"

"I really don't…" he started, but then he didn't finish his thought. He took a deep breath and thought through what he knew about P. She said she lived in Lexingar, so she wouldn't need such a space to talk or meet. This meant that the tents belonged to someone else, but who? Who would set up thin tents and a fire, and then not be around enjoying the warmth of the fire? What else did he know about her? He looked around, trying to remember their conversation in town. He concentrated, thinking about everything he knew about her. She had watched the archery tournament, which meant she was probably looking for an assassin, but she had already told him that. She had chosen to follow him specifically after the tournament, which meant she needed a long range archer. After several minutes of piecing together what he knew, he spoke.

"There are people not from this area watching from the darkness over there," Kaz pointed across the fire. "From my position here they think they are safe from being seen because eyes can't normally focus on dark and light at the same time. They are probably listeners, eavesdropping on our conversation, testing me to see if I'm the right person to kill for you."

Smiling, P waved toward the spot where Kaz had pointed, and two men came walking over. "Well done, Kaz. Digger has a proposal for you."

Digger, the leader of the pair, walked up to the fire and shook his head. Digger was a thin man with tight, strong muscles. He wore woven wool pants and a shirt that had been worn thin by overuse. Even before he had drawn near the light, Kaz could see his questioning look.

"Him? I thought you were bringing me a warrior." The man continued to shake his head. "I don't need a boy; I have a village of boys. What I need is a man."

"You also seem to have a village of men," Kaz said, standing up, "but they haven't done you much good." P was just as surprised as Digger by this outburst. "Why don't you explain your troubles and I'll decide if I can help." With that Kaz sat down and waited for the others to join him.

Digger slowly and reluctantly joined him in a tight circle around the fire.

"P, I like this one," Digger said with a smile. Then he spoke to Kaz. "We come from the village of Hess."

"I've never heard of that place," Kaz interrupted.

"I suspect that nobody has," the man said with a downcast look. "Hess is an entire village that is kept secret from the king because we are a village of slaves."

"That's impossible," Kaz declared. "Slavery was dissolved over a hundred years ago."

The man did not respond with words, but instead held up his left arm. It was branded with the letter O. Kaz had heard of slaves being branded like cattle to mark them as property, but he never thought he would see a person treated that way. "We *are* slaves and we are kept from the knowledge of the king, so that our master can treat us how he wants, use us how he wants, and never answer for his actions."

"How could a thing like that be kept from the king all this time?" Kaz asked, still not completely convinced. "Why don't you go to the king now? He's in Lexingar. I'm sure he'd help if he knew."

P interjected, "It's not just a petty crook keeping them there. He has kept the entire country oblivious to the village of Hess for years. He has an appointment from the king, and the king has visited his land several times and never seen Hess."

"Who are you talking about?" Kaz asked in frustration.

P looked at Kaz, then around the small fire for approval. "If I tell you, you'll need to come with us. There will be no choice after that."

Kaz sat silently for several moments not knowing how to respond.

"I want to tell you a little more about the target," P began. "He has groups of guards, and he also has agreements with a group of outlaws."

Kaz scrunched his brow in confusion, "That makes no sense."

"It makes perfect sense," Digger cut in. "His land seems to be overrun with thieves and bandits, then his soldiers come riding in to save the day. The people feel they are indebted to him for their safety, and he takes their money, takes their magical items, and keeps them living in fear of ever going exploring on his estates."

Kaz placed his head in his hands, "Oh my goodness!" As soon as Digger explained the plot, Kaz knew it was true. And he knew who the target was. Baron Omer was the man they were speaking of. The attacks that ended Garin's life and led to Bendar's disappearance were all a part of a scheme to steal from those who travelled through his land and keep a slave village secret. In a moment of clarity, Kaz finally found the direction in his life that he had been seeking. Although he didn't have all the answers, he knew what he needed to do.

"What?" P asked, leaning in close.

"I'm going with you. We're going to bring Omer to justice."

CHAPTER 38

Dune led the way through the crowded streets as Trae carried his cargo, trying not to attract too much attention. When they approached the stadium, the people were densely clustered. Wearing the long, dark, magician's robe, Dune pressed into the people, who, upon seeing a magician, opened a small passage. Trae kept close, making sure to not lose his place in the wake of his friend.

From the outside walls of the stadium they could hear the boisterous cheers of the fans as the horses galloped toward each other, then an explosion of applause and shouts when lances clashed on armor and shields. Dune moved along the perimeter away from the entrance. The farther he got from the entrance, the more room they had, until they were almost entirely alone moving into a small back alley between the stadium and the city wall.

"Where are we going?" Trae asked.

Dune answered by stopping alongside the city wall and pressing on some stones. The stone gave way and opened to reveal a narrow staircase cut into a hollow in the wall. Dune proceeded quickly as Trae struggled to maneuver his baggage. They descended the stairs in the dark. The only light flickered from the bottom. When they entered the lighted room they were surrounded by armed guards.

"What is your purpose here?" a well-built soldier addressed Dune. In the small entrance, all eyes were on the magician, not knowing his intentions. Dune did not have time to answer as a clatter from up the stairs announced Trae's arrival. From the darkness rolled an unusual canvas bag.

"Sorry, he slipped," Trae was saying as he entered the room. He quieted when he saw the group with weapons drawn.

"This is my purpose," Dune answered pointing at the sack. "I need to speak with Sir Theodore."

"Sir Theodore is away on urgent business."

Dune reached down and pulled open the sack. At his movement, the men visibly tensed. Dune pulled the seeker's elixir vial from the man and held it up.

"Get this man to a secluded cell, keep that container close. The moment Sir Theodore arrives, notify him that we have one of Mordyar's seekers." Some men in the group gasped at this last remark.

"Let's go," Dune said. He began walking up the stairs.

"Wait. Who are you?" a guard called after them. Dune continued to walk, ignoring the questions that followed them as the two men ascended and exited.

Dune led the way through the streets of Lexingar, passing people who didn't have any idea what had happened.

"It is amazing to me," he remarked, "that we were able to find the leader of the seekers, poison her elixir, and quite possibly cripple Mordyar's supporters inside of Denall."

Trae looked at his friend questioningly, "I'm getting pretty tired of asking this," Trae began, "but this isn't done yet is it?"

"Well," Dune said with a mischievous grin, "I'd sure hate to miss the reaction on Melna's face when she realizes what we've done."

"Speaking of the look on people's faces," Trae added as they made their way to the south gate, "When am I going to have my own face again?"

* * * * *

Sir Theodore entered the training ground under the Lexingar stadium followed by a proud young man with a great warhorse. The moment Sir Theodore entered the room, there was a flurry of action. "We have a prisoner, delivered by a magician," one guard said as he saluted his superior officer.

"Where is he?" Sir Theodore responded, running to look up a flight of stairs that led to one of the closest entrances.

"In the dungeon, in isolation."

"Not the prisoner, where is Dune?" Sir Theodore asked, turning on his soldier.

The corporal was partly embarrassed and partly confused by his misunderstanding.

"The magician never gave his name, but he went back out

that way," he pointed up the stairs, confirming that where Sir Theodore was looking was the direction Dune had gone.

Without a word to Mylot, Sir Theodore rushed up the steps. In a few short moments, he returned.

"He's gone," he said to nobody, then to the corporal, "Take me to the prisoner." The two men disappeared through an iron reinforced door.

Mylot felt unsure what to do as he looked around the room of unfamiliar faces. After having accompanied Sir Theodore as he made various offers to candidates who had performed well in earlier events, even being ordered to stand on the outskirts of a caravan as he had discussed a position on the king's guard with Farin, his final opponent from the single-handed sword competition, Mylot was feeling thoroughly deflated and frustrated. He stood still and tried to look confident.

"The stables are that way." He turned to see a woman in her late twenties pointing down a well-lit passageway.

"Thank you," Mylot said, absently handing her the reins.

She dropped the reins to the ground, and shook her head. "Do I look like your stable boy?" She gestured to her armor and crest that bore the mark of the king's guard. Without waiting for a response, she turned away. "What a fool." Some of the nearby soldiers began laughing at Mylot as he retrieved his horses' reins. Mylot's face contorted in anger.

"How dare you treat me like this, do you not know who I am?"

"Yeah, we know who you are," one man started folding his arms across his chest.

"You're the coward who fled from the jousting tournament," the woman added, not even turning to look at him. She grabbed an apple from a fruit basket and took a bite.

A third man joined in, "I believe the new stage name for you is Mylot the Mouse."

Mylot pushed his horse out of the way and stepped toe to toe with the three soldiers. "You know nothing, and will all answer for this impudence!"

Mylot advanced on the woman, but she continued to chew

on her apple without seeming to notice him.

"Wow, I've never been accused of being impudent to a mouse before," she then turned and glared at Mylot, "and if you don't quickly learn your place, you'll always be a mouse."

"That's better than being a stubborn, smart mouthed spinster, which is where you'll end up no doubt."

The woman shot out her hand with lightning speed and grabbed him by the breastplate with one hand and pulled him until he was an inch from her face.

"What was that?" She threw Mylot to the stone floor, and took another bite of her apple as if the fruit was more interesting than he was.

Mylot stood up slowly, dusting himself off. "I have never seen someone move so quickly," his amazement overshadowed his anger and he extended his hand.

The woman placed her apple core in Mylot's open palm. "The stalls are down that way," she chuckled again and turned to talk to the other men who were watching in amusement. Mylot stood for a moment taking in all the emotions from the time he had left the joust to follow Sir Theodore. *What have I done?*

After brushing down his horse, Mylot sat on a small stool in the stalls, not knowing what else he should do. He had never been so completely ignored before. After sitting for several minutes, he heard a familiar voice from down the passage.

"Where is he?"

"I don't know," came the response from the cocky woman. "Maybe he's still with the horses."

After a short silence, Sir Theodore came into view followed by the woman who had bested Mylot unarmed.

"This is Captain Conrad. She will be helping you get situated. I have some paperwork to do regarding some new recruits."

Captain Conrad looked at Sir Theodore, completely disregarding Mylot, "Did you speak to Farin and that girl from the single combat? They were very impressive."

"There were many fine soldiers this year." Without another

word to Mylot, Sir Theodore left.

Captain Conrad saluted to Sir Theodore, then watched as he walked away. When he was out of sight, she exhaled loudly, then turned to look at Mylot.

"Come on this way," she motioned with her hand for him to follow. Mylot sat still for a moment glaring up at her. "Or you can stay here, I really don't care either way."

She led Mylot down the hall, and as they walked, he tried to engage her in conversation. Despite her complete lack of respect, she seemed to be an amazing warrior, and having already achieved the rank of captain, she was due a measure of respect.

"So, Captain Conrad, why don't you compete in the tournaments? With your reflexes, you could easily win."

She squared on Mylot, "If you are going to join with us, you really need to stop thinking about tournaments, and winning, and being the center of attention. We work behind the scenes to keep the kingdom safe. If you want recognition and awards, go somewhere else, and take that pampered horse of yours with you." She held Mylot's eyes for a moment as if anticipating Mylot leaving. Mylot gave a look of determination. His commanding officer nodded and continued down the hallway.

"Very well. Welcome to the king's guard. Let's see if you can survive the training."

* * * * *

Kaz unconsciously rubbed his shirt before remembering that the Sight Stone was no longer hanging there. As insurance that he would not go running off to warn Omer, P had taken it and his magical rings before she let him return to say goodbye to his friends.

When he entered the circle of wagons, he headed right for Blade's home. Farin and Angela were quietly sitting by Blade's wagon when Kaz walked into the light of the campfire. Despite all the popularity and fame they had gained in a single day, they both looked glum.

"What's going on?" Kaz asked, sincerely concerned for his friends.

Angela looked up and was the first to respond. "Oh, hi Kaz. We didn't see you coming," she said rather flatly. Then, as her eyes looked downward again she said more quietly, "Just talking about what we're going to do."

Kaz looked quizzically at them. "We? Can't you do whatever *you* want?" Then to Farin who was silent, "Farin, you've always wanted to train for the king's army, now you have the chance to be on the king's personal guard."

"I know," he began, "but the truth is, I'm not sure I want that anymore."

"He's being ridiculous!" Angela began. She sat up straight and threw her arms in the air in frustration. "He is going with them in the morning."

Then Farin turned on her, "You can't tell me what to do." He emphasized his words by pointing back at her. "I like it here, and Blade can train me just as well as anyone else."

"You're bull headed and stubborn, and maybe *I* don't want you around!" Angela said this with no regard for anyone who was listening, then she stood up, and with a stamp of her foot, turned and stalked away.

Kaz sat down next to his friend. "What is going on?"

Farin looked frustrated. "I don't want Blade to think I'm abandoning him, and I like the life of peace and trading with the caravan." He seemed to struggle for more reasons. "We'll see all kinds of places, and I don't need to fight, and…"

Kaz cut him off, "And you'll get to stay with Angela." He looked down at Farin and waited for Farin to meet his eyes. "So your little huff here is a lover's quarrel?" Kaz began to laugh.

Farin shoved Kaz off the seat and Kaz rolled on the ground still laughing. He then started stalking close to Farin, ready to pounce. Farin normally wouldn't have worried about Kaz wrestling him, but remembering the sharp pains caused by the rings, Farin looked at Kaz' hands in the darkness. "Kaz, where are your rings? I'm not getting sucker punched with ice again."

Kaz stood up from his crouched position. In the moment

of youthful fun, he had almost forgotten his own obligations. Instead of wrestling his friend, he walked to him, and as Farin stood up, Kaz caught him completely by surprise in a full bear hug.

"I have to go," was all Kaz could say.

Farin stood solid as a pillar not knowing what to do. Eventually he gave Kaz a reassuring, but awkward pat on the back.

"It's all right, buddy."

Kaz released Farin. "Sorry, I just… We just started with… more. And now I'm leaving you too."

Farin looked at Kaz quizzically, but knew that this was not the time to make fun of Kaz's outburst of emotion.

"What's going on? Where are you going?"

"This past couple of months I've felt a little lost. Like I'm wandering around without getting anything done. Now I've found something really important, and I feel like my journey to being a man is taking me down a new path. And it starts with going back for Bendar," he answered, not sure how else he could explain himself. "I made some friends who are headed to Omer's keep, and I'm going with them."

Farin stood up, "Then I'm going too."

"No," Kaz said, holding up his hand, "you have a great offer here. Angela's right, you can't throw your future away. It's what you've always wanted."

Farin began pacing back and forth, "I'm not really sure what I want anymore, Kaz. It seems this journey of finding myself has done the opposite."

Kaz grabbed Farin by the shoulders and stopped him from walking, "Then take some time to figure out what you want. Either way I can't take you with me. These friends of mine hired me as an archer to help them hunt as they travel," he lied. He couldn't think of any better way to keep Farin from getting into the danger he would certainly face. "We're leaving tonight, heading west, and then up to Omer's keep. When I get there I'll find Bendar."

"Then we'll all meet together back at Dungan to be

welcomed as men," Farin finished Kaz's sentence.

"So now you're going to go back for that?" Kaz asked, somewhat surprised.

"I need to go back and tell the folks about Garin," he said with a sad look. "They deserve to hear it from me."

Kaz nodded and took Farin by the hand in a firm clasp. "I will see you at the summer festival. Now you need to get going over there and make up with your girl." With that, he playfully slapped Farin on the rump. With a smile, Kaz walked to Boon's wagon, fearing that he would not see his friend again.

Boon was sitting by the edge of a fire that was set a safe distance from the wagon. When Kaz came, he followed the young man into the wagon where he had some supplies stored.

"So it looks like you are gathering your things," Boon said, as Kaz was packing his belongings. "Did you decide then, to become an assassin?" Kaz motioned for Boon to be silent, but Boon continued, "These curtains are designed to foil eavesdroppers -- you are safe to talk here."

Kaz shook his head, "Farin told me he could still hear through the thin walls of the wagons. If he can hear through, then this conversation is not as private as you might think."

Boon looked shocked, but then reasoned, "Farin was always close to the wagon. To listen through from a distance would require the Hearing Stone. Now let me know what is bothering you."

With Boon's declaration, Kaz slapped his hands together, "Of course!" he said.

"What?" Boon asked. Kaz looked at Boon and pulled open the collar of his shirt. "Where is your stone?" Boon asked, surprised and upset.

"She has it." At this statement from Kaz, Boon drew himself up and looked ready to explode in anger. "It's all right," Kaz reassured him, "I willingly gave it to her as a sign of trust between us; a guarantee that I would return. But I never thought about why she asked for the stone before this moment. The only way she could know of its great worth is if she has one of her own," Kaz said with resignation. "She is probably listening to me right now," he added with a grin.

"Why are you doing this?" Boon asked.

Kaz stopped packing and looked Boon in the eyes. With his voice filled with emotions he explained.

"When I was young, my dad told me to always live with integrity. He said I needed to do what was right, even when it was hard, or when nobody would know the difference. When the drams attacked, I was terrified. I thought I would die, and I hadn't really done anything important in life. I've spent the time since wondering when my purpose would become clear to me."

Boon held up his hand to stop Kaz, "You also saved a caravan, developed your skills…"

"I know that," Kaz continued, "but that all happened so quickly, there wasn't really another option. The point is that now I have a choice, I really think I can do a lot of good, I can help people who aren't strong enough to stand up for themselves. I think going with them would make my father proud."

Boon grabbed Kaz in a bear hug. With emotion in his voice he spoke, "I'm certain that he already is. I also know that when you look back on the past year, you'll see that you did have a choice, every time you helped someone, every time you made someone smile, and even when you saved the caravan. The iron ash bow couldn't go to a more worthy archer. I'm proud to have brought it to you. Each of those moments and a thousand others have led you here, and if you feel your path is going with these people," he pointed in the direction P had been standing, "then the bow must certainly go with you. I know it's the right path for you. You are a great man."

"Not yet," Kaz corrected, with a grin to try to hide that he was on the edge of tears. "My Troven isn't quite over yet."

Boon shook his head and helped Kaz pack his remaining items. As they left the wagon, Boon led Kaz toward the line of horses, on their way out of the circle of wagons.

When they passed the tall gelding which had previously been owned by one of the bandits who had attacked the caravan, Kaz noticed that it was saddled and had full saddle bags for traveling.

"I figured you would be leaving tonight," Boon said, holding the reins of the horse. "Odon told me to let you have him whenever you wanted to leave, so he's ready for you."

"Thank you," was all Kaz could say. He embraced the older man one final time, and this time he was answered with a stronger, tighter bear hug than he thought the man could give.

"Be safe and remember who you are," were Boon's final words of advice as Kaz swung into the saddle and trotted toward the camp of his new traveling companions.

Kaz rode with his bow in hand, scanning his surroundings as he returned to the tattered tents. Kaz felt a keen loss, realizing how much better his vision had been with the Sight Stone, but he also was pleased to realize that his vision without the stone had grown in strength through the exercises that Boon had shown him. When he arrived at their campsite, P was mounted and waiting for him, while the other two men had gathered their belongings and were standing ready. P reached out her hand and returned the rings and Sight Stone.

"As promised," she said.

Kaz urged his horse forward, down an unfamiliar path. Despite the uncertain future, for the first time since the dram attack, he felt like he was in control of his Troven. He was finding who he was meant to become.

ABOUT THE AUTHOR

Eric Buffington was born in Ontario Canada, where he lived until he was eighteen. After that he traveled with a Canadian government program, for one year (what he did is top secret), he then moved to California to serve a two year mission working with the Laotian people. Shortly after returning home he met the love of his life, moved to Pennsylvania and married her. He has since completed a Bachelor's and Master's degree in education. He currently lives in Pennsylvania with his wonderfully supportive wife, and their four children. He currently works as a High School math teacher in an online cyber school.

Thanks for reading The Troven!

Tell your friends about it, and please consider leaving a review on Amazon or Goodreads.

Be sure to check out other great stories brought to you by Dragon Scale Publishing
Go to:

www.dragonscalebooks.com

You can enter monthly give aways for books and other prizes by signing up for Dragon Scale Publishing's newsletter and keeping up with the authors and publishing company via Twitter, Facebook, and Goodreads.

The adventures of the stone holders continue
Fall 2016 in

The Secrets at the Keep

Will Kaz and P be able to bring Omer down and free the slaves from Hess?

What will Farin choose? Will he follow Angela and stay with the Algernons, or will he follow his life-long dream of joining the King's Guard?

Will Dune and Trae's plan to poison the seekers prove successful, or does Melna have another trick up her sleeve?

Will Mylot ever be able to deliver the mysterious jeweled chest to Maggie?

What has become of Bendar?

Answer these questions and more when you purchase your copy of The Secrets at the Keep. For now, please enjoy this excerpt:

...

Through the gaping hole in the side of the tent, Dune saw Melna rushing about now, handing out the poisoned Han'Or. She also must have known that the local guards would be on their way; her hurried attempts to fill the bottles that hung from the seekers' belts resulted in more of the precious elixir sloshing to the ground than he could imagine a seeker would normally ever allow for. After giving it to all the gathered seekers, she held her own bottle up in the air.

Dune held his breath as he watched her slowly bring the bottle to her mouth. The other seekers followed her lead and began to drink the poisoned liquid. As she was about to tilt the bottle back, she seemed to notice that someone was watching her. She leaned her head to the side and made eye contact with Dune before he could avert his gaze. It only took a small moment for recognition to set in.

"Put them down! Don't drink that!" she began to scream, smashing her own bottle to the ground. But her words went unheeded as seekers who had gone weeks on half rations eagerly drank their hard won Han'Or.

Dune stood up and began running towards the tent. Most of the seekers would be dead momentarily and he wasn't going to let Melna escape. Trae rushed up next to him with his mace in one hand and shield in the other.

"What's the plan?"

"Stop Melna!"

While they were still several yards from the tent, Dune saw that some of the seekers were falling to the ground, grasping at their throats. The poison was working, but there were others who were not affected by it. When he was about to reach the tent, a huge explosion erupted, blasting him onto his back. His ears were filled with a deafening ringing, and his world began to tilt back and forth.

39784537R00229

Made in the USA
Middletown, DE
25 January 2017